Stephen Crane (November 1, 1871 - June 5, 1900) was an American poet, novelist, and short story writer. Prolific throughout his short life, he wrote notable works in the Realist tradition as well as early examples of American Naturalism and Impressionism. He is recognized by modern critics as one of the most innovative writers of his generation. The ninth surviving child of Methodist parents, Crane began writing at the age of four and had published several articles by the age of 16. Having little interest in university studies though he was active in a fraternity, he left Syracuse University in 1891 to work as a reporter and writer. Crane's first novel was the 1893 Bowery tale Maggie: A Girl of the Streets, generally considered by critics to be the first work of American literary Naturalism. He won international acclaim in 1895 for his Civil War novel The Red Badge of Courage, which he wrote without having any battle experience. (Source: Wikipedia)

Literary works:

Maggie: A Girl of the Streets (1893)
The Red Badge of Courage (1895)
The Black Riders and Other Lines (1895)
George's Mother (1896)
The Third Violet (1897)
The Open Boat and Other Tales of Adventure (1898)
War is Kind (1899)
Active Service (1899)
The Monster and Other Stories (1899)
Wounds in the Rain (1900)
Great Battles of the World
The O'Ruddy (1903)
The Monster. London
Last Words. London
Whilomville Stories

THRONE CLASSICS

THE MONSTER AND OTHER STORIES,

THE LITTLE REGIMENT, AND OTHER EPISODES OF

THE AMERICAN CIVIL WAR

&

LAST WORDS

Stephen Crane

This is a work of fiction. Names, characters, places, and incidents either are the product of the author's imagination or are used fictitiously. Any resemblance to actual persons, living or dead, events, or locales is entirely coincidental.

First Printing: 2019

ISBN 978-93-5383-916-1 (paperback)

ISBN 978-93-5383-917-8 (Hardcover)

Published by Throne Classics

www.throneclassics.com

Contents

THE MONSTER AND OTHER STORIES,

THE LITTLE REGIMENT, AND OTHER EPISODES OF

THE AMERICAN CIVIL WAR

&

LAST WORDS

THE MONSTER AND OTHER STORIES

THE MONSTER

I

Little Jim was, for the time, engine Number 36, and he was making the run between Syracuse and Rochester. He was fourteen minutes behind time, and the throttle was wide open. In consequence, when he swung around the curve at the flower-bed, a wheel of his cart destroyed a peony. Number 36 slowed down at once and looked guiltily at his father, who was mowing the lawn. The doctor had his back to this accident, and he continued to pace slowly to and fro, pushing the mower.

Jim dropped the tongue of the cart. He looked at his father and at the broken flower. Finally he went to the peony and tried to stand it on its pins, resuscitated, but the spine of it was hurt, and it would only hang limply from his hand. Jim could do no reparation. He looked again towards his father.

He went on to the lawn, very slowly, and kicking wretchedly at the turf. Presently his father came along with the whirring machine, while the sweet, new grass blades spun from the knives. In a low voice, Jim said, "Pa!"

The doctor was shaving this lawn as if it were a priest's chin. All during the season he had worked at it in the coolness and peace of the evenings after supper. Even in the shadow of the cherry-trees the grass was strong and healthy. Jim raised his voice a trifle. "Pa!"

The doctor paused, and with the howl of the machine no longer occupying the sense, one could hear the robins in the cherry-trees arranging their affairs. Jim's hands were behind his back, and sometimes his fingers clasped and unclasped. Again he said, "Pa!" The child's fresh and rosy lip was lowered.

The doctor stared down at his son, thrusting his head forward and frowning attentively. "What is it, Jimmie?"

"Pa!" repeated the child at length. Then he raised his finger and pointed at the flowerbed. "There!"

"What?" said the doctor, frowning more. "What is it, Jim?"

After a period of silence, during which the child may have undergone a severe mental tumult, he raised his finger and repeated his former word—"There!" The father had respected this silence with perfect courtesy. Afterwards his glance carefully followed the direction indicated by the child's finger, but he could see nothing which explained to him. "I don't understand what you mean, Jimmie," he said.

It seemed that the importance of the whole thing had taken away the boy's vocabulary, He could only reiterate, "There!"

The doctor mused upon the situation, but he could make nothing of it. At last he said, "Come, show me."

Together they crossed the lawn towards the flower-bed. At some yards from the broken peony Jimmie began to lag. "There!" The word came almost breathlessly.

"Where?" said the doctor.

Jimmie kicked at the grass. "There!" he replied.

The doctor was obliged to go forward alone. After some trouble he found the subject of the incident, the broken flower. Turning then, he saw the child lurking at the rear and scanning his countenance.

The father reflected. After a time he said, "Jimmie, come here." With an infinite modesty of demeanor the child came forward. "Jimmie, how did this happen?"

The child answered, "Now—I was playin' train—and—now—I runned over it."

"You were doing what?"

"I was playin' train."

The father reflected again. "Well, Jimmie," he said, slowly, "I guess you had better not play train any more to-day. Do you think you had better?"

"No, sir," said Jimmie.

During the delivery of the judgment the child had not faced his father, and afterwards he went away, with his head lowered, shuffling his feet.

II

It was apparent from Jimmie's manner that he felt some kind of desire to efface himself. He went down to the stable. Henry Johnson, the negro who cared for the doctor's horses, was sponging the buggy. He grinned fraternally when he saw Jimmie coming. These two were pals. In regard to almost everything in life they seemed to have minds precisely alike. Of course there were points of emphatic divergence. For instance, it was plain from Henry's talk that he was a very handsome negro, and he was known to be a light, a weight, and an eminence in the suburb of the town, where lived the larger number of the negroes, and obviously this glory was over Jimmie's horizon; but he vaguely appreciated it and paid deference to Henry for it mainly because Henry appreciated it and deferred to himself. However, on all points of conduct as related to the doctor, who was the moon, they were in complete but unexpressed understanding. Whenever Jimmie became the victim of an eclipse he went to the stable to solace himself with Henry's crimes. Henry, with the elasticity of his race, could usually provide a sin to place himself on a footing with the disgraced one. Perhaps he would remember that he had forgotten to put the hitching-strap in the back of the buggy on some recent occasion, and had been reprimanded by the doctor. Then these two would commune subtly and without words concerning their moon, holding themselves sympathetically as people who had committed similar treasons. On the other hand, Henry would sometimes choose to absolutely repudiate this idea, and when Jimmie appeared in his shame would bully him most virtuously, preaching with assurance the precepts of the doctor's creed, and pointing out to Jimmie all his abominations. Jimmie did not discover that this was odious in his comrade. He accepted it and lived in its shadow with humility, merely trying to conciliate the saintly Henry with acts of deference.

Won by this attitude, Henry would sometimes allow the child to enjoy the felicity of squeezing the sponge over a buggy-wheel, even when Jimmie was still gory from unspeakable deeds.

Whenever Henry dwelt for a time in sackcloth, Jimmie did not patronize him at all. This was a justice of his age, his condition. He did not know. Besides, Henry could drive a horse, and Jimmie had a full sense of this sublimity. Henry personally conducted the moon during the splendid journeys through the country roads, where farms spread on all sides, with sheep, cows, and other marvels abounding.

"Hello, Jim!" said Henry, poising his sponge. Water was dripping from the buggy. Sometimes the horses in the stalls stamped thunderingly on the pine floor. There was an atmosphere of hay and of harness.

For a minute Jimmie refused to take an interest in anything. He was very downcast. He could not even feel the wonders of wagon washing. Henry, while at his work, narrowly observed him.

"Your pop done wallop yer, didn't he?" he said at last.

"No," said Jimmie, defensively; "he didn't."

After this casual remark Henry continued his labor, with a scowl of occupation. Presently he said: "I done tol' yer many's th' time not to go a-foolin' an' a-projjeckin' with them flowers. Yer pop don' like it nohow." As a matter of fact, Henry had never mentioned flowers to the boy.

Jimmie preserved a gloomy silence, so Henry began to use seductive wiles in this affair of washing a wagon. It was not until he began to spin a wheel on the tree, and the sprinkling water flew everywhere, that the boy was visibly moved. He had been seated on the sill of the carriage-house door, but at the beginning of this ceremony he arose and circled towards the buggy, with an interest that slowly consumed the remembrance of a late disgrace.

Johnson could then display all the dignity of a man whose duty it was to protect Jimmie from a splashing. "Look out, boy! look out! You done gwi' spile yer pants. I raikon your mommer don't 'low this foolishness, she know it. I ain't gwi' have you round yere spilin' yer pants, an' have Mis' Trescott light on me pressen'ly. 'Deed I ain't." He spoke with an air of great irritation, but he was not annoyed at all. This tone was merely a part of his importance. In reality he was always delighted to have the child there to witness the business of the stable. For one thing, Jimmie was invariably overcome with reverence when he was told how beautifully a harness was polished or a horse groomed. Henry explained each detail of this kind with unction, procuring great joy from the child's admiration.

III

After Johnson had taken his supper in the kitchen, he went to his loft in the carriage house and dressed himself with much care. No belle of a court circle could bestow more mind on a toilet than did Johnson. On second thought, he was more like a priest arraying himself for some parade of the church. As he emerged from his room and sauntered down the carriage-drive, no one would have suspected him of ever having washed a buggy.

It was not altogether a matter of the lavender trousers, nor yet the straw hat with its bright silk band. The change was somewhere, far in the interior of Henry. But there was no cake-walk hyperbole in it. He was simply a quiet, well-bred gentleman of position, wealth, and other necessary achievements out for an evening stroll, and he had never washed a wagon in his life.

In the morning, when in his working-clothes, he had met a friend—"Hello, Pete!" "Hello, Henry!" Now, in his effulgence, he encountered this same friend. His bow was not at all haughty. If it expressed anything, it expressed consummate generosity—"Good-evenin', Misteh Washington." Pete, who was very dirty, being at work in a potato-patch, responded in a mixture of abasement and appreciation—Good-evenin', Misteh Johnsing."

The shimmering blue of the electric arc lamps was strong in the main street of the town. At numerous points it was conquered by the orange glare of the outnumbering gaslights in the windows of shops. Through this radiant lane moved a crowd, which culminated in a throng before the post-office, awaiting the distribution of the evening mails. Occasionally there came into it a shrill electric street-car, the motor singing like a cageful of grasshoppers, and possessing a great gong that clanged forth both warnings and simple noise. At the little theatre, which was a varnish and red plush miniature of one of the famous New York theatres, a company of strollers was to play "East Lynne." The young men of the town were mainly gathered at the corners, in distinctive groups, which expressed various shades and lines of chumship, and had little to do with any social gradations. There they discussed everything with critical insight, passing the whole town in review as it swarmed in the street. When the gongs of the electric cars ceased for a moment to harry the ears, there could be heard the sound of the feet of the leisurely crowd on the bluestone pavement, and it was like the peaceful evening lashing at the shore of a lake. At the foot of the hill, where two lines of maples sentinelled the way, an electric lamp glowed high among the embowering branches, and made most wonderful shadow-etchings on the road below it.

When Johnson appeared amid the throng a member of one of the profane groups at a corner instantly telegraphed news of this extraordinary arrival to his companions. They hailed him. "Hello, Henry! Going to walk for a cake to-night?"

"Ain't he smooth?"

"Why, you've got that cake right in your pocket, Henry!"

"Throw out your chest a little more."

Henry was not ruffled in any way by these quiet admonitions and compliments. In reply he laughed a supremely good-natured, chuckling laugh, which nevertheless expressed an underground complacency of superior metal.

Young Griscom, the lawyer, was just emerging from Reifsnyder's barber shop, rubbing his chin contentedly. On the steps he dropped his hand and looked with wide eyes into the crowd. Suddenly he bolted back into the shop. "Wow!" he cried to the parliament; "you ought to see the coon that's coming!"

Reifsnyder and his assistant instantly poised their razors high and turned towards the window. Two belathered heads reared from the chairs. The electric shine in the street caused an effect like water to them who looked through the glass from the yellow glamour of Reifsnyder's shop. In fact, the people without resembled the inhabitants of a great aquarium that here had a square pane in it. Presently into this frame swam the graceful form of Henry Johnson.

"Chee!" said Reifsnyder. He and his assistant with one accord threw their obligations to the winds, and leaving their lathered victims helpless, advanced to the window. "Ain't he a taisy?" said Reifsnyder, marvelling.

But the man in the first chair, with a grievance in his mind, had found a weapon. "Why, that's only Henry Johnson, you blamed idiots! Come on now, Reif, and shave me. What do you think I am—a mummy?"

Reifsnyder turned, in a great excitement. "I bait you any money that vas not Henry Johnson! Henry Johnson! Rats!" The scorn put into this last word made it an explosion. "That man was a Pullman-car porter or someding. How could that be Henry Johnson?" he demanded, turbulently. "You vas crazy."

The man in the first chair faced the barber in a storm of indignation. "Didn't I give him those lavender trousers?" he roared.

And young Griscom, who had remained attentively at the window, said: "Yes, I guess that was Henry. It looked like him."

"Oh, vell," said Reifsnyder, returning to his business, "if you think so! Oh, vell!" He implied that he was submitting for the sake of amiability.

Finally the man in the second chair, mumbling from a mouth made timid by adjacent lather, said: "That was Henry Johnson all right. Why, he always dresses like that when he wants to make a front! He's the biggest dude in town—anybody knows that."

"Chinger!" said Reifsnyder.

Henry was not at all oblivious of the wake of wondering ejaculation that streamed out behind him. On other occasions he had reaped this same joy, and he always had an eye for the demonstration. With a face beaming with happiness he turned away from the scene of his victories into a narrow side street, where the electric light still hung high, but only to exhibit a row of tumble-down houses leaning together like paralytics.

The saffron Miss Bella Farragut, in a calico frock, had been crouched on the front stoop, gossiping at long range, but she espied her approaching caller at a distance. She dashed around the corner of the house, galloping like a horse. Henry saw it all, but he preserved the polite demeanor of a guest when a waiter spills claret down his cuff. In this awkward situation he was simply perfect.

The duty of receiving Mr. Johnson fell upon Mrs. Farragut, because Bella, in another room, was scrambling wildly into her best gown. The fat old woman met him with a great ivory smile, sweeping back with the door, and bowing low. "Walk in, Misteh Johnson, walk in. How is you dis ebenin', Misteh Johnson—how is you?"

Henry's face showed like a reflector as he bowed and bowed, bending almost from his head to his ankles, "Good-evenin', Mis' Fa'gut; good-evenin'. How is you dis evenin'? Is all you' folks well, Mis' Fa'gut?"

After a great deal of kowtow, they were planted in two chairs opposite each other in the living-room. Here they exchanged the most tremendous civilities, until Miss Bella swept into the room, when there was more kowtow on all sides, and a smiling show of teeth that was like an illumination.

The cooking-stove was of course in this drawing-room, and on the fire was some kind of a long-winded stew. Mrs. Farragut was obliged to arise and attend to it from time to time. Also young Sim came in and went to bed on his pallet in the corner. But to all these domesticities the three maintained an absolute dumbness. They bowed and smiled and ignored and imitated until a late hour, and if they had been the occupants of the most gorgeous salon in the world they could not have been more like three monkeys.

After Henry had gone, Bella, who encouraged herself in the appropriation of phrases, said, "Oh, ma, isn't he divine?"

IV

A Saturday evening was a sign always for a larger crowd to parade the thoroughfare. In summer the band played until ten o'clock in the little park. Most of the young men of the town affected to be superior to this band, even to despise it; but in the still and fragrant evenings they invariably turned out in force, because the girls were sure to attend this concert, strolling slowly over the grass, linked closely in pairs, or preferably in threes, in the curious public dependence upon one another which was their inheritance. There was no particular social aspect to this gathering, save that group regarded group with interest, but mainly in silence. Perhaps one girl would nudge another girl and suddenly say, "Look! there goes Gertie Hodgson and her sister!" And they would appear to regard this as an event of importance.

On a particular evening a rather large company of young men were gathered on the sidewalk that edged the park. They remained thus beyond the borders of the festivities because of their dignity, which would not exactly allow them to appear in anything which was so much fun for the younger lads. These latter were careering madly through the crowd, precipitating minor accidents from time to time, but usually fleeing like mist swept by the wind before retribution could lay hands upon them.

The band played a waltz which involved a gift of prominence to the bass horn, and one of the young men on the sidewalk said that the music reminded him of the new engines on the hill pumping water into the reservoir. A similarity of this kind was not inconceivable, but the young man did not say it because he disliked the band's playing. He said it because it was fashionable to say that manner of thing concerning the band. However, over in the stand, Billie Harris, who played the snare-drum, was always surrounded by a throng of boys, who adored his every whack.

After the mails from New York and Rochester had been finally distributed, the crowd from the post-office added to the mass already in the park. The wind waved the leaves of the maples, and, high in the air, the blue-burning globes of the arc lamps caused the wonderful traceries of leaf shadows on the ground. When the light fell upon the upturned face of a girl, it caused it to glow with a wonderful pallor. A policeman came suddenly from the darkness and chased a gang of obstreperous little boys. They hooted him from a distance. The leader of the band had some of the mannerisms of the great musicians, and during a period of silence the crowd smiled when they saw him raise his hand to his brow, stroke it sentimentally, and glance upward with a look of poetic anguish. In the shivering light, which gave to the park an effect like a great vaulted hall, the throng swarmed, with a gentle murmur of dresses switching the turf, and with a steady hum of voices.

Suddenly, without preliminary bars, there arose from afar the great hoarse roar of a factory whistle. It raised and swelled to a sinister note, and then it sang on the night wind one long call that held the crowd in the park immovable, speechless. The band-master had been about to vehemently let fall his hand to start the band on a thundering career through a popular march, but, smitten by this giant voice from the night, his hand dropped slowly to his knee, and, his mouth agape, he looked at his men in silence. The cry died away to a wail and then to stillness. It released the muscles of the company of young men on the sidewalk, who had been like statues, posed eagerly, lithely, their ears turned. And then they wheeled upon each other simultaneously, and, in a single explosion, they shouted, "One!"

Again the sound swelled in the night and roared its long ominous cry, and as it died away the crowd of young men wheeled upon each other and, in chorus, yelled, "Two!"

There was a moment of breathless waiting. Then they bawled, "Second district!" In a flash the company of indolent and cynical young men had vanished like a snowball disrupted by dynamite.

V

Jake Rogers was the first man to reach the home of Tuscarora Hose Company Number Six. He had wrenched his key from his pocket as he tore down the street, and he jumped at the spring-lock like a demon. As the doors flew back before his hands he leaped and kicked the wedges from a pair of wheels, loosened a tongue from its clasp, and in the glare of the electric light which the town placed before each of its hose-houses the next comers beheld the spectacle of Jake Rogers bent like hickory in the manfulness of his pulling, and the heavy cart was moving slowly towards the doors. Four men joined him at the time, and as they swung with the cart out into the street, dark figures sped towards them from the ponderous shadows back of the electric lamps. Some set up the inevitable question, "What district?"

"Second," was replied to them in a compact howl. Tuscarora Hose Company Number Six swept on a perilous wheel into Niagara Avenue, and as the men, attached to the cart by the rope which had been paid out from the windlass under the tongue, pulled madly in their fervor and abandon, the gong under the axle clanged incitingly. And sometimes the same cry was heard, "What district?"

"Second."

On a grade Johnnie Thorpe fell, and exercising a singular muscular ability, rolled out in time from the track of the on-coming wheel, and arose, dishevelled and aggrieved, casting a look of mournful disenchantment upon the black crowd that poured after the machine. The cart seemed to be the apex of a dark wave that was whirling as if it had been a broken dam. Back of the lad were stretches of lawn, and in that direction front-doors were banged by men who hoarsely shouted out into the clamorous avenue, "What district?"

At one of these houses a woman came to the door bearing a lamp, shielding her face from its rays with her hands. Across the cropped grass the avenue represented to her a kind of black torrent, upon which, nevertheless, fled numerous miraculous figures upon bicycles. She did not know that the towering light at the corner was continuing its nightly whine.

Suddenly a little boy somersaulted around the corner of the house as if he had been projected down a flight of stairs by a catapultian boot. He halted himself in front of the house by dint of a rather extraordinary evolution with his legs. "Oh, ma," he gasped, "can I go? Can I, ma?"

She straightened with the coldness of the exterior mother-judgment, although the hand that held the lamp trembled slightly. "No, Willie; you had better come to bed."

Instantly he began to buck and fume like a mustang. "Oh, ma," he cried, contorting himself—"oh, ma, can't I go? Please, ma, can't I go? Can't I go, ma?"

"It's half-past nine now, Willie."

He ended by wailing out a compromise: "Well, just down to the corner, ma? Just down to the corner?"

From the avenue came the sound of rushing men who wildly shouted. Somebody had grappled the bell-rope in the Methodist church, and now over the town rang this solemn and terrible voice, speaking from the clouds. Moved from its peaceful business, this bell gained a new spirit in the portentous night, and it swung the heart to and fro, up and down, with each peal of it.

"Just down to the corner, ma?"

"Willie, it's half-past nine now."

VI

The outlines of the house of Dr. Trescott had faded quietly into the evening, hiding a shape such as we call Queen Anne against the pall of the blackened sky. The neighborhood was at this time so quiet, and seemed so devoid of obstructions, that Hannigan's dog thought it a good opportunity to prowl in forbidden precincts, and so came and pawed Trescott's lawn, growling, and considering himself a formidable beast. Later, Peter Washington strolled past the house and whistled, but there was no dim light shining from Henry's loft, and presently Peter went his way. The rays from the street, creeping in silvery waves over the grass, caused the row of shrubs along the drive to throw a clear, bold shade.

A wisp of smoke came from one of the windows at the end of the house and drifted quietly into the branches of a cherry-tree. Its companions followed it in slowly increasing numbers, and finally there was a current controlled by invisible banks which poured into the fruit-laden boughs of the cherry-tree. It was no more to be noted than if a troop of dim and silent gray monkeys had been climbing a grapevine into the clouds.

After a moment the window brightened as if the four panes of it had been stained with blood, and a quick ear might have been led to imagine the fire-imps calling and calling, clan joining clan, gathering to the colors. From the street, however, the house maintained its dark quiet, insisting to a passer-by that it was the safe dwelling of people who chose to retire early to tranquil dreams. No one could have heard this low droning of the gathering clans.

Suddenly the panes of the red window tinkled and crashed to the ground, and at other windows there suddenly reared other flames, like bloody spectres at the apertures of a haunted house. This outbreak had been well planned, as if by professional revolutionists.

A man's voice suddenly shouted: "Fire! Fire! Fire!" Hannigan had flung his pipe frenziedly from him because his lungs demanded room. He tumbled down from his perch, swung over the fence, and ran shouting towards the front-door of the Trescotts'. Then he hammered on the door, using his fists as if they were mallets. Mrs. Trescott instantly came to one of the windows on the second floor. Afterwards she knew she had been about to say, "The doctor is not at home, but if you will leave your name, I will let him know as soon as he comes."

Hannigan's bawling was for a minute incoherent, but she understood that it was not about croup.

"What?" she said, raising the window swiftly.

"Your house is on fire! You're all ablaze! Move quick if—" His cries were resounding, in the street as if it were a cave of echoes. Many feet pattered swiftly on the stones. There was one man who ran with an almost fabulous speed. He wore lavender trousers. A straw hat with a bright silk band was held half crumpled in his hand.

As Henry reached the front-door, Hannigan had just broken the lock with a kick. A thick cloud of smoke poured over them, and Henry, ducking his head, rushed into it. From Hannigan's clamor he knew only one thing, but it turned him blue with horror. In the hall a lick of flame had found the cord that supported "Signing the Declaration." The engraving slumped suddenly down at one end, and then dropped to the floor, where it burst with the sound of a bomb. The fire was already roaring like a winter wind among the pines.

At the head of the stairs Mrs. Trescott was waving her arms as if they were two reeds.

"Jimmie! Save Jimmie!" she screamed in Henry's face. He plunged past her and disappeared, taking the long-familiar routes among these upper chambers, where he had once held office as a sort of second assistant housemaid.

Hannigan had followed him up the stairs, and grappled the arm of the maniacal woman there. His face was black with rage. "You must come down," he bellowed.

She would only scream at him in reply: "Jimmie! Jimmie! Save Jimmie!" But he dragged her forth while she babbled at him.

As they swung out into the open air a man ran across the lawn, and seizing a shutter, pulled it from its hinges and flung it far out upon the grass. Then he frantically attacked the other shutters one by one. It was a kind of temporary insanity.

"Here, you," howled Hannigan, "hold Mrs. Trescott—And stop—"

The news had been telegraphed by a twist of the wrist of a neighbor who had gone to the fire-box at the corner, and the time when Hannigan and his charge struggled out of the house was the time when the whistle roared its hoarse night call, smiting the crowd in the park, causing the leader of the band, who was about to order the first triumphal clang of a military march, to let his hand drop slowly to his knees.

VII

Henry pawed awkwardly through the smoke in the upper halls. He had attempted to guide himself by the walls, but they were too hot. The paper was crimpling, and he expected at any moment to have a flame burst from under his hands.

"Jimmie!"

He did not call very loud, as if in fear that the humming flames below would overhear him.

"Jimmie! Oh, Jimmie!"

Stumbling and panting, he speedily reached the entrance to Jimmie's room and flung open the door. The little chamber had no smoke in it at all. It was faintly illuminated by a beautiful rosy light reflected circuitously from the flames that were consuming the house. The boy had apparently just been aroused by the noise. He sat in his bed, his lips apart, his eyes wide, while upon his little white-robed figure played caressingly the light from the fire. As the door flew open he had before him this apparition of his pal, a terror-stricken negro, all tousled and with wool scorching, who leaped upon him and bore him up in a blanket as if the whole affair were a case of kidnapping by a dreadful robber chief. Without waiting to go through the usual short but complete process of wrinkling up his face, Jimmie let out a gorgeous bawl, which resembled the expression of a calf's deepest terror. As Johnson, bearing him, reeled into the smoke of the hall, he flung his arms about his neck and buried his face in the blanket. He called twice in muffled tones: "Mam-ma! Mam-ma!" When Johnson came to the top of the stairs with his burden, he took a quick step backward. Through the smoke that rolled to him he could see that the lower hall was all ablaze. He cried out then in a howl that resembled Jimmie's former achievement. His legs gained a frightful faculty of bending sideways. Swinging about precariously on these reedy legs, he made his way back slowly, back along the upper hall. From the way of him then, he had given up almost all idea of escaping from the burning house, and with it the desire. He was submitting, submitting because of his fathers, bending his mind in a most perfect slavery to this conflagration.

He now clutched Jimmie as unconsciously as when, running toward the house, he had clutched the hat with the bright silk band.

Suddenly he remembered a little private staircase which led from a bedroom to an apartment which the doctor had fitted up as a laboratory and work-house, where he used some of his leisure, and also hours when he might have been sleeping, in devoting himself to experiments which came in the way of his study and interest.

When Johnson recalled this stairway the submission to the blaze departed instantly. He had been perfectly familiar with it, but his confusion had destroyed the memory of it.

In his sudden momentary apathy there had been little that resembled fear, but now, as a way of safety came to him, the old frantic terror caught him. He was no longer creature to the flames, and he was afraid of the battle with them. It was a singular and swift set of alternations in which he feared twice without submission, and submitted once without fear.

"Jimmie!" he wailed, as he staggered on his way. He wished this little inanimate body at his breast to participate in his tremblings. But the child had lain limp and still during these headlong charges and countercharges, and no sign came from him.

Johnson passed through two rooms and came to the head of the stairs. As he opened the door great billows of smoke poured out, but gripping Jimmie closer, he plunged down through them. All manner of odors assailed him during this flight. They seemed to be alive with envy, hatred, and malice. At the entrance to the laboratory he confronted a strange spectacle. The room was like a garden in the region where might be burning flowers. Flames of violet, crimson, green, blue, orange, and purple were blooming everywhere. There was one blaze that was precisely the hue of a delicate coral. In another place was a mass that lay merely in phosphorescent inaction like a pile of emeralds. But all these marvels were to be seen dimly through clouds of heaving, turning, deadly smoke.

Johnson halted for a moment on the threshold. He cried out again in the negro wail that had in it the sadness of the swamps. Then he rushed across the room. An orange-colored flame leaped like a panther at the lavender trousers. This animal bit deeply into Johnson. There was an explosion at one side, and suddenly before him there reared a delicate, trembling sapphire shape like a fairy lady. With a quiet smile she blocked his path and doomed him and Jimmie. Johnson shrieked, and then ducked in the manner of his race in fights. He aimed to pass under the left guard of the sapphire lady. But she was swifter than eagles, and her talons caught in him as he plunged past her. Bowing his head as if his neck had been struck, Johnson lurched forward, twisting this way and that way. He fell on his back. The still form in the blanket flung from his arms, rolled to the edge of the floor and beneath the window.

Johnson had fallen with his head at the base of an old-fashioned desk.

There was a row of jars upon the top of this desk. For the most part, they were silent amid this rioting, but there was one which seemed to hold a scintillant and writhing serpent.

Suddenly the glass splintered, and a ruby-red snakelike thing poured its thick length out upon the top of the old desk. It coiled and hesitated, and then began to swim a languorous way down the mahogany slant. At the angle it waved its sizzling molten head to and fro over the closed eyes of the man beneath it. Then, in a moment, with a mystic impulse, it moved again, and the red snake flowed directly down into Johnson's upturned face.

Afterwards the trail of this creature seemed to reek, and amid flames and low explosions drops like red-hot jewels pattered softly down it at leisurely intervals.

VIII

Suddenly all roads led to Dr. Trescott's. The whole town flowed towards one point. Chippeway Hose Company Number One toiled desperately up Bridge Street Hill even as the Tuscaroras came in an impetuous sweep down Niagara Avenue. Meanwhile the machine of the hook-and-ladder experts from across the creek was spinning on its way. The chief of the fire department had been playing poker in the rear room of Whiteley's cigar-store, but at the first breath of the alarm he sprang through the door like a man escaping with the kitty.

In Whilomville, on these occasions, there was always a number of people who instantly turned their attention to the bells in the churches and school-houses. The bells not only emphasized the alarm, but it was the habit to send these sounds rolling across the sky in a stirring brazen uproar until the flames were practically vanquished. There was also a kind of rivalry as to which bell should be made to produce the greatest din. Even the Valley Church, four miles away among the farms, had heard the voices of its brethren, and immediately added a quaint little yelp.

Dr. Trescott had been driving homeward, slowly smoking a cigar, and feeling glad that this last case was now in complete obedience to him, like a wild animal that he had subdued, when he heard the long whistle, and chirped to his horse under the unlicensed but perfectly distinct impression that a fire had broken out in Oakhurst, a new and rather high-flying suburb of the town which was at least two miles from his own home. But in the second blast and in the ensuing silence he read the designation of his own district. He was then only a few blocks from his house. He took out the whip and laid it lightly on the mare. Surprised and frightened at this extraordinary action, she leaped forward, and as the reins straightened like steel bands, the doctor leaned backward a trifle. When the mare whirled him up to the closed gate he was wondering whose house could be afire. The man who had rung the signal-box yelled something at him, but he already knew. He left the mare to her will.

In front of his door was a maniacal woman in a wrapper. "Ned!" she screamed at sight of him. "Jimmie! Save Jimmie!"

Trescott had grown hard and chill. "Where?" he said. "Where?"

Mrs. Trescott's voice began to bubble. "Up—up—up—" She pointed at the second-story windows.

Hannigan was already shouting: "Don't go in that way! You can't go in that way!"

Trescott ran around the corner of the house and disappeared from them. He knew from the view he had taken of the main hall that it would be impossible to ascend from there. His hopes were fastened now to the stairway which led from the laboratory. The door which opened from this room out upon the lawn was fastened with a bolt and lock, but he kicked close to the lock and then close to the bolt. The door with a loud crash flew back. The doctor recoiled from the roll of smoke, and then bending low, he stepped into the garden of burning flowers. On the floor his stinging eyes could make out a form in a smouldering blanket near the window. Then, as he carried his son towards the door, he saw that the whole lawn seemed now alive with men and boys, the leaders in the great charge that the whole town was making. They seized him and his burden, and overpowered him in wet blankets and water.

But Hannigan was howling: "Johnson is in there yet! Henry Johnson is in there yet! He went in after the kid! Johnson is in there yet!"

These cries penetrated to the sleepy senses of Trescott, and he struggled with his captors, swearing, unknown to him and to them, all the deep blasphemies of his medical-student days. He rose to his feet and went again towards the door of the laboratory. They endeavored to restrain him, although they were much affrighted at him.

But a young man who was a brakeman on the railway, and lived in one of the rear streets near the Trescotts, had gone into the laboratory and brought forth a thing which he laid on the grass.

IX

There were hoarse commands from in front of the house. "Turn on your water, Five!" "Let 'er go, One!" The gathering crowd swayed this way and that way. The flames, towering high, cast a wild red light on their faces. There came the clangor of a gong from along some adjacent street. The crowd exclaimed at it. "Here comes Number Three!" "That's Three a-comin'!" A panting and irregular mob dashed into view, dragging a hose-cart. A cry of exultation arose from the little boys. "Here's Three!" The lads welcomed Never-Die Hose Company Number Three as if it was composed of a chariot dragged by a band of gods. The perspiring citizens flung themselves into the fray. The boys danced in impish joy at the displays of prowess. They acclaimed the approach of Number Two. They welcomed Number Four with cheers. They were so deeply moved by this whole affair that they bitterly guyed the late appearance of the hook and ladder company, whose heavy apparatus had almost stalled them on the Bridge Street hill. The lads hated and feared a fire, of course. They did not particularly want to have anybody's house burn, but still it was fine to see the gathering of the companies, and amid a great noise to watch their heroes perform all manner of prodigies.

They were divided into parties over the worth of different companies, and supported their creeds with no small violence. For instance, in that part of the little city where Number Four had its home it would be most daring for a boy to contend the superiority of any other company. Likewise, in another quarter, where a strange boy was asked which fire company was the best in

Whilomville, he was expected to answer "Number One." Feuds, which the boys forgot and remembered according to chance or the importance of some recent event, existed all through the town.

They did not care much for John Shipley, the chief of the department. It was true that he went to a fire with the speed of a falling angel, but when there he invariably lapsed into a certain still mood, which was almost a preoccupation, moving leisurely around the burning structure and surveying it, putting meanwhile at a cigar. This quiet man, who even when life was in danger seldom raised his voice, was not much to their fancy. Now old Sykes Huntington, when he was chief, used to bellow continually like a bull and gesticulate in a sort of delirium. He was much finer as a spectacle than this Shipley, who viewed a fire with the same steadiness that he viewed a raise in a large jack-pot. The greater number of the boys could never understand why the members of these companies persisted in re-electing Shipley, although they often pretended to understand it, because "My father says" was a very formidable phrase in argument, and the fathers seemed almost unanimous in advocating Shipley.

At this time there was considerable discussion as to which company had gotten the first stream of water on the fire. Most of the boys claimed that Number Five owned that distinction, but there was a determined minority who contended for Number One. Boys who were the blood adherents of other companies were obliged to choose between the two on this occasion, and the talk waxed warm.

But a great rumor went among the crowds. It was told with hushed voices. Afterwards a reverent silence fell even upon the boys. Jimmie Trescott and Henry Johnson had been burned to death, and Dr. Trescott himself had been most savagely hurt. The crowd did not even feel the police pushing at them. They raised their eyes, shining now with awe, towards the high flames.

The man who had information was at his best. In low tones he described the whole affair. "That was the kid's room—in the corner there. He had measles or somethin', and this coon—Johnson—was a-settin' up with 'im, and Johnson got sleepy or somethin' and upset the lamp, and the doctor he was down in his office, and he came running up, and they all got burned together till they dragged 'em out."

Another man, always preserved for the deliverance of the final judgment, was saying: "Oh, they'll die sure. Burned to flinders. No chance. Hull lot of 'em. Anybody can see." The crowd concentrated its gaze still more closely upon these flags of fire which waved joyfully against the black sky. The bells of the town were clashing unceasingly.

A little procession moved across the lawn and towards the street. There were three cots, borne by twelve of the firemen. The police moved sternly, but it needed no effort of theirs to open a lane for this slow cortege. The men who bore the cots were well known to the crowd, but in this solemn parade during the ringing of the bells and the shouting, and with the red glare upon the sky, they seemed utterly foreign, and Whilomville paid them a deep respect. Each man in this stretcher party had gained a reflected majesty. They were footmen to death, and the crowd made subtle obeisance to this august dignity derived from three prospective graves. One woman turned away with a shriek at sight of the covered body on the first stretcher, and people faced her suddenly in silent and mournful indignation. Otherwise there was barely a sound as these twelve important men with measured tread carried their burdens through the throng.

The little boys no longer discussed the merits of the different fire companies. For the greater part they had been routed. Only the more courageous viewed closely the three figures veiled in yellow blankets.

X

Old Judge Denning Hagenthorpe, who lived nearly opposite the Trescotts, had thrown his door wide open to receive the afflicted family. When it was publicly learned that the doctor and his son and the negro were still alive, it required a specially detailed policeman to prevent people from scaling the front porch and interviewing these sorely wounded. One old lady appeared with a miraculous poultice, and she quoted most damning Scripture to the officer when he said that she could not pass him. Throughout the night some lads old enough to be given privileges or to compel them from their mothers remained vigilantly upon the kerb in anticipation of a death or some such event. The reporter of the Morning Tribune rode thither on his bicycle every hour until three o'clock.

Six of the ten doctors in Whilomville attended at Judge Hagenthorpe's house.

Almost at once they were able to know that Trescott's burns were not vitally important. The child would possibly be scarred badly, but his life was undoubtedly safe. As for the negro Henry Johnson, he could not live. His body was frightfully seared, but more than that, he now had no face. His face had simply been burned away.

Trescott was always asking news of the two other patients. In the morning he seemed fresh and strong, so they told him that Johnson was doomed. They then saw him stir on the bed, and sprang quickly to see if the bandages needed readjusting. In the sudden glance he threw from one to another he impressed them as being both leonine and impracticable.

The morning paper announced the death of Henry Johnson. It contained a long interview with Edward J. Hannigan, in which the latter described in full the performance of Johnson at the fire. There was also an editorial built from all the best words in the vocabulary of the staff. The town halted in its accustomed road of thought, and turned a reverent attention to the memory of this hostler. In the breasts of many people was the regret that they had not known enough to give him a hand and a lift when he was alive, and they judged themselves stupid and ungenerous for this failure.

The name of Henry Johnson became suddenly the title of a saint to the little boys. The one who thought of it first could, by quoting it in an argument, at once overthrow his antagonist, whether it applied to the subject or whether it did not.

"Nigger, nigger, never die.

Black face and shiny eye."

Boys who had called this odious couplet in the rear of Johnson's march buried the fact at the bottom of their hearts.

Later in the day Miss Bella Farragut, of No. 7 Watermelon Alley, announced that she had been engaged to marry Mr. Henry Johnson.

XI

The old judge had a cane with an ivory head. He could never think at his best until he was leaning slightly on this stick and smoothing the white top with slow movements of his hands. It was also to him a kind of narcotic. If by any chance he mislaid it, he grew at once very irritable, and was likely to speak sharply to his sister, whose mental incapacity he had patiently endured for thirty years in the old mansion on Ontario Street. She was not at all aware of her brother's opinion of her endowments, and so it might be said that the judge had successfully dissembled for more than a quarter of a century, only risking the truth at the times when his cane was lost.

On a particular day the judge sat in his armchair on the porch. The sunshine sprinkled through the lilac-bushes and poured great coins on the boards. The sparrows disputed in the trees that lined the pavements. The judge mused deeply, while his hands gently caressed the ivory head of his cane.

Finally he arose and entered the house, his brow still furrowed in a thoughtful frown. His stick thumped solemnly in regular beats. On the second floor he entered a room where Dr. Trescott was working about the bedside of Henry Johnson. The bandages on the negro's head allowed only one thing to appear, an eye, which unwinkingly stared at the judge. The later spoke to Trescott on the condition of the patient. Afterward he evidently had something further to say, but he seemed to be kept from it by the scrutiny of the unwinking eye, at which he furtively glanced from time to time.

When Jimmie Trescott was sufficiently recovered, his mother had taken him to pay a visit to his grandparents in Connecticut. The doctor had remained to take care of his patients, but as a matter of truth he spent most of his time at Judge Hagenthorpe's house, where lay Henry Johnson. Here he slept and ate almost every meal in the long nights and days of his vigil.

At dinner, and away from the magic of the unwinking eye, the judge said, suddenly, "Trescott, do you think it is—" As Trescott paused expectantly, the judge fingered his knife. He said, thoughtfully, "No one wants to advance such ideas, but somehow I think that that poor fellow ought to die."

There was in Trescott's face at once a look of recognition, as if in this tangent of the judge he saw an old problem. He merely sighed and answered, "Who knows?" The words were spoken in a deep tone that gave them an elusive kind of significance.

The judge retreated to the cold manner of the bench. "Perhaps we may not talk with propriety of this kind of action, but I am induced to say that you are performing a questionable charity in preserving this negro's life. As near as I can understand, he will hereafter be a monster, a perfect monster, and probably with an affected brain. No man can observe you as I have observed you and not know that it was a matter of conscience with you, but I am afraid, my friend, that it is one of the blunders of virtue." The judge had delivered his views with his habitual oratory. The last three words he spoke with a particular emphasis, as if the phrase was his discovery.

The doctor made a weary gesture. "He saved my boy's life."

"Yes," said the judge, swiftly—"yes, I know!"

"And what am I to do?" said Trescott, his eyes suddenly lighting like an outburst from smouldering peat. "What am I to do? He gave himself for—for Jimmie. What am I to do for him?"

The judge abased himself completely before these words. He lowered his eyes for a moment. He picked at his cucumbers.

Presently he braced himself straightly in his chair. "He will be your creation, you understand. He is purely your creation. Nature has very evidently given him up. He is dead. You are restoring him to life. You are making him, and he will be a monster, and with no mind.

"He will be what you like, judge," cried Trescott, in sudden, polite fury. "He will be anything, but, by God! he saved my boy."

The judge interrupted in a voice trembling with emotion: "Trescott!

Trescott! Don't I know?"

Trescott had subsided to a sullen mood. "Yes, you know," he answered, acidly; "but you don't know all about your own boy being saved from death." This was a perfectly childish allusion to the judge's bachelorhood. Trescott knew that the remark was infantile, but he seemed to take desperate delight in it.

But it passed the judge completely. It was not his spot.

"I am puzzled," said he, in profound thought. "I don't know what to say."

Trescott had become repentant. "Don't think I don't appreciate what you say, judge. But—"

"Of course!" responded the judge, quickly. "Of course."

"It—" began Trescott.

"Of course," said the judge.

In silence they resumed their dinner.

"Well," said the judge, ultimately, "it is hard for a man to know what to do."

"It is," said the doctor, fervidly.

There was another silence. It was broken by the judge:

"Look here, Trescott; I don't want you to think—"

"No, certainly not," answered the doctor, earnestly.

"Well, I don't want you to think I would say anything to—It was only that I thought that I might be able to suggest to you that—perhaps—the affair was a little dubious."

With an appearance of suddenly disclosing his real mental perturbation, the doctor said: "Well, what would you do? Would you kill him?" he asked, abruptly and sternly.

"Trescott, you fool," said the old man, gently.

"Oh, well, I know, judge, but then—" He turned red, and spoke with new violence: "Say, he saved my boy—do you see? He saved my boy."

"You bet he did," cried the judge, with enthusiasm. "You bet he did." And they remained for a time gazing at each other, their faces illuminated with memories of a certain deed.

After another silence, the judge said, "It is hard for a man to know what to do."

XII

Late one evening Trescott, returning from a professional call, paused his buggy at the Hagenthorpe gate. He tied the mare to the old tin-covered post, and entered the house. Ultimately he appeared with a companion—a man who walked slowly and carefully, as if he were learning. He was wrapped to the heels in an old-fashioned ulster. They entered the buggy and drove away.

After a silence only broken by the swift and musical humming of the wheels on the smooth road, Trescott spoke. "Henry," he said, "I've got you a home here with old Alek Williams. You will have everything you want to eat and a good place to sleep, and I hope you will get along there all right. I will pay all your expenses, and come to see you as often as I can. If you don't get along, I want you to let me know as soon as possible, and then we will do what we can to make it better."

The dark figure at the doctor's side answered with a cheerful laugh. "These buggy wheels don' look like I washed 'em yesterday, docteh," he said.

Trescott hesitated for a moment, and then went on insistently, "I am taking you to Alek Williams, Henry, and I—"

The figure chuckled again. "No, 'deed! No, seh! Alek Williams don' know a hoss! 'Deed he don't. He don' know a hoss from a pig." The laugh that followed was like the rattle of pebbles.

Trescott turned and looked sternly and coldly at the dim form in the gloom from the buggy-top. "Henry," he said, "I didn't say anything about horses. I was saying—"

"Hoss? Hoss?" said the quavering voice from these near shadows. "Hoss? 'Deed I don' know all erbout a boss! 'Deed I don't." There was a satirical chuckle.

At the end of three miles the mare slackened and the doctor leaned forward, peering, while holding tight reins. The wheels of the buggy bumped often over out-cropping bowlders. A window shone forth, a simple square of topaz on a great black hill-side. Four dogs charged the buggy with ferocity, and when it did not promptly retreat, they circled courageously around the flanks, baying. A door opened near the window in the hill-side, and a man came and stood on a beach of yellow light.

"Yah! yah! You Roveh! You Susie! Come yah! Come yah this minit!"

Trescott called across the dark sea of grass, "Hello, Alek!"

"Hello!"

"Come down here and show me where to drive."

The man plunged from the beach into the surf, and Trescott could then only trace his course by the fervid and polite ejaculations of a host who was somewhere approaching. Presently Williams took the mare by the head, and uttering cries of welcome and scolding the swarming dogs, led the equipage towards the lights. When they halted at the door and Trescott was climbing out, Williams cried, "Will she stand, docteh?"

"She'll stand all right, but you better hold her for a minute. Now, Henry." The doctor turned and held both arms to the dark figure. It crawled to him painfully like a man going down a ladder. Williams took the mare away to be tied to a little tree, and when he returned he found them awaiting him in the gloom beyond the rays from the door.

He burst out then like a siphon pressed by a nervous thumb. "Hennery! Hennery, ma ol' frien'. Well, if I ain' glade. If I ain' glade!"

Trescott had taken the silent shape by the arm and led it forward into the full revelation of the light. "Well, now, Alek, you can take Henry and put him to bed, and in the morning I will—"

Near the end of this sentence old Williams had come front to front with Johnson. He gasped for a second, and then yelled the yell of a man stabbed in the heart.

For a fraction of a moment Trescott seemed to be looking for epithets. Then he roared: "You old black chump! You old black—Shut up! Shut up! Do you hear?"

Williams obeyed instantly in the matter of his screams, but he continued in a lowered voice: "Ma Lode amassy! Who'd ever think? Ma Lode amassy!"

Trescott spoke again in the manner of a commander of a battalion. "Alek!"

The old negro again surrendered, but to himself he repeated in a whisper, "Ma Lode!" He was aghast and trembling.

As these three points of widening shadows approached the golden doorway a hale old negress appeared there, bowing. "Good-evenin', docteh! Good-evenin'! Come in! come in!" She had evidently just retired from a tempestuous struggle to place the room in order, but she was now bowing rapidly. She made the effort of a person swimming.

"Don't trouble yourself, Mary," said Trescott, entering. "I've brought Henry for you to take care of, and all you've got to do is to carry out what I tell you." Learning that he was not followed, he faced the door, and said, "Come in, Henry."

Johnson entered. "Whee!" shrieked Mrs. Williams. She almost achieved a back somersault. Six young members of the tribe of Williams made a simultaneous plunge for a position behind the stove, and formed a wailing heap.

XIII

"You know very well that you and your family lived usually on less than three dollars a week, and now that Dr. Trescott pays you five dollars a week for Johnson's board, you live like millionaires. You haven't done a stroke of work since Johnson began to board with you—everybody knows that—and so what are you kicking about?"

The judge sat in his chair on the porch, fondling his cane, and gazing down at old Williams, who stood under the lilac-bushes. "Yes, I know, jedge," said the negro, wagging his head in a puzzled manner. "Tain't like as if I didn't 'preciate what the docteh done, but—but—well, yeh see, jedge," he added, gaining a new impetus, "it's—it's hard wuk. This ol' man nev' did wuk so hard. Lode, no."

"Don't talk such nonsense, Alek," spoke the judge, sharply. "You have never really worked in your life—anyhow, enough to support a family of sparrows, and now when you are in a more prosperous condition than ever before, you come around talking like an old fool."

The negro began to scratch his head. "Yeh see, jedge," he said at last, "my ol' 'ooman she cain't 'ceive no lady callahs, nohow."

"Hang lady callers'" said the judge, irascibly. "If you have flour in the barrel and meat in the pot, your wife can get along without receiving lady callers, can't she?"

"But they won't come ainyhow, jedge," replied Williams, with an air of still deeper stupefaction. "Noner ma wife's frien's ner noner ma frien's 'll come near ma res'dence."

"Well, let them stay home if they are such silly people."

The old negro seemed to be seeking a way to elude this argument, but evidently finding none, he was about to shuffle meekly off. He halted, however. "Jedge," said he, "ma ol' 'ooman's near driv' abstracted."

"Your old woman is an idiot," responded the judge.

Williams came very close and peered solemnly through a branch of lilac. "Judge," he whispered, "the chillens."

"What about them?"

Dropping his voice to funereal depths, Williams said, "They—they cain't eat."

"Can't eat!" scoffed the judge, loudly. "Can't eat! You must think I am as big an old fool as you are. Can't eat—the little rascals! What's to prevent them from eating?"

In answer, Williams said, with mournful emphasis, "Hennery." Moved with a kind of satisfaction at his tragic use of the name, he remained staring at the judge for a sign of its effect.

The judge made a gesture of irritation. "Come, now, you old scoundrel, don't beat around the bush any more. What are you up to? What do you want? Speak out like a man, and don't give me any more of this tiresome rigamarole."

"I ain't er-beatin' round 'bout nuffin, jedge," replied Williams, indignantly. "No, seh; I say whatter got to say right out. 'Deed I do."

"Well, say it, then."

"Jedge," began the negro, taking off his hat and switching his knee with it, "Lode knows I'd do jes 'bout as much fer five dollehs er week as ainy cul'd man, but—but this yere business is awful, jedge. I raikon 'ain't been no sleep in—in my house sence docteh done fetch 'im."

"Well, what do you propose to do about it?"

Williams lifted his eyes from the ground and gazed off through the trees. "Raikon I got good appetite, an' sleep jes like er dog, but he—he's done broke me all up. 'Tain't no good, nohow. I wake up in the night; I hear 'im, mebbe, er-whimperin' an' er-whimperin', an' I sneak an' I sneak until I try th' do' to see if he locked in. An' he keep me er-puzzlin' an' er-quakin' all night long. Don't know how'll do in th' winter. Can't let 'im out where th' chillen is. He'll done freeze where he is now." Williams spoke these sentences as if he were talking to himself. After a silence of deep reflection he continued: "Folks go round sayin' he ain't Hennery Johnson at all. They say he's er devil!"

"What?" cried the judge.

"Yesseh," repeated Williams, in tones of injury, as if his veracity had been challenged. "Yesseh. I'm er-tellin' it to yeh straight, jedge. Plenty cul'd people folks up my way say it is a devil."

"Well, you don't think so yourself, do you?"

"No. 'Tain't no devil. It's Hennery Johnson."

"Well, then, what is the matter with you? You don't care what a lot of foolish people say. Go on 'tending to your business, and pay no attention to such idle nonsense."

"'Tis nonsense, jedge; but he looks like er devil."

"What do you care what he looks like?" demanded the judge.

"Ma rent is two dollehs and er half er month," said Williams, slowly.

"It might just as well be ten thousand dollars a month," responded the judge. "You never pay it, anyhow."

"Then, anoth' thing," continued Williams, in his reflective tone. "If he was all right in his haid I could stan' it; but, jedge, he's crazier 'n er loon. Then when he looks like er devil, an' done skears all ma frien's away, an' ma chillens cain't eat, an' ma ole 'ooman jes raisin' Cain all the time, an' ma rent two dollehs an' er half er month, an' him not right in his haid, it seems like five dollehs er week—"

The judge's stick came down sharply and suddenly upon the floor of the porch. "There," he said, "I thought that was what you were driving at."

Williams began swinging his head from side to side in the strange racial mannerism. "Now hol' on a minnet, jedge," he said, defensively. "'Tain't like as if I didn't 'preciate what the docteh done. 'Tain't that. Docteh Trescott is er kind man, an' 'tain't like as if I didn't 'preciate what he done; but—but—"

"But what? You are getting painful, Alek. Now tell me this: did you ever have five dollars a week regularly before in your life?"

Williams at once drew himself up with great dignity, but in the pause after that question he drooped gradually to another attitude. In the end he answered, heroically: "No, jedge, I 'ain't. An' 'tain't like as if I was er-sayin' five dollehs wasn't er lot er money for a man like me. But, jedge, what er man oughter git fer this kinder wuk is er salary. Yesseh, jedge," he repeated, with a great impressive gesture; "fer this kinder wuk er man oughter git er Salary." He laid a terrible emphasis upon the final word.

The judge laughed. "I know Dr. Trescott's mind concerning this affair, Alek; and if you are dissatisfied with your boarder, he is quite ready to move him to some other place; so, if you care to leave word with me that you are tired of the arrangement and wish it changed, he will come and take Johnson away."

Williams scratched his head again in deep perplexity. "Five dollehs is er big price fer bo'd, but 'tain't no big price fer the bo'd of er crazy man," he said, finally.

"What do you think you ought to get?" asked the judge.

"Well," answered Alek, in the manner of one deep in a balancing of the scales, "he looks like er devil, an' done skears e'rybody, an' ma chillens cain't eat, an' I cain't sleep, an' he ain't right in his haid, an'—"

"You told me all those things."

After scratching his wool, and beating his knee with his hat, and gazing off through the trees and down at the ground, Williams said, as he kicked nervously at the gravel, "Well, jedge, I think it is wuth—" He stuttered.

"Worth what?"

"Six dollehs," answered Williams, in a desperate outburst.

The judge lay back in his great arm-chair and went through all the motions of a man laughing heartily, but he made no sound save a slight cough. Williams had been watching him with apprehension.

"Well," said the judge, "do you call six dollars a salary?"

"No, seh," promptly responded Williams. "'Tain't a salary. No, 'deed!

'Tain't a salary." He looked with some anger upon the man who questioned his intelligence in this way.

"Well, supposing your children can't eat?"

"I—"

"And supposing he looks like a devil? And supposing all those things continue? Would you be satisfied with six dollars a week?"

Recollections seemed to throng in Williams's mind at these interrogations, and he answered dubiously. "Of co'se a man who ain't right in his haid, an' looks like er devil—But six dollehs—" After these two attempts at a sentence Williams suddenly appeared as an orator, with a great shiny palm waving in the air. "I tell yeh, jedge, six dollehs is six dollehs, but if I git six dollehs for bo'ding Hennery Johnson, I uhns it! I uhns it!"

"I don't doubt that you earn six dollars for every week's work you do," said the judge.

"Well, if I bo'd Hennery Johnson fer six dollehs er week, I uhns it! I uhns it!" cried Williams, wildly.

XIV

Reifsnyder's assistant had gone to his supper, and the owner of the shop was trying to placate four men who wished to be shaved at once. Reifsnyder was very garrulous—a fact which made him rather remarkable among barbers, who, as a class, are austerely speechless, having been taught silence by the hammering reiteration of a tradition. It is the customers who talk in the ordinary event.

As Reifsnyder waved his razor down the cheek of a man in the chair, he turned often to cool the impatience of the others with pleasant talk, which they did not particularly heed.

"Oh, he should have let him die," said Bainbridge, a railway engineer, finally replying to one of the barber's orations. "Shut up, Reif, and go on with your business!"

Instead, Reifsnyder paused shaving entirely, and turned to front the speaker. "Let him die?" he demanded. "How vas that? How can you let a man die?"

"By letting him die, you chump," said the engineer. The others laughed a little, and Reifsnyder turned at once to his work, sullenly, as a man overwhelmed by the derision of numbers.

"How vas that?" he grumbled later. "How can you let a man die when he vas done so much for you?"

"'When he vas done so much for you?'" repeated Bainbridge. "You better shave some people. How vas that? Maybe this ain't a barber shop?"

A man hitherto silent now said, "If I had been the doctor, I would have done the same thing."

"Of course," said Reifsnyder. "Any man could do it. Any man that vas not like you, you—old—flint-hearted—fish." He had sought the final words with painful care, and he delivered the collection triumphantly at Bainbridge. The engineer laughed.

The man in the chair now lifted himself higher, while Reifsnyder began an elaborate ceremony of anointing and combing his hair. Now free to join comfortably in the talk, the man said: "They say he is the most terrible thing in the world. Young Johnnie Bernard—that drives the grocery wagon—saw him up at Alek Williams's shanty, and he says he couldn't eat anything for two days."

"Chee!" said Reifsnyder.

"Well, what makes him so terrible?" asked another.

"Because he hasn't got any face," replied the barber and the engineer in duct.

"Hasn't got any face!" repeated the man. "How can he do without any face?"

"He has no face in the front of his head.

In the place where his face ought to grow."

Bainbridge sang these lines pathetically as he arose and hung his hat on a hook. The man in the chair was about to abdicate in his favor. "Get a gait on you now," he said to Reifsnyder. "I go out at 7.31."

As the barber foamed the lather on the cheeks of the engineer he seemed to be thinking heavily. Then suddenly he burst out. "How would you like to be with no face?" he cried to the assemblage.

"Oh, if I had to have a face like yours—" answered one customer.

Bainbridge's voice came from a sea of lather. "You're kicking because if losing faces became popular, you'd have to go out of business."

"I don't think it will become so much popular," said Reifsnyder.

"Not if it's got to be taken off in the way his was taken off," said another man. "I'd rather keep mine, if you don't mind."

"I guess so!" cried the barber. "Just think!"

The shaving of Bainbridge had arrived at a time of comparative liberty for him. "I wonder what the doctor says to himself?" he observed. "He may be sorry he made him live."

"It was the only thing he could do," replied a man. The others seemed to agree with him.

"Supposing you were in his place," said one, "and Johnson had saved your kid. What would you do?"

"Certainly!"

"Of course! You would do anything on earth for him. You'd take all the trouble in the world for him. And spend your last dollar on him. Well, then?"

"I wonder how it feels to be without any face?" said Reifsnyder, musingly.

The man who had previously spoken, feeling that he had expressed himself well, repeated the whole thing. "You would do anything on earth for him. You'd take all the trouble in the world for him. And spend your last dollar on him. Well, then?"

"No, but look," said Reifsnyder; "supposing you don't got a face!"

XV

As soon as Williams was hidden from the view of the old judge he began to gesture and talk to himself. An elation had evidently penetrated to his vitals, and caused him to dilate as if he had been filled with gas. He snapped his fingers in the air, and whistled fragments of triumphal music. At times, in his progress towards his shanty, he indulged in a shuffling movement that was really a dance. It was to be learned from the intermediate monologue that he had emerged from his trials laurelled and proud. He was the unconquerable Alexander Williams. Nothing could exceed the bold self-reliance of his manner. His kingly stride, his heroic song, the derisive flourish of his hands—all betokened a man who had successfully defied the world.

On his way he saw Zeke Paterson coming to town. They hailed each other at a distance of fifty yards.

"How do, Broth' Paterson?"

"How do, Broth' Williams?"

They were both deacons.

"Is you' folks well, Broth' Paterson?"

"Middlin', middlin'. How's you' folks, Broth' Williams?"

Neither of them had slowed his pace in the smallest degree. They had simply begun this talk when a considerable space separated them, continued it as they passed, and added polite questions as they drifted steadily apart. Williams's mind seemed to be a balloon. He had been so inflated that he had not noticed that Paterson had definitely shied into the dry ditch as they came to the point of ordinary contact.

Afterwards, as he went a lonely way, he burst out again in song and pantomimic celebration of his estate. His feet moved in prancing steps.

When he came in sight of his cabin, the fields were bathed in a blue dusk, and the light in the window was pale. Cavorting and gesticulating, he gazed joyfully for some moments upon this light. Then suddenly another idea seemed to attack his mind, and he stopped, with an air of being suddenly dampened. In the end he approached his home as if it were the fortress of an enemy.

Some dogs disputed his advance for a loud moment, and then discovering their lord, slunk away embarrassed. His reproaches were addressed to them in muffled tones.

Arriving at the door, he pushed it open with the timidity of a new thief. He thrust his head cautiously sideways, and his eyes met the eyes of his wife, who sat by the table, the lamp-light defining a half of her face. "'Sh!" he said, uselessly. His glance travelled swiftly to the inner door which shielded the one bed-chamber. The pickaninnies, strewn upon the floor of the living-room, were softly snoring. After a hearty meal they had promptly dispersed themselves about the place and gone to sleep. "'Sh!" said Williams again to his motionless and silent wife. He had allowed only his head to appear. His wife, with one hand upon the edge of the table and the other at her knee, was regarding him with wide eyes and parted lips as if he were a spectre. She looked to be one who was living in terror, and even the familiar face at the door had thrilled her because it had come suddenly.

Williams broke the tense silence. "Is he all right?" he whispered, waving his eyes towards the inner door. Following his glance timorously, his wife nodded, and in a low tone answered:

"I raikon he's done gone t' sleep."

Williams then slunk noiselessly across his threshold.

He lifted a chair, and with infinite care placed it so that it faced the dreaded inner door. His wife moved slightly, so as to also squarely face it. A silence came upon them in which they seemed to be waiting for a calamity, pealing and deadly.

Williams finally coughed behind his hand. His wife started, and looked upon him in alarm. "Pears like he done gwine keep quiet ternight," he breathed. They continually pointed their speech and their looks at the inner door, paying it the homage due to a corpse or a phantom. Another long stillness followed this sentence. Their eyes shone white and wide. A wagon rattled down the distant road. From their chairs they looked at the window, and the effect of the light in the cabin was a presentation of an intensely black and solemn night. The old woman adopted the attitude used always in church at funerals. At times she seemed to be upon the point of breaking out in prayer.

"He mighty quiet ter-night," whispered Williams. "Was he good ter-day?" For answer his wife raised her eyes to the ceiling in the supplication of Job. Williams moved restlessly. Finally he tiptoed to the door. He knelt slowly and without a sound, and placed his ear near the key-hole. Hearing a noise behind him, he turned quickly. His wife was staring at him aghast. She stood in front of the stove, and her arms were spread out in the natural movement to protect all her sleeping ducklings.

But Williams arose without having touched the door. "I raikon he er-sleep," he said, fingering his wool. He debated with himself for some time. During this interval his wife remained, a great fat statue of a mother shielding her children.

It was plain that his mind was swept suddenly by a wave of temerity. With a sounding step he moved towards the door. His fingers were almost upon the knob when he swiftly ducked and dodged away, clapping his hands to the back of his head. It was as if the portal had threatened him. There was a little tumult near the stove, where Mrs. Williams's desperate retreat had involved her feet with the prostrate children.

After the panic Williams bore traces of a feeling of shame. He returned to the charge. He firmly grasped the knob with his left hand, and with his other hand turned the key in the lock. He pushed the door, and as it swung portentously open he sprang nimbly to one side like the fearful slave liberating the lion. Near the stove a group had formed, the terror stricken mother, with her arms stretched, and the aroused children clinging frenziedly to her skirts.

The light streamed after the swinging door, and disclosed a room six feet one way and six feet the other way. It was small enough to enable the radiance to lay it plain. Williams peered warily around the corner made by the door-post.

Suddenly he advanced, retired, and advanced again with a howl. His palsied family had expected him to spring backward, and at his howl they heaped themselves wondrously. But Williams simply stood in the little room emitting his howls before an open window. "He's gone! He's gone! He's gone!" His eye and his hand had speedily proved the fact. He had even thrown open a little cupboard.

Presently he came flying out. He grabbed his hat, and hurled the outer door back upon its hinges. Then he tumbled headlong into the night. He was yelling: "Docteh Trescott! Docteh Trescott!" He ran wildly through the fields, and galloped in the direction of town. He continued to call to Trescott, as if the latter was within easy hearing. It was as if Trescott was poised in the contemplative sky over the running negro, and could heed this reaching voice—"Docteh Trescott!"

In the cabin, Mrs. Williams, supported by relays from the battalion of children, stood quaking watch until the truth of daylight came as a reinforcement and made the arrogant, strutting, swashbuckler children, and a mother who proclaimed her illimitable courage.

XVI

Theresa Page was giving a party. It was the outcome of a long series of arguments addressed to her mother, which had been overheard in part by her father. He had at last said five words, "Oh, let her have it." The mother had then gladly capitulated.

Theresa had written nineteen invitations, and distributed them at recess to her schoolmates. Later her mother had composed five large cakes, and still later a vast amount of lemonade.

So the nine little girls and the ten little boys sat quite primly in the dining-room, while Theresa and her mother plied them with cake and lemonade, and also with ice-cream. This primness sat now quite strangely upon them. It was owing to the presence of Mrs. Page. Previously in the parlor alone with their games they had overturned a chair; the boys had let more or less of their hoodlum spirit shine forth. But when circumstances could be possibly magnified to warrant it, the girls made the boys victims of an insufferable pride, snubbing them mercilessly. So in the dining-room they resembled a class at Sunday-school, if it were not for the subterranean smiles, gestures, rebuffs, and poutings which stamped the affair as a children's party.

Two little girls of this subdued gathering were planted in a settle with their backs to the broad window. They were beaming lovingly upon each other with an effect of scorning the boys.

Hearing a noise behind her at the window, one little girl turned to face it. Instantly she screamed and sprang away, covering her face with her hands. "What was it? What was it?" cried every one in a roar. Some slight movement of the eyes of the weeping and shuddering child informed the company that she had been frightened by an appearance at the window. At once they all faced the imperturbable window, and for a moment there was a silence. An astute lad made an immediate census of the other lads. The prank of slipping out and looming spectrally at a window was too venerable. But the little boys were all present and astonished.

As they recovered their minds they uttered warlike cries, and through a side door sallied rapidly out against the terror. They vied with each other in daring.

None wished particularly to encounter a dragon in the darkness of the garden, but there could be no faltering when the fair ones in the dining-room were present. Calling to each other in stern voices, they went dragooning over the lawn, attacking the shadows with ferocity, but still with the caution of reasonable beings. They found, however, nothing new to the peace of the night. Of course there was a lad who told a great lie. He described a grim figure, bending low and slinking off along the fence. He gave a number of details, rendering his lie more splendid by a repetition of certain forms which he recalled from romances. For instance, he insisted that he had heard the creature emit a hollow laugh.

Inside the house the little girl who had raised the alarm was still shuddering and weeping. With the utmost difficulty was she brought to a state approximating calmness by Mrs. Page. Then she wanted to go home at once.

Page entered the house at this time. He had exiled himself until he concluded that this children's party was finished and gone. He was obliged to escort the little girl home because she screamed again when they opened the door and she saw the night.

She was not coherent even to her mother. Was it a man? She didn't know. It was simply a thing, a dreadful thing.

XVII

In Watermelon Alley the Farraguts were spending their evening as usual on the little rickety porch. Sometimes they howled gossip to other people on other rickety porches. The thin wail of a baby arose from a near house. A man had a terrific altercation with his wife, to which the alley paid no attention at all.

There appeared suddenly before the Farraguts a monster making a low and sweeping bow. There was an instant's pause, and then occurred something that resembled the effect of an upheaval of the earth's surface. The old woman hurled herself backward with a dreadful cry. Young Sim had been perched gracefully on a railing. At sight of the monster he simply fell over it to the ground. He made no sound, his eyes stuck out, his nerveless hands tried to grapple the rail to prevent a tumble, and then he vanished. Bella, blubbering, and with her hair suddenly and mysteriously dishevelled, was crawling on her hands and knees fearsomely up the steps.

Standing before this wreck of a family gathering, the monster continued to bow. It even raised a deprecatory claw. "Doh' make no botheration 'bout me, Miss Fa'gut," it said, politely. "No, 'deed. I jes drap in ter ax if yer well this evenin', Miss Fa'gut. Don' make no botheration. No, 'deed. I gwine ax you to go to er daince with me, Miss Fa'gut. I ax you if I can have the magnifercent gratitude of you' company on that 'casion, Miss Fa'gut."

The girl cast a miserable glance behind her. She was still crawling away. On the ground beside the porch young Sim raised a strange bleat, which expressed both his fright and his lack of wind. Presently the monster, with a fashionable amble, ascended the steps after the girl.

She grovelled in a corner of the room as the creature took a chair. It seated itself very elegantly on the edge. It held an old cap in both hands. "Don' make no botheration, Miss Fa'gut. Don' make no botherations. No, 'deed. I jes drap in ter ax you if you won' do me the proud of acceptin' ma humble invitation to er daince, Miss Fa'gut."

She shielded her eyes with her arms and tried to crawl past it, but the genial monster blocked the way. "I jes drap in ter ax you 'bout er daince, Miss Fa'gut. I ax you if I kin have the magnifercent gratitude of you' company on that 'casion, Miss Fa'gut."

In a last outbreak of despair, the girl, shuddering and wailing, threw herself face downward on the floor, while the monster sat on the edge of the chair gabbling courteous invitations, and holding the old hat daintily to his stomach.

At the back of the house, Mrs. Farragut, who was of enormous weight, and who for eight years had done little more than sit in an armchair and describe her various ailments, had with speed and agility scaled a high board fence.

XVIII

The black mass in the middle of Trescott's property was hardly allowed to cool before the builders were at work on another house. It had sprung upward at a fabulous rate. It was like a magical composition born of the ashes. The doctor's office was the first part to be completed, and he had already moved in his new books and instruments and medicines.

Trescott sat before his desk when the chief of police arrived. "Well, we found him," said the latter.

"Did you?" cried the doctor. "Where?"

"Shambling around the streets at daylight this morning. I'll be blamed if I can figure on where he passed the night."

"Where is he now?"

"Oh, we jugged him. I didn't know what else to do with him. That's what I want you to tell me. Of course we can't keep him. No charge could be made, you know."

"I'll come down and get him."

The official grinned retrospectively. "Must say he had a fine career while he was out. First thing he did was to break up a children's party at Page's. Then he went to Watermelon Alley. Whoo! He stampeded the whole outfit. Men, women, and children running pell-mell, and yelling. They say one old woman broke her leg, or something, shinning over a fence. Then he went right out on the main street, and an Irish girl threw a fit, and there was a sort of a riot. He began to run, and a big crowd chased him, firing rocks. But he gave them the slip somehow down there by the foundry and in the railroad yard. We looked for him all night, but couldn't find him."

"Was he hurt any? Did anybody hit him with a stone?"

"Guess there isn't much of him to hurt any more, is there? Guess he's been hurt up to the limit. No. They never touched him. Of course nobody really wanted to hit him, but you know how a crowd gets. It's like—it's like—"

"Yes, I know."

For a moment the chief of the police looked reflectively at the floor. Then he spoke hesitatingly. "You know Jake Winter's little girl was the one that he scared at the party. She is pretty sick, they say."

"Is she? Why, they didn't call me. I always attend the Winter family."

"No? Didn't they?" asked the chief, slowly. "Well—you know—Winter is—well, Winter has gone clean crazy over this business. He wanted—he wanted to have you arrested."

"Have me arrested? The idiot! What in the name of wonder could he have me arrested for?"

"Of course. He is a fool. I told him to keep his trap shut. But then you know how he'll go all over town yapping about the thing. I thought I'd better tip you."

"Oh, he is of no consequence; but then, of course, I'm obliged to you, Sam."

"That's all right. Well, you'll be down tonight and take him out, eh? You'll get a good welcome from the jailer. He don't like his job for a cent. He says you can have your man whenever you want him. He's got no use for him."

"But what is this business of Winter's about having me arrested?"

"Oh, it's a lot of chin about your having no right to allow this—this—this man to be at large. But I told him to tend to his own business. Only I thought I'd better let you know. And I might as well say right now, doctor, that there is a good deal of talk about this thing. If I were you, I'd come to the jail pretty late at night, because there is likely to be a crowd around the door, and I'd bring a—er—mask, or some kind of a veil, anyhow."

XIX

Martha Goodwin was single, and well along into the thin years. She lived with her married sister in Whilomville. She performed nearly all the housework in exchange for the privilege of existence. Every one tacitly recognized her labor as a form of penance for the early end of her betrothed, who had died of small-pox, which he had not caught from her.

But despite the strenuous and unceasing workaday of her life, she was a woman of great mind. She had adamantine opinions upon the situation in Armenia, the condition of women in China, the flirtation between Mrs. Minster of Niagara Avenue and young Griscom, the conflict in the Bible class of the Baptist Sunday-school, the duty of the United States towards the Cuban insurgents, and many other colossal matters. Her fullest experience of violence was gained on an occasion when she had seen a hound clubbed, but in the plan which she had made for the reform of the world she advocated drastic measures. For instance, she contended that all the Turks should be pushed into the sea and drowned, and that Mrs. Minster and young Griscom should be hanged side by side on twin gallows. In fact, this woman of peace, who had seen only peace, argued constantly for a creed of illimitable ferocity. She was invulnerable on these questions, because eventually she overrode all opponents with a sniff. This sniff was an active force. It was to her antagonists like a bang over the head, and none was known to recover from this expression of exalted contempt. It left them windless and conquered. They never again came forward as candidates for suppression. And Martha walked her kitchen with a stern brow, an invincible being like Napoleon.

Nevertheless her acquaintances, from the pain of their defeats, had been long in secret revolt. It was in no wise a conspiracy, because they did not care to state their open rebellion, but nevertheless it was understood that any woman who could not coincide with one of Martha's contentions was entitled to the support of others in the small circle. It amounted to an arrangement by which all were required to disbelieve any theory for which Martha fought. This, however, did not prevent them from speaking of her mind with profound respect.

Two people bore the brunt of her ability. Her sister Kate was visibly afraid of her, while Carrie Dungen sailed across from her kitchen to sit respectfully at Martha's feet and learn the business of the world. To be sure, afterwards, under another sun, she always laughed at Martha and pretended to deride her ideas, but in the presence of the sovereign she always remained silent or admiring. Kate, the sister, was of no consequence at all. Her principal delusion was that she did all the work in the up-stairs rooms of the house, while Martha did it down-stairs. The truth was seen only by the husband, who treated Martha with a kindness that was half banter, half deference. Martha herself had no suspicion that she was the only pillar of the domestic edifice. The situation was without definitions. Martha made definitions, but she devoted them entirely to the Armenians and Griscom and the Chinese and other subjects. Her dreams, which in early days had been of love of meadows and the shade of trees, of the face of a man, were now involved otherwise, and they were companioned in the kitchen curiously, Cuba, the hot-water kettle, Armenia, the washing of the dishes, and the whole thing being jumbled. In regard to social misdemeanors, she who was simply the mausoleum of a dead passion was probably the most savage critic in town. This unknown woman, hidden in a kitchen as in a well, was sure to have a considerable effect of the one kind or the other in the life of the town. Every time it moved a yard, she had personally contributed an inch. She could hammer so stoutly upon the door of a proposition that it would break from its hinges and fall upon her, but at any rate it moved. She was an engine, and the fact that she did not know that she was an engine contributed largely to the effect. One reason that she was formidable was that she did not even imagine that she was formidable. She remained a weak, innocent, and pig-headed creature, who alone would defy the universe if she thought the universe merited this proceeding.

One day Carrie Dungen came across from her kitchen with speed. She had a great deal of grist. "Oh," she cried, "Henry Johnson got away from where they was keeping him, and came to town last night, and scared everybody almost to death."

Martha was shining a dish-pan, polishing madly. No reasonable person could see cause for this operation, because the pan already glistened like silver. "Well!" she ejaculated. She imparted to the word a deep meaning. "This, my prophecy, has come to pass." It was a habit.

The overplus of information was choking Carrie. Before she could go on she was obliged to struggle for a moment. "And, oh, little Sadie Winter is awful sick, and they say Jake Winter was around this morning trying to get Doctor Trescott arrested. And poor old Mrs. Farragut sprained her ankle in trying to climb a fence. And there's a crowd around the jail all the time. They put Henry in jail because they didn't know what else to do with him, I guess. They say he is perfectly terrible."

Martha finally released the dish-pan and confronted the headlong speaker. "Well!" she said again, poising a great brown rag. Kate had heard the excited new-comer, and drifted down from the novel in her room. She was a shivery little woman. Her shoulder-blades seemed to be two panes of ice, for she was constantly shrugging and shrugging. "Serves him right if he was to lose all his patients," she said suddenly, in blood-thirsty tones. She snipped her words out as if her lips were scissors.

"Well, he's likely to," shouted Carrie Dungen. "Don't a lot of people say that they won't have him any more? If you're sick and nervous, Doctor Trescott would scare the life out of you, wouldn't he? He would me. I'd keep thinking."

Martha, stalking to and fro, sometimes surveyed the two other women with a contemplative frown.

XX

After the return from Connecticut, little Jimmie was at first much afraid of the monster who lived in the room over the carriage-house. He could not identify it in any way. Gradually, however, his fear dwindled under the influence of a weird fascination. He sidled into closer and closer relations with it.

One time the monster was seated on a box behind the stable basking in the rays of the afternoon sun. A heavy crepe veil was swathed about its head.

Little Jimmie and many companions came around the corner of the stable. They were all in what was popularly known as the baby class, and consequently escaped from school a half-hour before the other children. They halted abruptly at sight of the figure on the box. Jimmie waved his hand with the air of a proprietor.

"There he is," he said.

"O-o-o!" murmured all the little boys—"o-o-o!" They shrank back, and grouped according to courage or experience, as at the sound the monster slowly turned its head. Jimmie had remained in the van alone. "Don't be afraid! I won't let him hurt you," he said, delighted.

"Huh!" they replied, contemptuously. "We ain't afraid."

Jimmie seemed to reap all the joys of the owner and exhibitor of one of the world's marvels, while his audience remained at a distance—awed and entranced, fearful and envious.

One of them addressed Jimmie gloomily. "Bet you dassent walk right up to him." He was an older boy than Jimmie, and habitually oppressed him to a small degree. This new social elevation of the smaller lad probably seemed revolutionary to him.

"Huh!" said Jimmie, with deep scorn. "Dassent I? Dassent I, hey? Dassent I?"

The group was immensely excited. It turned its eyes upon the boy that Jimmie addressed. "No, you dassent," he said, stolidly, facing a moral defeat. He could see that Jimmie was resolved. "No, you dassent," he repeated, doggedly.

"Ho?" cried Jimmie. "You just watch!—you just watch!"

Amid a silence he turned and marched towards the monster. But possibly the palpable wariness of his companions had an effect upon him that weighed more than his previous experience, for suddenly, when near to the monster, he halted dubiously. But his playmates immediately uttered a derisive shout, and it seemed to force him forward. He went to the monster and laid his hand delicately on its shoulder. "Hello, Henry," he said, in a voice that trembled a trifle. The monster was crooning a weird line of negro melody that was scarcely more than a thread of sound, and it paid no heed to the boy.

Jimmie: strutted back to his companions. They acclaimed him and hooted his opponent. Amid this clamor the larger boy with difficulty preserved a dignified attitude.

"I dassent, dassent I?" said Jimmie to him.

"Now, you're so smart, let's see you do it!"

This challenge brought forth renewed taunts from the others. The larger boy puffed out his checks. "Well, I ain't afraid," he explained, sullenly. He had made a mistake in diplomacy, and now his small enemies were tumbling his prestige all about his ears. They crowed like roosters and bleated like lambs, and made many other noises which were supposed to bury him in ridicule and dishonor. "Well, I ain't afraid," he continued to explain through the din.

Jimmie, the hero of the mob, was pitiless. "You ain't afraid, hey?" he sneered. "If you ain't afraid, go do it, then."

"Well, I would if I wanted to," the other retorted. His eyes wore an expression of profound misery, but he preserved steadily other portions of a pot-valiant air. He suddenly faced one of his persecutors. "If you're so smart, why don't you go do it?" This persecutor sank promptly through the group to the rear. The incident gave the badgered one a breathing-spell, and for a moment even turned the derision in another direction. He took advantage of his interval. "I'll do it if anybody else will," he announced, swaggering to and fro.

Candidates for the adventure did not come forward. To defend themselves from this counter-charge, the other boys again set up their crowing and bleating. For a while they would hear nothing from him. Each time he opened his lips their chorus of noises made oratory impossible. But at last he was able to repeat that he would volunteer to dare as much in the affair as any other boy.

"Well, you go first," they shouted.

But Jimmie intervened to once more lead the populace against the large boy. "You're mighty brave, ain't you?" he said to him. "You dared me to do it, and I did—didn't I? Now who's afraid?" The others cheered this view loudly, and they instantly resumed the baiting of the large boy.

He shamefacedly scratched his left shin with his right foot. "Well, I ain't afraid." He cast an eye at the monster. "Well, I ain't afraid." With a glare of hatred at his squalling tormentors, he finally announced a grim intention. "Well, I'll do it, then, since you're so fresh. Now!"

The mob subsided as with a formidable countenance he turned towards the impassive figure on the box. The advance was also a regular progression from high daring to craven hesitation. At last, when some yards from the monster, the lad came to a full halt, as if he had encountered a stone wall. The observant little boys in the distance promptly hooted. Stung again by these cries, the lad sneaked two yards forward. He was crouched like a young cat ready for a backward spring. The crowd at the rear, beginning to respect this display, uttered some encouraging cries. Suddenly the lad gathered himself together, made a white and desperate rush forward, touched the monster's shoulder with a far-outstretched finger, and sped away, while his laughter rang out wild, shrill, and exultant.

The crowd of boys reverenced him at once, and began to throng into his camp, and look at him, and be his admirers. Jimmie was discomfited for a moment, but he and the larger boy, without agreement or word of any kind, seemed to recognize a truce, and they swiftly combined and began to parade before the others.

"Why, it's just as easy as nothing," puffed the larger boy. "Ain't it, Jim?"

"Course," blew Jimmie. "Why, it's as e-e-easy."

They were people of another class. If they had been decorated for courage on twelve battle-fields, they could not have made the other boys more ashamed of the situation.

Meanwhile they condescended to explain the emotions of the excursion, expressing unqualified contempt for any one who could hang back. "Why, it ain't nothin'. He won't do nothin' to you," they told the others, in tones of exasperation.

One of the very smallest boys in the party showed signs of a wistful desire to distinguish himself, and they turned their attention to him, pushing at his shoulders while he swung away from them, and hesitated dreamily. He was eventually induced to make furtive expedition, but it was only for a few yards. Then he paused, motionless, gazing with open mouth. The vociferous entreaties of Jimmie and the large boy had no power over him.

Mrs. Hannigan had come out on her back porch with a pail of water. From this coign she had a view of the secluded portion of the Trescott grounds that was behind the stable. She perceived the group of boys, and the monster on the box. She shaded her eyes with her hand to benefit her vision. She screeched then as if she was being murdered. "Eddie! Eddie! You come home this minute!"

Her son querulously demanded, "Aw, what for?"

"You come home this minute. Do you hear?"

The other boys seemed to think this visitation upon one of their number required them to preserve for a time the hang-dog air of a collection of culprits, and they remained in guilty silence until the little Hannigan, wrathfully protesting, was pushed through the door of his home. Mrs. Hannigan cast a piercing glance over the group, stared with a bitter face at the Trescott house, as if this new and handsome edifice was insulting her, and then followed her son.

There was wavering in the party. An inroad by one mother always caused them to carefully sweep the horizon to see if there were more coming. "This is my yard," said Jimmie, proudly. "We don't have to go home."

The monster on the box had turned its black crepe countenance towards the sky, and was waving its arms in time to a religious chant. "Look at him now," cried a little boy. They turned, and were transfixed by the solemnity and mystery of the indefinable gestures. The wail of the melody was mournful and slow. They drew back. It seemed to spellbind them with the power of a funeral. They were so absorbed that they did not hear the doctor's buggy drive up to the stable. Trescott got out, tied his horse, and approached the group. Jimmie saw him first, and at his look of dismay the others wheeled.

"What's all this, Jimmie?" asked Trescott, in surprise.

The lad advanced to the front of his companions, halted, and said nothing. Trescott's face gloomed slightly as he scanned the scene.

"What were you doing, Jimmie?"

"We was playin'," answered Jimmie, huskily.

"Playing at what?"

"Just playin'."

Trescott looked gravely at the other boys, and asked them to please go home. They proceeded to the street much in the manner of frustrated and revealed assassins. The crime of trespass on another boy's place was still a crime when they had only accepted the other boy's cordial invitation, and they were used to being sent out of all manner of gardens upon the sudden appearance of a father or a mother. Jimmie had wretchedly watched the departure of his companions. It involved the loss of his position as a lad who controlled the privileges of his father's grounds, but then he knew that in the beginning he had no right to ask so many boys to be his guests.

Once on the sidewalk, however, they speedily forgot their shame as trespassers, and the large boy launched forth in a description of his success in the late trial of courage. As they went rapidly up the street, the little boy who had made the furtive expedition cried out confidently from the rear, "Yes, and I went almost up to him, didn't I, Willie?"

The large boy crushed him in a few words. "Huh!" he scoffed. "You only went a little way. I went clear up to him."

The pace of the other boys was so manly that the tiny thing had to trot, and he remained at the rear, getting entangled in their legs in his attempts to reach the front rank and become of some importance, dodging this way and that way, and always piping out his little claim to glory.

XXI

"By-the-way, Grace," said Trescott, looking into the dining-room from his office door, "I wish you would send Jimmie to me before school-time."

When Jimmie came, he advanced so quietly that Trescott did not at first note him. "Oh," he said, wheeling from a cabinet, "here you are, young man."

"Yes, sir."

Trescott dropped into his chair and tapped the desk with a thoughtful finger. "Jimmie, what were you doing in the back garden yesterday—you and the other boys—to Henry?"

"We weren't doing anything, pa."

Trescott looked sternly into the raised eyes of his son. "Are you sure you were not annoying him in any way? Now what were you doing, exactly?"

"Why, we—why, we—now—Willie Dalzel said I dassent go right up to him, and I did; and then he did; and then—the other boys were 'fraid; and then—you comed."

Trescott groaned deeply. His countenance was so clouded in sorrow that the lad, bewildered by the mystery of it, burst suddenly forth in dismal lamentations. "There, there. Don't cry, Jim," said Trescott, going round the desk. "Only—" He sat in a great leather reading-chair, and took the boy on his knee. "Only I want to explain to you—"

After Jimmie had gone to school, and as Trescott was about to start on his round of morning calls, a message arrived from Doctor Moser. It set forth that the latter's sister was dying in the old homestead, twenty miles away up the valley, and asked Trescott to care for his patients for the day at least. There was also in the envelope a little history of each case and of what had already been done. Trescott replied to the messenger that he would gladly assent to the arrangement.

He noted that the first name on Moser's list was Winter, but this did not seem to strike him as an important fact. When its turn came, he rang the Winter bell. "Good-morning, Mrs. Winter," he said, cheerfully, as the door was opened. "Doctor Moser has been obliged to leave town to-day, and he has asked me to come in his stead. How is the little girl this morning?"

Mrs. Winter had regarded him in stony surprise. At last she said: "Come in! I'll see my husband." She bolted into the house. Trescott entered the hall, and turned to the left into the sitting-room.

Presently Winter shuffled through the door. His eyes flashed towards Trescott. He did not betray any desire to advance far into the room. "What do you want?" he said.

"What do I want? What do I want?" repeated Trescott, lifting his head suddenly. He had heard an utterly new challenge in the night of the jungle.

"Yes, that's what I want to know," snapped Winter. "What do you want?"

Trescott was silent for a moment. He consulted Moser's memoranda. "I see that your little girl's case is a trifle serious," he remarked. "I would advise you to call a physician soon. I will leave you a copy of Dr. Moser's record to give to any one you may call." He paused to transcribe the record on a page of his note-book. Tearing out the leaf, he extended it to Winter as he moved towards the door. The latter shrunk against the wall. His head was hanging as he reached for the paper. This caused him to grasp air, and so Trescott simply let the paper flutter to the feet of the other man.

"Good-morning," said Trescott from the hall. This placid retreat seemed to suddenly arouse Winter to ferocity. It was as if he had then recalled all the truths which he had formulated to hurl at Trescott. So he followed him into the hall, and down the hall to the door, and through the door to the porch, barking in fiery rage from a respectful distance. As Trescott imperturbably turned the mare's head down the road, Winter stood on the porch, still yelping. He was like a little dog.

XXII

"Have you heard the news?" cried Carrie Dungen as she sped towards Martha's kitchen. "Have you heard the news?" Her eyes were shining with delight.

"No," answered Martha's sister Kate, bending forward eagerly. "What was it? What was it?"

Carrie appeared triumphantly in the open door. "Oh, there's been an awful scene between Doctor Trescott and Jake Winter. I never thought that Jake Winter had any pluck at all, but this morning he told the doctor just what he thought of him."

"Well, what did he think of him?" asked Martha.

"Oh, he called him everything. Mrs. Howarth heard it through her front blinds. It was terrible, she says. It's all over town now. Everybody knows it."

"Didn't the doctor answer back?"

"No! Mrs. Howarth—she says he never said a word. He just walked down to his buggy and got in, and drove off as co-o-o-l. But Jake gave him jinks, by all accounts."

"But what did he say?" cried Kate, shrill and excited. She was evidently at some kind of a feast.

"Oh, he told him that Sadie had never been well since that night Henry Johnson frightened her at Theresa Page's party, and he held him responsible, and how dared he cross his threshold—and—and—and—"

"And what?" said Martha.

"Did he swear at him?" said Kate, in fearsome glee.

"No—not much. He did swear at him a little, but not more than a man does anyhow when he is real mad, Mrs. Howarth says."

"O-oh!" breathed Kate. "And did he call him any names?"

Martha, at her work, had been for a time in deep thought. She now interrupted the others. "It don't seem as if Sadie Winter had been sick since that time Henry Johnson got loose. She's been to school almost the whole time since then, hasn't she?"

They combined upon her in immediate indignation. "School? School? I should say not. Don't think for a moment. School!"

Martha wheeled from the sink. She held an iron spoon, and it seemed as if she was going to attack them. "Sadie Winter has passed here many a morning since then carrying her schoolbag. Where was she going? To a wedding?"

The others, long accustomed to a mental tyranny, speedily surrendered.

"Did she?" stammered Kate. "I never saw her."

Carrie Dungen made a weak gesture.

"If I had been Doctor Trescott," exclaimed Martha, loudly, "I'd have knocked that miserable Jake Winter's head off."

Kate and Carrie, exchanging glances, made an alliance in the air. "I don't see why you say that, Martha," replied Carrie, with considerable boldness, gaining support and sympathy from Kate's smile. "I don't see how anybody can be blamed for getting angry when their little girl gets almost scared to death and gets sick from it, and all that. Besides, everybody says—"

"Oh, I don't care what everybody says," said Martha.

"Well, you can't go against the whole town," answered Carrie, in sudden sharp defiance.

"No, Martha, you can't go against the whole town," piped Kate, following her leader rapidly.

"'The whole town,'" cried Martha. "I'd like to know what you call 'the whole town.' Do you call these silly people who are scared of Henry Johnson 'the whole town'?"

"Why, Martha," said Carrie, in a reasoning tone, "you talk as if you wouldn't be scared of him!"

"No more would I," retorted Martha.

"O-oh, Martha, how you talk!" said Kate. "Why, the idea! Everybody's afraid of him."

Carrie was grinning. "You've never seen him, have you?" she asked, seductively.

"No," admitted Martha.

"Well, then, how do you know that you wouldn't be scared?"

Martha confronted her. "Have you ever seen him? No? Well, then, how do you know you would be scared?"

The allied forces broke out in chorus: "But, Martha, everybody says so. Everybody says so."

"Everybody says what?"

"Everybody that's seen him say they were frightened almost to death. Tisn't only women, but it's men too. It's awful."

Martha wagged her head solemnly. "I'd try not to be afraid of him."

"But supposing you could not help it?" said Kate.

"Yes, and look here," cried Carrie. "I'll tell you another thing. The Hannigans are going to move out of the house next door."

"On account of him?" demanded Martha.

Carrie nodded. "Mrs. Hannigan says so herself."

"Well, of all things!" ejaculated Martha. "Going to move, eh? You don't say so! Where they going to move to?"

"Down on Orchard Avenue."

"Well, of all things! Nice house?"

"I don't know about that. I haven't heard. But there's lots of nice houses on Orchard."

"Yes, but they're all taken," said Kate. "There isn't a vacant house on Orchard Avenue."

"Oh yes, there is," said Martha. "The old Hampstead house is vacant."

"Oh, of course," said Kate. "But then I don't believe Mrs. Hannigan would like it there. I wonder where they can be going to move to?"

"I'm sure I don't know," sighed Martha. "It must be to some place we don't know about."

"Well." said Carrie Dungen, after a general reflective silence, "it's easy enough to find out, anyhow."

"Who knows—around here?" asked Kate.

"Why, Mrs. Smith, and there she is in her garden," said Carrie, jumping to her feet. As she dashed out of the door, Kate and Martha crowded at the window. Carrie's voice rang out from near the steps. "Mrs. Smith! Mrs. Smith! Do you know where the Hannigans are going to move to?"

XXIII

The autumn smote the leaves, and the trees of Whilomville were panoplied in crimson and yellow. The winds grew stronger, and in the melancholy purple of the nights the home shine of a window became a finer thing. The little boys, watching the sear and sorrowful leaves drifting down from the maples, dreamed of the near time when they could heap bushels in the streets and burn them during the abrupt evenings.

Three men walked down the Niagara Avenue. As they approached Judge Hagenthorpe's house he came down his walk to meet them in the manner of one who has been waiting.

"Are you ready, judge?" one said.

"All ready," he answered.

The four then walked to Trescott's house. He received them in his office, where he had been reading. He seemed surprised at this visit of four very active and influential citizens, but he had nothing to say of it.

After they were all seated, Trescott looked expectantly from one face to another. There was a little silence. It was broken by John Twelve, the wholesale grocer, who was worth $400,000, and reported to be worth over a million.

"Well, doctor," he said, with a short laugh, "I suppose we might as well admit at once that we've come to interfere in something which is none of our business."

"Why, what is it?" asked Trescott, again looking from one face to another. He seemed to appeal particularly to Judge Hagenthorpe, but the old man had his chin lowered musingly to his cane, and would not look at him.

"It's about what nobody talks of—much," said Twelve. "It's about Henry Johnson."

Trescott squared himself in his chair. "Yes?" he said.

Having delivered himself of the title, Twelve seemed to become more easy. "Yes," he answered, blandly, "we wanted to talk to you about it."

"Yes?" said Trescott.

Twelve abruptly advanced on the main attack. "Now see here, Trescott, we like you, and we have come to talk right out about this business. It may be none of our affairs and all that, and as for me, I don't mind if you tell me so; but I am not going to keep quiet and see you ruin yourself. And that's how we all feel."

"I am not ruining myself," answered Trescott.

"No, maybe you are not exactly ruining yourself," said Twelve, slowly, "but you are doing yourself a great deal of harm. You have changed from being the leading doctor in town to about the last one. It is mainly because there are always a large number of people who are very thoughtless fools, of course, but then that doesn't change the condition."

A man who had not heretofore spoken said, solemnly, "It's the women."

"Well, what I want to say is this," resumed Twelve: "Even if there are a lot of fools in the world, we can't see any reason why you should ruin yourself by opposing them. You can't teach them anything, you know."

"I am not trying to teach them anything." Trescott smiled wearily. "I—It is a matter of—well—"

"And there are a good many of us that admire you for it immensely," interrupted Twelve; "but that isn't going to change the minds of all those ninnies."

"It's the women," stated the advocate of this view again.

"Well, what I want to say is this," said Twelve. "We want you to get out of this trouble and strike your old gait again. You are simply killing your practice through your infernal pigheadedness. Now this thing is out of the ordinary, but there must be ways to—to beat the game somehow, you see. So we've talked it over—about a dozen of us—and, as I say, if you want to tell us to mind our own business, why, go ahead; but we've talked it over, and we've come to the conclusion that the only way to do is to get Johnson a place somewhere off up the valley, and—"

Trescott wearily gestured. "You don't know, my friend. Everybody is so afraid of him, they can't even give him good care. Nobody can attend to him as I do myself."

"But I have a little no-good farm up beyond Clarence Mountain that I was going to give to Henry," cried Twelve, aggrieved. "And if you—and if you—if you—through your house burning down, or anything—why, all the boys were prepared to take him right off your hands, and—and—"

Trescott arose and went to the window. He turned his back upon them. They sat waiting in silence. When he returned he kept his face in the shadow. "No, John Twelve," he said, "it can't be done."

There was another stillness. Suddenly a man stirred on his chair.

"Well, then, a public institution—" he began.

"No," said Trescott; "public institutions are all very good, but he is not going to one."

In the background of the group old Judge Hagenthorpe was thoughtfully smoothing the polished ivory head of his cane.

XXIV

Trescott loudly stamped the snow from his feet and shook the flakes from his shoulders. When he entered the house he went at once to the dining-room, and then to the sitting-room. Jimmie was there, reading painfully in a large book concerning giraffes and tigers and crocodiles.

"Where is your mother, Jimmie?" asked Trescott.

"I don't know, pa," answered the boy. "I think she is up-stairs."

Trescott went to the foot of the stairs and called, but there came no answer. Seeing that the door of the little drawing-room was open, he entered. The room was bathed in the half-light that came from the four dull panes of mica in the front of the great stove. As his eyes grew used to the shadows he saw his wife curled in an arm-chair. He went to her. "Why, Grace." he said, "didn't you hear me calling you?"

She made no answer, and as he bent over the chair he heard her trying to smother a sob in the cushion.

"Grace!" he cried. "You're crying!"

She raised her face. "I've got a headache, a dreadful headache, Ned."

"A headache?" he repeated, in surprise and incredulity.

He pulled a chair close to hers. Later, as he cast his eye over the zone of light shed by the dull red panes, he saw that a low table had been drawn close to the stove, and that it was burdened with many small cups and plates of uncut tea-cake. He remembered that the day was Wednesday, and that his wife received on Wednesdays.

"Who was here to-day, Gracie?" he asked.

From his shoulder there came a mumble, "Mrs. Twelve."

"Was she—um," he said. "Why—didn't Anna Hagenthorpe come over?"

The mumble from his shoulder continued, "She wasn't well enough."

Glancing down at the cups, Trescott mechanically counted them. There were fifteen of them. "There, there," he said. "Don't cry, Grace. Don't cry."

The wind was whining round the house, and the snow beat aslant upon the windows. Sometimes the coal in the stove settled with a crumbling sound, and the four panes of mica flashed a sudden new crimson. As he sat holding her head on his shoulder, Trescott found himself occasionally trying to count the cups. There were fifteen of them.

THE BLUE HOTEL

I

The Palace Hotel at Fort Romper was painted a light blue, a shade that is on the legs of a kind of heron, causing the bird to declare its position against any background. The Palace Hotel, then, was always screaming and howling in a way that made the dazzling winter landscape of Nebraska seem only a gray swampish hush. It stood alone on the prairie, and when the snow was falling the town two hundred yards away was not visible. But when the traveller alighted at the railway station he was obliged to pass the Palace Hotel before he could come upon the company of low clapboard houses which composed Fort Romper, and it was not to be thought that any traveller could pass the Palace Hotel without looking at it. Pat Scully, the proprietor, had proved himself a master of strategy when he chose his paints. It is true that on clear days, when the great trans-continental expresses, long lines of swaying Pullmans, swept through Fort Romper, passengers were overcome at the sight, and the cult that knows the brown-reds and the subdivisions of the dark greens of the East expressed shame, pity, horror, in a laugh. But to the citizens of this prairie town and to the people who would naturally stop there, Pat Scully had performed a feat. With this opulence and splendor, these creeds, classes, egotisms, that streamed through Romper on the rails day after day, they had no color in common.

As if the displayed delights of such a blue hotel were not sufficiently enticing, it was Scully's habit to go every morning and evening to meet the leisurely trains that stopped at Romper and work his seductions upon any man that he might see wavering, gripsack in hand.

One morning, when a snow-crusted engine dragged its long string of freight cars and its one passenger coach to the station, Scully performed the marvel of catching three men. One was a shaky and quick-eyed Swede, with a great shining cheap valise; one was a tall bronzed cowboy, who was on his way to a ranch near the Dakota line; one was a little silent man from the East, who didn't look it, and didn't announce it. Scully practically made them prisoners. He was so nimble and merry and kindly that each probably felt it would be the height of brutality to try to escape. They trudged off over the creaking board sidewalks in the wake of the eager little Irishman. He wore a heavy fur cap squeezed tightly down on his head. It caused his two red ears to stick out stiffly, as if they were made of tin.

At last, Scully, elaborately, with boisterous hospitality, conducted them through the portals of the blue hotel. The room which they entered was small. It seemed to be merely a proper temple for an enormous stove, which, in the centre, was humming with godlike violence. At various points on its surface the iron had become luminous and glowed yellow from the heat. Beside the stove Scully's son Johnnie was playing High-Five with an old farmer who had whiskers both gray and sandy. They were quarrelling. Frequently the old farmer turned his face towards a box of sawdust—colored brown from tobacco juice—that was behind the stove, and spat with an air of great impatience and irritation. With a loud flourish of words Scully destroyed the game of cards, and bustled his son up-stairs with part of the baggage of the new guests. He himself conducted them to three basins of the coldest water in the world. The cowboy and the Easterner burnished themselves fiery-red with this water, until it seemed to be some kind of a metal polish. The Swede, however, merely dipped his fingers gingerly and with trepidation. It was notable that throughout this series of small ceremonies the three travellers were made to feel that Scully was very benevolent. He was conferring great favors upon them. He handed the towel from one to the other with an air of philanthropic impulse.

Afterwards they went to the first room, and, sitting about the stove, listened to Scully's officious clamor at his daughters, who were preparing the mid-day meal. They reflected in the silence of experienced men who tread carefully amid new people. Nevertheless, the old farmer, stationary, invincible in his chair near the warmest part of the stove, turned his face from the sawdust box frequently and addressed a glowing commonplace to the strangers. Usually he was answered in short but adequate sentences by either the cowboy or the Easterner. The Swede said nothing. He seemed to be occupied in making furtive estimates of each man in the room. One might have thought that he had the sense of silly suspicion which comes to guilt. He resembled a badly frightened man.

Later, at dinner, he spoke a little, addressing his conversation entirely to Scully. He volunteered that he had come from New York, where for ten years he had worked as a tailor. These facts seemed to strike Scully as fascinating, and afterwards he volunteered that he had lived at Romper for fourteen years. The Swede asked about the crops and the price of labor. He seemed barely to listen to Scully's extended replies. His eyes continued to rove from man to man.

Finally, with a laugh and a wink, he said that some of these Western communities were very dangerous; and after his statement he straightened his legs under the table, tilted his head, and laughed again, loudly. It was plain that the demonstration had no meaning to the others. They looked at him wondering and in silence.

II

As the men trooped heavily back into the front-room, the two little windows presented views of a turmoiling sea of snow. The huge arms of the wind were making attempts—mighty, circular, futile—to embrace the flakes as they sped. A gate-post like a still man with a blanched face stood aghast amid this profligate fury. In a hearty voice Scully announced the presence of a blizzard. The guests of the blue hotel, lighting their pipes, assented with grunts of lazy masculine contentment. No island of the sea could be exempt in the degree of this little room with its humming stove. Johnnie, son of Scully, in a tone which defined his opinion of his ability as a card-player, challenged the old farmer of both gray and sandy whiskers to a game of High-Five. The farmer agreed with a contemptuous and bitter scoff. They sat close to the stove, and squared their knees under a wide board. The cowboy and the Easterner watched the game with interest. The Swede remained near the window, aloof, but with a countenance that showed signs of an inexplicable excitement.

The play of Johnnie and the gray-beard was suddenly ended by another quarrel. The old man arose while casting a look of heated scorn at his adversary. He slowly buttoned his coat, and then stalked with fabulous dignity from the room. In the discreet silence of all other men the Swede laughed. His laughter rang somehow childish. Men by this time had begun to look at him askance, as if they wished to inquire what ailed him.

A new game was formed jocosely. The cowboy volunteered to become the partner of Johnnie, and they all then turned to ask the Swede to throw in his lot with the little Easterner, He asked some questions about the game, and, learning that it wore many names, and that he had played it when it was under an alias, he accepted the invitation. He strode towards the men nervously, as if he expected to be assaulted. Finally, seated, he gazed from face to face and laughed shrilly. This laugh was so strange that the Easterner looked up quickly, the cowboy sat intent and with his mouth open, and Johnnie paused, holding the cards with still fingers.

Afterwards there was a short silence. Then Johnnie said, "Well, let's get at it. Come on now!" They pulled their chairs forward until their knees were bunched under the board. They began to play, and their interest in the game caused the others to forget the manner of the Swede.

The cowboy was a board-whacker. Each time that he held superior cards he whanged them, one by one, with exceeding force, down upon the improvised table, and took the tricks with a glowing air of prowess and pride that sent thrills of indignation into the hearts of his opponents. A game with a board-whacker in it is sure to become intense. The countenances of the Easterner and the Swede were miserable whenever the cowboy thundered down his aces and kings, while Johnnie, his eyes gleaming with joy, chuckled and chuckled.

Because of the absorbing play none considered the strange ways of the Swede. They paid strict heed to the game. Finally, during a lull caused by a new deal, the Swede suddenly addressed Johnnie: "I suppose there have been a good many men killed in this room." The jaws of the others dropped and they looked at him.

"What in hell are you talking about?" said Johnnie.

The Swede laughed again his blatant laugh, full of a kind of false courage and defiance. "Oh, you know what I mean all right," he answered.

"I'm a liar if I do!" Johnnie protested. The card was halted, and the men stared at the Swede. Johnnie evidently felt that as the son of the proprietor he should make a direct inquiry. "Now, what might you be drivin' at, mister?" he asked. The Swede winked at him. It was a wink full of cunning. His fingers shook on the edge of the board. "Oh, maybe you think I have been to nowheres. Maybe you think I'm a tenderfoot?"

"I don't know nothin' about you," answered Johnnie, "and I don't give a damn where you've been. All I got to say is that I don't know what you're driving at. There hain't never been nobody killed in this room."

The cowboy, who had been steadily gazing at the Swede, then spoke: "What's wrong with you, mister?"

Apparently it seemed to the Swede that he was formidably menaced. He shivered and turned white near the corners of his mouth. He sent an appealing glance in the direction of the little Easterner. During these moments he did not forget to wear his air of advanced pot-valor. "They say they don't know what I mean," he remarked mockingly to the Easterner.

The latter answered after prolonged and cautious reflection. "I don't understand you," he said, impassively.

The Swede made a movement then which announced that he thought he had encountered treachery from the only quarter where he had expected sympathy, if not help. "Oh, I see you are all against me. I see—"

The cowboy was in a state of deep stupefaction. "Say." he cried, as he tumbled the deck violently down upon the board "—say, what are you gittin' at, hey?"

The Swede sprang up with the celerity of a man escaping from a snake on the floor. "I don't want to fight!" he shouted. "I don't want to fight!"

The cowboy stretched his long legs indolently and deliberately. His hands were in his pockets. He spat into the sawdust box. "Well, who the hell thought you did?" he inquired.

The Swede backed rapidly towards a corner of the room. His hands were out protectingly in front of his chest, but he was making an obvious struggle to control his fright. "Gentlemen," he quavered, "I suppose I am going to be killed before I can leave this house! I suppose I am going to be killed before I can leave this house!" In his eyes was the dying-swan look. Through the windows could be seen the snow turning blue in the shadow of dusk. The wind tore at the house and some loose thing beat regularly against the clapboards like a spirit tapping.

A door opened, and Scully himself entered. He paused in surprise as he noted the tragic attitude of the Swede. Then he said, "What's the matter here?"

The Swede answered him swiftly and eagerly: "These men are going to kill me."

"Kill you!" ejaculated Scully. "Kill you! What are you talkin'?"

The Swede made the gesture of a martyr.

Scully wheeled sternly upon his son. "What is this, Johnnie?"

The lad had grown sullen. "Damned if I know," he answered. "I can't make no sense to it." He began to shuffle the cards, fluttering them together with an angry snap. "He says a good many men have been killed in this room, or something like that. And he says he's goin' to be killed here too. I don't know what ails him. He's crazy, I shouldn't wonder."

Scully then looked for explanation to the cowboy, but the cowboy simply shrugged his shoulders.

"Kill you?" said Scully again to the Swede. "Kill you? Man, you're off your nut."

"Oh, I know." burst out the Swede. "I know what will happen. Yes, I'm crazy—yes. Yes, of course, I'm crazy—yes. But I know one thing—" There was a sort of sweat of misery and terror upon his face. "I know I won't get out of here alive."

The cowboy drew a deep breath, as if his mind was passing into the last stages of dissolution. "Well, I'm dog-goned," he whispered to himself.

Scully wheeled suddenly and faced his son. "You've been troublin' this man!"

Johnnie's voice was loud with its burden of grievance. "Why, good Gawd, I ain't done nothin' to 'im."

The Swede broke in. "Gentlemen, do not disturb yourselves. I will leave this house. I will go away because"—he accused them dramatically with his glance—"because I do not want to be killed."

Scully was furious with his son. "Will you tell me what is the matter, you young divil? What's the matter, anyhow? Speak out!"

"Blame it!" cried Johnnie in despair, "don't I tell you I don't know. He—he says we want to kill him, and that's all I know. I can't tell what ails him."

The Swede continued to repeat: "Never mind, Mr. Scully; nevermind. I will leave this house. I will go away, because I do not wish to be killed. Yes, of course, I am crazy—yes. But I know one thing! I will go away. I will leave this house. Never mind, Mr. Scully; never mind. I will go away."

"You will not go 'way," said Scully. "You will not go 'way until I hear the reason of this business. If anybody has troubled you I will take care of him. This is my house. You are under my roof, and I will not allow any peaceable man to be troubled here." He cast a terrible eye upon Johnnie, the cowboy, and the Easterner.

"Never mind, Mr. Scully; never mind. I will go away. I do not wish to be killed." The Swede moved towards the door, which opened upon the stairs. It was evidently his intention to go at once for his baggage.

"No, no," shouted Scully peremptorily; but the white-faced man slid by him and disappeared. "Now," said Scully severely, "what does this mane?"

Johnnie and the cowboy cried together: "Why, we didn't do nothin' to 'im!"

Scully's eyes were cold. "No," he said, "you didn't?"

Johnnie swore a deep oath. "Why this is the wildest loon I ever see. We didn't do nothin' at all. We were jest sittin' here play in' cards, and he—"

The father suddenly spoke to the Easterner. "Mr. Blanc," he asked, "what has these boys been doin'?"

The Easterner reflected again. "I didn't see anything wrong at all," he said at last, slowly.

Scully began to howl. "But what does it mane?" He stared ferociously at his son. "I have a mind to lather you for this, me boy."

Johnnie was frantic. "Well, what have I done?" he bawled at his father.

III

"I think you are tongue-tied," said Scully finally to his son, the cowboy, and the Easterner; and at the end of this scornful sentence he left the room.

Up-stairs the Swede was swiftly fastening the straps of his great valise. Once his back happened to be half turned towards the door, and, hearing a noise there, he wheeled and sprang up, uttering a loud cry. Scully's wrinkled visage showed grimly in the light of the small lamp he carried. This yellow effulgence, streaming upward, colored only his prominent features, and left his eyes, for instance, in mysterious shadow. He resembled a murderer.

"Man! man!" he exclaimed, "have you gone daffy?"

"Oh, no! Oh, no!" rejoined the other. "There are people in this world who know pretty nearly as much as you do—understand?"

For a moment they stood gazing at each other. Upon the Swede's deathly pale checks were two spots brightly crimson and sharply edged, as if they had been carefully painted. Scully placed the light on the table and sat himself on the edge of the bed. He spoke ruminatively. "By cracky, I never heard of such a thing in my life. It's a complete muddle. I can't, for the soul of me, think how you ever got this idea into your head." Presently he lifted his eyes and asked: "And did you sure think they were going to kill you?"

The Swede scanned the old man as if he wished to see into his mind. "I did," he said at last. He obviously suspected that this answer might precipitate an outbreak. As he pulled on a strap his whole arm shook, the elbow wavering like a bit of paper.

Scully banged his hand impressively on the foot-board of the bed. "Why, man, we're goin' to have a line of ilictric street-cars in this town next spring."

"'A line of electric street-cars,'" repeated the Swede, stupidly.

"And," said Scully, "there's a new railroad goin' to be built down from Broken Arm to here. Not to mintion the four churches and the smashin' big brick school-house. Then there's the big factory, too. Why, in two years Romper 'll be a metropolis."

Having finished the preparation of his baggage, the Swede straightened himself. "Mr. Scully," he said, with sudden hardihood, "how much do I owe you?"

"You don't owe me anythin'," said the old man, angrily.

"Yes, I do," retorted the Swede. He took seventy-five cents from his pocket and tendered it to Scully; but the latter snapped his fingers in disdainful refusal. However, it happened that they both stood gazing in a strange fashion at three silver pieces on the Swede's open palm.

"I'll not take your money," said Scully at last. "Not after what's been goin' on here." Then a plan seemed to strike him. "Here," he cried, picking up his lamp and moving towards the door. "Here! Come with me a minute."

"No," said the Swede, in overwhelming alarm.

"Yes," urged the old man. "Come on! I want you to come and see a picter—just across the hall—in my room."

The Swede must have concluded that his hour was come. His jaw dropped and his teeth showed like a dead man's. He ultimately followed Scully across the corridor, but he had the step of one hung in chains.

Scully flashed the light high on the wall of his own chamber. There was revealed a ridiculous photograph of a little girl. She was leaning against a balustrade of gorgeous decoration, and the formidable bang to her hair was prominent. The figure was as graceful as an upright sled-stake, and, withal, it was of the hue of lead. "There," said Scully, tenderly, "that's the picter of my little girl that died. Her name was Carrie. She had the purtiest hair you ever saw! I was that fond of her, she—"

Turning then, he saw that the Swede was not contemplating the picture at all, but, instead, was keeping keen watch on the gloom in the rear.

"Look, man!" cried Scully, heartily. "That's the picter of my little gal that died. Her name was Carrie. And then here's the picter of my oldest boy, Michael. He's a lawyer in Lincoln, an' doin' well. I gave that boy a grand eddycation, and I'm glad for it now. He's a fine boy. Look at 'im now. Ain't he bold as blazes, him there in Lincoln, an honored an' respicted gintleman. An honored an' respicted gintleman," concluded Scully with a flourish. And, so saying, he smote the Swede jovially on the back.

The Swede faintly smiled.

"Now," said the old man, "there's only one more thing." He dropped suddenly to the floor and thrust his head beneath the bed. The Swede could hear his muffled voice. "I'd keep it under me piller if it wasn't for that boy Johnnie. Then there's the old woman—Where is it now? I never put it twice in the same place. Ah, now come out with you!"

Presently he backed clumsily from under the bed, dragging with him an old coat rolled into a bundle. "I've fetched him," he muttered. Kneeling on the floor, he unrolled the coat and extracted from its heart a large yellow-brown whiskey bottle.

His first maneuver was to hold the bottle up to the light. Reassured, apparently, that nobody had been tampering with it, he thrust it with a generous movement towards the Swede.

The weak-kneed Swede was about to eagerly clutch this element of strength, but he suddenly jerked his hand away and cast a look of horror upon Scully.

"Drink," said the old man affectionately. He had risen to his feet, and now stood facing the Swede.

There was a silence. Then again Scully said: "Drink!"

The Swede laughed wildly. He grabbed the bottle, put it to his mouth, and as his lips curled absurdly around the opening and his throat worked, he kept his glance, burning with hatred, upon the old man's face.

IV

After the departure of Scully the three men, with the card-board still upon their knees, preserved for a long time an astounded silence. Then Johnnie said: "That's the dod-dangest Swede I ever see."

"He ain't no Swede," said the cowboy, scornfully.

"Well, what is he then?" cried Johnnie. "What is he then?"

"It's my opinion," replied the cowboy deliberately, "he's some kind of a Dutchman." It was a venerable custom of the country to entitle as Swedes all light-haired men who spoke with a heavy tongue. In consequence the idea of the cowboy was not without its daring. "Yes, sir," he repeated. "It's my opinion this feller is some kind of a Dutchman."

"Well, he says he's a Swede, anyhow," muttered Johnnie, sulkily. He turned to the Easterner: "What do you think, Mr. Blanc?"

"Oh, I don't know," replied the Easterner.

"Well, what do you think makes him act that way?" asked the cowboy.

"Why, he's frightened." The Easterner knocked his pipe against a rim of the stove. "He's clear frightened out of his boots."

"What at?" cried Johnnie and cowboy together.

The Easterner reflected over his answer.

"What at?" cried the others again.

"Oh, I don't know, but it seems to me this man has been reading dime-novels, and he thinks he's right out in the middle of it—the shootin' and stabbin' and all."

"But," said the cowboy, deeply scandalized, "this ain't Wyoming, ner none of them places. This is Nebrasker."

"Yes," added Johnnie, "an' why don't he wait till he gits out West?"

The travelled Easterner laughed. "It isn't different there even—not in these days. But he thinks he's right in the middle of hell."

Johnnie and the cowboy mused long.

"It's awful funny," remarked Johnnie at last.

"Yes," said the cowboy. "This is a queer game. I hope we don't git snowed in, because then we'd have to stand this here man bein' around with us all the time. That wouldn't be no good."

"I wish pop would throw him out," said Johnnie.

Presently they heard a loud stamping on the stairs, accompanied by ringing jokes in the voice of old Scully, and laughter, evidently from the Swede. The men around the stove stared vacantly at each other. "Gosh!" said the cowboy. The door flew open, and old Scully, flushed and anecdotal, came into the room. He was jabbering at the Swede, who followed him, laughing bravely. It was the entry of two roisterers from a banquet-hall.

"Come now," said Scully sharply to the three seated men, "move up and give us a chance at the stove." The cowboy and the Easterner obediently sidled their chairs to make room for the new-comers. Johnnie, however, simply arranged himself in a more indolent attitude, and then remained motionless.

"Come! Git over, there," said Scully.

"Plenty of room on the other side of the stove," said Johnnie.

"Do you think we want to sit in the draught?" roared the father.

But the Swede here interposed with a grandeur of confidence. "No, no.

Let the boy sit where he likes," he cried in a bullying voice to the father.

"All right! All right!" said Scully, deferentially. The cowboy and the Easterner exchanged glances of wonder.

The five chairs were formed in a crescent about one side of the stove. The Swede began to talk; he talked arrogantly, profanely, angrily. Johnnie, the cowboy, and the Easterner maintained a morose silence, while old Scully appeared to be receptive and eager, breaking in constantly with sympathetic ejaculations.

Finally the Swede announced that he was thirsty. He moved in his chair, and said that he would go for a drink of water.

"I'll git it for you," cried Scully at once.

"No," said the Swede, contemptuously. "I'll get it for myself." He arose and stalked with the air of an owner off into the executive parts of the hotel.

As soon as the Swede was out of hearing Scully sprang to his feet and whispered intensely to the others: "Up-stairs he thought I was tryin' to poison 'im."

"Say," said Johnnie, "this makes me sick. Why don't you throw 'im out in the snow?"

"Why, he's all right now," declared Scully. "It was only that he was from the East, and he thought this was a tough place. That's all. He's all right now."

The cowboy looked with admiration upon the Easterner. "You were straight," he said. "You were on to that there Dutchman."

"Well," said Johnnie to his father, "he may be all right now, but I don't see it. Other time he was scared, but now he's too fresh."

Scully's speech was always a combination of Irish brogue and idiom, Western twang and idiom, and scraps of curiously formal diction taken from the story-books and newspapers, He now hurled a strange mass of language at the head of his son. "What do I keep? What do I keep? What do I keep?" he demanded, in a voice of thunder. He slapped his knee impressively, to indicate that he himself was going to make reply, and that all should heed. "I keep a hotel," he shouted. "A hotel, do you mind? A guest under my roof has sacred privileges. He is to be intimidated by none. Not one word shall he hear that would prejudice him in favor of goin' away. I'll not have it. There's no place in this here town where they can say they iver took in a guest of mine because he was afraid to stay here." He wheeled suddenly upon the cowboy and the Easterner. "Am I right?"

"Yes, Mr. Scully," said the cowboy, "I think you're right."

"Yes, Mr. Scully," said the Easterner, "I think you're right."

V

At six-o'clock supper, the Swede fizzed like a fire-wheel. He sometimes seemed on the point of bursting into riotous song, and in all his madness he was encouraged by old Scully. The Easterner was incased in reserve; the cowboy sat in wide-mouthed amazement, forgetting to eat, while Johnnie wrathily demolished great plates of food. The daughters of the house, when they were obliged to replenish the biscuits, approached as warily as Indians, and, having succeeded in their purpose, fled with ill-concealed trepidation. The Swede domineered the whole feast, and he gave it the appearance of a cruel bacchanal. He seemed to have grown suddenly taller; he gazed, brutally disdainful, into every face. His voice rang through the room. Once when he jabbed out harpoon-fashion with his fork to pinion a biscuit, the weapon nearly impaled the hand of the Easterner which had been stretched quietly out for the same biscuit.

After supper, as the men filed towards the other room, the Swede smote Scully ruthlessly on the shoulder. "Well, old boy, that was a good, square meal." Johnnie looked hopefully at his father; he knew that shoulder was tender from an old fall; and, indeed, it appeared for a moment as if Scully was going to flame out over the matter, but in the end he smiled a sickly smile and remained silent. The others understood from his manner that he was admitting his responsibility for the Swede's new view-point.

Johnnie, however, addressed his parent in an aside. "Why don't you license somebody to kick you down-stairs?" Scully scowled darkly by way of reply.

When they were gathered about the stove, the Swede insisted on another game of High Five. Scully gently deprecated the plan at first, but the Swede turned a wolfish glare upon him. The old man subsided, and the Swede canvassed the others. In his tone there was always a great threat. The cowboy and the Easterner both remarked indifferently that they would play. Scully said that he would presently have to go to meet the 6.58 train, and so the Swede turned menacingly upon Johnnie. For a moment their glances crossed like blades, and then Johnnie smiled and said, "Yes, I'll play."

They formed a square, with the little board on their knees. The Easterner and the Swede were again partners. As the play went on, it was noticeable that the cowboy was not board-whacking as usual. Meanwhile, Scully, near the lamp, had put on his spectacles and, with an appearance curiously like an old priest, was reading a newspaper. In time he went out to meet the 6.58 train, and, despite his precautions, a gust of polar wind whirled into the room as he opened the door. Besides scattering the cards, it dulled the players to the marrow. The Swede cursed frightfully. When Scully returned, his entrance disturbed a cosey and friendly scene. The Swede again cursed. But presently they were once more intent, their heads bent forward and their hands moving swiftly. The Swede had adopted the fashion of board-whacking.

Scully took up his paper and for a long time remained immersed in matters which were extraordinarily remote from him. The lamp burned badly, and once he stopped to adjust the wick. The newspaper, as he turned from page to page, rustled with a slow and comfortable sound. Then suddenly he heard three terrible words: "You are cheatin'!"

Such scenes often prove that there can be little of dramatic import in environment. Any room can present a tragic front; any room can be comic. This little den was now hideous as a torture-chamber. The new faces of the men themselves had changed it upon the instant. The Swede held a huge fist in front of Johnnie's face, while the latter looked steadily over it into the blazing orbs of his accuser. The Easterner had grown pallid; the cowboy's jaw had dropped in that expression of bovine amazement which was one of his important mannerisms. After the three words, the first sound in the room was made by Scully's paper as it floated forgotten to his feet. His spectacles had also fallen from his nose, but by a clutch he had saved them in air. His hand, grasping the spectacles, now remained poised awkwardly and near his shoulder. He stared at the card-players.

Probably the silence was while a second elapsed. Then, if the floor had been suddenly twitched out from under the men they could not have moved quicker. The five had projected themselves headlong towards a common point. It happened that Johnnie, in rising to hurl himself upon the Swede, had stumbled slightly because of his curiously instinctive care for the cards and the board. The loss of the moment allowed time for the arrival of Scully, and also allowed the cowboy time to give the Swede a great push which sent him staggering back. The men found tongue together, and hoarse shouts of rage, appeal, or fear burst from every throat. The cowboy pushed and jostled feverishly at the Swede, and the Easterner and Scully clung wildly to Johnnie; but, through the smoky air, above the swaying bodies of the peace-compellers, the eyes of the two warriors ever sought each other in glances of challenge that were at once hot and steely.

Of course the board had been overturned, and now the whole company of cards was scattered over the floor, where the boots of the men trampled the fat and painted kings and queens as they gazed with their silly eyes at the war that was waging above them.

Scully's voice was dominating the yells. "Stop now? Stop, I say! Stop, now—"

Johnnie, as he struggled to burst through the rank formed by Scully and the Easterner, was crying, "Well, he says I cheated! He says I cheated! I won't allow no man to say I cheated! If he says I cheated, he's a ——— ———!"

The cowboy was telling the Swede, "Quit, now! Quit, d'ye hear—"

The screams of the Swede never ceased: "He did cheat! I saw him! I saw him—"

As for the Easterner, he was importuning in a voice that was not heeded:

"Wait a moment, can't you? Oh, wait a moment. What's the good of a fight over a game of cards? Wait a moment—"

In this tumult no complete sentences were clear. "Cheat"—"Quit"—"He says"—these fragments pierced the uproar and rang out sharply. It was remarkable that, whereas Scully undoubtedly made the most noise, he was the least heard of any of the riotous band.

Then suddenly there was a great cessation. It was as if each man had paused for breath; and although the room was still lighted with the anger of men, it could be seen that there was no danger of immediate conflict, and at once Johnnie, shouldering his way forward, almost succeeded in confronting the Swede. "What did you say I cheated for? What did you say I cheated for? I don't cheat, and I won't let no man say I do!"

The Swede said, "I saw you! I saw you!"

"Well," cried Johnnie, "I'll fight any man what says I cheat!"

"No, you won't," said the cowboy. "Not here."

"Ah, be still, can't you?" said Scully, coming between them.

The quiet was sufficient to allow the Easterner's voice to be heard. He was repealing, "Oh, wait a moment, can't you? What's the good of a fight over a game of cards? Wait a moment!"

Johnnie, his red face appearing above his father's shoulder, hailed the Swede again. "Did you say I cheated?"

The Swede showed his teeth. "Yes."

"Then," said Johnnie, "we must fight."

"Yes, fight," roared the Swede. He was like a demoniac. "Yes, fight! I'll show you what kind of a man I am! I'll show you who you want to fight! Maybe you think I can't fight! Maybe you think I can't! I'll show you, you skin, you card-sharp! Yes, you cheated! You cheated! You cheated!"

"Well, let's go at it, then, mister," said Johnnie, coolly.

The cowboy's brow was beaded with sweat from his efforts in intercepting all sorts of raids. He turned in despair to Scully. "What are you goin' to do now?"

A change had come over the Celtic visage of the old man. He now seemed all eagerness; his eyes glowed.

"We'll let them fight," he answered, stalwartly. "I can't put up with it any longer. I've stood this damned Swede till I'm sick. We'll let them fight."

VI

The men prepared to go out-of-doors. The Easterner was so nervous that he had great difficulty in getting his arms into the sleeves of his new leather coat. As the cowboy drew his fur cap down over his cars his hands trembled. In fact, Johnnie and old Scully were the only ones who displayed no agitation. These preliminaries were conducted without words.

Scully threw open the door. "Well, come on," he said. Instantly a terrific wind caused the flame of the lamp to struggle at its wick, while a puff of black smoke sprang from the chimney-top. The stove was in mid-current of the blast, and its voice swelled to equal the roar of the storm. Some of the scarred and bedabbled cards were caught up from the floor and dashed helplessly against the farther wall. The men lowered their heads and plunged into the tempest as into a sea.

No snow was falling, but great whirls and clouds of flakes, swept up from the ground by the frantic winds, were streaming southward with the speed of bullets. The covered land was blue with the sheen of an unearthly satin, and there was no other hue save where, at the low, black railway station—which seemed incredibly distant—one light gleamed like a tiny jewel. As the men floundered into a thigh deep drift, it was known that the Swede was bawling out something. Scully went to him, put a hand on his shoulder and projected an ear. "What's that you say?" he shouted.

"I say," bawled the Swede again, "I won't stand much show against this gang. I know you'll all pitch on me."

Scully smote him reproachfully on the arm. "Tut, man!" he yelled. The wind tore the words from Scully's lips and scattered them far alee.

"You are all a gang of—" boomed the Swede, but the storm also seized the remainder of this sentence.

Immediately turning their backs upon the wind, the men had swung around a corner to the sheltered side of the hotel. It was the function of the little house to preserve here, amid this great devastation of snow, an irregular V-shape of heavily incrusted grass, which crackled beneath the feet. One could imagine the great drifts piled against the windward side. When the party reached the comparative peace of this spot it was found that the Swede was still bellowing.

"Oh, I know what kind of a thing this is! I know you'll all pitch on me. I can't lick you all!"

Scully turned upon him panther fashion. "You'll not have to whip all of us. You'll have to whip my son Johnnie. An' the man what troubles you durin' that time will have me to dale with."

The arrangements were swiftly made. The two men faced each other, obedient to the harsh commands of Scully, whose face, in the subtly luminous gloom, could be seen set in the austere impersonal lines that are pictured on the countenances of the Roman veterans. The Easterner's teeth were chattering, and he was hopping up and down like a mechanical toy. The cowboy stood rock-like.

The contestants had not stripped off any clothing. Each was in his ordinary attire. Their fists were up, and they eyed each other in a calm that had the elements of leonine cruelty in it.

During this pause, the Easterner's mind, like a film, took lasting impressions of three men—the iron-nerved master of the ceremony; the Swede, pale, motionless, terrible; and Johnnie, serene yet ferocious, brutish yet heroic. The entire prelude had in it a tragedy greater than the tragedy of action, and this aspect was accentuated by the long, mellow cry of the blizzard, as it sped the tumbling and wailing flakes into the black abyss of the south.

"Now!" said Scully.

The two combatants leaped forward and crashed together like bullocks. There was heard the cushioned sound of blows, and of a curse squeezing out from between the tight teeth of one.

As for the spectators, the Easterner's pent-up breath exploded from him with a pop of relief, absolute relief from the tension of the preliminaries. The cowboy bounded into the air with a yowl. Scully was immovable as from supreme amazement and fear at the fury of the fight which he himself had permitted and arranged.

For a time the encounter in the darkness was such a perplexity of flying arms that it presented no more detail than would a swiftly revolving wheel. Occasionally a face, as if illumined by a flash of light, would shine out, ghastly and marked with pink spots. A moment later, the men might have been known as shadows, if it were not for the involuntary utterance of oaths that came from them in whispers.

Suddenly a holocaust of warlike desire caught the cowboy, and he bolted forward with the speed of a broncho. "Go it, Johnnie! go it! Kill him! Kill him!"

Scully confronted him. "Kape back," he said; and by his glance the cowboy could tell that this man was Johnnie's father.

To the Easterner there was a monotony of unchangeable fighting that was an abomination. This confused mingling was eternal to his sense, which was concentrated in a longing for the end, the priceless end. Once the fighters lurched near him, and as he scrambled hastily backward he heard them breathe like men on the rack.

"Kill him, Johnnie! Kill him! Kill him! Kill him!" The cowboy's face was contorted like one of those agony masks in museums.

"Keep still," said Scully, icily.

Then there was a sudden loud grunt, incomplete, cut short, and Johnnie's body swung away from the Swede and fell with sickening heaviness to the grass. The cowboy was barely in time to prevent the mad Swede from flinging himself upon his prone adversary. "No, you don't," said the cowboy, interposing an arm. "Wait a second."

Scully was at his son's side. "Johnnie! Johnnie, me boy!" His voice had a quality of melancholy tenderness. "Johnnie! Can you go on with it?" He looked anxiously down into the bloody, pulpy face of his son.

There was a moment of silence, and then Johnnie answered in his ordinary voice, "Yes, I—it—yes."

Assisted by his father he struggled to his feet. "Wait a bit now till you git your wind," said the old man.

A few paces away the cowboy was lecturing the Swede. "No, you don't! Wait a second!"

The Easterner was plucking at Scully's sleeve. "Oh, this is enough," he pleaded. "This is enough! Let it go as it stands. This is enough!"

"Bill," said Scully, "git out of the road." The cowboy stepped aside. "Now." The combatants were actuated by a new caution as they advanced towards collision. They glared at each other, and then the Swede aimed a lightning blow that carried with it his entire weight. Johnnie was evidently half stupid from weakness, but he miraculously dodged, and his fist sent the over-balanced Swede sprawling.

The cowboy, Scully, and the Easterner burst into a cheer that was like a chorus of triumphant soldiery, but before its conclusion the Swede had scuffled agilely to his feet and come in berserk abandon at his foe. There was another perplexity of flying arms, and Johnnie's body again swung away and fell, even as a bundle might fall from a roof. The Swede instantly staggered to a little wind-waved tree and leaned upon it, breathing like an engine, while his savage and flame-lit eyes roamed from face to face as the men bent over Johnnie. There was a splendor of isolation in his situation at this time which the Easterner felt once when, lifting his eyes from the man on the ground, he beheld that mysterious and lonely figure, waiting.

"Arc you any good yet, Johnnie?" asked Scully in a broken voice.

The son gasped and opened his eyes languidly. After a moment he answered, "No—I ain't—any good—any—more." Then, from shame and bodily ill he began to weep, the tears furrowing down through the blood-stains on his face. "He was too—too—too heavy for me."

Scully straightened and addressed the waiting figure. "Stranger," he said, evenly, "it's all up with our side." Then his voice changed into that vibrant huskiness which is commonly the tone of the most simple and deadly announcements. "Johnnie is whipped."

Without replying, the victor moved off on the route to the front door of the hotel.

The cowboy was formulating new and un-spellable blasphemies. The Easterner was startled to find that they were out in a wind that seemed to come direct from the shadowed arctic floes. He heard again the wail of the snow as it was flung to its grave in the south. He knew now that all this time the cold had been sinking into him deeper and deeper, and he wondered that he had not perished. He felt indifferent to the condition of the vanquished man.

"Johnnie, can you walk?" asked Scully.

"Did I hurt—hurt him any?" asked the son.

"Can you walk, boy? Can you walk?"

Johnnie's voice was suddenly strong. There was a robust impatience in it. "I asked you whether I hurt him any!"

"Yes, yes, Johnnie," answered the cowboy, consolingly; "he's hurt a good deal."

They raised him from the ground, and as soon as he was on his feet he went tottering off, rebuffing all attempts at assistance. When the party rounded the corner they were fairly blinded by the pelting of the snow. It burned their faces like fire. The cowboy carried Johnnie through the drift to the door. As they entered some cards again rose from the floor and beat against the wall.

The Easterner rushed to the stove. He was so profoundly chilled that he almost dared to embrace the glowing iron. The Swede was not in the room. Johnnie sank into a chair, and, folding his arms on his knees, buried his face in them. Scully, warming one foot and then the other at a rim of the stove, muttered to himself with Celtic mournfulness. The cowboy had removed his fur cap, and with a dazed and rueful air he was running one hand through his tousled locks. From overhead they could hear the creaking of boards, as the Swede tramped here and there in his room.

The sad quiet was broken by the sudden flinging open of a door that led towards the kitchen. It was instantly followed by an inrush of women. They precipitated themselves upon Johnnie amid a chorus of lamentation. Before they carried their prey off to the kitchen, there to be bathed and harangued with that mixture of sympathy and abuse which is a feat of their sex, the mother straightened herself and fixed old Scully with an eye of stern reproach. "Shame be upon you, Patrick Scully!" she cried. "Your own son, too. Shame be upon you!"

"There, now! Be quiet, now!" said the old man, weakly.

"Shame be upon you, Patrick Scully!" The girls, rallying to this slogan, sniffed disdainfully in the direction of those trembling accomplices, the cowboy and the Easterner. Presently they bore Johnnie away, and left the three men to dismal reflection.

VII

"I'd like to fight this here Dutchman myself," said the cowboy, breaking a long silence.

Scully wagged his head sadly. "No, that wouldn't do. It wouldn't be right. It wouldn't be right."

"Well, why wouldn't it?" argued the cowboy. "I don't see no harm in it."

"No," answered Scully, with mournful heroism. "It wouldn't be right. It was Johnnie's fight, and now we mustn't whip the man just because he whipped Johnnie."

"Yes, that's true enough," said the cowboy; "but—he better not get fresh with me, because I couldn't stand no more of it."

"You'll not say a word to him," commanded Scully, and even then they heard the tread of the Swede on the stairs. His entrance was made theatric. He swept the door back with a bang and swaggered to the middle of the room. No one looked at him. "Well," he cried, insolently, at Scully, "I s'pose you'll tell me now how much I owe you?"

The old man remained stolid. "You don't owe me nothin'."

"Huh!" said the Swede, "huh! Don't owe 'im nothin'."

The cowboy addressed the Swede. "Stranger, I don't see how you come to be so gay around here."

Old Scully was instantly alert. "Stop!" he shouted, holding his hand forth, fingers upward. "Bill, you shut up!"

The cowboy spat carelessly into the sawdust box. "I didn't say a word, did I?" he asked.

"Mr. Scully," called the Swede, "how much do I owe you?" It was seen that he was attired for departure, and that he had his valise in his hand.

"You don't owe me nothin'," repeated Scully in his same imperturbable way.

"Huh!" said the Swede. "I guess you're right. I guess if it was any way at all, you'd owe me somethin'. That's what I guess." He turned to the cowboy. "'Kill him! Kill him! Kill him!'" he mimicked, and then guffawed victoriously. "'Kill him!'" He was convulsed with ironical humor.

But he might have been jeering the dead. The three men were immovable and silent, staring with glassy eyes at the stove.

The Swede opened the door and passed into the storm, giving one derisive glance backward at the still group.

As soon as the door was closed, Scully and the cowboy leaped to their feet and began to curse. They trampled to and fro, waving their arms and smashing into the air with their fists. "Oh, but that was a hard minute!" wailed Scully. "That was a hard minute! Him there leerin' and scoffin'! One bang at his nose was worth forty dollars to me that minute! How did you stand it, Bill?"

"How did I stand it?" cried the cowboy in a quivering voice. "How did I stand it? Oh!"

The old man burst into sudden brogue. "I'd loike to take that Swade," he wailed, "and hould 'im down on a shtone flure and bate 'im to a jelly wid a shtick!"

The cowboy groaned in sympathy. "I'd like to git him by the neck and ha-ammer him "—he brought his hand down on a chair with a noise like a pistol-shot—"hammer that there Dutchman until he couldn't tell himself from a dead coyote!"

"I'd bate 'im until he—"

"I'd show him some things—"

And then together they raised a yearning, fanatic cry—"Oh-o-oh! if we only could—"

"Yes!"

"Yes!"

"And then I'd—"

"O-o-oh!"

VIII

The Swede, tightly gripping his valise, tacked across the face of the storm as if he carried sails. He was following a line of little naked, gasping trees, which he knew must mark the way of the road. His face, fresh from the pounding of Johnnie's fists, felt more pleasure than pain in the wind and the driving snow. A number of square shapes loomed upon him finally, and he knew them as the houses of the main body of the town. He found a street and made travel along it, leaning heavily upon the wind whenever, at a corner, a terrific blast caught him.

He might have been in a deserted village. We picture the world as thick with conquering and elate humanity, but here, with the bugles of the tempest pealing, it was hard to imagine a peopled earth. One viewed the existence of man then as a marvel, and conceded a glamour of wonder to these lice which were caused to cling to a whirling, fire-smote, ice-locked, disease-stricken, space-lost bulb. The conceit of man was explained by this storm to be the very engine of life. One was a coxcomb not to die in it. However, the Swede found a saloon.

In front of it an indomitable red light was burning, and the snow-flakes were made blood color as they flew through the circumscribed territory of the lamp's shining. The Swede pushed open the door of the saloon and entered. A sanded expanse was before him, and at the end of it four men sat about a table drinking. Down one side of the room extended a radiant bar, and its guardian was leaning upon his elbows listening to the talk of the men at the table. The Swede dropped his valise upon the floor, and, smiling fraternally upon the barkeeper, said, "Gimme some whiskey, will you?" The man placed a bottle, a whiskey-glass, and a glass of ice-thick water upon the bar. The Swede poured himself an abnormal portion of whiskey and drank it in three gulps. "Pretty bad night," remarked the bartender, indifferently. He was making the pretension of blindness which is usually a distinction of his class; but it could have been seen that he was furtively studying the half-erased blood-stains on the face of the Swede. "Bad night," he said again.

"Oh, it's good enough for me," replied the Swede, hardily, as he poured himself some more whiskey. The barkeeper took his coin and maneuvered it through its reception by the highly nickelled cash-machine. A bell rang; a card labelled "20 cts." had appeared.

"No," continued the Swede, "this isn't too bad weather. It's good enough for me."

"So?" murmured the barkeeper, languidly.

The copious drams made the Swede's eyes swim, and he breathed a trifle heavier. "Yes, I like this weather. I like it. It suits me." It was apparently his design to impart a deep significance to these words.

"So?" murmured the bartender again. He turned to gaze dreamily at the scroll-like birds and bird-like scrolls which had been drawn with soap upon the mirrors back of the bar.

"Well, I guess I'll take another drink," said the Swede, presently. "Have something?"

"No, thanks; I'm not drinkin'," answered the bartender. Afterwards he asked, "How did you hurt your face?"

The Swede immediately began to boast loudly. "Why, in a fight. I thumped the soul out of a man down here at Scully's hotel."

The interest of the four men at the table was at last aroused.

"Who was it?" said one.

"Johnnie Scully," blustered the Swede. "Son of the man what runs it. He will be pretty near dead for some weeks, I can tell you. I made a nice thing of him, I did. He couldn't get up. They carried him in the house. Have a drink?"

Instantly the men in some subtle way incased themselves in reserve. "No, thanks," said one. The group was of curious formation. Two were prominent local business men; one was the district-attorney; and one was a professional gambler of the kind known as "square." But a scrutiny of the group would not have enabled an observer to pick the gambler from the men of more reputable pursuits. He was, in fact, a man so delicate in manner, when among people of fair class, and so judicious in his choice of victims, that in the strictly masculine part of the town's life he had come to be explicitly trusted and admired. People called him a thoroughbred. The fear and contempt with which his craft was regarded was undoubtedly the reason that his quiet dignity shone conspicuous above the quiet dignity of men who might be merely hatters, billiard markers, or grocery-clerks. Beyond an occasional unwary traveller, who came by rail, this gambler was supposed to prey solely upon reckless and senile farmers, who, when flush with good crops, drove into town in all the pride and confidence of an absolutely invulnerable stupidity. Hearing at times in circuitous fashion of the despoilment of such a farmer, the important men of Romper invariably laughed in contempt of the victim, and, if they thought of the wolf at all, it was with a kind of pride at the knowledge that he would never dare think of attacking their wisdom and courage. Besides, it was popular that this gambler had a real wife and two real children in a neat cottage in a suburb, where he led an exemplary home life; and when any one even suggested a discrepancy in his character, the crowd immediately vociferated descriptions of this virtuous family circle. Then men who led exemplary home lives, and men who did not lead exemplary home lives, all subsided in a bunch, remarking that there was nothing more to be said.

However, when a restriction was placed upon him—as, for instance, when a strong clique of members of the new Pollywog Club refused to permit him, even as a spectator, to appear in the rooms of the organization—the candor and gentleness with which he accepted the judgment disarmed many of his foes and made his friends more desperately partisan. He invariably distinguished between himself and a respectable Romper man so quickly and frankly that his manner actually appeared to be a continual broadcast compliment.

And one must not forget to declare the fundamental fact of his entire position in Romper. It is irrefutable that in all affairs outside of his business, in all matters that occur eternally and commonly between man and man, this thieving card-player was so generous, so just, so moral, that, in a contest, he could have put to flight the consciences of nine-tenths of the citizens of Romper.

And so it happened that he was seated in this saloon with the two prominent local merchants and the district-attorney.

The Swede continued to drink raw whiskey, meanwhile babbling at the barkeeper and trying to induce him to indulge in potations. "Come on. Have a drink. Come on. What—no? Well, have a little one, then. By gawd, I've whipped a man to-night, and I want to celebrate. I whipped him good, too. Gentlemen," the Swede cried to the men at the table, "have a drink?"

"Ssh!" said the barkeeper.

The group at the table, although furtively attentive, had been pretending to be deep in talk, but now a man lifted his eyes towards the Swede and said, shortly, "Thanks. We don't want any more."

At this reply the Swede ruffled out his chest like a rooster. "Well," he exploded, "it seems I can't get anybody to drink with me in this town. Seems so, don't it? Well!"

"Ssh!" said the barkeeper.

"Say," snarled the Swede, "don't you try to shut me up. I won't have it. I'm a gentleman, and I want people to drink with me. And I want 'em to drink with me now. Now—do you understand?" He rapped the bar with his knuckles.

Years of experience had calloused the bartender. He merely grew sulky. "I hear you," he answered.

"Well," cried the Swede, "listen hard then. See those men over there? Well, they're going to drink with me, and don't you forget it. Now you watch."

"Hi!" yelled the barkeeper, "this won't do!"

"Why won't it?" demanded the Swede. He stalked over to the table, and by chance laid his hand upon the shoulder of the gambler. "How about this?" he asked, wrathfully. "I asked you to drink with me."

The gambler simply twisted his head and spoke over his shoulder. "My friend, I don't know you."

"Oh, hell!" answered the Swede, "come and have a drink."

"Now, my boy," advised the gambler, kindly, "take your hand off my shoulder and go 'way and mind your own business." He was a little, slim man, and it seemed strange to hear him use this tone of heroic patronage to the burly Swede. The other men at the table said nothing.

"What! You won't drink with me, you little dude? I'll make you then! I'll make you!" The Swede had grasped the gambler frenziedly at the throat, and was dragging him from his chair. The other men sprang up. The barkeeper dashed around the corner of his bar. There was a great tumult, and then was seen a long blade in the hand of the gambler. It shot forward, and a human body, this citadel of virtue, wisdom, power, was pierced as easily as if it had been a melon. The Swede fell with a cry of supreme astonishment.

The prominent merchants and the district attorney must have at once tumbled out of the place backward. The bartender found himself hanging limply to the arm of a chair and gazing into the eyes of a murderer.

"Henry," said the latter, as he wiped his knife on one of the towels that hung beneath the bar-rail, "you tell 'em where to find me. I'll be home, waiting for 'em." Then he vanished. A moment afterwards the barkeeper was in the street dinning through the storm for help, and, moreover, companionship.

The corpse of the Swede, alone in the saloon, had its eyes fixed upon a dreadful legend that dwelt atop of the cash-machine: "This registers the amount of your purchase."

IX

Months later, the cowboy was frying pork over the stove of a little ranch near the Dakota line, when there was a quick thud of hoofs outside, and presently the Easterner entered with the letters and the papers.

"Well," said the Easterner at once, "the chap that killed the Swede has got three years. Wasn't much, was it?"

"He has? Three years?" The cowboy poised his pan of pork, while he ruminated upon the news. "Three years. That ain't much."

"No. It was a light sentence," replied the Easterner as he unbuckled his spurs. "Seems there was a good deal of sympathy for him in Romper."

"If the bartender had been any good," observed the cowboy, thoughtfully, "he would have gone in and cracked that there Dutchman on the head with a bottle in the beginnin' of it and stopped all this here murderin'."

"Yes, a thousand things might have happened," said the Easterner, tartly.

The cowboy returned his pan of pork to the fire, but his philosophy continued. "It's funny, ain't it? If he hadn't said Johnnie was cheatin' he'd be alive this minute. He was an awful fool. Game played for fun, too. Not for money. I believe he was crazy."

"I feel sorry for that gambler," said the Easterner.

"Oh, so do I," said the cowboy. "He don't deserve none of it for killin' who he did."

"The Swede might not have been killed if everything had been square."

"Might not have been killed?" exclaimed the cowboy. "Everythin' square? Why, when he said that Johnnie was cheatin' and acted like such a jackass? And then in the saloon he fairly walked up to git hurt?" With these arguments the cowboy browbeat the Easterner and reduced him to rage.

"You're a fool!" cried the Easterner, viciously. "You're a bigger jackass than the Swede by a million majority. Now let me tell you one thing. Let me tell you something. Listen! Johnnie was cheating!"

"'Johnnie,'" said the cowboy, blankly. There was a minute of silence, and then he said, robustly, "Why, no. The game was only for fun."

"Fun or not," said the Easterner, "Johnnie was cheating. I saw him. I know it. I saw him. And I refused to stand up and be a man. I let the Swede fight it out alone. And you—you were simply puffing around the place and wanting to fight. And then old Scully himself! We are all in it! This poor gambler isn't even a noun. He is kind of an adverb. Every sin is the result of a collaboration. We, five of us, have collaborated in the murder of this Swede. Usually there are from a dozen to forty women really involved in every murder, but in this case it seems to be only five men—you, I, Johnnie, old Scully, and that fool of an unfortunate gambler came merely as a culmination, the apex of a human movement, and gets all the punishment."

The cowboy, injured and rebellious, cried out blindly into this fog of mysterious theory: "Well, I didn't do anythin', did I?"

HIS NEW MITTENS

I

Little Horace was walking home from school, brilliantly decorated by a pair of new red mittens. A number of boys were snowballing gleefully in a field. They hailed him. "Come on, Horace! We're having a battle."

Horace was sad. "No," he said, "I can't. I've got to go home." At noon his mother had admonished him: "Now, Horace, you come straight home as soon as school is out. Do you hear? And don't you get them nice new mittens all wet, either. Do you hear?" Also his aunt had said: "I declare, Emily, it's a shame the way you allow that child to ruin his things." She had meant mittens. To his mother, Horace had dutifully replied, "Yes'm." But he now loitered in the vicinity of the group of uproarious boys, who were yelling like hawks as the white balls flew.

Some of them immediately analyzed this extraordinary hesitancy. "Hah!" they paused to scoff, "afraid of your new mittens, ain't you?" Some smaller boys, who were not yet so wise in discerning motives, applauded this attack with unreasonable vehemence. "A-fray-ed of his mit-tens! A-fray-ed of his mit-tens." They sang these lines to cruel and monotonous music which is as old perhaps as American childhood, and which it is the privilege of the emancipated adult to completely forget. "Afray-ed of his mit-tens!"

Horace cast a tortured glance towards his playmates, and then dropped his eyes to the snow at his feet. Presently he turned to the trunk of one of the great maple-trees that lined the curb. He made a pretence of closely examining the rough and virile bark. To his mind, this familiar street of Whilomville seemed to grow dark in the thick shadow of shame. The trees and the houses were now palled in purple.

"A-fray-ed of his mit-tens!" The terrible music had in it a meaning from the moonlit war-drums of chanting cannibals.

At last Horace, with supreme effort, raised his head. "'Tain't them I care about," he said, gruffly. "I've got to go home. That's all."

Whereupon each boy held his left forefinger as if it were a pencil and began to sharpen it derisively with his right forefinger. They came closer, and sang like a trained chorus, "A-fray-ed of his mittens!"

When he raised his voice to deny the charge it was simply lost in the screams of the mob. He was alone, fronting all the traditions of boyhood held before him by inexorable representatives. To such a low state had he fallen that one lad, a mere baby, outflanked him and then struck him in the cheek with a heavy snowball. The act was acclaimed with loud jeers. Horace turned to dart at his assailant, but there was an immediate demonstration on the other flank, and he found himself obliged to keep his face towards the hilarious crew of tormentors. The baby retreated in safety to the rear of the crowd, where he was received with fulsome compliments upon his daring. Horace retreated slowly up the walk. He continually tried to make them heed him, but the only sound was the chant, "A-fray-ed of his mit-tens!" In this desperate withdrawal the beset and haggard boy suffered more than is the common lot of man.

Being a boy himself, he did not understand boys at all. He had, of course, the dismal conviction that they were going to dog him to his grave. But near the corner of the field they suddenly seemed to forget all about it. Indeed, they possessed only the malevolence of so many flitter-headed sparrows. The interest had swung capriciously to some other matter. In a moment they were off in the field again, carousing amid the snow. Some authoritative boy had probably said, "Aw, come on!"

As the pursuit ceased, Horace ceased his retreat. He spent some time in what was evidently an attempt to adjust his self respect, and then began to wander furtively down towards the group. He, too, had undergone an important change. Perhaps his sharp agony was only as durable as the malevolence of the others. In this boyish life obedience to some unformulated creed of manners was enforced with capricious but merciless rigor. However, they were, after all, his comrades, his friends.

They did not heed his return. They were engaged in an altercation. It had evidently been planned that this battle was between Indians and soldiers. The smaller and weaker boys had been induced to appear as Indians in the initial skirmish, but they were now very sick of it, and were reluctantly but steadfastly, affirming their desire for a change of caste. The larger boys had all won great distinction, devastating Indians materially, and they wished the war to go on as planned. They explained vociferously that it was proper for the soldiers always to thrash the Indians. The little boys did not pretend to deny the truth of this argument; they confined themselves to the simple statement that, in that case, they wished to be soldiers. Each little boy willingly appealed to the others to remain Indians, but as for himself he reiterated his desire to enlist as a soldier. The larger boys were in despair over this dearth of enthusiasm in the small Indians. They alternately wheedled and bullied, but they could not persuade the little boys, who were really suffering dreadful humiliation rather than submit to another onslaught of soldiers. They were called all the baby names that had the power of stinging deep into their pride, but they remained firm.

Then a formidable lad, a leader of reputation, one who could whip many boys that wore long trousers, suddenly blew out his checks and shouted, "Well, all right then. I'll be an Indian myself. Now." The little boys greeted with cheers this addition to their wearied ranks, and seemed then content. But matters were not mended in the least, because all of the personal following of the formidable lad, with the addition of every outsider, spontaneously forsook the flag and declared themselves Indians. There were now no soldiers. The Indians had carried everything unanimously. The formidable lad used his influence, but his influence could not shake the loyalty of his friends, who refused to fight under any colors but his colors.

Plainly there was nothing for it but to coerce the little ones. The formidable lad again became a soldier, and then graciously permitted to join him all the real fighting strength of the crowd, leaving behind a most forlorn band of little Indians. Then the soldiers attacked the Indians, exhorting them to opposition at the same time.

The Indians at first adopted a policy of hurried surrender, but this had no success, as none of the surrenders were accepted. They then turned to flee, bawling out protests. The ferocious soldiers pursued them amid shouts. The battle widened, developing all manner of marvellous detail.

Horace had turned towards home several times, but, as a matter of fact, this scene held him in a spell. It was fascinating beyond anything which the grown man understands. He had always in the back of his head a sense of guilt, even a sense of impending punishment for disobedience, but they could not weigh with the delirium of this snow-battle.

II

One of the raiding soldiers, espying Horace, called out in passing, "A-fray-ed of his mit-tens!" Horace flinched at this renewal, and the other lad paused to taunt him again. Horace scooped some snow, moulded it into a ball, and flung it at the other. "Ho!" cried the boy, "you're an Indian, are you? Hey, fellers, here's an Indian that ain't been killed yet." He and Horace engaged in a duel in which both were in such haste to mould snowballs that they had little time for aiming.

Horace once struck his opponent squarely in the chest. "Hey," he shouted, "you're dead. You can't fight any more, Pete. I killed you. You're dead."

The other boy flushed red, but he continued frantically to make ammunition. "You never touched me!" he retorted, glowering. "You never touched me! Where, now?" he added, defiantly. "Where did you hit me?"

"On the coat! Right on your breast! You can't fight any more! You're dead!"

"You never!"

"I did, too! Hey, fellers, ain't he dead? I hit 'im square!"

"He never!"

Nobody had seen the affair, but some of the boys took sides in absolute accordance with their friendship for one of the concerned parties. Horace's opponent went about contending, "He never touched me! He never came near me! He never came near me!"

The formidable leader now came forward and accosted Horace. "What was you? An Indian? Well, then, you're dead—that's all. He hit you. I saw him."

"Me?" shrieked Horace. "He never came within a mile of me——"

At that moment he heard his name called in a certain familiar tune of two notes, with the last note shrill and prolonged. He looked towards the sidewalk, and saw his mother standing there in her widow's weeds, with two brown paper parcels under her arm. A silence had fallen upon all the boys. Horace moved slowly towards his mother. She did not seem to note his approach; she was gazing austerely off through the naked branches of the maples where two crimson sunset bars lay on the deep blue sky.

At a distance of ten paces Horace made a desperate venture. "Oh, ma," he whined, "can't I stay out for a while?"

"No," she answered solemnly, "you come with me." Horace knew that profile; it was the inexorable profile. But he continued to plead, because it was not beyond his mind that a great show of suffering now might diminish his suffering later.

He did not dare to look back at his playmates. It was already a public scandal that he could not stay out as late as other boys, and he could imagine his standing now that he had been again dragged off by his mother in sight of the whole world. He was a profoundly miserable human being.

Aunt Martha opened the door for them. Light streamed about her straight skirt. "Oh," she said, "so you found him on the road, eh? Well, I declare! It was about time!"

Horace slunk into the kitchen. The stove, straddling out on its four iron legs, was gently humming. Aunt Martha had evidently just lighted the lamp, for she went to it and began to twist the wick experimentally.

"Now," said the mother, "let's see them mittens."

Horace's chin sank. The aspiration of the criminal, the passionate desire for an asylum from retribution, from justice, was aflame in his heart. "I—I—

don't—don't know where they are." he gasped finally, as he passed his hand over his pockets.

"Horace," intoned his mother, "you are tellin' me a story!"

"'Tain't a story," he answered, just above his breath. He looked like a sheep-stealer.

His mother held him by the arm, and began to search his pockets. Almost at once she was able to bring forth a pair of very wet mittens. "Well, I declare!" cried Aunt Martha. The two women went close to the lamp, and minutely examined the mittens, turning them over and over. Afterwards, when Horace looked up, his mother's sad-lined, homely face was turned towards him. He burst into tears.

His mother drew a chair near the stove. "Just you sit there now, until I tell you to git off." He sidled meekly into the chair. His mother and his aunt went briskly about the business of preparing supper. They did not display a knowledge of his existence; they carried an effect of oblivion so far that they even did not speak to each other. Presently they went into the dining and living room; Horace could hear the dishes rattling. His Aunt Martha brought a plate of food, placed it on a chair near him, and went away without a word.

Horace instantly decided that he would not touch a morsel of the food. He had often used this ruse in dealing with his mother. He did not know why it brought her to terms, but certainly it sometimes did.

The mother looked up when the aunt returned to the other room. "Is he eatin' his supper?" she asked.

The maiden aunt, fortified in ignorance, gazed with pity and contempt upon this interest. "Well, now, Emily, how do I know?" she queried. "Was I goin' to stand over 'im? Of all the worryin' you do about that child! It's a shame the way you're bringin' up that child."

"Well, he ought to eat somethin'. It won't do fer him to go without eatin'," the mother retorted, weakly.

Aunt Martha, profoundly scorning the policy of concession which these words meant, uttered a long, contemptuous sigh.

III

Alone in the kitchen, Horace stared with sombre eyes at the plate of food. For a long time he betrayed no sign of yielding. His mood was adamantine. He was resolved not to sell his vengeance for bread, cold ham, and a pickle, and yet it must be known that the sight of them affected him powerfully. The pickle in particular was notable for its seductive charm. He surveyed it darkly.

But at last, unable to longer endure his state, his attitude in the presence of the pickle, he put out an inquisitive finger and touched it, and it was cool and green and plump. Then a full conception of the cruel woe of his situation swept upon him suddenly, and his eyes filled with tears, which began to move down his cheeks. He sniffled. His heart was black with hatred. He painted in his mind scenes of deadly retribution. His mother would be taught that he was not one to endure persecution meekly, without raising an arm in his defence. And so his dreams were of a slaughter of feelings, and near the end of them his mother was pictured as coming, bowed with pain, to his feet. Weeping, she implored his charity. Would he forgive her? No; his once tender heart had been turned to stone by her injustice. He could not forgive her. She must pay the inexorable penalty.

The first item in this horrible plan was the refusal of the food. This he knew by experience would work havoc in his mother's heart. And so he grimly waited.

But suddenly it occurred to him that the first part of his revenge was in danger of failing. The thought struck him that his mother might not capitulate in the usual way. According to his recollection, the time was more than due when she should come in, worried, sadly affectionate, and ask him if he was ill. It had then been his custom to hint in a resigned voice that he was the victim of secret disease, but that he preferred to suffer in silence and alone. If she was obdurate in her anxiety, he always asked her in a gloomy, low voice to go away and leave him to suffer in silence and alone in the darkness without food. He had known this maneuvering to result even in pie.

But what was the meaning of the long pause and the stillness? Had his old and valued ruse betrayed him? As the truth sank into his mind, he supremely loathed life, the world, his mother. Her heart was beating back the besiegers; he was a defeated child.

He wept for a time before deciding upon the final stroke. He would run away. In a remote corner of the world he would become some sort of bloody-handed person driven to a life of crime by the barbarity of his mother. She should never know his fate. He would torture her for years with doubts and doubts, and drive her implacably to a repentant grave. Nor would Aunt Martha escape. Some day, a century hence, when his mother was dead, he would write to his Aunt Martha, and point out her part in the blighting of his life. For one blow against him now he would, in time, deal back a thousand—aye, ten thousand.

He arose and took his coat and cap. As he moved stealthily towards the door he cast a glance backward at the pickle. He was tempted to take it, but he knew that if he left the plate inviolate his mother would feel even worse.

A blue snow was falling. People, bowed forward, were moving briskly along the walks. The electric lamps hummed amid showers of flakes. As Horace emerged from the kitchen, a shrill squall drove the flakes around the corner of the house. He cowered away from it, and its violence illumined his mind vaguely in new directions. He deliberated upon a choice of remote corners of the globe. He found that he had no plans which were definite enough in a geographical way, but without much loss of time he decided upon California. He moved briskly as far as his mother's front gate on the road to California. He was off at last. His success was a trifle dreadful; his throat choked.

But at the gate he paused. He did not know if his journey to California would be shorter if he went down Niagara Avenue or off through Hogan Street. As the storm was very cold and the point was very important, he decided to withdraw for reflection to the wood-shed. He entered the dark shanty, and took seat upon the old chopping-block upon which he was supposed to perform for a few minutes every afternoon when he returned from school. The wind screamed and shouted at the loose boards, and there was a rift of snow on the floor to leeward of a crack.

Here the idea of starting for California on such a night departed from his mind, leaving him ruminating miserably upon his martyrdom. He saw nothing for it but to sleep all night in the wood-shed and start for California in the morning bright and early. Thinking of his bed, he kicked over the floor and found that the innumerable chips were all frozen tightly, bedded in ice.

Later he viewed with joy some signs of excitement in the house. The flare of a lamp moved rapidly from window to window. Then the kitchen door slammed loudly and a shawled figure sped towards the gate. At last he was making them feel his power. The shivering child's face was lit with saturnine glee as in the darkness of the wood-shed he gloated over the evidences of consternation in his home. The shawled figure had been his Aunt Martha dashing with the alarm to the neighbors.

The cold of the wood-shed was tormenting him. He endured only because of the terror he was causing. But then it occurred to him that, if they instituted a search for him, they would probably examine the wood-shed. He knew that it would not be manful to be caught so soon. He was not positive now that he was going to remain away forever, but at any rate he was bound to inflict some more damage before allowing himself to be captured. If he merely succeeded in making his mother angry, she would thrash him on sight. He must prolong the time in order to be safe. If he held out properly, he was sure of a welcome of love, even though he should drip with crimes.

Evidently the storm had increased, for when he went out it swung him violently with its rough and merciless strength. Panting, stung, half blinded with the driving flakes, he was now a waif, exiled, friendless, and poor. With a bursting heart, he thought of his home and his mother. To his forlorn vision they were as far away as heaven.

IV

Horace was undergoing changes of feeling so rapidly that he was merely moved hither and then thither like a kite. He was now aghast at the merciless ferocity of his mother. It was she who had thrust him into this wild storm, and she was perfectly indifferent to his fate, perfectly indifferent. The forlorn wanderer could no longer weep. The strong sobs caught at his throat, making his breath come in short, quick snuffles. All in him was conquered save the enigmatical childish ideal of form, manner. This principle still held out, and it was the only thing between him and submission. When he surrendered, he must surrender in a way that deferred to the undefined code. He longed simply to go to the kitchen and stumble in, but his unfathomable sense of fitness forbade him.

Presently he found himself at the head of Niagara Avenue, staring through the snow into the blazing windows of Stickney's butcher-shop. Stickney was the family butcher, not so much because of a superiority to other Whilomville butchers as because he lived next door and had been an intimate friend of the father of Horace. Rows of glowing pigs hung head downward back of the tables, which bore huge pieces of red beef. Clumps of attenuated turkeys were suspended here and there. Stickney, hale and smiling, was bantering with a woman in a cloak, who, with a monster basket on her arm, was dickering for eight cents' worth of some thing. Horace watched them through a crusted pane. When the woman came out and passed him, he went towards the door. He touched the latch with his finger, but withdrew again suddenly to the sidewalk. Inside Stickney was whistling cheerily and assorting his knives.

Finally Horace went desperately forward, opened the door, and entered the shop. His head hung low. Stickney stopped whistling. "Hello, young man," he cried, "what brings you here?"

Horace halted, but said nothing. He swung one foot to and fro over the saw-dust floor.

Stickney had placed his two fat hands palms downward and wide apart on the table, in the attitude of a butcher facing a customer, but now he straightened.

"Here," he said, "what's wrong? What's wrong, kid?"

"Nothin'," answered Horace, huskily. He labored for a moment with something in his throat, and afterwards added, "O'ny——I've——I've run away, and—"

"Run away!" shouted Stickney. "Run away from what? Who?"

"From——home," answered Horace. "I don't like it there any more. I——" He had arranged an oration to win the sympathy of the butcher; he had prepared a table setting forth the merits of his case in the most logical fashion, but it was as if the wind had been knocked out of his mind. "I've run away. I——"

Stickney reached an enormous hand over the array of beef, and firmly grappled the emigrant. Then he swung himself to Horace's side. His face was stretched with laughter, and he playfully shook his prisoner. "Come——come——come. What dashed nonsense is this? Run away, hey? Run away?" Whereupon the child's long-tried spirit found vent in howls.

"Come, come," said Stickney, busily. "Never mind now, never mind. You just come along with me. It'll be all right. I'll fix it. Never you mind."

Five minutes later the butcher, with a great ulster over his apron, was leading the boy homeward.

At the very threshold, Horace raised his last flag of pride. "No——no," he sobbed. "I don't want to. I don't want to go in there." He braced his foot against the step and made a very respectable resistance.

"Now, Horace," cried the butcher. He thrust open the door with a bang. "Hello there!" Across the dark kitchen the door to the living-room opened and Aunt Martha appeared. "You've found him!" she screamed.

"We've come to make a call," roared the butcher. At the entrance to the living-room a silence fell upon them all. Upon a couch Horace saw his mother lying limp, pale as death, her eyes gleaming with pain. There was an electric pause before she swung a waxen hand towards Horace. "My child," she murmured, tremulously. Whereupon the sinister person addressed, with a prolonged wail of grief and joy, ran to her with speed. "Mam-ma! Mam-ma! Oh, mam-ma!" She was not able to speak in a known tongue as she folded him in her weak arms.

Aunt Martha turned defiantly upon the butcher because her face betrayed her. She was crying. She made a gesture half military, half feminine. "Won't you have a glass of our root-beer, Mr. Stickney? We make it ourselves."

THE LITTLE REGIMENT, AND OTHER EPISODES OF THE AMERICAN CIVIL WAR

THE LITTLE REGIMENT.

I.

The fog made the clothes of the men of the column in the roadway seem of a luminous quality. It imparted to the heavy infantry overcoats a new colour, a kind of blue which was so pale that a regiment might have been merely a long, low shadow in the mist. However, a muttering, one part grumble, three parts joke, hovered in the air above the thick ranks, and blended in an undertoned roar, which was the voice of the column.

The town on the southern shore of the little river loomed spectrally, a faint etching upon the gray cloud-masses which were shifting with oily languor. A long row of guns upon the northern bank had been pitiless in their hatred, but a little battered belfry could be dimly seen still pointing with invincible resolution toward the heavens.

The enclouded air vibrated with noises made by hidden colossal things. The infantry tramplings, the heavy rumbling of the artillery, made the earth speak of gigantic preparation. Guns on distant heights thundered from time to time with sudden, nervous roar, as if unable to endure in silence a knowledge of hostile troops massing, other guns going to position. These sounds, near and remote, defined an immense battle-ground, described the tremendous width of the stage of the prospective drama. The voices of the guns, slightly casual, unexcited in their challenges and warnings, could not destroy the unutterable eloquence of the word in the air, a meaning of impending struggle which made the breath halt at the lips.

The column in the roadway was ankle-deep in mud. The men swore piously at the rain which drizzled upon them, compelling them to stand always very erect in fear of the drops that would sweep in under their coat-collars. The fog was as cold as wet cloths. The men stuffed their hands deep in their pockets, and huddled their muskets in their arms. The machinery of orders had rooted these soldiers deeply into the mud precisely as almighty nature roots mullein stalks.

They listened and speculated when a tumult of fighting came from the dim town across the river. When the noise lulled for a time they resumed their descriptions of the mud and graphically exaggerated the number of hours they had been kept waiting. The general commanding their division rode along the ranks, and they cheered admiringly, affectionately, crying out to him gleeful prophecies of the coming battle. Each man scanned him with a peculiarly keen personal interest, and afterward spoke of him with unquestioning devotion and confidence, narrating anecdotes which were mainly untrue.

When the jokers lifted the shrill voices which invariably belonged to them, flinging witticisms at their comrades, a loud laugh would sweep from rank to rank, and soldiers who had not heard would lean forward and demand repetition. When were borne past them some wounded men with gray and blood-smeared faces, and eyes that rolled in that helpless beseeching for assistance from the sky which comes with supreme pain, the soldiers in the mud watched intently, and from time to time asked of the bearers an account of the affair. Frequently they bragged of their corps, their division, their brigade, their regiment. Anon they referred to the mud and the cold drizzle. Upon this threshold of a wild scene of death they, in short, defied the proportion of events with that splendour of heedlessness which belongs only to veterans.

"Like a lot of wooden soldiers," swore Billie Dempster, moving his feet in the thick mass, and casting a vindictive glance indefinitely; "standing in the mud for a hundred years."

"Oh, shut up!" murmured his brother Dan. The manner of his words implied that this fraternal voice near him was an indescribable bore.

"Why should I shut up?" demanded Billie.

"Because you're a fool," cried Dan, taking no time to debate it; "the biggest fool in the regiment."

There was but one man between them, and he was habituated. These insults from brother to brother had swept across his chest, flown past his face, many times during two long campaigns. Upon this occasion he simply grinned first at one, then at the other.

The way of these brothers was not an unknown topic in regimental gossip. They had enlisted simultaneously, with each sneering loudly at the other for doing it. They left their little town, and went forward with the flag, exchanging protestations of undying suspicion. In the camp life they so openly despised each other that, when entertaining quarrels were lacking, their companions often contrived situations calculated to bring forth display of this fraternal dislike.

Both were large-limbed, strong young men, and often fought with friends in camp unless one was near to interfere with the other. This latter happened rather frequently, because Dan, preposterously willing for any manner of combat, had a very great horror of seeing Billie in a fight; and Billie, almost odiously ready himself, simply refused to see Dan stripped to his shirt and with his fists aloft. This sat queerly upon them, and made them the objects of plots.

When Dan jumped through a ring of eager soldiers and dragged forth his raving brother by the arm, a thing often predicted would almost come to pass. When Billie performed the same office for Dan, the prediction would again miss fulfilment by an inch. But indeed they never fought together, although they were perpetually upon the verge.

They expressed longing for such conflict. As a matter of truth, they had at one time made full arrangement for it, but even with the encouragement and interest of half of the regiment they somehow failed to achieve collision.

If Dan became a victim of police duty, no jeering was so destructive to the feelings as Billie's comment. If Billie got a call to appear at the headquarters, none would so genially prophesy his complete undoing as Dan. Small misfortunes to one were, in truth, invariably greeted with hilarity by the other, who seemed to see in them great re-enforcement of his opinion.

As soldiers, they expressed each for each a scorn intense and blasting. After a certain battle, Billie was promoted to corporal. When Dan was told of it, he seemed smitten dumb with astonishment and patriotic indignation. He stared in silence, while the dark blood rushed to Billie's forehead, and he shifted his weight from foot to foot. Dan at last found his tongue, and said: "Well, I'm durned!" If he had heard that an army mule had been appointed to the post of corps commander, his tone could not have had more derision in it. Afterward, he adopted a fervid insubordination, an almost religious reluctance to obey the new corporal's orders, which came near to developing the desired strife.

It is here finally to be recorded also that Dan, most ferociously profane in speech, very rarely swore in the presence of his brother; and that Billie, whose oaths came from his lips with the grace of falling pebbles, was seldom known to express himself in this manner when near his brother Dan.

At last the afternoon contained a suggestion of evening. Metallic cries rang suddenly from end to end of the column. They inspired at once a quick, business-like adjustment. The long thing stirred in the mud. The men had hushed, and were looking across the river. A moment later the shadowy mass of pale blue figures was moving steadily toward the stream. There could be heard from the town a clash of swift fighting and cheering. The noise of the shooting coming through the heavy air had its sharpness taken from it, and sounded in thuds.

There was a halt upon the bank above the pontoons. When the column went winding down the incline, and streamed out upon the bridge, the fog had faded to a great degree, and in the clearer dusk the guns on a distant ridge were enabled to perceive the crossing. The long whirling outcries of the shells came into the air above the men. An occasional solid shot struck the surface of the river, and dashed into view a sudden vertical jet. The distance was subtly illuminated by the lightning from the deep-booming guns. One by one the batteries on the northern shore aroused, the innumerable guns bellowing in angry oration at the distant ridge. The rolling thunder crashed and reverberated as a wild surf sounds on a still night, and to this music the column marched across the pontoons.

The waters of the grim river curled away in a smile from the ends of the great boats, and slid swiftly beneath the planking. The dark, riddled walls of the town upreared before the troops, and from a region hidden by these hammered and tumbled houses came incessantly the yells and firings of a prolonged and close skirmish.

When Dan had called his brother a fool, his voice had been so decisive, so brightly assured, that many men had laughed, considering it to be great humour under the circumstances. The incident happened to rankle deep in Billie. It was not any strange thing that his brother had called him a fool. In fact, he often called him a fool with exactly the same amount of cheerful and prompt conviction, and before large audiences, too. Billie wondered in his own mind why he took such profound offence in this case; but, at any rate, as he slid down the bank and on to the bridge with his regiment, he was searching his knowledge for something that would pierce Dan's blithesome spirit. But he could contrive nothing at this time, and his impotency made the glance which he was once able to give his brother still more malignant.

The guns far and near were roaring a fearful and grand introduction for this column which was marching upon the stage of death. Billie felt it, but only in a numb way. His heart was cased in that curious dissonant metal which covers a man's emotions at such times. The terrible voices from the hills told him that in this wide conflict his life was an insignificant fact, and that his death would be an insignificant fact. They portended the whirlwind to which he would be as necessary as a butterfly's waved wing. The solemnity, the sadness of it came near enough to make him wonder why he was neither solemn nor sad. When his mind vaguely adjusted events according to their importance to him, it appeared that the uppermost thing was the fact that upon the eve of battle, and before many comrades, his brother had called him a fool.

Dan was in a particularly happy mood. "Hurray! Look at 'em shoot," he said, when the long witches' croon of the shells came into the air. It enraged Billie when he felt the little thorn in him, and saw at the same time that his brother had completely forgotten it.

The column went from the bridge into more mud. At this southern end there was a chaos of hoarse directions and commands. Darkness was coming upon the earth, and regiments were being hurried up the slippery bank. As Billie floundered in the black mud, amid the swearing, sliding crowd, he suddenly resolved that, in the absence of other means of hurting Dan, he would avoid looking at him, refrain from speaking to him, pay absolutely no heed to his existence; and this done skilfully would, he imagined, soon reduce his brother to a poignant sensitiveness.

At the top of the bank the column again halted and rearranged itself, as a man after a climb rearranges his clothing. Presently the great steel-backed brigade, an infinitely graceful thing in the rhythm and ease of its veteran movement, swung up a little narrow, slanting street.

Evening had come so swiftly that the fighting on the remote borders of the town was indicated by thin flashes of flame. Some building was on fire, and its reflection upon the clouds was an oval of delicate pink.

II.

All demeanour of rural serenity had been wrenched violently from the little town by the guns and by the waves of men which had surged through it. The hand of war laid upon this village had in an instant changed it to a thing of remnants. It resembled the place of a monstrous shaking of the earth itself. The windows, now mere unsightly holes, made the tumbled and blackened dwellings seem skeletons. Doors lay splintered to fragments. Chimneys had flung their bricks everywhere. The artillery fire had not neglected the rows of gentle shade-trees which had lined the streets. Branches and heavy trunks cluttered the mud in drift-wood tangles, while a few shattered forms had contrived to remain dejectedly, mournfully upright. They expressed an innocence, a helplessness, which perforce created a pity for their happening into this cauldron of battle. Furthermore, there was under foot a vast collection of odd things reminiscent of the charge, the fight, the retreat. There were boxes and barrels filled with earth, behind which riflemen had lain snugly, and in these little trenches were the dead in blue with the dead in gray, the poses eloquent of the struggles for possession of the town until the history of the whole conflict was written plainly in the streets.

And yet the spirit of this little city, its quaint individuality, poised in the air above the ruins, defying the guns, the sweeping volleys; holding in contempt those avaricious blazes which had attacked many dwellings. The hard earthen sidewalks proclaimed the games that had been played there during long lazy days, in the careful shadows of the trees. "General Merchandise," in faint letters upon a long board, had to be read with a slanted glance, for the sign dangled by one end; but the porch of the old store was a palpable legend of wide-hatted men, smoking.

This subtle essence, this soul of the life that had been, brushed like invisible wings the thoughts of the men in the swift columns that came up from the river.

In the darkness a loud and endless humming arose from the great blue crowds bivouacked in the streets. From time to time a sharp spatter of firing from far picket lines entered this bass chorus. The smell from the smouldering ruins floated on the cold night breeze.

Dan, seated ruefully upon the doorstep of a shot-pierced house, was proclaiming the campaign badly managed. Orders had been issued forbidding camp-fires.

Suddenly he ceased his oration, and scanning the group of his comrades, said: "Where's Billie? Do you know?"

"Gone on picket."

"Get out! Has he?" said Dan. "No business to go on picket. Why don't some of them other corporals take their turn?"

A bearded private was smoking his pipe of confiscated tobacco, seated comfortably upon a horse-hair trunk which he had dragged from the house. He observed: "Was his turn."

"No such thing," cried Dan. He and the man on the horse-hair trunk held discussion in which Dan stoutly maintained that if his brother had been sent on picket it was an injustice. He ceased his argument when another soldier, upon whose arms could faintly be seen the two stripes of a corporal, entered the circle. "Humph," said Dan, "where you been?"

The corporal made no answer. Presently Dan said: "Billie, where you been?"

His brother did not seem to hear these inquiries. He glanced at the house which towered above them, and remarked casually to the man on the horse-hair trunk: "Funny, ain't it? After the pelting this town got, you'd think there wouldn't be one brick left on another."

"Oh," said Dan, glowering at his brother's back. "Getting mighty smart, ain't you?"

The absence of camp-fires allowed the evening to make apparent its quality of faint silver light in which the blue clothes of the throng became black, and the faces became white expanses, void of expression. There was considerable excitement a short distance from the group around the doorstep. A soldier had chanced upon a hoop-skirt, and arrayed in it he was performing a dance amid the applause of his companions. Billie and a greater part of the men immediately poured over there to witness the exhibition.

"What's the matter with Billie?" demanded Dan of the man upon the horse-hair trunk.

"How do I know?" rejoined the other in mild resentment. He arose and walked away. When he returned he said briefly, in a weather-wise tone, that it would rain during the night.

Dan took a seat upon one end of the horse-hair trunk. He was facing the crowd around the dancer, which in its hilarity swung this way and that way. At times he imagined that he could recognise his brother's face.

He and the man on the other end of the trunk thoughtfully talked of the army's position. To their minds, infantry and artillery were in a most precarious jumble in the streets of the town; but they did not grow nervous over it, for they were used to having the army appear in a precarious jumble to their minds. They had learned to accept such puzzling situations as a consequence of their position in the ranks, and were now usually in possession of a simple but perfectly immovable faith that somebody understood the jumble. Even if they had been convinced that the army was a headless monster, they would merely have nodded with the veteran's singular cynicism. It was none of their business as soldiers. Their duty was to grab sleep and food when occasion permitted, and cheerfully fight wherever their feet were planted until more orders came. This was a task sufficiently absorbing.

They spoke of other corps, and this talk being confidential, their voices dropped to tones of awe. "The Ninth"—"The First"—"The Fifth"—"The Sixth"—"The Third"—the simple numerals rang with eloquence, each having a meaning which was to float through many years as no intangible arithmetical mist, but as pregnant with individuality as the names of cities.

Of their own corps they spoke with a deep veneration, an idolatry, a supreme confidence which apparently would not blanch to see it match against everything.

It was as if their respect for other corps was due partly to a wonder that organizations not blessed with their own famous numeral could take such an interest in war. They could prove that their division was the best in the corps, and that their brigade was the best in the division. And their regiment—it was plain that no fortune of life was equal to the chance which caused a man to be born, so to speak, into this command, the keystone of the defending arch.

At times Dan covered with insults the character of a vague, unnamed general to whose petulance and busy-body spirit he ascribed the order which made hot coffee impossible.

Dan said that victory was certain in the coming battle. The other man seemed rather dubious. He remarked upon the fortified line of hills, which had impressed him even from the other side of the river. "Shucks," said Dan. "Why, we—" He pictured a splendid overflowing of these hills by the sea of men in blue. During the period of this conversation Dan's glance searched the merry throng about the dancer. Above the babble of voices in the street a far-away thunder could sometimes be heard—evidently from the very edge of the horizon—the boom-boom of restless guns.

III.

Ultimately the night deepened to the tone of black velvet. The outlines of the fireless camp were like the faint drawings upon ancient tapestry. The glint of a rifle, the shine of a button, might have been of threads of silver and gold sewn upon the fabric of the night. There was little presented to the vision, but to a sense more subtle there was discernible in the atmosphere something like a pulse; a mystic beating which would have told a stranger of the presence of a giant thing—the slumbering mass of regiments and batteries.

With fires forbidden, the floor of a dry old kitchen was thought to be a good exchange for the cold earth of December, even if a shell had exploded in it and knocked it so out of shape that when a man lay curled in his blanket his last waking thought was likely to be of the wall that bellied out above him as if strongly anxious to topple upon the score of soldiers.

Billie looked at the bricks ever about to descend in a shower upon his face, listened to the industrious pickets plying their rifles on the border of the town, imagined some measure of the din of the coming battle, thought of Dan and Dan's chagrin, and rolling over in his blanket went to sleep with satisfaction.

At an unknown hour he was aroused by the creaking of boards. Lifting himself upon his elbow, he saw a sergeant prowling among the sleeping forms. The sergeant carried a candle in an old brass candle-stick. He would have resembled some old farmer on an unusual midnight tour if it were not for the significance of his gleaming buttons and striped sleeves.

Billie blinked stupidly at the light until his mind returned from the journeys of slumber. The sergeant stooped among the unconscious soldiers, holding the candle close, and peering into each face.

"Hello, Haines," said Billie. "Relief?"

"Hello, Billie," said the sergeant. "Special duty."

"Dan got to go?"

"Jameson, Hunter, McCormack, D. Dempster. Yes. Where is he?"

"Over there by the winder," said Billie, gesturing. "What is it for, Haines?"

"You don't think I know, do you?" demanded the sergeant. He began to pipe sharply but cheerily at men upon the floor. "Come, Mac, get up here. Here's a special for you. Wake up, Jameson. Come along, Dannie, me boy."

Each man at once took this call to duty as a personal affront. They pulled themselves out of their blankets, rubbed their eyes, and swore at whoever was responsible. "Them's orders," cried the sergeant. "Come! Get out of here." An undetailed head with dishevelled hair thrust out from a blanket, and a sleepy voice said: "Shut up, Haines, and go home."

When the detail clanked out of the kitchen, all but one of the remaining men seemed to be again asleep. Billie, leaning on his elbow, was gazing into darkness. When the footsteps died to silence, he curled himself into his blanket.

At the first cool lavender lights of daybreak he aroused again, and scanned his recumbent companions. Seeing a wakeful one he asked: "Is Dan back yet?"

The man said: "Hain't seen 'im."

Billie put both hands behind his head, and scowled into the air. "Can't see the use of these cussed details in the night-time," he muttered in his most unreasonable tones. "Darn nuisances. Why can't they—" He grumbled at length and graphically.

When Dan entered with the squad, however, Billie was convincingly asleep.

IV.

The regiment trotted in double time along the street, and the colonel seemed to quarrel over the right of way with many artillery officers. Batteries were waiting in the mud, and the men of them, exasperated by the bustle of this ambitious infantry, shook their fists from saddle and caisson, exchanging all manner of taunts and jests. The slanted guns continued to look reflectively at the ground.

On the outskirts of the crumbled town a fringe of blue figures were firing into the fog. The regiment swung out into skirmish lines, and the fringe of blue figures departed, turning their backs and going joyfully around the flank.

The bullets began a low moan off toward a ridge which loomed faintly in the heavy mist. When the swift crescendo had reached its climax, the missiles zipped just overhead, as if piercing an invisible curtain. A battery on the hill was crashing with such tumult that it was as if the guns had quarrelled and had fallen pell-mell and snarling upon each other. The shells howled on their journey toward the town. From short range distance there came a spatter of musketry, sweeping along an invisible line and making faint sheets of orange light.

Some in the new skirmish lines were beginning to fire at various shadows discerned in the vapour, forms of men suddenly revealed by some humour of the laggard masses of clouds. The crackle of musketry began to dominate the purring of the hostile bullets. Dan, in the front rank, held his rifle poised, and looked into the fog keenly, coldly, with the air of a sportsman. His nerves were so steady that it was as if they had been drawn from his body, leaving him merely a muscular machine; but his numb heart was somehow beating to the pealing march of the fight.

The waving skirmish line went backward and forward, ran this way and that way. Men got lost in the fog, and men were found again. Once they got too close to the formidable ridge, and the thing burst out as if repulsing a general attack. Once another blue regiment was apprehended on the very edge of firing into them. Once a friendly battery began an elaborate and scientific process of extermination. Always as busy as brokers, the men slid here and there over the plain, fighting their foes, escaping from their friends, leaving a history of many movements in the wet yellow turf, cursing the atmosphere, blazing away every time they could identify the enemy.

In one mystic changing of the fog, as if the fingers of spirits were drawing aside these draperies, a small group of the gray skirmishers, silent, statuesque, were suddenly disclosed to Dan and those about him. So vivid and near were they that there was something uncanny in the revelation.

There might have been a second of mutual staring. Then each rifle in each group was at the shoulder. As Dan's glance flashed along the barrel of his weapon, the figure of a man suddenly loomed as if the musket had been a telescope. The short black beard, the slouch hat, the pose of the man as he sighted to shoot, made a quick picture in Dan's mind. The same moment, it would seem, he pulled his own trigger, and the man, smitten, lurched forward, while his exploding rifle made a slanting crimson streak in the air, and the slouch hat fell before the body. The billows of the fog, governed by singular impulses, rolled between.

"You got that feller sure enough," said a comrade to Dan. Dan looked at him absent-mindedly.

V.

When the next morning calmly displayed another fog, the men of the regiment exchanged eloquent comments; but they did not abuse it at length, because the streets of the town now contained enough galloping aides to make three troops of cavalry, and they knew that they had come to the verge of the great fight.

Dan conversed with the man who had once possessed a horse-hair trunk; but they did not mention the line of hills which had furnished them in more careless moments with an agreeable topic. They avoided it now as condemned men do the subject of death, and yet the thought of it stayed in their eyes as they looked at each other and talked gravely of other things.

The expectant regiment heaved a long sigh of relief when the sharp call: "Fall in," repeated indefinitely, arose in the streets. It was inevitable that a bloody battle was to be fought, and they wanted to get it off their minds. They were, however, doomed again to spend a long period planted firmly in the mud. They craned their necks, and wondered where some of the other regiments were going.

At last the mists rolled carelessly away. Nature made at this time all provisions to enable foes to see each other, and immediately the roar of guns resounded from every hill. The endless cracking of the skirmishers swelled to rolling crashes of musketry. Shells screamed with panther-like noises at the houses. Dan looked at the man of the horse-hair trunk, and the man said: "Well, here she comes!"

The tenor voices of younger officers and the deep and hoarse voices of the older ones rang in the streets. These cries pricked like spurs. The masses of men vibrated from the suddenness with which they were plunged into the situation of troops about to fight. That the orders were long-expected did not concern the emotion.

Simultaneous movement was imparted to all these thick bodies of men and horses that lay in the town. Regiment after regiment swung rapidly into the streets that faced the sinister ridge.

This exodus was theatrical. The little sober-hued village had been like the cloak which disguises the king of drama. It was now put aside, and an army, splendid thing of steel and blue, stood forth in the sunlight.

Even the soldiers in the heavy columns drew deep breaths at the sight, more majestic than they had dreamed. The heights of the enemy's position were crowded with men who resembled people come to witness some mighty pageant. But as the column moved steadily to their positions, the guns, matter-of-fact warriors, doubled their number, and shells burst with red thrilling tumult on the crowded plain. One came into the ranks of the regiment, and after the smoke and the wrath of it had faded, leaving motionless figures, everyone stormed according to the limits of his vocabulary, for veterans detest being killed when they are not busy.

The regiment sometimes looked sideways at its brigade companions composed of men who had never been in battle; but no frozen blood could withstand the heat of the splendour of this army before the eyes on the plain, these lines so long that the flanks were little streaks, this mass of men of one intention. The recruits carried themselves heedlessly. At the rear was an idle battery, and three artillery men in a foolish row on a caisson nudged each other and grinned at the recruits. "You'll catch it pretty soon," they called out.

They were impersonally gleeful, as if they themselves were not also likely to catch it pretty soon. But with this picture of an army in their hearts, the new men perhaps felt the devotion which the drops may feel for the wave; they were of its power and glory; they smiled jauntily at the foolish row of gunners, and told them to go to blazes.

The column trotted across some little bridges, and spread quickly into lines of battle. Before them was a bit of plain, and back of the plain was the ridge. There was no time left for considerations. The men were staring at the plain, mightily wondering how it would feel to be out there, when a brigade in advance yelled and charged. The hill was all gray smoke and fire-points.

That fierce elation in the terrors of war, catching a man's heart and making it burn with such ardour that he becomes capable of dying, flashed in the faces of the men like coloured lights, and made them resemble leashed animals, eager, ferocious, daunting at nothing. The line was really in its first leap before the wild, hoarse crying of the orders.

The greed for close quarters which is the emotion of a bayonet charge, came then into the minds of the men and developed until it was a madness. The field, with its faded grass of a Southern winter, seemed to this fury miles in width.

High, slow-moving masses of smoke, with an odour of burning cotton, engulfed the line until the men might have been swimmers. Before them the ridge, the shore of this gray sea, was outlined, crossed, and re-crossed by sheets of flame. The howl of the battle arose to the noise of innumerable wind demons.

The line, galloping, scrambling, plunging like a herd of wounded horses, went over a field that was sown with corpses, the records of other charges.

Directly in front of the black-faced, whooping Dan, carousing in this onward sweep like a new kind of fiend, a wounded man appeared, raising his shattered body, and staring at this rush of men down upon him. It seemed to occur to him that he was to be trampled; he made a desperate, piteous effort to escape; then finally huddled in a waiting heap. Dan and the soldier near him widened the interval between them without looking down, without appearing to heed the wounded man. This little clump of blue seemed to reel past them as boulders reel past a train.

Bursting through a smoke-wave, the scampering, unformed bunches came upon the wreck of the brigade that had preceded them, a floundering mass stopped afar from the hill by the swirling volleys.

It was as if a necromancer had suddenly shown them a picture of the fate which awaited them; but the line with muscular spasm hurled itself over this wreckage and onward, until men were stumbling amid the relics of other assaults, the point where the fire from the ridge consumed.

The men, panting, perspiring, with crazed faces, tried to push against it; but it was as if they had come to a wall. The wave halted, shuddered in an agony from the quick struggle of its two desires, then toppled, and broke into a fragmentary thing which has no name.

Veterans could now at last be distinguished from recruits. The new regiments were instantly gone, lost, scattered, as if they never had been. But the sweeping failure of the charge, the battle, could not make the veterans forget their business. With a last throe, the band of maniacs drew itself up and blazed a volley at the hill, insignificant to those iron intrenchments, but nevertheless expressing that singular final despair which enables men coolly to defy the walls of a city of death.

After this episode the men renamed their command. They called it the Little Regiment.

VI.

"I seen Dan shoot a feller yesterday. Yes sir. I'm sure it was him that done it. And maybe he thinks about that feller now, and wonders if he tumbled down just about the same way. Them things come up in a man's mind."

Bivouac fires upon the sidewalks, in the streets, in the yards, threw high their wavering reflections, which examined, like slim, red fingers, the dingy, scarred walls and the piles of tumbled brick. The droning of voices again arose from great blue crowds.

The odour of frying bacon, the fragrance from countless little coffee-pails floated among the ruins. The rifles, stacked in the shadows, emitted flashes of steely light. Wherever a flag lay horizontally from one stack to another was the bed of an eagle which had led men into the mystic smoke.

The men about a particular fire were engaged in holding in check their jovial spirits. They moved whispering around the blaze, although they looked at it with a certain fine contentment, like labourers after a day's hard work.

There was one who sat apart. They did not address him save in tones suddenly changed. They did not regard him directly, but always in little sidelong glances.

At last a soldier from a distant fire came into this circle of light. He studied for a time the man who sat apart. Then he hesitatingly stepped closer, and said: "Got any news, Dan?"

"No," said Dan.

The new-comer shifted his feet. He looked at the fire, at the sky, at the other men, at Dan. His face expressed a curious despair; his tongue was plainly in rebellion. Finally, however, he contrived to say: "Well, there's some chance yet, Dan. Lots of the wounded are still lying out there, you know. There's some chance yet."

"Yes," said Dan.

The soldier shifted his feet again, and looked miserably into the air. After another struggle he said: "Well, there's some chance yet, Dan." He moved hastily away.

One of the men of the squad, perhaps encouraged by this example, now approached the still figure. "No news yet, hey?" he said, after coughing behind his hand.

"No," said Dan.

"Well," said the man, "I've been thinking of how he was fretting about you the night you went on special duty. You recollect? Well, sir, I was surprised.

He couldn't say enough about it. I swan, I don't believe he slep' a wink after you left, but just lay awake cussing special duty and worrying. I was surprised. But there he lay cussing. He——"

Dan made a curious sound, as if a stone had wedged in his throat. He said: "Shut up, will you?"

Afterward the men would not allow this moody contemplation of the fire to be interrupted.

"Oh, let him alone, can't you?"

"Come away from there, Casey!"

"Say, can't you leave him be?"

They moved with reverence about the immovable figure, with its countenance of mask-like invulnerability.

VII.

After the red round eye of the sun had stared long at the little plain and its burden, darkness, a sable mercy, came heavily upon it, and the wan hands of the dead were no longer seen in strange frozen gestures.

The heights in front of the plain shone with tiny camp-fires, and from the town in the rear, small shimmerings ascended from the blazes of the bivouac. The plain was a black expanse upon which, from time to time, dots of light, lanterns, floated slowly here and there. These fields were long steeped in grim mystery.

Suddenly, upon one dark spot, there was a resurrection. A strange thing had been groaning there, prostrate. Then it suddenly dragged itself to a sitting posture, and became a man.

The man stared stupidly for a moment at the lights on the hill, then turned and contemplated the faint colouring over the town. For some moments he remained thus, staring with dull eyes, his face unemotional, wooden.

Finally he looked around him at the corpses dimly to be seen. No change flashed into his face upon viewing these men. They seemed to suggest merely that his information concerning himself was not too complete. He ran his fingers over his arms and chest, bearing always the air of an idiot upon a bench at an almshouse door.

Finding no wound in his arms nor in his chest, he raised his hand to his head, and the fingers came away with some dark liquid upon them. Holding these fingers close to his eyes, he scanned them in the same stupid fashion, while his body gently swayed.

The soldier rolled his eyes again toward the town. When he arose, his clothing peeled from the frozen ground like wet paper. Hearing the sound of it, he seemed to see reason for deliberation. He paused and looked at the ground, then at his trousers, then at the ground.

Finally he went slowly off toward the faint reflection, holding his hands palm outward before him, and walking in the manner of a blind man.

VIII.

The immovable Dan again sat unaddressed in the midst of comrades, who did not joke aloud. The dampness of the usual morning fog seemed to make the little camp-fires furious.

Suddenly a cry arose in the streets, a shout of amazement and delight. The men making breakfast at the fire looked up quickly. They broke forth in clamorous exclamation: "Well! Of all things! Dan! Dan! Look who's coming! Oh, Dan!"

Dan the silent raised his eyes and saw a man, with a bandage of the size of a helmet about his head, receiving a furious demonstration from the company. He was shaking hands, and explaining, and haranguing to a high degree.

Dan started. His face of bronze flushed to his temples. He seemed about to leap from the ground, but then suddenly he sank back, and resumed his impassive gazing.

The men were in a flurry. They looked from one to the other. "Dan!

Look! See who's coming!" some cried again. "Dan! Look!"

He scowled at last, and moved his shoulders sullenly. "Well, don't I know it?"

But they could not be convinced that his eyes were in service. "Dan! Why can't you look? See who's coming!"

He made a gesture then of irritation and rage. "Curse it! Don't I know it?"

The man with a bandage of the size of a helmet moved forward, always shaking hands and explaining. At times his glance wandered to Dan, who saw with his eyes riveted.

After a series of shiftings, it occurred naturally that the man with the bandage was very near to the man who saw the flames. He paused, and there was a little silence. Finally he said: "Hello, Dan."

"Hello, Billie."

THREE MIRACULOUS SOLDIERS.

I.

The girl was in the front room on the second floor, peering through the blinds. It was the "best room." There was a very new rag carpet on the floor. The edges of it had been dyed with alternate stripes of red and green. Upon the wooden mantel there were two little puffy figures in clay—a shepherd and a shepherdess probably. A triangle of pink and white wool hung carefully over the edge of this shelf. Upon the bureau there was nothing at all save a spread newspaper, with edges folded to make it into a mat. The quilts and sheets had been removed from the bed and were stacked upon a chair. The pillows and the great feather mattress were muffled and tumbled until they resembled great dumplings. The picture of a man terribly leaden in complexion hung in an oval frame on one white wall and steadily confronted the bureau.

From between the slats of the blinds she had a view of the road as it wended across the meadow to the woods, and again where it reappeared crossing the hill, half a mile away. It lay yellow and warm in the summer sunshine. From the long grasses of the meadow came the rhythmic click of the insects. Occasional frogs in the hidden brook made a peculiar chug-chug sound, as if somebody throttled them. The leaves of the wood swung in gentle winds. Through the dark-green branches of the pines that grew in the front yard could be seen the mountains, far to the southeast, and inexpressibly blue.

Mary's eyes were fastened upon the little streak of road that appeared on the distant hill. Her face was flushed with excitement, and the hand which stretched in a strained pose on the sill trembled because of the nervous shaking of the wrist. The pines whisked their green needles with a soft, hissing sound against the house.

At last the girl turned from the window and went to the head of the stairs. "Well, I just know they're coming, anyhow," she cried argumentatively to the depths.

A voice from below called to her angrily: "They ain't. We've never seen one yet. They never come into this neighbourhood. You just come down here and 'tend to your work insteader watching for soldiers."

"Well, ma, I just know they're coming."

A voice retorted with the shrillness and mechanical violence of occasional housewives. The girl swished her skirts defiantly and returned to the window.

Upon the yellow streak of road that lay across the hillside there now was a handful of black dots—horsemen. A cloud of dust floated away. The girl flew to the head of the stairs and whirled down into the kitchen.

"They're coming! They're coming!"

It was as if she had cried "Fire!" Her mother had been peeling potatoes while seated comfortably at the table. She sprang to her feet. "No—it can't be—how you know it's them—where?" The stubby knife fell from her hand, and two or three curls of potato skin dropped from her apron to the floor.

The girl turned and dashed upstairs. Her mother followed, gasping for breath, and yet contriving to fill the air with questions, reproach, and remonstrance. The girl was already at the window, eagerly pointing. "There! There! See 'em! See 'em!"

Rushing to the window, the mother scanned for an instant the road on the hill. She crouched back with a groan. "It's them, sure as the world! It's them!" She waved her hands in despairing gestures.

The black dots vanished into the wood. The girl at the window was quivering and her eyes were shining like water when the sun flashes. "Hush! They're in the woods! They'll be here directly." She bent down and intently watched the green archway whence the road emerged. "Hush! I hear 'em coming," she swiftly whispered to her mother, for the elder woman had dropped dolefully upon the mattress and was sobbing. And indeed the girl could hear the quick, dull trample of horses. She stepped aside with sudden apprehension, but she bent her head forward in order to still scan the road.

"Here they are!"

There was something very theatrical in the sudden appearance of these men to the eyes of the girl. It was as if a scene had been shifted. The forest suddenly disclosed them—a dozen brown-faced troopers in blue—galloping.

"Oh, look!" breathed the girl. Her mouth was puckered into an expression of strange fascination as if she had expected to see the troopers change into demons and gloat at her. She was at last looking upon those curious beings who rode down from the North—those men of legend and colossal tale—they who were possessed of such marvellous hallucinations.

The little troop rode in silence. At its head was a youthful fellow with some dim yellow stripes upon his arm. In his right hand he held his carbine, slanting upward, with the stock resting upon his knee. He was absorbed in a scrutiny of the country before him.

At the heels of the sergeant the rest of the squad rode in thin column, with creak of leather and tinkle of steel and tin. The girl scanned the faces of the horsemen, seeming astonished vaguely to find them of the type she knew.

The lad at the head of the troop comprehended the house and its environments in two glances. He did not check the long, swinging stride of his horse. The troopers glanced for a moment like casual tourists, and then returned to their study of the region in front. The heavy thudding of the hoofs became a small noise. The dust, hanging in sheets, slowly sank.

The sobs of the woman on the bed took form in words which, while strong in their note of calamity, yet expressed a querulous mental reaching for some near thing to blame. "And it'll be lucky fer us if we ain't both butchered in our sleep—plundering and running off horses—old Santo's gone—you see if he ain't—plundering——"

"But, ma," said the girl, perplexed and terrified in the same moment, "they've gone."

"Oh, but they'll come back!" cried the mother, without pausing her wail. "They'll come back—trust them for that—running off horses. O John,

John! why did you, why did you?" She suddenly lifted herself and sat rigid, staring at her daughter. "Mary," she said in tragic whisper, "the kitchen door isn't locked!" Already she was bended forward to listen, her mouth agape, her eyes fixed upon her daughter.

"Mother," faltered the girl.

Her mother again whispered, "The kitchen door isn't locked."

Motionless and mute they stared into each other's eyes.

At last the girl quavered, "We better—we better go and lock it." The mother nodded. Hanging arm in arm they stole across the floor toward the head of the stairs. A board of the floor creaked. They halted and exchanged a look of dumb agony.

At last they reached the head of the stairs. From the kitchen came the bass humming of the kettle and frequent sputterings and cracklings from the fire. These sounds were sinister. The mother and the girl stood incapable of movement. "There's somebody down there!" whispered the elder woman.

Finally, the girl made a gesture of resolution. She twisted her arm from her mother's hands and went two steps downward. She addressed the kitchen: "Who's there?" Her tone was intended to be dauntless. It rang so dramatically in the silence that a sudden new panic seized them as if the suspected presence in the kitchen had cried out to them. But the girl ventured again: "Is there anybody there?" No reply was made save by the kettle and the fire.

With a stealthy tread the girl continued her journey. As she neared the last step the fire crackled explosively and the girl screamed. But the mystic presence had not swept around the corner to grab her, so she dropped to a seat on the step and laughed. "It was—was only the—the fire," she said, stammering hysterically.

Then she arose with sudden fortitude and cried: "Why, there isn't anybody there! I know there isn't." She marched down into the kitchen. In her face was dread, as if she half expected to confront something, but the room was empty. She cried joyously: "There's nobody here! Come on down, ma." She ran to the kitchen door and locked it.

The mother came down to the kitchen. "Oh, dear, what a fright I've had! It's given me the sick headache. I know it has."

"Oh, ma," said the girl.

"I know it has—I know it. Oh, if your father was only here! He'd settle those Yankees mighty quick—he'd settle 'em! Two poor helpless women——"

"Why, ma, what makes you act so? The Yankees haven't——"

"Oh, they'll be back—they'll be back. Two poor helpless women! Your father and your uncle Asa and Bill off galavanting around and fighting when they ought to be protecting their home! That's the kind of men they are. Didn't I say to your father just before he left——"

"Ma," said the girl, coming suddenly from the window, "the barn door is open. I wonder if they took old Santo?"

"Oh, of course they have—of course——Mary, I don't see what we are going to do—I don't see what we are going to do."

The girl said, "Ma, I'm going to see if they took old Santo."

"Mary," cried the mother, "don't you dare!"

"But think of poor old Sant, ma."

"Never you mind old Santo. We're lucky to be safe ourselves, I tell you. Never mind old Santo. Don't you dare to go out there, Mary—Mary!"

The girl had unlocked the door and stepped out upon the porch. The mother cried in despair, "Mary!"

"Why, there isn't anybody out here," the girl called in response. She stood for a moment with a curious smile upon her face as of gleeful satisfaction at her daring.

The breeze was waving the boughs of the apple trees. A rooster with an air importantly courteous was conducting three hens upon a foraging tour.

On the hillside at the rear of the gray old barn the red leaves of a creeper flamed amid the summer foliage. High in the sky clouds rolled toward the north. The girl swung impulsively from the little stoop and ran toward the barn.

The great door was open, and the carved peg which usually performed the office of a catch lay on the ground. The girl could not see into the barn because of the heavy shadows. She paused in a listening attitude and heard a horse munching placidly. She gave a cry of delight and sprang across the threshold. Then she suddenly shrank back and gasped. She had confronted three men in gray seated upon the floor with their legs stretched out and their backs against Santo's manger. Their dust-covered countenances were expanded in grins.

II.

As Mary sprang backward and screamed, one of the calm men in gray, still grinning, announced, "I knowed you'd holler." Sitting there comfortably the three surveyed her with amusement.

Mary caught her breath, throwing her hand up to her throat. "Oh!" she said, "you—you frightened me!"

"We're sorry, lady, but couldn't help it no way," cheerfully responded another. "I knowed you'd holler when I seen you coming yere, but I raikoned we couldn't help it no way. We hain't a-troubling this yere barn, I don't guess. We been doing some mighty tall sleeping yere. We done woke when them Yanks loped past."

"Where did you come from? Did—did you escape from the—the Yankees?" The girl still stammered and trembled. The three soldiers laughed. "No, m'm. No, m'm. They never cotch us. We was in a muss down the road yere about two mile. And Bill yere they gin it to him in the arm, kehplunk. And they pasted me thar, too. Curious. And Sim yere, he didn't get nothing, but they chased us all quite a little piece, and we done lose track of our boys."

"Was it—was it those who passed here just now? Did they chase you?"

The men in gray laughed again. "What—them? No, indeedee! There was a mighty big swarm of Yanks and a mighty big swarm of our boys, too. What—that little passel? No, m'm."

She became calm enough to scan them more attentively. They were much begrimed and very dusty. Their gray clothes were tattered. Splashed mud had dried upon them in reddish spots. It appeared, too, that the men had not shaved in many days. In the hats there was a singular diversity. One soldier wore the little blue cap of the Northern infantry, with corps emblem and regimental number; one wore a great slouch hat with a wide hole in the crown; and the other wore no hat at all. The left sleeve of one man and the right sleeve of another had been slit and the arms were neatly bandaged with clean cloth. "These hain't no more than two little cuts," explained one. "We stopped up yere to Mis' Leavitts—she said her name was—and she bind them for us. Bill yere, he had the thirst come on him. And the fever too. We——"

"Did you ever see my father in the army?" asked Mary. "John Hinckson—his name is."

The three soldiers grinned again, but they replied kindly: "No, m'm. No, m'm, we hain't never. What is he—in the cavalry?"

"No," said the girl. "He and my uncle Asa and my cousin—his name is Bill Parker—they are all with Longstreet—they call him."

"Oh," said the soldiers. "Longstreet? Oh, they're a good smart ways from yere. 'Way off up nawtheast. There hain't nothing but cavalry down yere. They're in the infantry, probably."

"We haven't heard anything from them for days and days," said Mary.

"Oh, they're all right in the infantry," said one man, to be consoling. "The infantry don't do much fighting. They go bellering out in a big swarm and only a few of 'em get hurt. But if they was in the cavalry—the cavalry——"

Mary interrupted him without intention. "Are you hungry?" she asked.

The soldiers looked at each other, struck by some sudden and singular shame. They hung their heads. "No, m'm," replied one at last.

Santo, in his stall, was tranquilly chewing and chewing. Sometimes he looked benevolently over at them. He was an old horse and there was something about his eyes and his forelock which created the impression that he wore spectacles. Mary went and patted his nose. "Well, if you are hungry, I can get you something," she told the men. "Or you might come to the house."

"We wouldn't dast go to the house," said one. "That passel of Yanks was only a scouting crowd, most like. Just an advance. More coming, likely."

"Well, I can bring you something," cried the girl eagerly. "Won't you let me bring you something?"

"Well," said a soldier with embarrassment, "we hain't had much. If you could bring us a little snack-like—just a snack—we'd——"

Without waiting for him to cease, the girl turned toward the door. But before she had reached it she stopped abruptly. "Listen!" she whispered. Her form was bent forward, her head turned and lowered, her hand extended toward the men in a command for silence.

They could faintly hear the thudding of many hoofs, the clank of arms, and frequent calling voices.

"By cracky, it's the Yanks!" The soldiers scrambled to their feet and came toward the door. "I knowed that first crowd was only an advance."

The girl and the three men peered from the shadows of the barn. The view of the road was intersected by tree trunks and a little henhouse. However, they could see many horsemen streaming down the road. The horsemen were in blue. "Oh, hide—hide—hide!" cried the girl, with a sob in her voice.

"Wait a minute," whispered a gray soldier excitedly. "Maybe they're going along by. No, by thunder, they hain't! They're halting. Scoot, boys!"

They made a noiseless dash into the dark end of the barn. The girl, standing by the door, heard them break forth an instant later in clamorous whispers. "Where'll we hide? Where'll we hide? There hain't a place to hide!" The girl turned and glanced wildly about the barn. It seemed true. The stock of hay had grown low under Santo's endless munching, and from occasional levyings by passing troopers in gray. The poles of the mow were barely covered, save in one corner where there was a little bunch.

The girl espied the great feed box. She ran to it and lifted the lid. "Here! here!" she called. "Get in here."

They had been tearing noiselessly around the rear part of the barn. At her low call they came and plunged at the box. They did not all get in at the same moment without a good deal of a tangle. The wounded men gasped and muttered, but they at last were flopped down on the layer of feed which covered the bottom. Swiftly and softly the girl lowered the lid and then turned like a flash toward the door.

No one appeared there, so she went close to survey the situation. The troopers had dismounted and stood in silence by their horses. A gray-bearded man, whose red cheeks and nose shone vividly above the whiskers, was strolling about with two or three others. They wore double-breasted coats, and faded yellow sashes were wound under their black leather sword belts. The gray-bearded soldier was apparently giving orders, pointing here and there.

Mary tiptoed to the feed box. "They've all got off their horses," she said to it. A finger projected from a knothole near the top and said to her very plainly, "Come closer." She obeyed, and then a muffled voice could be heard: "Scoot for the house, lady, and if we don't see you again, why, much obliged for what you done."

"Good-bye," she said to the feed box.

She made two attempts to walk dauntlessly from the barn, but each time she faltered and failed just before she reached the point where she could have been seen by the blue-coated troopers. At last, however, she made a sort of a rush forward and went out into the bright sunshine.

The group of men in double-breasted coats wheeled in her direction at the instant. The gray-bearded officer forgot to lower his arm which had been stretched forth in giving an order.

She felt that her feet were touching the ground in a most unnatural manner. Her bearing, she believed, was suddenly grown awkward and ungainly. Upon her face she thought that this sentence was plainly written: "There are three men hidden in the feed box."

The gray-bearded soldier came toward her. She stopped; she seemed about to run away. But the soldier doffed his little blue cap and looked amiable. "You live here, I presume?" he said.

"Yes," she answered.

"Well, we are obliged to camp here for the night, and as we've got two wounded men with us I don't suppose you'd mind if we put them in the barn."

"In—in the barn?"

He became aware that she was agitated. He smiled assuringly. "You needn't be frightened. We won't hurt anything around here. You'll all be safe enough."

The girl balanced on one foot and swung the other to and fro in the grass. She was looking down at it. "But—but I don't think ma would like it if—if you took the barn."

The old officer laughed. "Wouldn't she?" said he. "That's so. Maybe she wouldn't." He reflected for a time and then decided cheerfully: "Well, we will have to go ask her, anyhow. Where is she? In the house?"

"Yes," replied the girl, "she's in the house. She—she'll be scared to death when she sees you!"

"Well, you go and ask her then," said the soldier, always wearing a benign smile. "You go ask her and then come and tell me."

When the girl pushed open the door and entered the kitchen, she found it empty. "Ma!" she called softly. There was no answer. The kettle still was humming its low song. The knife and the curl of potato skin lay on the floor.

She went to her mother's room and entered timidly. The new, lonely aspect of the house shook her nerves. Upon the bed was a confusion of coverings. "Ma!" called the girl, quaking in fear that her mother was not there to reply. But there was a sudden turmoil of the quilts, and her mother's head was thrust forth. "Mary!" she cried, in what seemed to be a supreme astonishment, "I thought—I thought——"

"Oh, ma," blurted the girl, "there's over a thousand Yankees in the yard, and I've hidden three of our men in the feed box!"

The elder woman, however, upon the appearance of her daughter had begun to thrash hysterically about on the bed and wail.

"Ma," the girl exclaimed, "and now they want to use the barn—and our men in the feed box! What shall I do, ma? What shall I do?"

Her mother did not seem to hear, so absorbed was she in her grievous flounderings and tears. "Ma!" appealed the girl. "Ma!"

For a moment Mary stood silently debating, her lips apart, her eyes fixed. Then she went to the kitchen window and peeked.

The old officer and the others were staring up the road. She went to another window in order to get a proper view of the road, and saw that they were gazing at a small body of horsemen approaching at a trot and raising much dust. Presently she recognised them as the squad that had passed the house earlier, for the young man with the dim yellow chevron still rode at their head. An unarmed horseman in gray was receiving their close attention.

As they came very near to the house she darted to the first window again. The gray-bearded officer was smiling a fine broad smile of satisfaction. "So you got him?" he called out. The young sergeant sprang from his horse and his brown hand moved in a salute. The girl could not hear his reply. She saw the unarmed horseman in gray stroking a very black mustache and looking about him coolly and with an interested air. He appeared so indifferent that she did not understand he was a prisoner until she heard the graybeard call out: "Well, put him in the barn. He'll be safe there, I guess." A party of troopers moved with the prisoner toward the barn.

The girl made a sudden gesture of horror, remembering the three men in the feed box.

III.

The busy troopers in blue scurried about the long lines of stamping horses. Men crooked their backs and perspired in order to rub with cloths or bunches of grass these slim equine legs, upon whose splendid machinery they depended so greatly. The lips of the horses were still wet and frothy from the steel bars which had wrenched at their mouths all day. Over their backs and about their noses sped the talk of the men.

"Moind where yer plug is steppin', Finerty! Keep 'im aff me!"

"An ould elephant! He shtrides like a schoolhouse."

"Bill's little mar—she was plum beat when she come in with Crawford's crowd."

"Crawford's the hardest-ridin' cavalryman in the army. An he don't use up a horse, neither—much. They stay fresh when the others are most a-droppin'."

"Finerty, will yeh moind that cow a yours?"

Amid a bustle of gossip and banter, the horses retained their air of solemn rumination, twisting their lower jaws from side to side and sometimes rubbing noses dreamfully.

Over in front of the barn three troopers sat talking comfortably. Their carbines were leaned against the wall. At their side and outlined in the black of the open door stood a sentry, his weapon resting in the hollow of his arm. Four horses, saddled and accoutred, were conferring with their heads close together. The four bridle reins were flung over a post.

Upon the calm green of the land, typical in every way of peace, the hues of war brought thither by the troops shone strangely. Mary, gazing curiously, did not feel that she was contemplating a familiar scene. It was no longer the home acres. The new blue, steel, and faded yellow thoroughly dominated the old green and brown. She could hear the voices of the men, and it seemed from their tone that they had camped there for years. Everything with them was usual. They had taken possession of the landscape in such a way that even the old marks appeared strange and formidable to the girl.

Mary had intended to go and tell the commander in blue that her mother did not wish his men to use the barn at all, but she paused when she heard him speak to the sergeant. She thought she perceived then that it mattered little to him what her mother wished, and that an objection by her or by anybody would be futile. She saw the soldiers conduct the prisoner in gray into the barn, and for a long time she watched the three chatting guards and the pondering sentry. Upon her mind in desolate weight was the recollection of the three men in the feed box.

It seemed to her that in a case of this description it was her duty to be a heroine. In all the stories she had read when at boarding school in Pennsylvania, the girl characters, confronted with such difficulties, invariably did hair breadth things. True, they were usually bent upon rescuing and recovering their lovers, and neither the calm man in gray nor any of the three in the feed box was lover of hers, but then a real heroine would not pause over this minor question. Plainly a heroine would take measures to rescue the four men. If she did not at least make the attempt, she would be false to those carefully constructed ideals which were the accumulation of years of dreaming.

But the situation puzzled her. There was the barn with only one door, and with four armed troopers in front of this door, one of them with his back to the rest of the world, engaged, no doubt, in a steadfast contemplation of the calm man and, incidentally, of the feed box. She knew, too, that even if she should open the kitchen door, three heads and perhaps four would turn casually in her direction. Their ears were real ears.

Heroines, she knew, conducted these matters with infinite precision and despatch. They severed the hero's bonds, cried a dramatic sentence, and stood between him and his enemies until he had run far enough away. She saw well, however, that even should she achieve all things up to the point where she might take glorious stand between the escaping and the pursuers, those grim troopers in blue would not pause. They would run around her, make a circuit. One by one she saw the gorgeous contrivances and expedients of fiction fall before the plain, homely difficulties of this situation. They were of no service. Sadly, ruefully, she thought of the calm man and of the contents of the feed box.

The sum of her invention was that she could sally forth to the commander of the blue cavalry, and confessing to him that there were three of her friends and his enemies secreted in the feed box, pray him to let them depart unmolested. But she was beginning to believe the old graybeard to be a bear. It was hardly probable that he would give this plan his support. It was more probable that he and some of his men would at once descend upon the feed box and confiscate her three friends. The difficulty with her idea was that she could not learn its value without trying it, and then in case of failure it would be too late for remedies and other plans. She reflected that war made men very unreasonable.

All that she could do was to stand at the window and mournfully regard the barn. She admitted this to herself with a sense of deep humiliation. She was not, then, made of that fine stuff, that mental satin, which enabled some other beings to be of such mighty service to the distressed. She was defeated by a barn with one door, by four men with eight eyes and eight ears—trivialities that would not impede the real heroine.

The vivid white light of broad day began slowly to fade. Tones of gray came upon the fields, and the shadows were of lead. In this more sombre atmosphere the fires built by the troops down in the far end of the orchard grew more brilliant, becoming spots of crimson colour in the dark grove.

The girl heard a fretting voice from her mother's room. "Mary!" She hastily obeyed the call. She perceived that she had quite forgotten her mother's existence in this time of excitement.

The elder woman still lay upon the bed. Her face was flushed and perspiration stood amid new wrinkles upon her forehead. Weaving wild glances from side to side, she began to whimper. "Oh, I'm just sick—I'm just sick! Have those men gone yet? Have they gone?"

The girl smoothed a pillow carefully for her mother's head. "No, ma.

They're here yet. But they haven't hurt anything—it doesn't seem. Will I get you something to eat?"

Her mother gestured her away with the impatience of the ill. "No—no—just don't bother me. My head is splitting, and you know very well that nothing can be done for me when I get one of these spells. It's trouble—that's what makes them. When are those men going? Look here, don't you go 'way. You stick close to the house now."

"I'll stay right here," said the girl. She sat in the gloom and listened to her mother's incessant moaning. When she attempted to move, her mother cried out at her. When she desired to ask if she might try to alleviate the pain, she was interrupted shortly. Somehow her sitting in passive silence within hearing of this illness seemed to contribute to her mother's relief. She assumed a posture of submission. Sometimes her mother projected questions concerning the local condition, and although she laboured to be graphic and at the same time soothing, unalarming, her form of reply was always displeasing to the sick woman, and brought forth ejaculations of angry impatience.

Eventually the woman slept in the manner of one worn from terrible labour. The girl went slowly and softly to the kitchen. When she looked from the window, she saw the four soldiers still at the barn door. In the west, the sky was yellow. Some tree trunks intersecting it appeared black as streaks of ink. Soldiers hovered in blue clouds about the bright splendour of the fires in the orchard. There were glimmers of steel.

The girl sat in the new gloom of the kitchen and watched. The soldiers lit a lantern and hung it in the barn. Its rays made the form of the sentry seem gigantic. Horses whinnied from the orchard. There was a low hum of human voices. Sometimes small detachments of troopers rode past the front of the house. The girl heard the abrupt calls of sentries. She fetched some food and ate it from her hand, standing by the window. She was so afraid that something would occur that she barely left her post for an instant.

A picture of the interior of the barn hung vividly in her mind. She recalled the knot-holes in the boards at the rear, but she admitted that the prisoners could not escape through them. She remembered some inadequacies of the roof, but these also counted for nothing. When confronting the problem, she felt her ambitions, her ideals tumbling headlong like cottages of straw.

Once she felt that she had decided to reconnoitre at any rate. It was night; the lantern at the barn and the camp fires made everything without their circle into masses of heavy mystic blackness. She took two steps toward the door. But there she paused. Innumerable possibilities of danger had assailed her mind. She returned to the window and stood wavering. At last, she went swiftly to the door, opened it, and slid noiselessly into the darkness.

For a moment she regarded the shadows. Down in the orchard the camp fires of the troops appeared precisely like a great painting, all in reds upon a black cloth. The voices of the troopers still hummed. The girl started slowly off in the opposite direction. Her eyes were fixed in a stare; she studied the darkness in front for a moment, before she ventured upon a forward step. Unconsciously, her throat was arranged for a sudden shrill scream. High in the tree branches she could hear the voice of the wind, a melody of the night, low and sad, the plaint of an endless, incommunicable sorrow. Her own distress, the plight of the men in gray—these near matters as well as all she had known or imagined of grief—everything was expressed in this soft mourning of the wind in the trees. At first she felt like weeping. This sound told her of human impotency and doom. Then later the trees and the wind breathed strength to her, sang of sacrifice, of dauntless effort, of hard carven faces that did not blanch when Duty came at midnight or at noon.

She turned often to scan the shadowy figures that moved from time to time in the light at the barn door. Once she trod upon a stick, and it flopped, crackling in the intolerable manner of all sticks. At this noise, however, the guards at the barn made no sign. Finally, she was where she could see the knot-holes in the rear of the structure gleaming like pieces of metal from the effect of the light within. Scarcely breathing in her excitement she glided close and applied an eye to a knothole. She had barely achieved one glance at the interior before she sprang back shuddering.

For the unconscious and cheerful sentry at the door was swearing away in flaming sentences, heaping one gorgeous oath upon another, making a conflagration of his description of his troop horse.

"Why," he was declaring to the calm prisoner in gray, "you ain't got a horse in your hull —— army that can run forty rod with that there little mar'!"

As in the outer darkness Mary cautiously returned to the knothole, the three guards in front suddenly called in low tones: "S-s-s-h!"

"Quit, Pete; here comes the lieutenant." The sentry had apparently been about to resume his declamation, but at these warnings he suddenly posed in a soldierly manner.

A tall and lean officer with a smooth face entered the barn. The sentry saluted primly. The officer flashed a comprehensive glance about him. "Everything all right?"

"All right, sir."

This officer had eyes like the points of stilettos. The lines from his nose to the corners of his mouth were deep and gave him a slightly disagreeable aspect, but somewhere in his face there was a quality of singular thoughtfulness, as of the absorbed student dealing in generalities, which was utterly in opposition to the rapacious keenness of the eyes which saw everything.

Suddenly he lifted a long finger and pointed. "What's that?"

"That? That's a feed box, I suppose."

"What's in it?"

"I don't know. I——"

"You ought to know," said the officer sharply. He walked over to the feed box and flung up the lid. With a sweeping gesture, he reached down and scooped a handful of feed. "You ought to know what's in everything when you have prisoners in your care," he added, scowling.

During the time of this incident, the girl had nearly swooned. Her hands searched weakly over the boards for something to which to cling. With the pallor of the dying she had watched the downward sweep of the officer's arm, which after all had only brought forth a handful of feed. The result was a stupefaction of her mind. She was astonished out of her senses at this spectacle of three large men metamorphosed into a handful of feed.

IV.

It is perhaps a singular thing that this absence of the three men from the feed box at the time of the sharp lieutenant's investigation should terrify the girl more than it should joy her. That for which she had prayed had come to pass. Apparently the escape of these men in the face of every improbability had been granted her, but her dominating emotion was fright. The feed box was a mystic and terrible machine, like some dark magician's trap. She felt it almost possible that she should see the three weird men floating spectrally away through the air. She glanced with swift apprehension behind her, and when the dazzle from the lantern's light had left her eyes, saw only the dim hillside stretched in solemn silence.

The interior of the barn possessed for her another fascination because it was now uncanny. It contained that extraordinary feed box. When she peeped again at the knothole, the calm, gray prisoner was seated upon the feed box, thumping it with his dangling, careless heels as if it were in nowise his conception of a remarkable feed-box. The sentry also stood facing it. His carbine he held in the hollow of his arm. His legs were spread apart, and he mused. From without came the low mumble of the three other troopers. The sharp lieutenant had vanished.

The trembling yellow light of the lantern caused the figures of the men to cast monstrous wavering shadows. There were spaces of gloom which shrouded ordinary things in impressive garb. The roof presented an inscrutable blackness, save where small rifts in the shingles glowed phosphorescently. Frequently old Santo put down a thunderous hoof. The heels of the prisoner made a sound like the booming of a wild kind of drum. When the men moved their heads, their eyes shone with ghoulish whiteness, and their complexions were always waxen and unreal. And there was that profoundly strange feed box, imperturbable with its burden of fantastic mystery.

Suddenly from down near her feet the girl heard a crunching sound, a sort of a nibbling, as if some silent and very discreet terrier was at work upon the turf. She faltered back; here was no doubt another grotesque detail of this most unnatural episode. She did not run, because physically she was in the power of these events. Her feet chained her to the ground in submission to this march of terror after terror. As she stared at the spot from which this sound seemed to come, there floated through her mind a vague, sweet vision—a vision of her safe little room, in which at this hour she usually was sleeping.

The scratching continued faintly and with frequent pauses, as if the terrier was then listening. When the girl first removed her eyes from the knothole the scene appeared of one velvet blackness; then gradually objects loomed with a dim lustre. She could see now where the tops of the trees joined the sky and the form of the barn was before her dyed in heavy purple. She was ever about to shriek, but no sound came from her constricted throat. She gazed at the ground with the expression of countenance of one who watches the sinister-moving grass where a serpent approaches.

Dimly she saw a piece of sod wrenched free and drawn under the great foundation beam of the barn. Once she imagined that she saw human hands, not outlined at all, but sufficient in colour, form, or movement to make subtle suggestion.

Then suddenly a thought that illuminated the entire situation flashed in her mind like a light. The three men, late of the feed box, were beneath the floor of the barn and were now scraping their way under this beam. She did not consider for a moment how they could come there. They were marvellous creatures. The supernatural was to be expected of them. She no longer trembled, for she was possessed upon this instant of the most unchangeable species of conviction. The evidence before her amounted to no evidence at all, but nevertheless her opinion grew in an instant from an irresponsible acorn to a rooted and immovable tree. It was as if she was on a jury.

She stooped down hastily and scanned the ground. There she indeed saw a pair of hands hauling at the dirt where the sod had been displaced. Softly, in a whisper like a breath, she said, “Hey!”

The dim hands were drawn hastily under the barn. The girl reflected for a moment. Then she stooped and whispered: "Hey! It's me!"

After a time there was a resumption of the digging. The ghostly hands began once more their cautious mining. She waited. In hollow reverberations from the interior of the barn came the frequent sounds of old Santo's lazy movements. The sentry conversed with the prisoner.

At last the girl saw a head thrust slowly from under the beam. She perceived the face of one of the miraculous soldiers from the feed box. A pair of eyes glintered and wavered, then finally settled upon her, a pale statue of a girl. The eyes became lit with a kind of humorous greeting. An arm gestured at her.

Stooping, she breathed, "All right." The man drew himself silently back under the beam. A moment later the pair of hands resumed their cautious task. Ultimately the head and arms of the man were thrust strangely from the earth. He was lying on his back. The girl thought of the dirt in his hair. Wriggling slowly and pushing at the beam above him he forced his way out of the curious little passage. He twisted his body and raised himself upon his hands. He grinned at the girl and drew his feet carefully from under the beam. When he at last stood erect beside her, he at once began mechanically to brush the dirt from his clothes with his hands. In the barn the sentry and his prisoner were evidently engaged in an argument.

The girl and the first miraculous soldier signalled warily. It seemed that they feared that their arms would make noises in passing through the air. Their lips moved, conveying dim meanings.

In this sign language the girl described the situation in the barn. With guarded motions, she told him of the importance of absolute stillness. He nodded, and then in the same manner he told her of his two companions under the barn floor. He informed her again of their wounded state, and wagged his head to express his despair. He contorted his face, to tell how sore were their arms; and jabbed the air mournfully, to express their remote geographical position.

This signalling was interrupted by the sound of a body being dragged or dragging itself with slow, swishing sound under the barn. The sound was too loud for safety. They rushed to the hole and began to semaphore until a shaggy head appeared with rolling eyes and quick grin.

With frantic downward motions of their arms they suppressed this grin and with it the swishing noise. In dramatic pantomime they informed this head of the terrible consequences of so much noise. The head nodded, and painfully but with extreme care the second man pushed and pulled himself from the hole.

In a faint whisper the first man said, "Where's Sim?"

The second man made low reply. "He's right here." He motioned reassuringly toward the hole.

When the third head appeared, a soft smile of glee came upon each face, and the mute group exchanged expressive glances.

When they all stood together, free from this tragic barn, they breathed a long sigh that was contemporaneous with another smile and another exchange of glances.

One of the men tiptoed to a knothole and peered into the barn. The sentry was at that moment speaking. "Yes, we know 'em all. There isn't a house in this region that we don't know who is in it most of the time. We collar 'em once in a while—like we did you. Now, that house out yonder, we——"

The man suddenly left the knothole and returned to the others. Upon his face, dimly discerned, there was an indication that he had made an astonishing discovery. The others questioned him with their eyes, but he simply waved an arm to express his inability to speak at that spot. He led them back toward the hill, prowling carefully. At a safe distance from the barn he halted and as they grouped eagerly about him, he exploded in an intense undertone: "Why, that—that's Cap'n Sawyer they got in yonder."

"Cap'n Sawyer!" incredulously whispered the other men.

But the girl had something to ask. "How did you get out of that feed box?" He smiled. "Well, when you put us in there, we was just in a minute when we allowed it wasn't a mighty safe place, and we allowed we'd get out. And we did. We skedaddled 'round and 'round until it 'peared like we was going to get cotched, and then we flung ourselves down in the cow stalls where it's low-like—just dirt floor—and then we just naturally went a-whooping under the barn floor when the Yanks come. And we didn't know Cap'n Sawyer by his voice nohow. We heard 'im discoursing, and we allowed it was a mighty pert man, but we didn't know that it was him. No, m'm."

These three men, so recently from a situation of peril, seemed suddenly to have dropped all thought of it. They stood with sad faces looking at the barn. They seemed to be making no plans at all to reach a place of more complete safety. They were halted and stupefied by some unknown calamity.

"How do you raikon they cotch him, Sim?" one whispered mournfully.

"I don't know," replied another, in the same tone.

Another with a low snarl expressed in two words his opinion of the methods of Fate: "Oh, hell!"

The three men started then as if simultaneously stung and gazed at the young girl who stood silently near them. The man who had sworn began to make agitated apology: "Pardon, miss! 'Pon my soul I clean forgot you was by. 'Deed, and I wouldn't swear like that if I had knowed. 'Deed, I wouldn't."

The girl did not seem to hear him. She was staring at the barn. Suddenly she turned and whispered, "Who is he?"

"He's Cap'n Sawyer, m'm," they told her sorrowfully. "He's our own cap'n. He's been in command of us yere since a long time. He's got folks about yere. Raikon they cotch him while he was a-visiting."

She was still for a time and then, awed, she said, "Will they—will they hang him?"

"No, m'm. Oh, no, m'm. Don't raikon no such thing. No, m'm."

The group became absorbed in a contemplation of the barn. For a time no one moved nor spoke. At last the girl was aroused by slight sounds, and turning, she perceived that the three men who had so recently escaped from the barn were now advancing toward it.

V.

The girl, waiting in the darkness, expected to hear the sudden crash and uproar of a fight as soon as the three creeping men should reach the barn. She reflected in an agony upon the swift disaster that would befall any enterprise so desperate. She had an impulse to beg them to come away. The grass rustled in silken movements as she sped toward the barn.

When she arrived, however, she gazed about her bewildered. The men were gone. She searched with her eyes, trying to detect some moving thing, but she could see nothing.

Left alone again, she began to be afraid of the night. The great stretches of darkness could hide crawling dangers. From sheer desire to see a human, she was obliged to peep again at the knothole. The sentry had apparently wearied of talking. Instead, he was reflecting. The prisoner still sat on the feed box, moodily staring at the floor. The girl felt in one way that she was looking at a ghastly group in wax. She started when the old horse put down an echoing hoof. She wished the men would speak; their silence re-enforced the strange aspect. They might have been two dead men.

The girl felt impelled to look at the corner of the interior where were the cow stalls. There was no light there save the appearance of peculiar gray haze which marked the track of the dimming rays of the lantern. All else was sombre shadow. At last she saw something move there. It might have been as small as a rat, or it might have been a part of something as large as a man. At any rate, it proclaimed that something in that spot was alive. At one time she saw it plainly and at other times it vanished, because her fixture of gaze caused her occasionally to greatly tangle and blur those peculiar shadows and faint lights. At last, however, she perceived a human head. It was monstrously dishevelled and wild. It moved slowly forward until its glance could fall upon the prisoner and then upon the sentry. The wandering rays caused the eyes to glitter like silver. The girl's heart pounded so that she put her hand over it.

The sentry and the prisoner remained immovably waxen, and over in the gloom the head thrust from the floor watched them with its silver eyes.

Finally, the prisoner slipped from the feed box, and, raising his arms, yawned at great length. "Oh, well," he remarked, "you boys will get a good licking if you fool around here much longer. That's some satisfaction, anyhow, even if you did bag me. You'll get a good walloping." He reflected for a moment, and decided: "I'm sort of willing to be captured if you fellows only get a d——d good licking for being so smart."

The sentry looked up and smiled a superior smile. "Licking, hey? Nixey!" He winked exasperatingly at the prisoner. "You fellows are not fast enough, my boy. Why didn't you lick us at ——? and at ——? and at ----?" He named some of the great battles.

To this the captive officer blurted in angry astonishment, "Why, we did!"

The sentry winked again in profound irony. "Yes—I know you did. Of course. You whipped us, didn't you? Fine kind of whipping that was! Why, we——"

He suddenly ceased, smitten mute by a sound that broke the stillness of the night. It was the sharp crack of a distant shot that made wild echoes among the hills. It was instantly followed by the hoarse cry of a human voice, a far-away yell of warning, singing of surprise, peril, fear of death. A moment later there was a distant, fierce spattering of shots. The sentry and the prisoner stood facing each other, their lips apart, listening.

The orchard at that instant awoke to sudden tumult. There were the thud and scramble and scamper of feet, the mellow, swift clash of arms, men's voices in question, oath, command, hurried and unhurried, resolute and frantic. A horse sped along the road at a raging gallop. A loud voice shouted, "What is it, Ferguson?" Another voice yelled something incoherent. There was a sharp, discordant chorus of command. An uproarious volley suddenly rang from the orchard. The prisoner in gray moved from his intent, listening attitude. Instantly the eyes of the sentry blazed, and he said with a new and terrible sternness, "Stand where you are!"

The prisoner trembled in his excitement. Expressions of delight and triumph bubbled to his lips. "A surprise, by Gawd! Now—now, you'll see!"

The sentry stolidly swung his carbine to his shoulder. He sighted carefully along the barrel until it pointed at the prisoner's head, about at his nose. "Well, I've got you, anyhow. Remember that! Don't move!"

The prisoner could not keep his arms from nervously gesturing. "I won't; but——"

"And shut your mouth!"

The three comrades of the sentry flung themselves into view. "Pete—devil of a row!—can you——"

"I've got him," said the sentry calmly and without moving. It was as if the barrel of the carbine rested on piers of stone. The three comrades turned and plunged into the darkness.

In the orchard it seemed as if two gigantic animals were engaged in a mad, floundering encounter, snarling, howling in a whirling chaos of noise and motion. In the barn the prisoner and his guard faced each other in silence.

As for the girl at the knothole, the sky had fallen at the beginning of this clamour. She would not have been astonished to see the stars swinging from their abodes, and the vegetation, the barn, all blow away. It was the end of everything, the grand universal murder. When two of the three miraculous soldiers who formed the original feed-box corps emerged in detail from the hole under the beam and slid away into the darkness, she did no more than glance at them.

Suddenly she recollected the head with silver eyes. She started forward and again applied her eyes to the knothole. Even with the din resounding from the orchard, from up the road and down the road, from the heavens and from the deep earth, the central fascination was this mystic head. There, to her, was the dark god of the tragedy.

The prisoner in gray at this moment burst into a laugh that was no more than a hysterical gurgle. "Well, you can't hold that gun out forever! Pretty soon you'll have to lower it."

The sentry's voice sounded slightly muffled, for his cheek was pressed against the weapon. "I won't be tired for some time yet."

The girl saw the head slowly rise, the eyes fixed upon the sentry's face. A tall, black figure slunk across the cow stalls and vanished back of old Santo's quarters. She knew what was to come to pass. She knew this grim thing was upon a terrible mission, and that it would reappear again at the head of the little passage between Santo's stall and the wall, almost at the sentry's elbow; and yet when she saw a faint indication as of a form crouching there, a scream from an utterly new alarm almost escaped her.

The sentry's arms, after all, were not of granite. He moved restively. At last he spoke in his even, unchanging tone: "Well, I guess you'll have to climb into that feed box. Step back and lift the lid."

"Why, you don't mean——"

"Step back!"

The girl felt a cry of warning arising to her lips as she gazed at this sentry. She noted every detail of his facial expression. She saw, moreover, his mass of brown hair bunching disgracefully about his ears, his clear eyes lit now with a hard, cold light, his forehead puckered in a mighty scowl, the ring upon the third finger of the left hand. "Oh, they won't kill him! Surely they won't kill him!" The noise of the fight in the orchard was the loud music, the thunder and lightning, the rioting of the tempest which people love during the critical scene of a tragedy.

When the prisoner moved back in reluctant obedience, he faced for an instant the entrance of the little passage, and what he saw there must have been written swiftly, graphically in his eyes. And the sentry read it and knew then that he was upon the threshold of his death. In a fraction of time, certain information went from the grim thing in the passage to the prisoner, and from the prisoner to the sentry. But at that instant the black formidable figure arose, towered, and made its leap. A new shadow flashed across the floor when the blow was struck.

As for the girl at the knothole, when she returned to sense she found herself standing with clinched hands and screaming with her might.

As if her reason had again departed from her, she ran around the barn, in at the door, and flung herself sobbing beside the body of the soldier in blue.

The uproar of the fight became at last coherent, inasmuch as one party was giving shouts of supreme exultation. The firing no longer sounded in crashes; it was now expressed in spiteful crackles, the last words of the combat, spoken with feminine vindictiveness.

Presently there was a thud of flying feet. A grimy panting, red-faced mob of troopers in blue plunged into the barn, became instantly frozen to attitudes of amazement and rage, and then roared in one great chorus, "He's gone!"

The girl who knelt beside the body upon the floor turned toward them her lamenting eyes and cried: "He's not dead, is he? He can't be dead?"

They thronged forward. The sharp lieutenant who had been so particular about the feed box knelt by the side of the girl and laid his head against the chest of the prostrate soldier. "Why, no," he said, rising and looking at the man. "He's all right. Some of you boys throw some water on him."

"Are you sure?" demanded the girl, feverishly.

"Of course! He'll be better after awhile."

"Oh!" said she softly, and then looked down at the sentry. She started to arise, and the lieutenant reached down and hoisted rather awkwardly at her arm.

"Don't you worry about him. He's all right."

She turned her face with its curving lips and shining eyes once more toward the unconscious soldier upon the floor. The troopers made a lane to the door, the lieutenant bowed, the girl vanished.

"Queer," said a young officer. "Girl very clearly worst kind of rebel, and yet she falls to weeping and wailing like mad over one of her enemies. Be around in the morning with all sorts of doctoring—you see if she ain't. Queer."

The sharp lieutenant shrugged his shoulders. After reflection he shrugged his shoulders again. He said: "War changes many things; but it doesn't change everything, thank God!"

A MYSTERY OF HEROISM.

The dark uniforms of the men were so coated with dust from the incessant wrestling of the two armies that the regiment almost seemed a part of the clay bank which shielded them from the shells. On the top of the hill a battery was arguing in tremendous roars with some other guns, and to the eye of the infantry, the artillerymen, the guns, the caissons, the horses, were distinctly outlined upon the blue sky. When a piece was fired, a red streak as round as a log flashed low in the heavens, like a monstrous bolt of lightning. The men of the battery wore white duck trousers, which somehow emphasized their legs; and when they ran and crowded in little groups at the bidding of the shouting officers, it was more impressive than usual to the infantry.

Fred Collins, of A Company, was saying: "Thunder! I wisht I had a drink. Ain't there any water round here?" Then somebody yelled, "There goes th' bugler!"

As the eyes of half the regiment swept in one machinelike movement there was an instant's picture of a horse in a great convulsive leap of a death wound and a rider leaning back with a crooked arm and spread fingers before his face. On the ground was the crimson terror of an exploding shell, with fibres of flame that seemed like lances. A glittering bugle swung clear of the rider's back as fell headlong the horse and the man. In the air was an odour as from a conflagration.

Sometimes they of the infantry looked down at a fair little meadow which spread at their feet. Its long, green grass was rippling gently in a breeze. Beyond it was the gray form of a house half torn to pieces by shells and by the busy axes of soldiers who had pursued firewood. The line of an old fence was now dimly marked by long weeds and by an occasional post. A shell had blown the well-house to fragments. Little lines of gray smoke ribboning upward from some embers indicated the place where had stood the barn.

From beyond a curtain of green woods there came the sound of some stupendous scuffle, as if two animals of the size of islands were fighting. At a distance there were occasional appearances of swift-moving men, horses, batteries, flags, and, with the crashing of infantry volleys were heard, often, wild and frenzied cheers. In the midst of it all Smith and Ferguson, two privates of A Company, were engaged in a heated discussion, which involved the greatest questions of the national existence.

The battery on the hill presently engaged in a frightful duel. The white legs of the gunners scampered this way and that way, and the officers redoubled their shouts. The guns, with their demeanours of stolidity and courage, were typical of something infinitely self-possessed in this clamour of death that swirled around the hill.

One of a "swing" team was suddenly smitten quivering to the ground, and his maddened brethren dragged his torn body in their struggle to escape from this turmoil and danger. A young soldier astride one of the leaders swore and fumed in his saddle, and furiously jerked at the bridle. An officer screamed out an order so violently that his voice broke and ended the sentence in a falsetto shriek.

The leading company of the infantry regiment was somewhat exposed, and the colonel ordered it moved more fully under the shelter of the hill. There was the clank of steel against steel.

A lieutenant of the battery rode down and passed them, holding his right arm carefully in his left hand. And it was as if this arm was not at all a part of him, but belonged to another man. His sober and reflective charger went slowly. The officer's face was grimy and perspiring, and his uniform was tousled as if he had been in direct grapple with an enemy. He smiled grimly when the men stared at him. He turned his horse toward the meadow.

Collins, of A Company, said: "I wisht I had a drink. I bet there's water in that there ol' well yonder!"

"Yes; but how you goin' to git it?"

For the little meadow which intervened was now suffering a terrible onslaught of shells. Its green and beautiful calm had vanished utterly. Brown earth was being flung in monstrous handfuls. And there was a massacre of the young blades of grass. They were being torn, burned, obliterated. Some curious fortune of the battle had made this gentle little meadow the object of the red hate of the shells, and each one as it exploded seemed like an imprecation in the face of a maiden.

The wounded officer who was riding across this expanse said to himself, "Why, they couldn't shoot any harder if the whole army was massed here!"

A shell struck the gray ruins of the house, and as, after the roar, the shattered wall fell in fragments, there was a noise which resembled the flapping of shutters during a wild gale of winter. Indeed, the infantry paused in the shelter of the bank appeared as men standing upon a shore contemplating a madness of the sea. The angel of calamity had under its glance the battery upon the hill. Fewer white-legged men laboured about the guns. A shell had smitten one of the pieces, and after the flare, the smoke, the dust, the wrath of this blow were gone, it was possible to see white legs stretched horizontally upon the ground. And at that interval to the rear, where it is the business of battery horses to stand with their noses to the fight awaiting the command to drag their guns out of the destruction or into it or wheresoever these incomprehensible humans demanded with whip and spur—in this line of passive and dumb spectators, whose fluttering hearts yet would not let them forget the iron laws of man's control of them—in this rank of brute-soldiers there had been relentless and hideous carnage. From the ruck of bleeding and prostrate horses, the men of the infantry could see one animal raising its stricken body with its fore legs, and turning its nose with mystic and profound eloquence toward the sky.

Some comrades joked Collins about his thirst. "Well, if yeh want a drink so bad, why don't yeh go git it!"

"Well, I will in a minnet, if yeh don't shut up!"

A lieutenant of artillery floundered his horse straight down the hill with as great concern as if it were level ground. As he galloped past the colonel of the infantry, he threw up his hand in swift salute. "We've got to get out of that," he roared angrily. He was a black-bearded officer, and his eyes, which resembled beads, sparkled like those of an insane man. His jumping horse sped along the column of infantry.

The fat major, standing carelessly with his sword held horizontally behind him and with his legs far apart, looked after the receding horseman and laughed. "He wants to get back with orders pretty quick, or there'll be no batt'ry left," he observed.

The wise young captain of the second company hazarded to the lieutenant colonel that the enemy's infantry would probably soon attack the hill, and the lieutenant colonel snubbed him.

A private in one of the rear companies looked out over the meadow, and then turned to a companion and said, "Look there, Jim!" It was the wounded officer from the battery, who some time before had started to ride across the meadow, supporting his right arm carefully with his left hand. This man had encountered a shell apparently at a time when no one perceived him, and he could now be seen lying face downward with a stirruped foot stretched across the body of his dead horse. A leg of the charger extended slantingly upward precisely as stiff as a stake. Around this motionless pair the shells still howled.

There was a quarrel in A Company. Collins was shaking his fist in the faces of some laughing comrades. "Dern yeh! I ain't afraid t' go. If yeh say much, I will go!"

"Of course, yeh will! You'll run through that there medder, won't yeh?"

Collins said, in a terrible voice, "You see now!" At this ominous threat his comrades broke into renewed jeers.

Collins gave them a dark scowl and went to find his captain. The latter was conversing with the colonel of the regiment.

"Captain," said Collins, saluting and standing at attention—in those days all trousers bagged at the knees—"captain, I want t' get permission to go git some water from that there well over yonder!"

The colonel and the captain swung about simultaneously and stared across the meadow. The captain laughed. "You must be pretty thirsty, Collins?"

"Yes, sir, I am."

"Well—ah," said the captain. After a moment, he asked, "Can't you wait?"

"No, sir."

The colonel was watching Collins's face. "Look here, my lad," he said, in a pious sort of a voice—"look here, my lad"—Collins was not a lad—"don't you think that's taking pretty big risks for a little drink of water?"

"I dunno," said Collins uncomfortably. Some of the resentment toward his companions, which perhaps had forced him into this affair, was beginning to fade. "I dunno wether 'tis."

The colonel and the captain contemplated him for a time.

"Well," said the captain finally.

"Well," said the colonel, "if you want to go, why, go."

Collins saluted. "Much obliged t' yeh."

As he moved away the colonel called after him. "Take some of the other boys' canteens with you an' hurry back now."

"Yes, sir, I will."

The colonel and the captain looked at each other then, for it had suddenly occurred that they could not for the life of them tell whether Collins wanted to go or whether he did not.

They turned to regard Collins, and as they perceived him surrounded by gesticulating comrades, the colonel said: "Well, by thunder! I guess he's going."

Collins appeared as a man dreaming. In the midst of the questions, the advice, the warnings, all the excited talk of his company mates, he maintained a curious silence.

They were very busy in preparing him for his ordeal. When they inspected him carefully it was somewhat like the examination that grooms give a horse before a race; and they were amazed, staggered by the whole affair. Their astonishment found vent in strange repetitions.

"Are yeh sure a-goin'?" they demanded again and again.

"Certainly I am," cried Collins, at last furiously.

He strode sullenly away from them. He was swinging five or six canteens by their cords. It seemed that his cap would not remain firmly on his head, and often he reached and pulled it down over his brow.

There was a general movement in the compact column. The long animal-like thing moved slightly. Its four hundred eyes were turned upon the figure of Collins.

"Well, sir, if that ain't th' derndest thing! I never thought Fred Collins had the blood in him for that kind of business."

"What's he goin' to do, anyhow?"

"He's goin' to that well there after water."

"We ain't dyin' of thirst, are we? That's foolishness."

"Well, somebody put him up to it, an' he's doin' it."

"Say, he must be a desperate cuss."

When Collins faced the meadow and walked away from the regiment, he was vaguely conscious that a chasm, the deep valley of all prides, was suddenly between him and his comrades. It was provisional, but the provision was that he return as a victor. He had blindly been led by quaint emotions, and laid himself under an obligation to walk squarely up to the face of death.

But he was not sure that he wished to make a retraction, even if he could do so without shame. As a matter of truth, he was sure of very little. He was mainly surprised.

It seemed to him supernaturally strange that he had allowed his mind to man[oe]uvre his body into such a situation. He understood that it might be called dramatically great.

However, he had no full appreciation of anything, excepting that he was actually conscious of being dazed. He could feel his dulled mind groping after the form and colour of this incident. He wondered why he did not feel some keen agony of fear cutting his sense like a knife. He wondered at this, because human expression had said loudly for centuries that men should feel afraid of certain things, and that all men who did not feel this fear were phenomena—heroes.

He was, then, a hero. He suffered that disappointment which we would all have if we discovered that we were ourselves capable of those deeds which we most admire in history and legend. This, then, was a hero. After all, heroes were not much.

No, it could not be true. He was not a hero. Heroes had no shames in their lives, and, as for him, he remembered borrowing fifteen dollars from a friend and promising to pay it back the next day, and then avoiding that friend for ten months. When at home his mother had aroused him for the early labour of his life on the farm, it had often been his fashion to be irritable, childish, diabolical; and his mother had died since he had come to the war.

He saw that, in this matter of the well, the canteens, the shells, he was an intruder in the land of fine deeds.

He was now about thirty paces from his comrades. The regiment had just turned its many faces toward him.

From the forest of terrific noises there suddenly emerged a little uneven line of men. They fired fiercely and rapidly at distant foliage on which appeared little puffs of white smoke. The spatter of skirmish firing was added to the thunder of the guns on the hill. The little line of men ran forward. A colour sergeant fell flat with his flag as if he had slipped on ice. There was hoarse cheering from this distant field.

Collins suddenly felt that two demon fingers were pressed into his ears. He could see nothing but flying arrows, flaming red. He lurched from the shock of this explosion, but he made a mad rush for the house, which he viewed as a man submerged to the neck in a boiling surf might view the shore. In the air, little pieces of shell howled and the earthquake explosions drove him insane with the menace of their roar. As he ran the canteens knocked together with a rhythmical tinkling.

As he neared the house, each detail of the scene became vivid to him. He was aware of some bricks of the vanished chimney lying on the sod. There was a door which hung by one hinge.

Rifle bullets called forth by the insistent skirmishers came from the far-off bank of foliage. They mingled with the shells and the pieces of shells until the air was torn in all directions by hootings, yells, howls. The sky was full of fiends who directed all their wild rage at his head.

When he came to the well, he flung himself face downward and peered into its darkness. There were furtive silver glintings some feet from the surface. He grabbed one of the canteens and, unfastening its cap, swung it down by the cord. The water flowed slowly in with an indolent gurgle.

And now as he lay with his face turned away he was suddenly smitten with the terror. It came upon his heart like the grasp of claws. All the power faded from his muscles. For an instant he was no more than a dead man.

The canteen filled with a maddening slowness, in the manner of all bottles. Presently he recovered his strength and addressed a screaming oath to it. He leaned over until it seemed as if he intended to try to push water into it with his hands. His eyes as he gazed down into the well shone like two pieces of metal and in their expression was a great appeal and a great curse. The stupid water derided him.

There was the blaring thunder of a shell. Crimson light shone through the swift-boiling smoke and made a pink reflection on part of the wall of the well. Collins jerked out his arm and canteen with the same motion that a man would use in withdrawing his head from a furnace.

He scrambled erect and glared and hesitated. On the ground near him lay the old well bucket, with a length of rusty chain. He lowered it swiftly into the well. The bucket struck the water and then, turning lazily over, sank. When, with hand reaching tremblingly over hand, he hauled it out, it knocked often against the walls of the well and spilled some of its contents.

In running with a filled bucket, a man can adopt but one kind of gait. So through this terrible field over which screamed practical angels of death Collins ran in the manner of a farmer chased out of a dairy by a bull.

His face went staring white with anticipation—anticipation of a blow that would whirl him around and down. He would fall as he had seen other men fall, the life knocked out of them so suddenly that their knees were no more quick to touch the ground than their heads. He saw the long blue line of the regiment, but his comrades were standing looking at him from the edge of an impossible star. He was aware of some deep wheel ruts and hoofprints in the sod beneath his feet.

The artillery officer who had fallen in this meadow had been making groans in the teeth of the tempest of sound. These futile cries, wrenched from him by his agony, were heard only by shells, bullets. When wild-eyed Collins came running, this officer raised himself. His face contorted and blanched from pain, he was about to utter some great beseeching cry. But suddenly his face straightened and he called: "Say, young man, give me a drink of water, will you?"

Collins had no room amid his emotions for surprise. He was mad from the threats of destruction.

"I can't!" he screamed, and in his reply was a full description of his quaking apprehension. His cap was gone and his hair was riotous. His clothes made it appear that he had been dragged over the ground by the heels. He ran on.

The officer's head sank down and one elbow crooked. His foot in its brass-bound stirrup still stretched over the body of his horse and the other leg was under the steed.

But Collins turned. He came dashing back. His face had now turned gray and in his eyes was all terror. "Here it is! here it is!"

The officer was as a man gone in drink. His arm bent like a twig. His head drooped as if his neck were of willow. He was sinking to the ground, to lie face downward.

Collins grabbed him by the shoulder. "Here it is. Here's your drink. Turn over. Turn over, man, for God's sake!"

With Collins hauling at his shoulder, the officer twisted his body and fell with his face turned toward that region where lived the unspeakable noises of the swirling missiles. There was the faintest shadow of a smile on his lips as he looked at Collins. He gave a sigh, a little primitive breath like that from a child.

Collins tried to hold the bucket steadily, but his shaking hands caused the water to splash all over the face of the dying man. Then he jerked it away and ran on.

The regiment gave him a welcoming roar. The grimed faces were wrinkled in laughter.

His captain waved the bucket away. "Give it to the men!"

The two genial, skylarking young lieutenants were the first to gain possession of it. They played over it in their fashion.

When one tried to drink the other teasingly knocked his elbow. "Don't, Billie! You'll make me spill it," said the one. The other laughed.

Suddenly there was an oath, the thud of wood on the ground, and a swift murmur of astonishment among the ranks. The two lieutenants glared at each other. The bucket lay on the ground empty.

AN INDIANA CAMPAIGN.

I.

When the able-bodied citizens of the village formed a company and marched away to the war, Major Tom Boldin assumed in a manner the burden of the village cares. Everybody ran to him when they felt obliged to discuss their affairs. The sorrows of the town were dragged before him. His little bench at the sunny side of Migglesville tavern became a sort of an open court where people came to speak resentfully of their grievances. He accepted his position and struggled manfully under the load. It behooved him, as a man who had seen the sky red over the quaint, low cities of Mexico, and the compact Northern bayonets gleaming on the narrow roads.

One warm summer day the major sat asleep on his little bench. There was a lull in the tempest of discussion which usually enveloped him. His cane, by use of which he could make the most tremendous and impressive gestures, reposed beside him. His hat lay upon the bench, and his old bald head had swung far forward until his nose actually touched the first button of his waistcoat.

The sparrows wrangled desperately in the road, defying perspiration. Once a team went jangling and creaking past, raising a yellow blur of dust before the soft tones of the field and sky. In the long grass of the meadow across the road the insects chirped and clacked eternally.

Suddenly a frouzy-headed boy appeared in the roadway, his bare feet pattering rapidly. He was extremely excited. He gave a shrill whoop as he discovered the sleeping major and rushed toward him. He created a terrific panic among some chickens who had been scratching intently near the major's feet. They clamoured in an insanity of fear, and rushed hither and thither seeking a way of escape, whereas in reality all ways lay plainly open to them.

This tumult caused the major to arouse with a sudden little jump of amazement and apprehension. He rubbed his eyes and gazed about him. Meanwhile, some clever chicken had discovered a passage to safety and led the flock into the garden, where they squawked in sustained alarm.

Panting from his run and choked with terror, the little boy stood before the major, struggling with a tale that was ever upon the tip of his tongue.

"Major—now—major——"

The old man, roused from a delicious slumber, glared impatiently at the little boy. "Come, come! What's th' matter with yeh?" he demanded. "What's th' matter? Don't stand there shaking! Speak up!"

"Lots is th' matter!" the little boy shouted valiantly, with a courage born of the importance of his tale. "My ma's chickens 'uz all stole, an'—now—he's over in th' woods!"

"Who is? Who is over in the woods? Go ahead!"

"Now—th' rebel is!"

"What?" roared the major.

"Th' rebel!" cried the little boy, with the last of his breath.

The major pounced from his bench in tempestuous excitement. He seized the little boy by the collar and gave him a great jerk. "Where? Are yeh sure? Who saw 'im? How long ago? Where is he now? Did you see 'im?"

The little boy, frightened at the major's fury, began to sob. After a moment he managed to stammer: "He—now—he's in the woods. I saw 'im. He looks uglier'n anythin'."

The major released his hold upon the boy, and, pausing for a time, indulged in a glorious dream. Then he said: "By thunder! we'll ketch th' cuss. You wait here," he told the boy, "an' don't say a word t' anybody. Do yeh hear?"

The boy, still weeping, nodded, and the major hurriedly entered the inn. He took down from its pegs an awkward, smoothbore rifle and carefully examined the enormous percussion cap that was fitted over the nipple. Mistrusting the cap, he removed it and replaced it with a new one. He scrutinized the gun keenly, as if he could judge in this manner of the condition of the load. All his movements were deliberate and deadly.

When he arrived upon the porch of the tavern he beheld the yard filled with people. Peter Witheby, sooty-faced and grinning, was in the van. He looked at the major. "Well?" he said.

"Well?" returned the major, bridling.

"Well, what's 'che got?" said old Peter.

"'Got?' Got a rebel over in th' woods!" roared the major.

At this sentence the women and boys, who had gathered eagerly about him, gave vent to startled cries. The women had come from adjacent houses, but the little boys represented the entire village. They had miraculously heard the first whisper of rumour, and they performed wonders in getting to the spot. They clustered around the important figure of the major and gazed in silent awe. The women, however, burst forth. At the word "rebel," which represented to them all terrible things, they deluged the major with questions which were obviously unanswerable.

He shook them off with violent impatience. Meanwhile Peter Witheby was trying to force exasperating interrogations through the tumult to the major's ears. "What? No! Yes! How d' I know?" the maddened veteran snarled as he struggled with his friends. "No! Yes! What? How in thunder d' I know?" Upon the steps of the tavern the landlady sat, weeping forlornly.

At last the major burst through the crowd, and went to the roadway. There, as they all streamed after him, he turned and faced them. "Now, look a' here, I don't know any more about this than you do," he told them forcibly. "All that I know is that there's a rebel over in Smith's woods, an' all I know is that I'm agoin' after 'im."

"But hol' on a minnet," said old Peter. "How do yeh know he's a rebel?"

"I know he is!" cried the major. "Don't yeh think I know what a rebel is?"

Then, with a gesture of disdain at the babbling crowd, he marched determinedly away, his rifle held in the hollow of his arm. At this heroic moment a new clamour arose, half admiration, half dismay. Old Peter hobbled after the major, continually repeating, "Hol' on a minnet."

The little boy who had given the alarm was the centre of a throng of lads who gazed with envy and awe, discovering in him a new quality. He held forth to them eloquently. The women stared after the figure of the major and old Peter, his pursuer. Jerozel Bronson, a half-witted lad who comprehended nothing save an occasional genial word, leaned against the fence and grinned like a skull. The major and the pursuer passed out of view around the turn in the road where the great maples lazily shook the dust that lay on their leaves.

For a moment the little group of women listened intently as if they expected to hear a sudden shot and cries from the distance. They looked at each other, their lips a little ways apart. The trees sighed softly in the heat of the summer sun. The insects in the meadow continued their monotonous humming, and, somewhere, a hen had been stricken with fear and was cackling loudly.

Finally, Mrs. Goodwin said, "Well, I'm goin' up to th' turn a' th' road, anyhow." Mrs. Willets and Mrs. Joe Petersen, her particular friends, cried out at this temerity, but she said, "Well, I'm goin', anyhow."

She called Bronson. "Come on, Jerozel. You're a man, an' if he should chase us, why, you mus' pitch inteh 'im. Hey?"

Bronson always obeyed everybody. He grinned an assent, and went with her down the road.

A little boy attempted to follow them, but a shrill scream from his mother made him halt.

The remaining women stood motionless, their eyes fixed upon Mrs. Goodwin and Jerozel. Then at last one gave a laugh of triumph at her conquest of caution and fear, and cried, "Well, I'm goin' too!"

Another instantly said, "So am I." There began a general movement. Some of the little boys had already ventured a hundred feet away from the main body, and at this unanimous advance they spread out ahead in little groups. Some recounted terrible stories of rebel ferocity. Their eyes were large with excitement. The whole thing with its possible dangers had for them a delicious element. Johnnie Peterson, who could whip any boy present, explained what he would do in case the enemy should happen to pounce out at him.

The familiar scene suddenly assumed a new aspect. The field of corn which met the road upon the left was no longer a mere field of corn. It was a darkly mystic place whose recesses could contain all manner of dangers. The long green leaves, waving in the breeze, rustled from the passing of men. In the song of the insects there were now omens, threats.

There was a warning in the enamel blue of the sky, in the stretch of yellow road, in the very atmosphere. Above the tops of the corn loomed the distant foliage of Smith's woods, curtaining the silent action of a tragedy whose horrors they imagined.

The women and the little boys came to a halt, overwhelmed by the impressiveness of the landscape. They waited silently.

Mrs. Goodwin suddenly said, "I'm goin' back." The others, who all wished to return, cried at once disdainfully:

"Well, go back, if yeh want to!"

A cricket at the roadside exploded suddenly in his shrill song, and a woman who had been standing near shrieked in startled terror. An electric movement went through the group of women. They jumped and gave vent to sudden screams. With the fears still upon their agitated faces, they turned to berate the one who had shrieked. "My! what a goose you are, Sallie! Why, it took my breath away. Goodness sakes, don't holler like that again!"

II.

"Hol' on a minnet!" Peter Witheby was crying to the major, as the latter, full of the importance and dignity of his position as protector of Migglesville, paced forward swiftly. The veteran already felt upon his brow a wreath formed of the flowers of gratitude, and as he strode he was absorbed in planning a calm and self-contained manner of wearing it. "Hol' on a minnet!" piped old Peter in the rear.

At last the major, aroused from his dream of triumph, turned about wrathfully. "Well, what?"

"Now, look a' here," said Peter. "What 'che goin' t' do?"

The major, with a gesture of supreme exasperation, wheeled again and went on. When he arrived at the cornfield he halted and waited for Peter. He had suddenly felt that indefinable menace in the landscape.

"Well?" demanded Peter, panting.

The major's eyes wavered a trifle. "Well," he repeated—"well, I'm goin' in there an' bring out that there rebel."

They both paused and studied the gently swaying masses of corn, and behind them the looming woods, sinister with possible secrets.

"Well," said old Peter.

The major moved uneasily and put his hand to his brow. Peter waited in obvious expectation.

The major crossed through the grass at the roadside and climbed the fence. He put both legs over the topmost rail and then sat perched there, facing the woods. Once he turned his head and asked, "What?"

"I hain't said anythin'," answered Peter.

The major clambered down from the fence and went slowly into the corn, his gun held in readiness. Peter stood in the road.

Presently the major returned and said, in a cautious whisper, "If yeh hear anythin', you come a-runnin', will yeh?"

"Well, I hain't got no gun nor nuthin'," said Peter, in the same low tone; "what good 'ud I do?"

"Well, yeh might come along with me an' watch," said the major. "Four eyes is better'n two."

"If I had a gun——" began Peter.

"Oh, yeh don't need no gun," interrupted the major, waving his hand. "All I'm afraid of is that I won't find 'im. My eyes ain't so good as they was."

"Well——"

"Come along," whispered the major. "Yeh hain't afraid, are yeh?"

"No, but——"

"Well, come along, then. What's th' matter with yeh?"

Peter climbed the fence. He paused on the top rail and took a prolonged stare at the inscrutable woods. When he joined the major in the cornfield he said, with a touch of anger:

"Well, you got the gun. Remember that. If he comes for me, I hain't got a blame thing!"

"Shucks!" answered the major. "He ain't agoin' t' come for yeh."

The two then began a wary journey through the corn. One by one the long aisles between the rows appeared. As they glanced along each of them it seemed as if some gruesome thing had just previously vacated it. Old Peter halted once and whispered: "Say, look a' here; supposin'—supposin'——"

"Supposin' what?" demanded the major.

"Supposin'——" said Peter. "Well, remember you got th' gun, an' I hain't got anythin'."

"Thunder!" said the major.

When they got to where the stalks were very short because of the shade cast by the trees of the wood, they halted again. The leaves were gently swishing in the breeze. Before them stretched the mystic green wall of the forest, and there seemed to be in it eyes which followed each of their movements.

Peter at last said, "I don't believe there's anybody in there."

"Yes, there is, too," said the major. "I'll bet anythin' he's in there."

"How d' yeh know?" asked Peter. "I'll bet he ain't within a mile o' here."

The major suddenly ejaculated, "Listen!"

They bent forward, scarce breathing, their mouths agape, their eyes glinting. Finally, the major turned his head. "Did yeh hear that?" he said hoarsely.

"No," said Peter, in a low voice. "What was it?"

The major listened for a moment. Then he turned again. "I thought I heered somebody holler!" he explained cautiously.

They both bent forward and listened once more. Peter in the intentness of his attitude lost his balance and was obliged to lift his foot hastily and with noise. "S-s-sh!" hissed the major.

After a minute Peter spoke quite loudly, "Oh, shucks! I don't believe yeh heered anythin'."

The major made a frantic downward gesture with his hand. "Shet up, will yeh!" he said, in an angry undertone.

Peter became silent for a moment, but presently he said again, "Oh, yeh didn't hear anythin'."

The major turned to glare at his companion in despair and wrath.

"What's th' matter with yeh? Can't yeh shet up?"

"Oh, this here ain't no use. If you're goin' in after 'im, why don't yeh go in after 'im?"

"Well, gimme time, can't yeh?" said the major, in a growl. And, as if to add more to this reproach, he climbed the fence that compassed the woods, looking resentfully back at his companion.

"Well," said Peter, when the major paused.

The major stepped down upon the thick carpet of brown leaves that stretched under the trees. He turned then to whisper, "You wait here, will yeh?" His face was red with determination.

"Well, hol' on a minnet!" said Peter. "You—I—we'd better——"

"No," said the major. "You wait here."

He went stealthily into the thickets. Peter watched him until he grew to be a vague, slow-moving shadow. From time to time he could hear the leaves crackle and twigs snap under the major's awkward tread. Peter, intent, breathless, waited for the peal of sudden tragedy. Finally, the woods grew silent in a solemn and impressive hush that caused Peter to feel the thumping of his heart. He began to look about him to make sure that nothing should spring upon him from the sombre shadows. He scrutinized this cool gloom before him, and at times he thought he could perceive the moving of swift silent shapes. He concluded that he had better go back and try to muster some assistance to the major.

As Peter came through the corn, the women in the road caught sight of the glittering figure and screamed. Many of them began to run. The little boys, with all their valour, scurried away in clouds. Mrs. Joe Peterson, however, cast a glance over her shoulders as she, with her skirts gathered up, was running as best she could. She instantly stopped and, in tones of deepest scorn, called out to the others, "Why, it's on'y Pete Witheby!" They came faltering back then, those who had been naturally swiftest in the race avoiding the eyes of those whose limbs had enabled them to flee a short distance.

Peter came rapidly, appreciating the glances of vivid interest in the eyes of the women. To their lightning-like questions, which hit all sides of the episode, he opposed a new tranquillity gained from his sudden ascent in importance. He made no answer to their clamour. When he had reached the top of the fence, he called out commandingly: "Here you, Johnnie, you and George, run an' git my gun! It's hangin' on th' pegs over th' bench in th' shop."

At this terrible sentence, a shuddering cry broke from the women. The boys named sped down the road, accompanied by a retinue of envious companions.

Peter swung his legs over the rail and faced the woods again. He twisted his head once to say: "Keep still, can't yeh? Quit scufflin' aroun'!" They could see by his manner that this was a supreme moment. The group became motionless and still. Later, Peter turned to say, "S-s-sh!" to a restless boy, and the air with which he said it smote them all with awe.

The little boys who had gone after the gun came pattering along hurriedly, the weapon borne in the midst of them. Each was anxious to share in the honour. The one who had been delegated to bring it was bullying and directing his comrades.

Peter said, "S-s-sh!" He took the gun and poised it in readiness to sweep the cornfield. He scowled at the boys and whispered angrily: "Why didn't yeh bring th' powder horn an' th' thing with th' bullets in? I told yeh t' bring 'em. I'll send somebody else next time."

"Yeh didn't tell us!" cried the two boys shrilly.

"S-s-sh! Quit yeh noise," said Peter, with a violent gesture.

However, this reproof enabled other boys to recover that peace of mind which they had lost when seeing their friends loaded with honours.

The women had cautiously approached the fence and, from time to time, whispered feverish questions; but Peter repulsed them savagely, with an air of being infinitely bothered by their interference in his intent watch. They were forced to listen again in silence to the weird and prophetic chanting of the insects and the mystic silken rustling of the corn.

At last the thud of hurrying feet in the soft soil of the field came to their ears. A dark form sped toward them. A wave of a mighty fear swept over the group, and the screams of the women came hoarsely from their choked throats. Peter swung madly from his perch, and turned to use the fence as a rampart.

But it was the major. His face was inflamed and his eyes were glaring. He clutched his rifle by the middle and swung it wildly. He was bounding at a great speed for his fat, short body.

"It's all right! it's all right!" he began to yell, some distance away. "It's all right! It's on'y ol' Milt' Jacoby!"

When he arrived at the top of the fence, he paused and mopped his brow.

"What?" they thundered, in an agony of sudden unreasoning disappointment.

Mrs. Joe Petersen, who was a distant connection of Milton Jacoby, thought to forestall any damage to her social position by saying at once disdainfully, "Drunk, I s'pose!"

"Yep," said the major, still on the fence, and mopped his brow. "Drunk as a fool. Thunder! I was surprised. I—I—thought it was a rebel, sure."

The thoughts of all these women wavered for a time. They were at a loss for precise expression of their emotion. At last, however, they hurled this superior sentence at the major:

"Well, yeh might have known."

A GRAY SLEEVE.

I.

"It looks as if it might rain this afternoon," remarked the lieutenant of artillery.

"So it does," the infantry captain assented. He glanced casually at the sky. When his eyes had lowered to the green-shadowed landscape before him, he said fretfully: "I wish those fellows out yonder would quit pelting at us. They've been at it since noon."

At the edge of a grove of maples, across wide fields, there occasionally appeared little puffs of smoke of a dull hue in this gloom of sky which expressed an impending rain. The long wave of blue and steel in the field moved uneasily at the eternal barking of the far-away sharpshooters, and the men, leaning upon their rifles, stared at the grove of maples. Once a private turned to borrow some tobacco from a comrade in the rear rank, but, with his hand still stretched out, he continued to twist his head and glance at the distant trees. He was afraid the enemy would shoot him at a time when he was not looking.

Suddenly the artillery officer said, "See what's coming!"

Along the rear of the brigade of infantry a column of cavalry was sweeping at a hard gallop. A lieutenant, riding some yards to the right of the column, bawled furiously at the four troopers just at the rear of the colours. They had lost distance and made a little gap, but at the shouts of the lieutenant they urged their horses forward. The bugler, careering along behind the captain of the troop, fought and tugged like a wrestler to keep his frantic animal from bolting far ahead of the column.

On the springy turf the innumerable hoofs thundered in a swift storm of sound. In the brown faces of the troopers their eyes were set like bits of flashing steel.

The long line of the infantry regiments standing at ease underwent a sudden movement at the rush of the passing squadron. The foot soldiers turned their heads to gaze at the torrent of horses and men.

The yellow folds of the flag fluttered back in silken, shuddering waves as if it were a reluctant thing. Occasionally a giant spring of a charger would rear the firm and sturdy figure of a soldier suddenly head and shoulders above his comrades. Over the noise of the scudding hoofs could be heard the creaking of leather trappings, the jingle and clank of steel, and the tense, low-toned commands or appeals of the men to their horses. And the horses were mad with the headlong sweep of this movement. Powerful under jaws bent back and straightened so that the bits were clamped as rigidly as vices upon the teeth, and glistening necks arched in desperate resistance to the hands at the bridles. Swinging their heads in rage at the granite laws of their lives, which compelled even their angers and their ardours to chosen directions and chosen faces, their flight was as a flight of harnessed demons.

The captain's bay kept its pace at the head of the squadron with the lithe bounds of a thoroughbred, and this horse was proud as a chief at the roaring trample of his fellows behind him. The captain's glance was calmly upon the grove of maples whence the sharpshooters of the enemy had been picking at the blue line. He seemed to be reflecting. He stolidly rose and fell with the plunges of his horse in all the indifference of a deacon's figure seated plumply in church. And it occurred to many of the watching infantry to wonder why this officer could remain imperturbable and reflective when his squadron was thundering and swarming behind him like the rushing of a flood.

The column swung in a sabre-curve toward a break in a fence, and dashed into a roadway. Once a little plank bridge was encountered, and the sound of the hoofs upon it was like the long roll of many drums. An old captain in the infantry turned to his first lieutenant and made a remark which was a compound of bitter disparagement of cavalry in general and soldiery admiration of this particular troop.

Suddenly the bugle sounded, and the column halted with a jolting upheaval amid sharp, brief cries. A moment later the men had tumbled from their horses, and, carbines in hand, were running in a swarm toward the grove of maples. In the road one of every four of the troopers was standing with braced legs, and pulling and hauling at the bridles of four frenzied horses.

The captain was running awkwardly in his boots. He held his sabre low so that the point often threatened to catch in the turf. His yellow hair ruffled out from under his faded cap. "Go in hard now!" he roared, in a voice of hoarse fury. His face was violently red.

The troopers threw themselves upon the grove like wolves upon a great animal. Along the whole front of woods there was the dry, crackling of musketry, with bitter, swift flashes and smoke that writhed like stung phantoms. The troopers yelled shrilly and spanged bullets low into the foliage.

For a moment, when near the woods, the line almost halted. The men struggled and fought for a time like swimmers encountering a powerful current. Then with a supreme effort they went on again. They dashed madly at the grove, whose foliage from the high light of the field was as inscrutable as a wall.

Then suddenly each detail of the calm trees became apparent, and with a few more frantic leaps the men were in the cool gloom of the woods. There was a heavy odour as from burned paper. Wisps of gray smoke wound upward. The men halted and, grimy, perspiring, and puffing, they searched the recesses of the woods with eager, fierce glances. Figures could be seen flitting afar off. A dozen carbines rattled at them in an angry volley.

During this pause the captain strode along the line, his face lit with a broad smile of contentment. "When he sends this crowd to do anything, I guess he'll find we do it pretty sharp," he said to the grinning lieutenant.

"Say, they didn't stand that rush a minute, did they?" said the subaltern. Both officers were profoundly dusty in their uniforms, and their faces were soiled like those of two urchins.

Out in the grass behind them were three tumbled and silent forms.

Presently the line moved forward again. The men went from tree to tree like hunters stalking game. Some at the left of the line fired occasionally, and those at the right gazed curiously in that direction. The men still breathed heavily from their scramble across the field.

Of a sudden a trooper halted and said: "Hello! there's a house!" Every one paused. The men turned to look at their leader.

The captain stretched his neck and swung his head from side to side. "By George, it is a house!" he said.

Through the wealth of leaves there vaguely loomed the form of a large, white house. These troopers, brown-faced from many days of campaigning, each feature of them telling of their placid confidence and courage, were stopped abruptly by the appearance of this house. There was some subtle suggestion—some tale of an unknown thing—which watched them from they knew not what part of it.

A rail fence girded a wide lawn of tangled grass. Seven pines stood along a drive-way which led from two distant posts of a vanished gate. The blue-clothed troopers moved forward until they stood at the fence peering over it.

The captain put one hand on the top rail and seemed to be about to climb the fence, when suddenly he hesitated, and said in a low voice, "Watson, what do you think of it?"

The lieutenant stared at the house. "Derned if I know!" he replied.

The captain pondered. It happened that the whole company had turned a gaze of profound awe and doubt upon this edifice which confronted them. The men were very silent.

At last the captain swore and said: "We are certainly a pack of fools. Derned old deserted house halting a company of Union cavalry, and making us gape like babies!"

"Yes, but there's something—something——" insisted the subaltern in a half stammer.

"Well, if there's 'something—something' in there, I'll get it out," said the captain. "Send Sharpe clean around to the other side with about twelve men, so we will sure bag your 'something—something,' and I'll take a few of the boys and find out what's in the d——d old thing!"

He chose the nearest eight men for his "storming party," as the lieutenant called it. After he had waited some minutes for the others to get into position, he said "Come ahead" to his eight men, and climbed the fence.

The brighter light of the tangled lawn made him suddenly feel tremendously apparent, and he wondered if there could be some mystic thing in the house which was regarding this approach. His men trudged silently at his back. They stared at the windows and lost themselves in deep speculations as to the probability of there being, perhaps, eyes behind the blinds—malignant eyes, piercing eyes.

Suddenly a corporal in the party gave vent to a startled exclamation, and half threw his carbine into position. The captain turned quickly, and the corporal said: "I saw an arm move the blinds. An arm with a gray sleeve!"

"Don't be a fool, Jones, now!" said the captain sharply.

"I swear t'——" began the corporal, but the captain silenced him.

When they arrived at the front of the house, the troopers paused, while the captain went softly up the front steps. He stood before the large front door and studied it. Some crickets chirped in the long grass, and the nearest pine could be heard in its endless sighs. One of the privates moved uneasily, and his foot crunched the gravel. Suddenly the captain swore angrily and kicked the door with a loud crash. It flew open.

II.

The bright lights of the day flashed into the old house when the captain angrily kicked open the door. He was aware of a wide hallway carpeted with matting and extending deep into the dwelling. There was also an old walnut hatrack and a little marble-topped table with a vase and two books upon it. Farther back was a great, venerable fireplace containing dreary ashes.

But directly in front of the captain was a young girl. The flying open of the door had obviously been an utter astonishment to her, and she remained transfixed there in the middle of the floor, staring at the captain with wide eyes.

She was like a child caught at the time of a raid upon the cake. She wavered to and fro upon her feet, and held her hands behind her. There were two little points of terror in her eyes, as she gazed up at the young captain in dusty blue, with his reddish, bronze complexion, his yellow hair, his bright sabre held threateningly.

These two remained motionless and silent, simply staring at each other for some moments.

The captain felt his rage fade out of him and leave his mind limp. He had been violently angry, because this house had made him feel hesitant, wary. He did not like to be wary. He liked to feel confident, sure. So he had kicked the door open, and had been prepared to march in like a soldier of wrath.

But now he began, for one thing, to wonder if his uniform was so dusty and old in appearance. Moreover, he had a feeling that his face was covered with a compound of dust, grime, and perspiration. He took a step forward and said, "I didn't mean to frighten you." But his voice was coarse from his battle-howling. It seemed to him to have hempen fibres in it.

The girl's breath came in little, quick gasps, and she looked at him as she would have looked at a serpent.

"I didn't mean to frighten you," he said again.

The girl, still with her hands behind her, began to back away.

"Is there any one else in the house?" he went on, while slowly following her. "I don't wish to disturb you, but we had a fight with some rebel skirmishers in the woods, and I thought maybe some of them might have come in here. In fact, I was pretty sure of it. Are there any of them here?"

The girl looked at him and said, "No!" He wondered why extreme agitation made the eyes of some women so limpid and bright.

"Who is here besides yourself?"

By this time his pursuit had driven her to the end of the hall, and she remained there with her back to the wall and her hands still behind her. When she answered this question, she did not look at him but down at the floor. She cleared her voice and then said, "There is no one here."

"No one?"

She lifted her eyes to him in that appeal that the human being must make even to falling trees, crashing bowlders, the sea in a storm, and said, "No, no, there is no one here." He could plainly see her tremble.

Of a sudden he bethought him that she continually kept her hands behind her. As he recalled her air when first discovered, he remembered she appeared precisely as a child detected at one of the crimes of childhood. Moreover, she had always backed away from him. He thought now that she was concealing something which was an evidence of the presence of the enemy in the house.

"What are you holding behind you?" he said suddenly.

She gave a little quick moan, as if some grim hand had throttled her.

"What are you holding behind you?"

"Oh, nothing—please. I am not holding anything behind me; indeed I'm not."

"Very well. Hold your hands out in front of you, then."

"Oh, indeed, I'm not holding anything behind me. Indeed, I'm not."

"Well," he began. Then he paused, and remained for a moment dubious. Finally, he laughed. "Well, I shall have my men search the house, anyhow. I'm sorry to trouble you, but I feel sure that there is some one here whom we want." He turned to the corporal, who with the other men was gaping quietly in at the door, and said, "Jones, go through the house."

As for himself, he remained planted in front of the girl, for she evidently did not dare to move and allow him to see what she held so carefully behind her back. So she was his prisoner.

The men rummaged around on the ground floor of the house. Sometimes the captain called to them, "Try that closet," "Is there any cellar?" But they found no one, and at last they went trooping toward the stairs which led to the second floor.

But at this movement on the part of the men the girl uttered a cry—a cry of such fright and appeal that the men paused. "Oh, don't go up there! Please don't go up there!—ple—ease! There is no one there! Indeed—indeed there is not! Oh, ple—ease!"

"Go on, Jones," said the captain calmly.

The obedient corporal made a preliminary step, and the girl bounded toward the stairs with another cry.

As she passed him, the captain caught sight of that which she had concealed behind her back, and which she had forgotten in this supreme moment. It was a pistol.

She ran to the first step, and standing there, faced the men, one hand extended with perpendicular palm, and the other holding the pistol at her side. "Oh, please, don't go up there! Nobody is there—indeed, there is not! P-l-e-a-s-e!" Then suddenly she sank swiftly down upon the step, and, huddling forlornly, began to weep in the agony and with the convulsive tremors of an infant. The pistol fell from her fingers and rattled down to the floor.

The astonished troopers looked at their astonished captain. There was a short silence.

Finally, the captain stooped and picked up the pistol. It was a heavy weapon of the army pattern. He ascertained that it was empty.

He leaned toward the shaking girl, and said gently, "Will you tell me what you were going to do with this pistol?"

He had to repeat the question a number of times, but at last a muffled voice said, "Nothing."

"Nothing!" He insisted quietly upon a further answer. At the tender tones of the captain's voice, the phlegmatic corporal turned and winked gravely at the man next to him.

"Won't you tell me?"

The girl shook her head.

"Please tell me!"

The silent privates were moving their feet uneasily and wondering how long they were to wait.

The captain said, "Please won't you tell me?"

Then this girl's voice began in stricken tones half coherent, and amid violent sobbing: "It was grandpa's. He—he—he said he was going to shoot anybody who came in here—he didn't care if there were thousands of 'em. And—and I know he would, and I was afraid they'd kill him. And so—and—so I stole away his pistol—and I was going to hide it when you—you—you kicked open the door."

The men straightened up and looked at each other. The girl began to weep again.

The captain mopped his brow. He peered down at the girl. He mopped his brow again. Suddenly he said, "Ah, don't cry like that."

He moved restlessly and looked down at his boots. He mopped his brow again.

Then he gripped the corporal by the arm and dragged him some yards back from the others. "Jones," he said, in an intensely earnest voice, "will you tell me what in the devil I am going to do?"

The corporal's countenance became illuminated with satisfaction at being thus requested to advise his superior officer. He adopted an air of great thought, and finally said: "Well, of course, the feller with the gray sleeve must be upstairs, and we must get past the girl and up there somehow. Suppose I take her by the arm and lead her——"

"What!" interrupted the captain from between his clinched teeth. As he turned away from the corporal, he said fiercely over his shoulder, "You touch that girl and I'll split your skull!"

III.

The corporal looked after his captain with an expression of mingled amazement, grief, and philosophy. He seemed to be saying to himself that there unfortunately were times, after all, when one could not rely upon the most reliable of men. When he returned to the group he found the captain bending over the girl and saying, "Why is it that you don't want us to search upstairs?"

The girl's head was buried in her crossed arms. Locks of her hair had escaped from their fastenings and these fell upon her shoulder.

"Won't you tell me?"

The corporal here winked again at the man next to him.

"Because," the girl moaned—"because—there isn't anybody up there."

The captain at last said timidly, "Well, I'm afraid—I'm afraid we'll have to——"

The girl sprang to her feet again, and implored him with her hands. She looked deep into his eyes with her glance, which was at this time like that of the fawn when it says to the hunter, "Have mercy upon me!"

These two stood regarding each other. The captain's foot was on the bottom step, but he seemed to be shrinking. He wore an air of being deeply wretched and ashamed. There was a silence.

Suddenly the corporal said in a quick, low tone, "Look out, captain!"

All turned their eyes swiftly toward the head of the stairs. There had appeared there a youth in a gray uniform. He stood looking coolly down at them. No word was said by the troopers. The girl gave vent to a little wail of desolation, "O Harry!"

He began slowly to descend the stairs. His right arm was in a white sling, and there were some fresh blood stains upon the cloth. His face was rigid and deathly pale, but his eyes flashed like lights. The girl was again moaning in an utterly dreary fashion, as the youth came slowly down toward the silent men in blue.

Six steps from the bottom of the flight he halted and said, "I reckon it's me you're looking for."

The troopers had crowded forward a trifle and, posed in lithe, nervous attitudes, were watching him like cats. The captain remained unmoved. At the youth's question he merely nodded his head and said, "Yes."

The young man in gray looked down at the girl, and then, in the same even tone which now, however, seemed to vibrate with suppressed fury, he said, "And is that any reason why you should insult my sister?"

At this sentence, the girl intervened, desperately, between the young man in gray and the officer in blue. "Oh, don't, Harry, don't! He was good to me! He was good to me, Harry—indeed he was!"

The youth came on in his quiet, erect fashion until the girl could have touched either of the men with her hand, for the captain still remained with his foot upon the first step. She continually repeated: "O Harry! O Harry!"

The youth in gray man[oe]uvred to glare into the captain's face, first over one shoulder of the girl and then over the other. In a voice that rang like metal, he said: "You are armed and unwounded, while I have no weapons and am wounded; but——"

The captain had stepped back and sheathed his sabre. The eyes of these two men were gleaming fire, but otherwise the captain's countenance was imperturbable. He said: "You are mistaken. You have no reason to——"

"You lie!"

All save the captain and the youth in gray started in an electric movement.

These two words crackled in the air like shattered glass. There was a breathless silence.

The captain cleared his throat. His look at the youth contained a quality of singular and terrible ferocity, but he said in his stolid tone, "I don't suppose you mean what you say now."

Upon his arm he had felt the pressure of some unconscious little fingers. The girl was leaning against the wall as if she no longer knew how to keep her balance, but those fingers—he held his arm very still. She murmured: "O Harry, don't! He was good to me—indeed he was!"

The corporal had come forward until he in a measure confronted the youth in gray, for he saw those fingers upon the captain's arm, and he knew that sometimes very strong men were not able to move hand nor foot under such conditions.

The youth had suddenly seemed to become weak. He breathed heavily and clung to the rail. He was glaring at the captain, and apparently summoning all his will power to combat his weakness. The corporal addressed him with profound straightforwardness, "Don't you be a derned fool!" The youth turned toward him so fiercely that the corporal threw up a knee and an elbow like a boy who expects to be cuffed.

The girl pleaded with the captain. "You won't hurt him, will you? He don't know what he's saying. He's wounded, you know. Please don't mind him!"

"I won't touch him," said the captain, with rather extraordinary earnestness; "don't you worry about him at all. I won't touch him!"

Then he looked at her, and the girl suddenly withdrew her fingers from his arm.

The corporal contemplated the top of the stairs, and remarked without surprise, "There's another of 'em coming!"

An old man was clambering down the stairs with much speed. He waved a cane wildly. "Get out of my house, you thieves! Get out! I won't have you cross my threshold! Get out!" He mumbled and wagged his head in an old man's fury. It was plainly his intention to assault them.

And so it occurred that a young girl became engaged in protecting a stalwart captain, fully armed, and with eight grim troopers at his back, from the attack of an old man with a walking-stick!

A blush passed over the temples and brow of the captain, and he looked particularly savage and weary. Despite the girl's efforts, he suddenly faced the old man.

"Look here," he said distinctly, "we came in because we had been fighting in the woods yonder, and we concluded that some of the enemy were in this house, especially when we saw a gray sleeve at the window. But this young man is wounded, and I have nothing to say to him. I will even take it for granted that there are no others like him upstairs. We will go away, leaving your d——d old house just as we found it! And we are no more thieves and rascals than you are!"

The old man simply roared: "I haven't got a cow nor a pig nor a chicken on the place! Your soldiers have stolen everything they could carry away. They have torn down half my fences for firewood. This afternoon some of your accursed bullets even broke my window panes!"

The girl had been faltering: "Grandpa! O grandpa!"

The captain looked at the girl. She returned his glance from the shadow of the old man's shoulder. After studying her face a moment, he said, "Well, we will go now." He strode toward the door and his men clanked docilely after him.

At this time there was the sound of harsh cries and rushing footsteps from without. The door flew open, and a whirlwind composed of blue-coated troopers came in with a swoop. It was headed by the lieutenant. "Oh, here you are!" he cried, catching his breath. "We thought——Oh, look at the girl!"

The captain said intensely, "Shut up, you fool!"

The men settled to a halt with a clash and a bang. There could be heard the dulled sound of many hoofs outside of the house.

"Did you order up the horses?" inquired the captain.

"Yes. We thought——"

"Well, then, let's get out of here," interrupted the captain morosely.

The men began to filter out into the open air. The youth in gray had been hanging dismally to the railing of the stairway. He now was climbing slowly up to the second floor. The old man was addressing himself directly to the serene corporal.

"Not a chicken on the place!" he cried.

"Well, I didn't take your chickens, did I?"

"No, maybe you didn't, but——"

The captain crossed the hall and stood before the girl in rather a culprit's fashion. "You are not angry at me, are you?" he asked timidly.

"No," she said. She hesitated a moment, and then suddenly held out her hand. "You were good to me—and I'm—much obliged."

The captain took her hand, and then he blushed, for he found himself unable to formulate a sentence that applied in any way to the situation.

She did not seem to heed that hand for a time.

He loosened his grasp presently, for he was ashamed to hold it so long without saying anything clever. At last, with an air of charging an intrenched brigade, he contrived to say, "I would rather do anything than frighten or trouble you."

His brow was warmly perspiring. He had a sense of being hideous in his dusty uniform and with his grimy face.

She said, "Oh, I'm so glad it was you instead of somebody who might have—might have hurt brother Harry and grandpa!"

He told her, "I wouldn't have hurt 'em for anything!"

There was a little silence.

"Well, good-bye!" he said at last.

"Good-bye!"

He walked toward the door past the old man, who was scolding at the vanishing figure of the corporal. The captain looked back. She had remained there watching him.

At the bugle's order, the troopers standing beside their horses swung briskly into the saddle. The lieutenant said to the first sergeant:

"Williams, did they ever meet before?"

"Hanged if I know!"

"Well, say——"

The captain saw a curtain move at one of the windows. He cantered from his position at the head of the column and steered his horse between two flower beds.

"Well, good-bye!"

The squadron trampled slowly past.

"Good-bye!"

They shook hands.

He evidently had something enormously important to say to her, but it seems that he could not manage it. He struggled heroically. The bay charger, with his great mystically solemn eyes, looked around the corner of his shoulder at the girl.

The captain studied a pine tree. The girl inspected the grass beneath the window. The captain said hoarsely, "I don't suppose—I don't suppose—I'll ever see you again!"

She looked at him affrightedly and shrank back from the window. He seemed to have woefully expected a reception of this kind for his question. He gave her instantly a glance of appeal.

She said, "Why, no, I don't suppose we will."

"Never?"

"Why, no, 'tain't possible. You—you are a—Yankee!"

"Oh, I know it, but——" Eventually he continued, "Well, some day, you know, when there's no more fighting, we might——" He observed that she had again withdrawn suddenly into the shadow, so he said, "Well, good-bye!"

When he held her fingers she bowed her head, and he saw a pink blush steal over the curves of her cheek and neck.

"Am I never going to see you again?"

She made no reply.

"Never?" he repeated.

After a long time, he bent over to hear a faint reply: "Sometimes—when there are no troops in the neighbourhood—grandpa don't mind if I—walk over as far as that old oak tree yonder—in the afternoons."

It appeared that the captain's grip was very strong, for she uttered an exclamation and looked at her fingers as if she expected to find them mere fragments. He rode away.

The bay horse leaped a flower bed. They were almost to the drive, when the girl uttered a panic-stricken cry.

The captain wheeled his horse violently and upon his return journey went straight through a flower bed.

The girl had clasped her hands. She beseeched him wildly with her eyes. "Oh, please, don't believe it! I never walk to the old oak tree. Indeed, I don't! I never—never—never walk there."

The bridle drooped on the bay charger's neck. The captain's figure seemed limp. With an expression of profound dejection and gloom he stared off at where the leaden sky met the dark green line of the woods. The long-impending rain began to fall with a mournful patter, drop and drop. There was a silence.

At last a low voice said, "Well—I might—sometimes I might—perhaps—but only once in a great while—I might walk to the old tree—in the afternoons."

THE VETERAN.

Out of the low window could be seen three hickory trees placed irregularly in a meadow that was resplendent in springtime green. Farther away, the old, dismal belfry of the village church loomed over the pines. A horse meditating in the shade of one of the hickories lazily swished his tail. The warm sunshine made an oblong of vivid yellow on the floor of the grocery.

"Could you see the whites of their eyes?" said the man who was seated on a soap box.

"Nothing of the kind," replied old Henry warmly. "Just a lot of flitting figures, and I let go at where they 'peared to be the thickest. Bang!"

"Mr. Fleming," said the grocer—his deferential voice expressed somehow the old man's exact social weight—"Mr. Fleming, you never was frightened much in them battles, was you?"

The veteran looked down and grinned. Observing his manner, the entire group tittered. "Well, I guess I was," he answered finally. "Pretty well scared, sometimes. Why, in my first battle I thought the sky was falling down. I thought the world was coming to an end. You bet I was scared."

Every one laughed. Perhaps it seemed strange and rather wonderful to them that a man should admit the thing, and in the tone of their laughter there was probably more admiration than if old Fleming had declared that he had always been a lion. Moreover, they knew that he had ranked as an orderly sergeant, and so their opinion of his heroism was fixed. None, to be sure, knew how an orderly sergeant ranked, but then it was understood to be somewhere just shy of a major general's stars. So, when old Henry admitted that he had been frightened, there was a laugh.

"The trouble was," said the old man, "I thought they were all shooting at me. Yes, sir, I thought every man in the other army was aiming at me in particular, and only me. And it seemed so darned unreasonable, you know. I wanted to explain to 'em what an almighty good fellow I was, because I thought then they might quit all trying to hit me. But I couldn't explain, and they kept on being unreasonable—blim!—blam!—bang! So I run!"

Two little triangles of wrinkles appeared at the corners of his eyes. Evidently he appreciated some comedy in this recital. Down near his feet, however, little Jim, his grandson, was visibly horror-stricken. His hands were clasped nervously, and his eyes were wide with astonishment at this terrible scandal, his most magnificent grandfather telling such a thing.

"That was at Chancellorsville. Of course, afterward I got kind of used to it. A man does. Lots of men, though, seem to feel all right from the start. I did, as soon as I 'got on to it,' as they say now; but at first I was pretty well flustered. Now, there was young Jim Conklin, old Si Conklin's son—that used to keep the tannery—you none of you recollect him—well, he went into it from the start just as if he was born to it. But with me it was different. I had to get used to it."

When little Jim walked with his grandfather he was in the habit of skipping along on the stone pavement in front of the three stores and the hotel of the town and betting that he could avoid the cracks. But upon this day he walked soberly, with his hand gripping two of his grandfather's fingers. Sometimes he kicked abstractedly at dandelions that curved over the walk. Any one could see that he was much troubled.

"There's Sickles's colt over in the medder, Jimmie," said the old man. "Don't you wish you owned one like him?"

"Um," said the boy, with a strange lack of interest. He continued his reflections. Then finally he ventured, "Grandpa—now—was that true what you was telling those men?"

"What?" asked the grandfather. "What was I telling them?"

"Oh, about your running."

"Why, yes, that was true enough, Jimmie. It was my first fight, and there was an awful lot of noise, you know."

Jimmie seemed dazed that this idol, of its own will, should so totter. His stout boyish idealism was injured.

Presently the grandfather said: "Sickles's colt is going for a drink. Don't you wish you owned Sickles's colt, Jimmie?"

The boy merely answered, "He ain't as nice as our'n." He lapsed then into another moody silence.

One of the hired men, a Swede, desired to drive to the county seat for purposes of his own. The old man loaned a horse and an unwashed buggy. It appeared later that one of the purposes of the Swede was to get drunk.

After quelling some boisterous frolic of the farm hands and boys in the garret, the old man had that night gone peacefully to sleep, when he was aroused by clamouring at the kitchen door. He grabbed his trousers, and they waved out behind as he dashed forward. He could hear the voice of the Swede, screaming and blubbering. He pushed the wooden button, and, as the door flew open, the Swede, a maniac, stumbled inward, chattering, weeping, still screaming: "De barn fire! Fire! Fire! De barn fire! Fire! Fire! Fire!"

There was a swift and indescribable change in the old man. His face ceased instantly to be a face; it became a mask, a gray thing, with horror written about the mouth and eyes. He hoarsely shouted at the foot of the little rickety stairs, and immediately, it seemed, there came down an avalanche of men. No one knew that during this time the old lady had been standing in her night clothes at the bedroom door, yelling: "What's th' matter? What's th' matter? What's th' matter?"

When they dashed toward the barn it presented to their eyes its usual appearance, solemn, rather mystic in the black night. The Swede's lantern was overturned at a point some yards in front of the barn doors. It contained a wild little conflagration of its own, and even in their excitement some of those who ran felt a gentle secondary vibration of the thrifty part of their minds at sight of this overturned lantern. Under ordinary circumstances it would have been a calamity.

But the cattle in the barn were trampling, trampling, trampling, and above this noise could be heard a humming like the song of innumerable bees. The old man hurled aside the great doors, and a yellow flame leaped out at one corner and sped and wavered frantically up the old gray wall. It was glad, terrible, this single flame, like the wild banner of deadly and triumphant foes.

The motley crowd from the garret had come with all the pails of the farm. They flung themselves upon the well. It was a leisurely old machine, long dwelling in indolence. It was in the habit of giving out water with a sort of reluctance. The men stormed at it, cursed it; but it continued to allow the buckets to be filled only after the wheezy windlass had howled many protests at the mad-handed men.

With his opened knife in his hand old Fleming himself had gone headlong into the barn, where the stifling smoke swirled with the air currents, and where could be heard in its fulness the terrible chorus of the flames, laden with tones of hate and death, a hymn of wonderful ferocity.

He flung a blanket over an old mare's head, cut the halter close to the manger, led the mare to the door, and fairly kicked her out to safety. He returned with the same blanket, and rescued one of the work horses. He took five horses out, and then came out himself, with his clothes bravely on fire. He had no whiskers, and very little hair on his head. They soused five pailfuls of water on him. His eldest son made a clean miss with the sixth pailful, because the old man had turned and was running down the decline and around to the basement of the barn, where were the stanchions of the cows. Some one noticed at the time that he ran very lamely, as if one of the frenzied horses had smashed his hip.

The cows, with their heads held in the heavy stanchions, had thrown themselves, strangled themselves, tangled themselves: done everything which the ingenuity of their exuberant fear could suggest to them.

Here, as at the well, the same thing happened to every man save one. Their hands went mad. They became incapable of everything save the power to rush into dangerous situations.

The old man released the cow nearest the door, and she, blind drunk with terror, crashed into the Swede. The Swede had been running to and fro babbling. He carried an empty milk pail, to which he clung with an unconscious, fierce enthusiasm. He shrieked like one lost as he went under the cow's hoofs, and the milk pail, rolling across the floor, made a flash of silver in the gloom.

Old Fleming took a fork, beat off the cow, and dragged the paralyzed Swede to the open air. When they had rescued all the cows save one, which had so fastened herself that she could not be moved an inch, they returned to the front of the barn and stood sadly, breathing like men who had reached the final point of human effort.

Many people had come running. Some one had even gone to the church, and now, from the distance, rang the tocsin note of the old bell. There was a long flare of crimson on the sky, which made remote people speculate as to the whereabouts of the fire.

The long flames sang their drumming chorus in voices of the heaviest bass. The wind whirled clouds of smoke and cinders into the faces of the spectators. The form of the old barn was outlined in black amid these masses of orange-hued flames.

And then came this Swede again, crying as one who is the weapon of the sinister fates. "De colts! De colts! You have forgot de colts!"

Old Fleming staggered. It was true; they had forgotten the two colts in the box stalls at the back of the barn. "Boys," he said, "I must try to get 'em out." They clamoured about him then, afraid for him, afraid of what they should see. Then they talked wildly each to each. "Why, it's sure death!" "He would never get out!" "Why, it's suicide for a man to go in there!" Old Fleming stared absent-mindedly at the open doors. "The poor little things!" he said. He rushed into the barn.

When the roof fell in, a great funnel of smoke swarmed toward the sky, as if the old man's mighty spirit, released from its body—a little bottle—had swelled like the genie of fable. The smoke was tinted rose-hue from the flames, and perhaps the unutterable midnights of the universe will have no power to daunt the colour of this soul.

THE END.

LAST WORDS

THE RELUCTANT VOYAGERS

CHAPTER I.

Two men sat by the sea waves.

"Well, I know I'm not handsome," said one gloomily. He was poking holes in the sand with a discontented cane.

The companion was watching the waves play. He seemed overcome with perspiring discomfort as a man who is resolved to set another man right.

Suddenly his mouth turned into a straight line. "To be sure you are not," he cried vehemently. "You look like thunder. I do not desire to be unpleasant, but I must assure you that your freckled skin continually reminds spectators of white wall paper with gilt roses on it. The top of your head looks like a little wooden plate. And your figure—heavens!"

For a time they were silent. They stared at the waves that purred near their feet like sleepy sea-kittens.

Finally the first man spoke.

"Well," said he, defiantly, "what of it?"

"What of it," exploded the other. "Why, it means that you'd look like blazes in a bathing-suit."

They were again silent. The freckled man seemed ashamed. His tall companion glowered at the scenery.

"I am decided," said the freckled man suddenly. He got boldly up from the sand and strode away. The tall man followed, walking sarcastically and glaring down at the round, resolute figure before him.

A bath-clerk was looking at the world with superior eyes through a hole in a board. To him the freckled man made application, waving his hands over his person in illustration of a snug fit. The bath-clerk thought profoundly. Eventually, he handed out a blue bundle with an air of having phenomenally solved the freckled man's dimensions.

The latter resumed his resolute stride.

"See here," said the tall man, following him, "I bet you've got a regular toga, you know. That fellow couldn't tell—"

"Yes, he could," interrupted the freckled man, "I saw correct mathematics in his eyes."

"Well, supposin' he has missed your size. Supposin'—"

"Tom," again interrupted the other, "produce your proud clothes and we'll go in."

The tall man swore bitterly. He went to one of a row of little wooden boxes and shut himself in it. His companion repaired to a similar box.

At first he felt like an opulent monk in a too-small cell, and he turned round two or three times to see if he could. He arrived finally into his bathing-dress. Immediately he dropped gasping upon a three-cornered bench. The suit fell in folds about his reclining form. There was silence, save for the caressing calls of the waves without.

Then he heard two shoes drop on the floor in one of the little coops. He began to clamour at the boards like a penitent at an unforgiving door.

"Tom," called he, "Tom—"

A voice of wrath, muffled by cloth, came through the walls. "You go t' blazes!"

The freckled man began to groan, taking the occupants of the entire row of coops into his confidence.

"Stop your noise," angrily cried the tall man from his hidden den. "You rented the bathing-suit, didn't you? Then—"

"It ain't a bathing-suit," shouted the freckled man at the boards. "It's an auditorium, a ballroom, or something. It ain't a bathing-suit."

The tall man came out of his box. His suit looked like blue skin. He walked with grandeur down the alley between the rows of coops. Stopping in front of his friend's door, he rapped on it with passionate knuckles.

"Come out of there, y' ol' fool," said he, in an enraged whisper. "It's only your accursed vanity. Wear it anyhow. What difference does it make? I never saw such a vain ol' idiot!"

As he was storming the door opened, and his friend confronted him. The tall man's legs gave way, and he fell against the opposite door.

The freckled man regarded him sternly.

"You're an ass," he said.

His back curved in scorn. He walked majestically down the alley. There was pride in the way his chubby feet patted the boards. The tall man followed, weakly, his eyes riveted upon the figure ahead.

As a disguise the freckled man had adopted the stomach of importance. He moved with an air of some sort of procession, across a board walk, down some steps, and out upon the sand.

There was a pug dog and three old women on a bench, a man and a maid with a book and a parasol, a seagull drifting high in the wind, and a distant, tremendous meeting of sea and sky. Down on the wet sand stood a girl being wooed by the breakers.

The freckled man moved with stately tread along the beach. The tall man, numb with amazement, came in the rear. They neared the girl.

Suddenly the tall man was seized with convulsions. He laughed, and the girl turned her head.

She perceived the freckled man in the bathing-suit. An expression of wonderment overspread her charming face. It changed in a moment to a pearly smile.

This smile seemed to smite the freckled man. He obviously tried to swell and fit his suit. Then he turned a shrivelling glance upon his companion, and fled up the beach. The tall man ran after him, pursuing with mocking cries that tingled his flesh like stings of insects. He seemed to be trying to lead the way out of the world. But at last he stopped and faced about.

"Tom Sharp," said he, between his clenched teeth, "you are an unutterable wretch! I could grind your bones under my heel."

The tall man was in a trance, with glazed eyes fixed on the bathing-dress. He seemed to be murmuring: "Oh, good Lord! Oh, good Lord! I never saw such a suit!"

The freckled man made the gesture of an assassin.

"Tom Sharp, you—"

The other was still murmuring: "Oh, good Lord! I never saw such a suit! I never—"

The freckled man ran down into the sea.

CHAPTER II.

The cool, swirling waters took his temper from him, and it became a thing that is lost in the ocean. The tall man floundered in, and the two forgot and rollicked in the waves.

The freckled man, in endeavouring to escape from mankind, had left all save a solitary fisherman under a large hat, and three boys in bathing-dress, laughing and splashing upon a raft made of old spars.

The two men swam softly over the ground swells.

The three boys dived from their raft, and turned their jolly faces shorewards. It twisted slowly around and around, and began to move seaward on some unknown voyage. The freckled man laid his face to the water and swam toward the raft with a practised stroke. The tall man followed, his bended arm appearing and disappearing with the precision of machinery.

The craft crept away, slowly and wearily, as if luring. The little wooden plate on the freckled man's head looked at the shore like a round, brown eye, but his gaze was fixed on the raft that slyly appeared to be waiting. The tall man used the little wooden plate as a beacon.

At length the freckled man reached the raft and climbed aboard. He lay down on his back and puffed. His bathing-dress spread about him like a dead balloon. The tall man came, snorted, shook his tangled locks and lay down by the side of his companion.

They were overcome with a delicious drowsiness. The planks of the raft seemed to fit their tired limbs. They gazed dreamily up into the vast sky of summer.

"This is great," said the tall man. His companion grunted blissfully.

Gentle hands from the sea rocked their craft and lulled them to peace. Lapping waves sang little rippling sea-songs about them. The two men issued contented groans.

"Tom," said the freckled man.

"What?" said the other.

"This is great."

They lay and thought.

A fish-hawk, soaring, suddenly turned and darted at the waves. The tall man indolently twisted his head and watched the bird plunge its claws into the water. It heavily arose with a silver gleaming fish.

"That bird has got his feet wet again. It's a shame," murmured the tall man sleepily. "He must suffer from an endless cold in the head. He should wear rubber boots. They'd look great, too. If I was him, I'd—Great Scott!"

He has partly arisen, and was looking at the shore.

He began to scream. "Ted! Ted! Ted! Look!"

"What's matter?" dreamily spoke the freckled man. "You remind me of when I put the bird-shot in your leg." He giggled softly.

The agitated tall man made a gesture of supreme eloquence. His companion up-reared and turned a startled gaze shoreward.

"Lord," he roared, as if stabbed.

The land was a long, brown streak with a rim of green, in which sparkled the tin roofs of huge hotels. The hands from the sea had pushed them away. The two men sprang erect, and did a little dance of perturbation.

"What shall we do? What shall we do?" moaned the freckled man, wriggling fantastically in his dead balloon.

The changing shore seemed to fascinate the tall man, and for a time he did not speak.

Suddenly he concluded his minuet of horror. He wheeled about and faced the freckled man. He elaborately folded his arms.

"So," he said, in slow, formidable tones. "So! This all comes from your accursed vanity, your bathing-suit, your idiocy; you have murdered your best friend."

He turned away. His companion reeled as if stricken by an unexpected arm.

He stretched out his hands. "Tom, Tom," wailed he, beseechingly, "don't be such a fool."

The broad back of his friend was occupied by a contemptuous sneer.

Three ships fell off the horizon. Landward, the hues were blending. The whistle of a locomotive sounded from an infinite distance as if tooting in heaven.

"Tom! Tom! My dear boy," quavered the freckled man, "don't speak that way to me."

"Oh, no, of course not," said the other, still facing away and throwing the words over his shoulder. "You suppose I am going to accept all this calmly, don't you? Not make the slightest objection? Make no protest at all, hey?"

"Well, I—I—" began the freckled man.

The tall man's wrath suddenly exploded. "You've abducted me! That's the whole amount of it! You've abducted me!"

"I ain't," protested the freckled man. "You must think I'm a fool."

The tall man swore, and sitting down, dangled his legs angrily in the water. Natural law compelled his companion to occupy the other end of the raft.

Over the waters little shoals of fish spluttered, raising tiny tempests. Languid jelly-fish floated near, tremulously waving a thousand legs. A row of porpoises trundled along like a procession of cog-wheels. The sky became greyed save where over the land sunset colours were assembling.

The two voyagers, back to back and at either end of the raft, quarrelled at length.

"What did you want to follow me for?" demanded the freckled man in a voice of indignation.

"If your figure hadn't been so like a bottle, we wouldn't be here," replied the tall man.

CHAPTER III.

The fires in the west blazed away, and solemnity spread over the sea. Electric lights began to blink like eyes. Night menaced the voyagers with a dangerous darkness, and fear came to bind their souls together. They huddled fraternally in the middle of the raft.

"I feel like a molecule," said the freckled man in subdued tones.

"I'd give two dollars for a cigar," muttered the tall man.

A V-shaped flock of ducks flew towards Barnegat, between the voyagers and a remnant of yellow sky. Shadows and winds came from the vanished eastern horizon.

"I think I hear voices," said the freckled man.

"That Dollie Ramsdell was an awfully nice girl," said the tall man.

When the coldness of the sea night came to them, the freckled man found he could by a peculiar movement of his legs and arms encase himself in his bathing-dress. The tall man was compelled to whistle and shiver. As night settled finally over the sea, red and green lights began to dot the blackness. There were mysterious shadows between the waves.

"I see things comin'," murmured the freckled man.

"I wish I hadn't ordered that new dress-suit for the hop to-morrow night," said the tall man reflectively.

The sea became uneasy and heaved painfully, like a lost bosom, when little forgotten heart-bells try to chime with a pure sound. The voyagers cringed at magnified foam on distant wave crests. A moon came and looked at them.

"Somebody's here," whispered the freckled man.

"I wish I had an almanac," remarked the tall man, regarding the moon.

Presently they fell to staring at the red and green lights that twinkled about them.

"Providence will not leave us," asserted the freckled man.

"Oh, we'll be picked up shortly. I owe money," said the tall man.

He began to thrum on an imaginary banjo.

"I have heard," said he, suddenly, "that captains with healthy ships beneath their feet will never turn back after having once started on a voyage. In that case we will be rescued by some ship bound for the golden seas of the south. Then, you'll be up to some of your confounded devilment, and we'll get put off. They'll maroon us! That's what they'll do! They'll maroon us! On an island with palm trees and sun-kissed maidens and all that. Sun-kissed maidens, eh? Great! They'd—"

He suddenly ceased and turned to stone. At a distance a great, green eye was contemplating the sea wanderers.

They stood up and did another dance. As they watched the eye grew larger.

Directly the form of a phantom-like ship came into view. About the great, green eye there bobbed small yellow dots. The wanderers could hear a far-away creaking of unseen tackle and flapping of shadowy sails. There came the melody of the waters as the ship's prow thrusted its way.

The tall man delivered an oration.

"Ha!" he exclaimed, "here comes our rescuers. The brave fellows! How I long to take the manly captain by the hand! You will soon see a white boat with a star on its bow drop from the side of yon ship. Kind sailors in blue and white will help us into the boat and conduct our wasted frames to the quarter-deck, where the handsome, bearded captain, with gold bands all around, will welcome us. Then in the hard-oak cabin, while the wine gurgles and the Havana's glow, we'll tell our tale of peril and privation."

The ship came on like a black hurrying animal with froth-filled maw. The two wanderers stood up and clasped hands. Then they howled out a wild duet that rang over the wastes of sea.

The cries seemed to strike the ship.

Men with boots on yelled and ran about the deck. They picked up heavy articles and threw them down. They yelled more. After hideous creakings and flappings, the vessel stood still.

In the meantime the wanderers had been chanting their song for help. Out in the blackness they beckoned to the ship and coaxed.

A voice came to them.

"Hello," it said.

They puffed out their cheeks and began to shout. "Hello! Hello! Hello!"

"Wot do yeh want?" said the voice.

The two wanderers gazed at each other, and sat suddenly down on the raft. Some pall came sweeping over the sky and quenched their stars.

But almost the tall man got up and brawled miscellaneous information. He stamped his foot, and frowning into the night, swore threateningly.

The vessel seemed fearful of these moaning voices that called from a hidden cavern of the water. And now one voice was filled with a menace. A number of men with enormous limbs that threw vast shadows over the sea as the lanterns flickered, held a debate and made gestures.

Off in the darkness, the tall man began to clamour like a mob. The freckled man sat in astounded silence, with his legs weak.

After a time one of the men of enormous limbs seized a rope that was tugging at the stern and drew a small boat from the shadows. Three giants clambered in and rowed cautiously toward the raft. Silver water flashed in the gloom as the oars dipped.

About fifty feet from the raft the boat stopped. "Who er you?" asked a voice.

The tall man braced himself and explained. He drew vivid pictures, his twirling fingers illustrating like live brushes.

"Oh," said the three giants.

The voyagers deserted the raft. They looked back, feeling in their hearts a mite of tenderness for the wet planks. Later, they wriggled up the side of the vessel and climbed over the railing.

On deck they met a man.

He held a lantern to their faces. "Got any chewin' tewbacca?" he inquired.

"No," said the tall man, "we ain't."

The man had a bronze face and solitary whiskers. Peculiar lines about his mouth were shaped into an eternal smile of derision. His feet were bare, and clung handily to crevices.

Fearful trousers were supported by a piece of suspender that went up the wrong side of his chest and came down the right side of his back, dividing him into triangles.

"Ezekiel P. Sanford, capt'in, schooner 'Mary Jones,' of N'yack, N.Y., genelmen," he said.

"Ah!" said the tall man, "delighted, I'm sure."

There were a few moments of silence. The giants were hovering in the gloom and staring.

Suddenly astonishment exploded the captain.

"Wot th' devil—" he shouted, "wot th' devil yeh got on?"

"Bathing-suits," said the tall man.

CHAPTER IV.

The schooner went on. The two voyagers sat down and watched. After a time they began to shiver. The soft blackness of the summer night passed away, and grey mists writhed over the sea. Soon lights of early dawn went changing across the sky, and the twin beacons on the highlands grew dim and sparkling faintly, as if a monster were dying. The dawn penetrated the marrow of the two men in bathing-dress.

The captain used to pause opposite them, hitch one hand in his suspender, and laugh.

"Well, I be dog-hanged," he frequently said.

The tall man grew furious. He snarled in a mad undertone to his companion. "This rescue ain't right. If I had known—"

He suddenly paused, transfixed by the captain's suspender. "It's goin' to break," cried he, in an ecstatic whisper. His eyes grew large with excitement as he watched the captain laugh. "It'll break in a minute, sure."

But the commander of the schooner recovered, and invited them to drink and eat. They followed him along the deck, and fell down a square black hole into the cabin.

It was a little den, with walls of a vanished whiteness. A lamp shed an orange light. In a sort of recess two little beds were hiding. A wooden table, immovable, as if the craft had been builded around it, sat in the middle of the floor. Overhead the square hole was studded with a dozen stars. A foot-worn ladder led to the heavens.

The captain produced ponderous crackers and some cold broiled ham. Then he vanished in the firmament like a fantastic comet.

The freckled man sat quite contentedly like a stout squaw in a blanket. The tall man walked about the cabin and sniffed. He was angered at the crudeness of the rescue, and his shrinking clothes made him feel too large. He contemplated his unhappy state.

Suddenly, he broke out. "I won't stand this, I tell you! Heavens and earth, look at the—say, what in the blazes did you want to get me in this thing for, anyhow? You're a fine old duffer, you are! Look at that ham!"

The freckled man grunted. He seemed somewhat blissful. He was seated upon a bench, comfortably enwrapped in his bathing-dress.

The tall man stormed about the cabin.

"This is an outrage! I'll see the captain! I'll tell him what I think of—"

He was interrupted by a pair of legs that appeared among the stars. The captain came down the ladder. He brought a coffee pot from the sky.

The tall man bristled forward. He was going to denounce everything.

The captain was intent upon the coffee pot, balancing it carefully, and leaving his unguided feet to find the steps of the ladder.

But the wrath of the tall man faded. He twirled his fingers in excitement, and renewed his ecstatic whisperings to the freckled man.

"It's going to break! Look, quick, look! It'll break in a minute!"

He was transfixed with interest, forgetting his wrongs in staring at the perilous passage.

But the captain arrived on the floor with triumphant suspenders.

"Well," said he, "after yeh have eat, maybe ye'd like t'sleep some! If so, yeh can sleep on them beds."

The tall man made no reply, save in a strained undertone. "It'll break in about a minute! Look, Ted, look quick!"

The freckled man glanced in a little bed on which were heaped boots and oilskins. He made a courteous gesture.

"My dear sir, we could not think of depriving you of your beds. No, indeed. Just a couple of blankets if you have them, and we'll sleep very comfortable on these benches."

The captain protested, politely twisting his back and bobbing his head. The suspenders tugged and creaked. The tall man partially suppressed a cry, and took a step forward.

The freckled man was sleepily insistent, and shortly the captain gave over his deprecatory contortions. He fetched a pink quilt with yellow dots on it to the freckled man, and a black one with red roses on it to the tall man.

Again he vanished in the firmament. The tall man gazed until the last remnant of trousers disappeared from the sky. Then he wrapped himself up in his quilt and lay down. The freckled man was puffing contentedly, swathed like an infant. The yellow polka-dots rose and fell on the vast pink of his chest.

The wanderers slept. In the quiet could be heard the groanings of timbers as the sea seemed to crunch them together. The lapping of water along the vessel's side sounded like gaspings. An hundred spirits of the wind had got their wings entangled in the rigging, and, in soft voices, were pleading to be loosened.

The freckled man was awakened by a foreign noise. He opened his eyes and saw his companion standing by his couch.

His comrade's face was wane with suffering. His eyes glowed in the darkness. He raised his arms, spreading them out like a clergyman at a grave. He groaned deep in his chest.

"Good Lord!" yelled the freckled man, starting up. "Tom, Tom, what's th' matter?"

The tall man spoke in a fearful voice. "To New York," he said, "to New York in our bathing-suits."

The freckled man sank back. The shadows of the cabin threw mysteries about the figure of the tall man, arrayed like some ancient and potent astrologer in the black quilt with the red roses on it.

CHAPTER V.

Directly the tall man went and lay down and began to groan.

The freckled man felt the miseries of the world upon him. He grew angry at the tall man awakening him. They quarrelled.

"Well," said the tall man, finally, "we're in a fix."

"I know that," said the other, sharply.

They regarded the ceiling in silence.

"What in the thunder are we going to do?" demanded the tall man, after a time. His companion was still silent. "Say," repeated he, angrily, "what in the thunder are we going to do?"

"I'm sure I don't know," said the freckled man in a dismal voice.

"Well, think of something," roared the other. "Think of something, you old fool. You don't want to make any more idiots of yourself, do you?"

"I ain't made an idiot of myself."

"Well, think. Know anybody in the city?"

"I know a fellow up in Harlem," said the freckled man.

"You know a fellow up in Harlem," howled the tall man. "Up in Harlem! How the dickens are we to—say, you're crazy!"

"We can take a cab," cried the other, waxing indignant.

The tall man grew suddenly calm. "Do you know any one else?" he asked, measuredly.

"I know another fellow somewhere on Park Place."

"Somewhere on Park Place," repeated the tall man in an unnatural manner. "Somewhere on Park Place." With an air of sublime resignation he turned his face to the wall.

The freckled man sat erect and frowned in the direction of his companion. "Well, now, I suppose you are going to sulk. You make me ill! It's the best we can do, ain't it? Hire a cab and go look that fellow up on Park—What's that? You can't afford it? What nonsense! You are getting—Oh! Well, maybe we can beg some clothes of the captain. Eh? Did I see 'im. Certainly, I saw 'im. Yes, it is improbable that a man who wears trousers like that can have clothes to lend. No, I won't wear oilskins and a sou'-wester. To Athens? Of course not! I don't know where it is. Do you? I thought not. With all your grumbling about other people, you never know anything important yourself. What? Broadway? I'll be hanged first. We can get off at Harlem, man alive. There are no cabs in Harlem. I don't think we can bribe a sailor to take us ashore and bring a cab to the dock, for the very simple reason that we have nothing to bribe him with. What? No, of course not. See here, Tom Sharp, don't you swear at me like that. I won't have it. What's that? I ain't, either. I ain't. What? I am not. It's no such thing. I ain't. I've got more than you have, anyway. Well, you ain't doing anything so very brilliant yourself—just lying there and cussin'." At length the tall man feigned to prodigiously snore. The freckled man thought with such vigour that he fell asleep.

After a time he dreamed that he was in a forest where bass drums grew on trees. There came a strong wind that banged the fruit about like empty pods. A frightful din was in his ears.

He awoke to find the captain of the schooner standing over him.

"We're at New York now," said the captain, raising his voice above the thumping and banging that was being done on deck, "an' I s'pose you fellers wanta go ashore." He chuckled in an exasperating manner. "Jes' sing out when yeh wanta go," he added, leering at the freckled man.

The tall man awoke, came over and grasped the captain by the throat.

"If you laugh again I'll kill you," he said.

The captain gurgled and waved his legs and arms.

"In the first place," the tall man continued, "you rescued us in a deucedly shabby manner. It makes me ill to think of it. I've a mind to mop you 'round just for that. In the second place, your vessel is bound for Athens, N.Y., and there's no sense in it. Now, will you or will you not turn this ship about and take us back where our clothes are, or to Philadelphia, where we belong?"

He furiously shook the captain. Then he eased his grip and awaited a reply.

"I can't," yelled the captain, "I can't. This vessel don't belong to me. I've got to—"

"Well, then," interrupted the tall man, "can you lend us some clothes?"

"Hain't got none," replied the captain, promptly. His face was red, and his eyes were glaring.

"Well, then," said the tall man, "can you lend us some money?"

"Hain't got none," replied the captain, promptly. Something overcame him and he laughed.

"Thunderation," roared the tall man. He seized the captain, who began to have wriggling contortions. The tall man kneaded him as if he were biscuits. "You infernal scoundrel," he bellowed, "this whole affair is some wretched plot, and you are in it. I am about to kill you."

The solitary whisker of the captain did acrobatic feats like a strange demon upon his chin. His eyes stood perilously from his head. The suspender wheezed and tugged like the tackle of a sail.

Suddenly the tall man released his hold. Great expectancy sat upon his features. "It's going to break," he cried, rubbing his hands.

But the captain howled and vanished in the sky.

The freckled man then came forward. He appeared filled with sarcasm.

"So!" said he. "So, you've settled the matter. The captain is the only man in the world who can help us, and I daresay he'll do anything he can now."

"That's all right," said the tall man. "If you don't like the way I run things you shouldn't have come on this trip at all."

They had another quarrel.

At the end of it they went on deck. The captain stood at the stern addressing the bow with opprobrious language. When he perceived the voyagers he began to fling his fists about in the air.

"I'm goin' to put yeh off," he yelled. The wanderers stared at each other.

"Hum," said the tall man.

The freckled man looked at his companion. "He's going to put us off, you see," he said, complacently.

The tall man began to walk about and move his shoulders. "I'd like to see you do it," he said, defiantly.

The captain tugged at a rope. A boat came at his bidding.

"I'd like to see you do it," the tall man repeated, continually. An imperturbable man in rubber boots climbed down in the boat and seized the oars. The captain motioned downward. His whisker had a triumphant appearance.

The two wanderers looked at the boat. "I guess we'll have to get in," murmured the freckled man.

The tall man was standing like a granite column. "I won't," said he. "I won't! I don't care what you do, but I won't!"

"Well, but—" expostulated the other. They held a furious debate.

In the meantime the captain was darting about making sinister gestures, but the back of the tall man held him at bay. The crew, much depleted by the departure of the imperturbable man into the boat, looked on from the bow.

"You're a fool," the freckled man concluded his argument.

"So?" inquired the tall man, highly exasperated.

"So? Well, if you think you're so bright, we'll go in the boat, and then you'll see."

He climbed down into the craft and seated himself in an ominous manner at the stern.

"You'll see," he said to his companion, as the latter floundered heavily down. "You'll see!"

The man in rubber boots calmly rowed the boat toward the shore. As they went, the captain leaned over the railing and laughed. The freckled man was seated very victoriously.

"Well, wasn't this the right thing after all?" he inquired in a pleasant voice. The tall man made no reply.

CHAPTER VI.

As they neared the dock something seemed suddenly to occur to the freckled man.

"Great heavens," he murmured. He stared at the approaching shore.

"My, what a plight, Tommy," he quavered.

"Do you think so?" spoke up the tall man, "Why, I really thought you liked it." He laughed in a hard voice. "Lord, what a figure you'll cut."

This laugh jarred the freckled man's soul. He became mad.

"Thunderation, turn the boat around," he roared. "Turn 'er round, quick. Man alive, we can't—turn 'er round, d'ye hear."

The tall man in the stern gazed at his companion with glowing eyes.

"Certainly not," he said. "We're going on. You insisted upon it." He began to prod his companion with words.

The freckled man stood up and waved his arms.

"Sit down," said the tall man. "You'll tip the boat over."

The other man began to shout.

"Sit down," said the tall man again.

Words bubbled from the freckled man's mouth. There was a little torrent of sentences that almost choked him. And he protested passionately with his hands.

But the boat went on to the shadow of the docks. The tall man was intent upon balancing it as it rocked dangerously during his comrade's oration.

"Sit down," he continually repeated.

"I won't," raged the freckled man. "I won't do anything." The boat wobbled with these words.

"Say," he continued, addressing the oarsman, "just turn this boat round, will you. Where in the thunder are you taking us to, anyhow?"

The oarsman looked at the sky and thought. Finally he spoke. "I'm doin' what the cap'n sed."

"Well, what in th' blazes do I care what the cap'n sed?" demanded the freckled man. He took a violent step. "You just turn this round or—"

The small craft reeled. Over one side water came flashing in. The freckled man cried out in fear, and gave a jump to the other side. The tall man roared orders, and the oarsman made efforts. The boat acted for a moment like an animal on a slackened wire. Then it upset.

"Sit down," said the tall man, in a final roar as he was plunged into the water. The oarsman dropped his oars to grapple with the gunwale. He went down saying unknown words. The freckled man's explanation or apology was strangled by the water.

Two or three tugs let off whistles of astonishment, and continued on their paths. A man dosing on a dock aroused and began to caper. The passengers of a ferry-boat all ran to the near railing.

A miraculous person in a small boat was bobbing on the waves near the piers. He sculled hastily toward the scene. It was a swirl of waters in the midst of which the dark bottom of the boat appeared, whale-like.

Two heads suddenly came up. "839," said the freckled man, chokingly. "That's it! 839!"

"What is?" said the tall man.

"That's the number of that feller on Park Place. I just remembered."

"You're the bloomingest—" the tall man said.

"It wasn't my fault," interrupted his companion. "If you hadn't—" He tried to gesticulate, but one hand held to the keel of the boat, and the other was supporting the form of the oarsman. The latter had fought a battle with his immense rubber boots and had been conquered.

The rescuer in the other small boat came fiercely. As his craft glided up, he reached out and grasped the tall man by the collar and dragged him into the boat, interrupting what was, under the circumstances, a very brilliant flow of rhetoric directed at the freckled man. The oarsman of the wrecked craft was taken tenderly over the gunwale and laid in the bottom of the boat. Puffing and blowing, the freckled man climbed in.

"You'll upset this one before we can get ashore," the other voyager remarked.

As they turned toward the land they saw that the nearest dock was lined with people. The freckled man gave a little moan.

But the staring eyes of the crowd were fixed on the limp form of the man in rubber boots. A hundred hands reached down to help lift the body up. On the dock some men grabbed it and began to beat it and roll it. A policeman tossed the spectators about. Each individual in the heaving crowd sought to fasten his eyes on the blue-tinted face of the man in the rubber boots. They surged to and fro, while the policeman beat them indiscriminately.

The wanderers came modestly up the dock and gazed shrinkingly at the throng. They stood for a moment, holding their breath to see the first finger of amazement levelled at them.

But the crowd bended and surged in absorbing anxiety to view the man in rubber boots, whose face fascinated them. The sea-wanderers were as though they were not there.

They stood without the jam and whispered hurriedly.

"839," said the freckled man.

"All right," said the tall man.

Under the pommeling hands the oarsman showed signs of life. The voyagers watched him make a protesting kick at the leg of the crowd, the while uttering angry groans.

"He's better," said the tall man, softly; "let's make off."

Together they stole noiselessly up the dock. Directly in front of it they found a row of six cabs.

The drivers on top were filled with a mighty curiosity. They had driven hurriedly from the adjacent ferry-house when they had seen the first running sign of an accident. They were straining on their toes and gazing at the tossing backs of the men in the crowd.

The wanderers made a little detour, and then went rapidly towards a cab. They stopped in front of it and looked up.

"Driver," called the tall man, softly.

The man was intent.

"Driver," breathed the freckled man. They stood for a moment and gazed imploringly.

The cabman suddenly moved his feet. "By Jimmy, I bet he's a gonner," he said, in an ecstacy, and he again relapsed into a statue.

The freckled man groaned and wrung his hands. The tall man climbed into the cab.

"Come in here," he said to his companion. The freckled man climbed in, and the tall man reached over and pulled the door shut. Then he put his head out the window.

"Driver," he roared, sternly, "839 Park Place—and quick."

The driver looked down and met the eye of the tall man. "Eh?—Oh—839? Park Place? Yessir." He reluctantly gave his horse a clump on the back. As the conveyance rattled off the wanderers huddled back among the dingy cushions and heaved great breaths of relief.

"Well, it's all over," said the freckled man, finally. "We're about out of it. And quicker than I expected. Much quicker. It looked to me sometimes that we were doomed. I am thankful to find it not so. I am rejoiced. And I hope and trust that you—well, I don't wish, to—perhaps it is not the proper time to—that is, I don't wish to intrude a moral at an inopportune moment, but, my dear, dear fellow, I think the time is ripe to point out to you that your obstinacy, your selfishness, your villainous temper, and your various other faults can make it just as unpleasant for your ownself, my dear boy, as they frequently do for other people. You can see what you brought us to, and I most sincerely hope, my dear, dear fellow, that I shall soon see those signs in you which shall lead me to believe that you have become a wiser man."

SPITZBERGEN TALES

THE KICKING TWELFTH

The Spitzbergen army was backed by tradition of centuries of victory. In its chronicles, occasional defeats were not printed in italics, but were likely to appear as glorious stands against overwhelming odds. A favourite way to dispose of them was frankly to attribute them to the blunders of the civilian heads of government. This was very good for the army, and probably no army had more self-confidence. When it was announced that an expeditionary force was to be sent to Rostina to chastise an impudent people, a hundred barrack squares filled with excited men, and a hundred sergeant-majors hurried silently through the groups, and succeeded in looking as if they were the repositories of the secrets of empire. Officers on leave sped joyfully back to their harness, and recruits were abused with unflagging devotion by every man, from colonels to privates of experience.

The Twelfth Regiment of the Line—the Kicking Twelfth—was consumed with a dread that it was not to be included in the expedition, and the regiment formed itself into an informal indignation meeting. Just as they had proved that a great outrage was about to be perpetrated, warning orders arrived to hold themselves in readiness for active service abroad—in Rostina. The barrack yard was in a flash transferred into a blue-and-buff pandemonium, and the official bugle itself hardly had power to quell the glad disturbance.

Thus it was that early in the spring the Kicking Twelfth—sixteen hundred men in service equipment—found itself crawling along a road in Rostina. They did not form part of the main force, but belonged to a column of four regiments of foot, two batteries of field guns, a battery of mountain howitzers, a regiment of horse, and a company of engineers. Nothing had happened. The long column had crawled without amusement of any kind through a broad green valley. Big white farm-houses dotted the slopes; but there was no sign of man or beast, and no smoke from the chimneys. The column was operating from its own base, and its general was expected to form a junction with the main body at a given point.

A squadron of the cavalry was fanned out ahead, scouting, and day by day the trudging infantry watched the blue uniforms of the horsemen as they came and went. Sometimes there would sound the faint thuds of a few shots, but the cavalry was unable to find anything to engage.

The Twelfth had no record of foreign service, and it could hardly be said that it had served as a unit in the great civil war, when His Majesty the King had whipped the Pretender. At that time the regiment had suffered from two opinions, so that it was impossible for either side to depend upon it. Many men had deserted to the standard of the Pretender, and a number of officers had drawn their swords for him. When the King, a thorough soldier, looked at the remnant, he saw that they lacked the spirit to be of great help to him in the tremendous battles which he was waging for his throne. And so this emaciated Twelfth was sent off to a corner of the kingdom to guard a dockyard, where some of the officers so plainly expressed their disapproval of this policy that the regiment received its steadfast name, the Kicking Twelfth.

At the time of which I am writing the Twelfth had a few veteran officers and well-bitten sergeants; but the body of the regiment was composed of men who had never heard a shot fired excepting on the rifle-range. But it was an experience for which they longed, and when the moment came for the corps' cry—"Kim up, the Kickers"—there was not likely to be a man who would not go tumbling after his leaders.

Young Timothy Lean was a second lieutenant in the first company of the third battalion, and just at this time he was pattering along at the flank of the men, keeping a fatherly lookout for boots that hurt and packs that sagged. He was extremely bored. The mere far-away sound of desultory shooting was not war as he had been led to believe it.

It did not appear that behind that freckled face and under that red hair there was a mind which dreamed of blood. He was not extremely anxious to kill somebody, but he was very fond of soldiering—it had been the career of his father and of his grandfather—and he understood that the profession of arms lost much of its point unless a man shot at people and had people shoot at him. Strolling in the sun through a practically deserted country might be a proper occupation for a divinity student on a vacation, but the soul of Timothy Lean was in revolt at it. Some times at night he would go morosely to the camp of the cavalry and hear the infant subalterns laughingly exaggerate the comedy side of the adventures which they had had out with small patrols far ahead. Lean would sit and listen in glum silence to these tales, and dislike the young officers—many of them old military school friends—for having had experience in modern warfare.

"Anyhow," he said savagely, "presently you'll be getting into a lot of trouble, and then the Foot will have to come along and pull you out. We always do. That's history."

"Oh, we can take care of ourselves," said the Cavalry, with good-natured understanding of his mood.

But the next day even Lean blessed the cavalry, for excited troopers came whirling back from the front, bending over their speeding horses, and shouting wildly and hoarsely for the infantry to clear the way. Men yelled at them from the roadside as courier followed courier, and from the distance ahead sounded in quick succession six booms from field guns. The information possessed by the couriers was no longer precious. Everybody knew what a battery meant when it spoke. The bugles cried out, and the long column jolted into a halt. Old Colonel Sponge went bouncing in his saddle back to see the general, and the regiment sat down in the grass by the roadside, and waited in silence. Presently the second squadron of the cavalry trotted off along the road in a cloud of dust, and in due time old Colonel Sponge came bouncing back, and palavered his three majors and his adjutant. Then there was more talk by the majors, and gradually through the correct channels spread information which in due time reached Timothy Lean.

The enemy, 5000 strong, occupied a pass at the head of the valley some four miles beyond. They had three batteries well posted. Their infantry was entrenched. The ground in their front was crossed and lined with many ditches and hedges; but the enemy's batteries were so posted that it was doubtful if a ditch would ever prove convenient as shelter for the Spitzbergen infantry.

There was a fair position for the Spitzbergen artillery 2300 yards from the enemy. The cavalry had succeeded in driving the enemy's skirmishers back upon the main body; but, of course, had only tried to worry them a little. The position was almost inaccessible on the enemy's right, owing to steep hills, which had been crowned by small parties of infantry. The enemy's left, although guarded by a much larger force, was approachable, and might be flanked. This was what the cavalry had to say, and it added briefly a report of two troopers killed and five wounded.

Whereupon Major-General Richie, commanding a force of 7500 men of His Majesty of Spitzbergen, set in motion, with a few simple words, the machinery which would launch his army at the enemy. The Twelfth understood the orders when they saw the smart young aide approaching old Colonel Sponge, and they rose as one man, apparently afraid that they would be late. There was a clank of accoutrements. Men shrugged their shoulders tighter against their packs, and thrusting their thumbs between their belts and their tunics, they wriggled into a closer fit with regard to the heavy ammunition equipment. It is curious to note that almost every man took off his cap, and looked contemplatively into it as if to read a maker's name. Then they replaced their caps with great care. There was little talking, and it was not observable that a single soldier handed a token or left a comrade with a message to be delivered in case he should be killed. They did not seem to think of being killed; they seemed absorbed in a desire to know what would happen, and how it would look when it was happening. Men glanced continually at their officers in a plain desire to be quick to understand the very first order that would be given; and officers looked gravely at their men, measuring them, feeling their temper, worrying about them.

A bugle called; there were sharp cries, and the Kicking Twelfth was off to battle.

The regiment had the right of line in the infantry brigade, and the men tramped noisily along the white road, every eye was strained ahead; but, after all, there was nothing to be seen but a dozen farms—in short, a country-side. It resembled the scenery in Spitzbergen; every man in the Kicking Twelfth had often confronted a dozen such farms with a composure which amounted to indifference. But still down the road came galloping troopers, who delivered information to Colonel Sponge and then galloped on. In time the Twelfth came to the top of a rise, and below them on the plain was the heavy black streak of a Spitzbergen squadron, and behind the squadron loomed the grey bare hill of the Rostina position.

There was a little of skirmish firing. The Twelfth reached a knoll, which the officers easily recognised as the place described by the cavalry as suitable for the Spitzbergen guns. The men swarmed up it in a peculiar formation. They resembled a crowd coming off a race track; but, nevertheless, there was no stray sheep. It was simply that the ground on which actual battles are fought is not like a chess board. And after them came swinging a six-gun battery, the guns wagging from side to side as the long line turned out of the road, and the drivers using their whips as the leading horses scrambled at the hill. The halted Twelfth lifted its voice and spoke amiably, but with point, to the battery.

"Go on, Guns! We'll take care of you. Don't be afraid. Give it to them!" The teams—lead, swing and wheel—struggled and slipped over the steep and uneven ground; and the gunners, as they clung to their springless positions, wore their usual and natural airs of unhappiness. They made no reply to the infantry. Once upon the top of the hill, however, these guns were unlimbered in a flash, and directly the infantry could hear the loud voice of an officer drawling out the time for fuses. A moment later the first 3·2 bellowed out, and there could be heard the swish and the snarl of a fleeting shell.

Colonel Sponge and a number of officers climbed to the battery's position; but the men of the regiment sat in the shelter of the hill, like so many blindfolded people, and wondered what they would have been able to see if they had been officers. Sometimes the shells of the enemy came sweeping over the top of the hill, and burst in great brown explosions in the fields to the rear. The men looked after them and laughed. To the rear could be seen also the mountain battery coming at a comic trot, with every man obviously in a deep rage with every mule. If a man can put in long service with a mule battery and come out of it with an amiable disposition, he should be presented with a medal weighing many ounces. After the mule battery came a long black winding thing, which was three regiments of Spitzbergen infantry; and at the backs of them and to the right was an inky square, which was the remaining Spitzbergen guns. General Richie and his staff clattered up the hill. The blindfolded Twelfth sat still. The inky square suddenly became a long racing line. The howitzers joined their little bark to the thunder of the guns on the hill, and the three regiments of infantry came on. The Twelfth sat still.

Of a sudden a bugle rang its warning, and the officers shouted. Some used the old cry, "Attention! Kim up, the Kickers!"—and the Twelfth knew that it had been told to go on. The majority of the men expected to see great things as soon as they rounded the shoulder of the hill; but there was nothing to be seen save a complicated plain and the grey knolls occupied by the enemy. Many company commanders in low voices worked at their men, and said things which do not appear in the written reports. They talked soothingly; they talked indignantly; and they talked always like fathers. And the men heard no sentences completely; they heard no specific direction, these wide-eyed men. They understood that there was being delivered some kind of exhortation to do as they had been taught, and they also understood that a superior intelligence was anxious over their behaviour and welfare.

There was a great deal of floundering through hedges, climbing of walls and jumping of ditches. Curiously original privates tried to find new and easier ways for themselves, instead of following the men in front of them. Officers had short fits of fury over these people. The more originality they possessed, the more likely they were to become separated from their companies. Colonel Sponge was making an exciting progress on a big charger. When the first song of the bullets came from above, the men wondered why he sat so high; the charger seemed as tall as the Eiffel Tower. But if he was high in the air, he had a fine view, and that supposedly is why people ascend the Eiffel Tower. Very often he had been a joke to them, but when they saw this fat, old gentleman so coolly treating the strange new missiles which hummed in the air, it struck them suddenly that they had wronged him seriously; and a man who could attain the command of a Spitzbergen regiment was entitled to general respect. And they gave him a sudden, quick affection—an affection that would make them follow him heartily, trustfully, grandly—this fat, old gentleman, seated on a too-big horse. In a flash his tousled grey head, his short, thick legs, even his paunch, had become specially and humorously endeared to them. And this is the way of soldiers.

But still the Twelfth had not yet come to the place where tumbling bodies begin their test of the very heart of a regiment. They backed through more hedges, jumped more ditches, slid over more walls. The Rostina artillery had seemed to be asleep; but suddenly the guns aroused like dogs from their kennels, and around the Twelfth there began a wild, swift screeching. There arose cries to hurry, to come on; and, as the rifle bullets began to plunge into them, the men saw the high, formidable hills of the enemy's right, and perfectly understood that they were doomed to storm them. The cheering thing was the sudden beginning of a tremendous uproar on the enemy's left.

Every man ran, hard, tense, breathless. When they reached the foot of the hills, they thought they had won the charge already, but they were electrified to see officers above them waving their swords and yelling with anger, surprise, and shame. With a long murmurous outcry the Twelfth began to climb the hill; and as they went and fell, they could hear frenzied shouts—"Kim up, the Kickers!" The pace was slow. It was like the rising of a tide; it was determined, almost relentless in its appearance, but it was slow. If a man fell there was a chance that he would land twenty yards below the point where he was hit. The Kickers crawled, their rifles in their left hands as they pulled and tugged themselves up with their right hands. Ever arose the shout, "Kim up, the Kickers!" Timothy Lean, his face flaming, his eyes wild, yelled it back as if he were delivering the gospel.

The Kickers came up. The enemy—they had been in small force, thinking the hills safe enough from attack—retreated quickly from this preposterous advance, and not a bayonet in the Twelfth saw blood; bayonets very seldom do.

The homing of this successful charge wore an unromantic aspect. About twenty windless men suddenly arrived, and threw themselves upon the crest of the hill, and breathed. And these twenty were joined by others, and still others, until almost 1100 men of the Twelfth lay upon the hilltop, while the regiment's track was marked by body after body, in groups and singly. The first officer—perchance the first man, one never can be certain—the first officer to gain the top of the hill was Timothy Lean, and such was the situation that he had the honour to receive his colonel with a bashful salute.

The regiment knew exactly what it had done; it did not have to wait to be told by the Spitzbergen newspapers. It had taken a formidable position with the loss of about five hundred men, and it knew it. It knew, too, that it was great glory for the Kicking Twelfth; and as the men lay rolling on their bellies, they expressed their joy in a wild cry—"Kim up, the Kickers!" For a moment there was nothing but joy, and then suddenly company commanders were besieged by men who wished to go down the path of the charge and look for their mates. The answers were without the quality of mercy; they were short, snapped, quick words, "No; you can't."

The attack on the enemy's left was sounding in great rolling crashes. The shells in their flight through the air made a noise as of red-hot iron plunged into water, and stray bullets nipped near the ears of the Kickers.

The Kickers looked and saw. The battle was below them. The enemy were indicated by a long, noisy line of gossamer smoke, although there could be seen a toy battery with tiny men employed at the guns. All over the field the shrapnel was bursting, making quick bulbs of white smoke. Far away, two regiments of Spitzbergen infantry were charging, and at the distance this charge looked like a casual stroll. It appeared that small black groups of men were walking meditatively toward the Rostina entrenchments.

There would have been orders given sooner to the Twelfth, but unfortunately Colonel Sponge arrived on top of the hill without a breath of wind in his body. He could not have given an order to save the regiment from being wiped off the earth. Finally he was able to gasp out something and point at the enemy. Timothy Lean ran along the line yelling to the men to sight at 800 yards; and like a slow and ponderous machine the regiment again went to work. The fire flanked a great part of the enemy's trenches.

It could be said that there were only two prominent points of view expressed by the men after their victorious arrival on the crest. One was defined in the exulting use of the corps' cry. The other was a grief-stricken murmur which is invariably heard after a fight—"My God, we're all cut to pieces!"

Colonel Sponge sat on the ground and impatiently waited for his wind to return. As soon as it did, he arose and cried out, "Form up, and we'll charge again! We will win this battle as soon as we can hit them!" The shouts of the officers sounded wild, like men yelling on ship-board in a gale. And the obedient Kickers arose for their task. It was running down hill this time. The mob of panting men poured over the stones.

But the enemy had not been blind to the great advantage gained by the Twelfth, and they now turned upon them a desperate fire of small arms. Men fell in every imaginable way, and their accoutrements rattled on the rocky ground. Some landed with a crash, floored by some tremendous blows; others dropped gently down like sacks of meal; with others, it would positively appear that some spirit had suddenly seized them by their ankles and jerked their legs from under them. Many officers were down, but Colonel Sponge, stuttering and blowing, was still upright. He was almost the last man in the charge, but not to his shame, rather to his stumpy legs. At one time it seemed that the assault would be lost. The effect of the fire was somewhat as if a terrible cyclone were blowing in the men's faces. They wavered, lowering their heads and shouldering weakly, as if it were impossible to make headway against the wind of battle. It was the moment of despair, the moment of the heroism which comes to the chosen of the war-god.

The colonel's cry broke and screeched absolute hatred; other officers simply howled; and the men, silent, debased, seemed to tighten their muscles for one last effort. Again they pushed against this mysterious power of the air, and once more the regiment was charging. Timothy Lean, agile and strong, was well in advance; and afterwards he reflected that the men who had been nearest to him were an old grizzled sergeant who would have gone to hell for the honour of the regiment, and a pie-faced lad who had been obliged to lie about his age in order to get into the army.

There was no shock of meeting. The Twelfth came down on a corner of the trenches, and as soon as the enemy had ascertained that the Twelfth was certain to arrive, they scuttled out, running close to the earth and spending no time in glances backward. In these days it is not discreet to wait for a charge to come home. You observe the charge, you attempt to stop it, and if you find that you can't, it is better to retire immediately to some other place. The Rostina soldiers were not heroes, perhaps, but they were men of sense. A maddened and badly-frightened mob of Kickers came tumbling into the trench, and shot at the backs of fleeing men. And at that very moment the action was won, and won by the Kickers. The enemy's flank was entirely crippled, and, knowing this, he did not await further and more disastrous information. The Twelfth looked at themselves and knew that they had a record. They sat down and grinned patronisingly as they saw the batteries galloping to advance position to shell the retreat, and they really laughed as the cavalry swept tumultuously forward.

The Twelfth had no more concern with the battle. They had won it, and the subsequent proceedings were only amusing.

There was a call from the flank, and the men wearily adjusted themselves as General Richie, stern and grim as a Roman, looked with his straight glance at a hammered and thin and dirty line of figures, which was His Majesty's Twelfth Regiment of the Line. When opposite old Colonel Sponge, a podgy figure standing at attention, the general's face set in still more grim and stern lines. He took off his helmet. "Kim up, the Kickers!" said he. He replaced his helmet and rode off. Down the cheeks of the little fat colonel rolled tears. He stood like a stone for a long moment, and wheeled in supreme wrath upon his surprised adjutant. "Delahaye, you d—d fool, don't stand there staring like a monkey! Go, tell young Lean I want to see him." The adjutant jumped as if he were on springs, and went after Lean. That young officer presented himself directly, his face covered with disgraceful smudges, and he had also torn his breeches. He had never seen the colonel in such a rage. "Lean, you young whelp! you—you're a good boy." And even as the general had turned away from the colonel, the colonel turned away from the lieutenant.

THE UPTURNED FACE.

"What will we do now?" said the adjutant, troubled and excited.

"Bury him," said Timothy Lean.

The two officers looked down close to their toes where lay the body of their comrade. The face was chalk-blue; gleaming eyes stared at the sky. Over the two upright figures was a windy sound of bullets, and on the top of the hill Lean's prostrate company of Spitzbergen infantry was firing measured volleys.

"Don't you think it would be better—" began the adjutant, "we might leave him until to-morrow."

"No," said Lean. "I can't hold that post an hour longer. I've got to fall back, and we've got to bury old Bill."

"Of course," said the adjutant, at once. "Your men got intrenching tools?"

Lean shouted back to his little line, and two men came slowly, one with a pick, one with a shovel. They started in the direction of the Rostina sharpshooters. Bullets cracked near their ears. "Dig here," said Lean gruffly. The men, thus caused to lower their glances to the turf, became hurried and frightened merely because they could not look to see whence the bullets came. The dull beat of the pick striking the earth sounded amid the swift snap of close bullets. Presently the other private began to shovel.

"I suppose," said the adjutant, slowly, "we'd better search his clothes for—things."

Lean nodded. Together in curious abstraction they looked at the body. Then Lean stirred his shoulders suddenly, arousing himself.

"Yes," he said, "we'd better see what he's got." He dropped to his knees, and his hands approached the body of the dead officer. But his hands wavered over the buttons of the tunic. The first button was brick-red with drying blood, and he did not seem to dare touch it.

"Go on," said the adjutant, hoarsely.

Lean stretched his wooden hand, and his fingers fumbled the blood-stained buttons. At last he rose with ghastly face. He had gathered a watch, a whistle, a pipe, a tobacco pouch, a handkerchief, a little case of cards and papers. He looked at the adjutant. There was a silence. The adjutant was feeling that he had been a coward to make Lean do all the grizzly business.

"Well," said Lean, "that's all, I think. You have his sword and revolver?"

"Yes," said the adjutant, his face working, and then he burst out in a sudden strange fury at the two privates. "Why don't you hurry up with that grave? What are you doing, anyhow? Hurry, do you hear? I never saw such stupid—"

Even as he cried out in his passion the two men were labouring for their lives. Ever overhead the bullets were spitting.

The grave was finished. It was not a masterpiece—a poor little shallow thing. Lean and the adjutant again looked at each other in a curious silent communication.

Suddenly the adjutant croaked out a weird laugh. It was a terrible laugh, which had its origin in that part of the mind which is first moved by the singing of the nerves. "Well," he said, humorously to Lean, "I suppose we had best tumble him in."

"Yes," said Lean. The two privates stood waiting, bent over their implements. "I suppose," said Lean, "it would be better if we laid him in ourselves."

"Yes," said the adjutant. Then apparently remembering that he had made Lean search the body, he stooped with great fortitude and took hold of the dead officer's clothing. Lean joined him. Both were particular that their fingers should not feel the corpse. They tugged away; the corpse lifted, heaved, toppled, flopped into the grave, and the two officers, straightening, looked again at each other—they were always looking at each other. They sighed with relief.

The adjutant said, "I suppose we should—we should say something. Do you know the service, Tim?"

"They don't read the service until the grave is filled in," said Lean, pressing his lips to an academic expression.

"Don't they?" said the adjutant, shocked that he had made the mistake.

"Oh, well," he cried, suddenly, "let us—let us say something—while he can hear us."

"All right," said Lean. "Do you know the service?"

"I can't remember a line of it," said the adjutant.

Lean was extremely dubious. "I can repeat two lines, but—"

"Well, do it," said the adjutant. "Go as far as you can. That's better than nothing. And the beasts have got our range exactly."

Lean looked at his two men. "Attention," he barked. The privates came to attention with a click, looking much aggrieved. The adjutant lowered his helmet to his knee. Lean, bareheaded, stood over the grave. The Rostina sharpshooters fired briskly.

"Oh Father, our friend has sunk in the deep waters of death, but his spirit has leaped toward Thee as the bubble arises from the lips of the drowning. Perceive, we beseech, Oh Father, the little flying bubble, and—"

Lean, although husky and ashamed, had suffered no hesitation up to this point, but he stopped with a hopeless feeling and looked at the corpse.

The adjutant moved uneasily. "And from Thy superb heights—" he began, and then he too came to an end.

"And from Thy superb heights," said Lean.

The adjutant suddenly remembered a phrase in the back part of the Spitzbergen burial service, and he exploited it with the triumphant manner of a man who has recalled everything, and can go on.

"Oh God, have mercy—"

"Oh God, have mercy—" said Lean.

"Mercy," repeated the adjutant, in quick failure.

"Mercy," said Lean. And then he was moved by some violence of feeling, for he turned suddenly upon his two men and tigerishly said, "Throw the dirt in."

The fire of the Rostina sharpshooters was accurate and continuous.

* * * * * * *

One of the aggrieved privates came forward with his shovel. He lifted his first shovel-load of earth, and for a moment of inexplicable hesitation it was held poised above this corpse, which from its chalk-blue face looked keenly out from the grave. Then the soldier emptied his shovel on—on the feet.

Timothy Lean felt as if tons had been swiftly lifted from off his forehead. He had felt that perhaps the private might empty the shovel on—on the face. It had been emptied on the feet. There was a great point gained there—ha, ha!—the first shovelful had been emptied on the feet. How satisfactory!

The adjutant began to babble. "Well, of course—a man we've messed with all these years—impossible—you can't, you know, leave your intimate friends rotting on the field. Go on, for God's sake, and shovel, you."

The man with the shovel suddenly ducked, grabbed his left arm with his right hand, and looked at his officer for orders. Lean picked the shovel from the ground. "Go to the rear," he said to the wounded man. He also addressed the other private. "You get under cover, too; I'll finish this business."

The wounded man scrambled hard still for the top of the ridge without devoting any glances to the direction from whence the bullets came, and the other man followed at an equal pace; but he was different, in that he looked back anxiously three times.

This is merely the way—often—of the hit and unhit.

Timothy Lean filled the shovel, hesitated, and then in a movement which was like a gesture of abhorrence he flung the dirt into the grave, and as it landed it made a sound—plop. Lean suddenly stopped and mopped his brow—a tired labourer.

"Perhaps we have been wrong," said the adjutant. His glance wavered stupidly. "It might have been better if we hadn't buried him just at this time. Of course, if we advance to-morrow the body would have been—"

"Damn you," said Lean, "shut your mouth." He was not the senior officer.

He again filled the shovel and flung the earth. Always the earth made that sound—plop. For a space Lean worked frantically, like a man digging himself out of danger.

Soon there was nothing to be seen but the chalk-blue face. Lean filled the shovel. "Good God," he cried to the adjutant. "Why didn't you turn him somehow when you put him in? This—" Then Lean began to stutter.

The adjutant understood. He was pale to the lips. "Go on, man," he cried, beseechingly, almost in a shout. Lean swung back the shovel. It went forward in a pendulum curve. When the earth landed it made a sound—plop.

THE SHRAPNEL OF THEIR FRIENDS.

From over the knolls came the tiny sound of a cavalry bugle singing out the recall, and later, detached parties of His Majesty's 2nd Hussars came trotting back to where the Spitzbergen infantry sat complacently on the captured Rostina position. The horsemen were well pleased, and they told how they had ridden thrice through the helterskelter of the fleeing enemy. They had ultimately been checked by the great truth, and when a good enemy runs away in daylight he sooner or later finds a place where he fetches up with a jolt, and turns face the pursuit—notably if it is a cavalry pursuit. The Hussars had discreetly withdrawn, displaying no foolish pride of corps at that time.

There was a general admission that the Kicking Twelfth had taken the chief honours of the day, but the artillery added that if the guns had not shelled so accurately the Twelfth's charge could not have been made so successfully, and the three other regiments of infantry, of course, did not conceal their feelings, that their attack on the enemy's left had withdrawn many rifles that would have been pelting at the Twelfth. The cavalry simply said that but for them the victory would not have been complete.

Corps' prides met each other face to face at every step, but the Kickers smiled easily and indulgently. A few recruits bragged, but they bragged because they were recruits. The older men did not wish it to appear that they were surprised and rejoicing at the performance of the regiment. If they were congratulated they simply smirked, suggesting that the ability of the Twelfth had been long known to them, and that the charge had been a little thing, you know, just turned off in the way of an afternoon's work.

Major-General Richie encamped his troops on the position which they had from the enemy. Old Colonel Sponge of the Twelfth redistributed his officers, and the losses had been so great that Timothy Lean got command of a company. It was not much of a company. Fifty-three smudged and sweating men faced their new commander. The company had gone into action with a strength of eighty-six. The heart of Timothy Lean beat high with pride. He intended to be some day a general, and if he ever became a general, that moment of promotion was not equal in joy to the moment when he looked at his new possession of fifty-three vagabonds. He scanned the faces, and recognised with satisfaction one old sergeant and two bright young corporals. "Now," said he to himself, "I have here a snug little body of men with which I can do something." In him burned the usual fierce fire to make them the best company in the regiment. He had adopted them; they were his men. "I will do what I can for you," he said. "Do you the same for me."

The Twelfth bivouacked on the ridge. Little fires were built, and there appeared among the men innumerable blackened tin cups, which were so treasured that a faint suspicion in connection with the loss of one could bring on the grimmest of fights. Meantime certain of the privates silently readjusted their kits as their names were called out by the sergeants. These were the men condemned to picket duty after a hard day of marching and fighting. The dusk came slowly, and the colour of the countless fires, spotting the ridge and the plain, grew in the falling darkness. Far-away pickets fired at something.

One by one the men's heads were lowered to the earth until the ridge was marked by two long shadowy rows of men. Here and there an officer sat musing in his dark cloak with a ray of a weakening fire gleaming on his sword-hilt. From the plain there came at times the sound of battery horses moving restlessly at their tethers, and one could imagine he heard the throaty, grumbling curse of the drivers. The moon died swiftly through flying light clouds. Far-away pickets fired at something.

In the morning the infantry and guns breakfasted to the music of a racket between the cavalry and the enemy, which was taking place some miles up the valley.

The ambitious Hussars had apparently stirred some kind of a hornet's nest, and they were having a good fight with no officious friends near enough to interfere. The remainder of the army looked toward the fight musingly over the tops of tin cups. In time the column crawled lazily forward to see.

The Twelfth, as it crawled, saw a regiment deploy to the right, and saw a battery dash to take position. The cavalry jingled back grinning with pride and expecting to be greatly admired. Presently the Twelfth was bidden to take seat by the roadside and await its turn. Instantly the wise men—and there were more than three—came out of the east and announced that they had divined the whole plan. The Kicking Twelfth was to be held in reserve until the critical moment of the fight, and then they were to be sent forward to win a victory. In corroboration, they pointed to the fact that the general in command was sticking close to them, in order, they said, to give the word quickly at the proper moment. And in truth, on a small hill to the right, Major-General Richie sat on his horse and used his glasses, while back of him his staff and the orderlies bestrode their champing, dancing mounts.

It is always good to look hard at a general, and the Kickers were transfixed with interest. The wise men again came out of the east and told what was inside the Richie head, but even the wise men wondered what was inside the Richie head.

Suddenly an exciting thing happened. To the left and ahead was a pounding Spitzbergen battery, and a toy suddenly appeared on the slope behind the guns. The toy was a man with a flag—the flag was white save for a square of red in the centre. And this toy began to wig-wag wag-wig, and it spoke to General Richie under the authority of the captain of the battery. It said: "The 88th are being driven on my centre and right."

Now, when the Kicking Twelfth had left Spitzbergen there was an average of six signalmen in each company. A proportion of these signallers had been destroyed in the first engagement, but enough remained so that the Kicking Twelfth read, as a unit, the news of the 88th. The word ran quickly. "The 88th are being driven on my centre and right."

Richie rode to where Colonel Sponge sat aloft on his big horse, and a moment later a cry ran along the column: "Kim up, the Kickers." A large number of the men were already in the road, hitching and twisting at their belts and packs. The Kickers moved forward.

They deployed and passed in a straggling line through the battery, and to the left and right of it. The gunners called out to them carefully, telling them not to be afraid.

The scene before them was startling. They were facing a country cut up by many steep-sided ravines, and over the resultant hills were retreating little squads of the 88th. The Twelfth laughed in its exultation. The men could now tell by the volume of fire that the 88th were retreating for reasons which were not sufficiently expressed in the noise of the Rostina shooting. Held together by the bugle, the Kickers swarmed up the first hill and laid on the crest. Parties of the 88th went through their lines, and the Twelfth told them coarsely its several opinions. The sights were clicked up to 600 yards, and, with a crashing volley, the regiment entered its second battle.

A thousand yards away on the right the cavalry and a regiment of infantry were creeping onward. Sponge decided not to be backward, and the bugle told the Twelfth to go ahead once more. The Twelfth charged, followed by a rabble of rallied men of the 88th, who were crying aloud that it had been all a mistake.

A charge in these days is not a running match. Those splendid pictures of levelled bayonets, dashing at headlong pace towards the closed ranks of the enemy are absurd as soon as they are mistaken for the actuality of the present. In these days charges are likely to cover at least the half of a mile, and to go at the pace exhibited in the pictures a man would be obliged to have a little steam engine inside of him.

The charge of the Kicking Twelfth somewhat resembled the advance of a great crowd of beaters who, for some reason, passionately desired to start the game. Men stumbled; men fell; men swore; there were cries: "This way!" "Come this way!" "Don't go that way!" "You can't get up that way!" Over the rocks the Twelfth scrambled, red in the face, sweating and angry. Soldiers fell because they were struck by bullets, and because they had not an ounce of strength left in them. Colonel Sponge, with a face like a red cushion, was being dragged windless up the steeps by devoted and athletic men. Three of the older captains lay afar back, and swearing with their eyes because their tongues were temporarily out of service.

And yet-and-yet, the speed of the charge was slow. From the position of the battery, it looked as if the Kickers were taking a walk over some extremely difficult country.

The regiment ascended a superior height, and found trenches and dead men. They took seat with the dead, satisfied with this company until they could get their wind. For thirty minutes purple-faced stragglers rejoined from the rear. Colonel Sponge looked behind him, and saw that Richie, with his staff, had approached by another route, and had evidently been near enough to see the full extent of the Kickers' exertions. Presently Richie began to pick a way for his horse towards the captured position. He disappeared in a gully between two hills.

Now it came to pass that a Spitzbergen battery on the far right took occasion to mistake the identity of the Kicking Twelfth, and the captain of these guns, not having anything to occupy him in front, directed his six 3·2's upon the ridge where the tired Kickers lay side by side with the Rostina dead. A shrapnel came swinging over the Kickers, seething and fuming. It burst directly over the trenches, and the shrapnel, of course, scattered forward, hurting nobody. But a man screamed out to his officer: "By God, sir, that is one of our own batteries!" The whole line quivered with fright. Five more shells streaked overhead, and one flung its hail into the middle of the 3rd battalion's line, and the Kicking Twelfth shuddered to the very centre of its heart, and arose, like one man, and fled.

Colonel Sponge, fighting, frothing at the month, dealing blows with his fist right and left, found himself confronting a fury on horseback. Richie was as pale as death, and his eyes sent out sparks. "What does this conduct mean?" he flashed out between his fastened teeth.

Sponge could only gurgle: "The battery—the battery—the battery!"

"The battery?" cried Richie, in a voice which sounded like pistol shots. "Are you afraid of the guns you almost took yesterday? Go back there, you white-livered cowards! You swine! You dogs! Curs! Curs! Curs! Go back there!"

Most of the men halted and crouched under the lashing tongue of their maddened general. But one man found desperate speech, and yelled: "General, it is our own battery that is firing on us!"

Many say that the General's face tightened until it looked like a mask. The Kicking Twelfth retired to a comfortable place, where they were only under the fire of the Rostina artillery. The men saw a staff officer riding over the obstructions in a manner calculated to break his neck directly.

The Kickers were aggrieved, but the heart of the colonel was cut in twain. He even babbled to his major, talking like a man who is about to die of simple rage. "Did you hear what he said to me? Did you hear what he called us? Did you hear what he called us?"

The majors searched their minds for words to heal a deep wound.

The Twelfth received orders to go into camp upon the hill where they had been insulted. Old Sponge looked as if he were about to knock the aide out of the saddle, but he saluted, and took the regiment back to the temporary companionship of the Rostina dead.

Major-General Richie never apologised to Colonel Sponge. When you are a commanding officer you do not adopt the custom of apologising for the wrong done to your subordinates. You ride away; and they understand, and are confident of the restitution to honour. Richie never opened his stern, young lips to Sponge in reference to the scene near the hill of the Rostina dead, but in time there was a general order No. 20, which spoke definitely of the gallantry of His Majesty's 12th regiment of the line and its colonel. In the end Sponge was given a high decoration, because he had been badly used by Richie on that day. Richie knew that it is hard for men to withstand the shrapnel of their friends.

A few days later the Kickers, marching in column on the road, came upon their friend the battery, halted in a field; and they addressed the battery, and the captain of the battery blanched to the tips of his ears. But the men of the battery told the Kickers to go to the devil—frankly, freely, placidly, told the Kickers to go to the devil.

And this story proves that it is sometimes better to be a private.

"AND IF HE WILLS, WE MUST DIE."

A sergeant, a corporal, and fourteen men of the Twelfth Regiment of the Line had been sent out to occupy a house on the main highway. They would be at least a half of a mile in advance of any other picket of their own people. Sergeant Morton was deeply angry at being sent on this duty. He said that he was over-worked. There were at least two sergeants, he claimed furiously, whose turn it should have been to go on this arduous mission. He was treated unfairly; he was abused by his superiors; why did any damned fool ever join the army? As for him he would get out of it as soon as possible; he was sick of it; the life of a dog. All this he said to the corporal, who listened attentively, giving grunts of respectful assent. On the way to this post two privates took occasion to drop to the rear and pilfer in the orchard of a deserted plantation. When the sergeant discovered this absence, he grew black with a rage which was an accumulation of all his irritations. "Run, you!" he howled. "Bring them here! I'll show them—" A private ran swiftly to the rear. The remainder of the squad began to shout nervously at the two delinquents, whose figures they could see in the deep shade of the orchard, hurriedly picking fruit from the ground and cramming it within their shirts, next to their skins. The beseeching cries of their comrades stirred the criminals more than did the barking of the sergeant. They ran to rejoin the squad, while holding their loaded bosoms and with their mouths open with aggrieved explanations.

Jones faced the sergeant with a horrible cancer marked in bumps on his left side. The disease of Patterson showed quite around the front of his waist in many protuberances. "A nice pair!" said the sergeant, with sudden frigidity. "You're the kind of soldiers a man wants to choose for a dangerous outpost duty, ain't you?"

The two privates stood at attention, still looking much aggrieved. "We only—" began Jones huskily.

"Oh, you 'only!'" cried the sergeant. "Yes, you 'only.' I know all about that. But if you think you are going to trifle with me—"

A moment later the squad moved on towards its station. Behind the sergeant's back Jones and Patterson were slyly passing apples and pears to their friends while the sergeant expounded eloquently to the corporal "You see what kind of men are in the army now. Why, when I joined the regiment it was a very different thing, I can tell you. Then a sergeant had some authority, and if a man disobeyed orders, he had a very small chance of escaping something extremely serious. But now! Good God! If I report these men, the captain will look over a lot of beastly orderly sheets and say—'Haw, eh, well, Sergeant Morton, these men seem to have very good records; very good records, indeed. I can't be too hard on them; no, not too hard.'" Continued the sergeant: "I tell you, Flagler, the army is no place for a decent man."

Flagler, the corporal, answered with a sincerity of appreciation which with him had become a science. "I think you are right, sergeant," he answered.

Behind them the privates mumbled discreetly. "Damn this sergeant of ours. He thinks we are made of wood. I don't see any reason for all this strictness when we are on active service. It isn't like being at home in barracks! There is no great harm in a couple of men dropping out to raid an orchard of the enemy when all the world knows that we haven't had a decent meal in twenty days."

The reddened face of Sergeant Morton suddenly showed to the rear. "A little more marching and less talking," he said.

When he came to the house he had been ordered to occupy the sergeant sniffed with disdain. "These people must have lived like cattle," he said angrily. To be sure, the place was not alluring. The ground floor had been used for the housing of cattle, and it was dark and terrible. A flight of steps led to the lofty first floor, which was denuded but respectable. The sergeant's visage lightened when he saw the strong walls of stone and cement. "Unless they turn guns on us, they will never get us out of here," he said cheerfully to the squad. The men, anxious to keep him in an amiable mood, all hurriedly grinned and seemed very appreciative and pleased. "I'll make this into a fortress," he announced. He sent Jones and Patterson, the two orchard thiefs, out on sentry-duty. He worked the others, then, until he could think of no more things to tell them to do. Afterwards he went forth, with a major-general's serious scowl, and examined the ground in front of his position. In returning he came upon a sentry, Jones, munching an apple. He sternly commanded him to throw it away.

The men spread their blankets on the floors of the bare rooms, and putting their packs under their heads and lighting their pipes, they lived in easy peace. Bees hummed in the garden, and a scent of flowers came through the open window. A great fan-shaped bit of sunshine smote the face of one man, and he indolently cursed as he moved his primitive bed to a shadier place.

Another private explained to a comrade: "This is all nonsense anyhow. No sense in occupying this post. They—"

"But, of course," said the corporal, "when she told me herself that she cared more for me than she did for him, I wasn't going to stand any of his talk—" The corporal's listener was so sleepy that he could only grunt his sympathy.

There was a sudden little spatter of shooting. A cry from Jones rang out. With no intermediate scrambling, the sergeant leaped straight to his feet. "Now," he cried, "let us see what you are made of! If," he added bitterly, "you are made of anything!"

A man yelled: "Good God, can't you see you're all tangled up in my cartridge belt?"

Another man yelled: "Keep off my legs! Can't you walk on the floor?"

To the windows there was a blind rush of slumberous men, who brushed hair from their eyes even as they made ready their rifles. Jones and Patterson came stumbling up the steps, crying dreadful information. Already the enemy's bullets were spitting and singing over the house.

The sergeant suddenly was stiff and cold with a sense of the importance of the thing. "Wait until you see one," he drawled loudly and calmly, "then shoot."

For some moments the enemy's bullets swung swifter than lightning over the house without anybody being able to discover a target. In this interval a man was shot in the throat. He gurgled, and then lay down on the floor. The blood slowly waved down the brown skin of his neck while he looked meekly at his comrades.

There was a howl. "There they are! There they come!" The rifles crackled. A light smoke drifted idly through the rooms. There was a strong odour as if from burnt paper and the powder of fire-crackers. The men were silent. Through the windows and about the house the bullets of an entirely invisible enemy moaned, hummed, spat, burst, and sang.

The men began to curse. "Why can't we see them?" they muttered through their teeth. The sergeant was still frigid. He answered soothingly as if he were directly reprehensible for this behaviour of the enemy. "Wait a moment. You will soon be able to see them. There! Give it to them." A little skirt of black figures had appeared in a field. It was really like shooting at an upright needle from the full length of a ball-room. But the men's spirits improved as soon as the enemy—this mysterious enemy—became a tangible thing, and far off. They had believed the foe to be shooting at them from the adjacent garden.

"Now," said the sergeant ambitiously, "we can beat them off easily if you men are good enough."

A man called out in a tone of quick, great interest. "See that fellow on horseback, Bill? Isn't he on horseback? I thought he was on horseback."

There was a fusilade against another side of the house. The sergeant dashed into the room which commanded that situation. He found a dead soldier on the floor. He rushed out howling: "When was Knowles killed? When was Knowles killed? Damn it, when was Knowles killed?" It was absolutely essential to find out the exact moment this man died. A blackened private turned upon his sergeant and demanded: "How in hell do I know?" Sergeant Morton had a sense of anger so brief that in the next second he cried: "Patterson!" He had even forgotten his vital interest in the time of Knowles' death.

"Yes?" said Patterson, his face set with some deep-rooted quality of determination. Still, he was a mere farm boy.

"Go in to Knowles' window and shoot at those people," said the sergeant hoarsely. Afterwards he coughed. Some of the fumes of the fight had made way to his lungs.

Patterson looked at the door into this other room. He looked at it as if he suspected it was to be his death-chamber. Then he entered and stood across the body of Knowles and fired vigorously into a group of plum trees.

"They can't take this house," declared the sergeant in a contemptuous and argumentative tone. He was apparently replying to somebody. The man who had been shot in the throat looked up at him. Eight men were firing from the windows. The sergeant detected in a corner three wounded men talking together feebly. "Don't you think there is anything to do?" he bawled. "Go and get Knowles' cartridges and give them to somebody who can use them! Take Simpson's too." The man who had been shot in the throat looked at him. Of the three wounded men who had been talking, one said: "My leg is all doubled up under me, sergeant." He spoke apologetically.

Meantime the sergeant was re-loading his rifle. His foot slipped in the blood of the man who had been shot in the throat, and the military boot made a greasy red streak on the floor.

"Why, we can hold this place," shouted the sergeant jubilantly. "Who says we can't?"

Corporal Flagler suddenly spun away from his window and fell in a heap.

"Sergeant," murmured a man as he dropped to a seat on the floor out of danger, "I can't stand this. I swear I can't. I think we should run away."

Morton, with the kindly eyes of a good shepherd, looked at the man. "You are afraid, Johnston, you are afraid," he said softly. The man struggled to his feet, cast upon the sergeant a gaze full of admiration, reproach, and despair, and returned to his post. A moment later he pitched forward, and thereafter his body hung out of the window, his arms straight and the fists clenched. Incidentally this corpse was pierced afterwards by chance three times by bullets of the enemy.

The sergeant laid his rifle against the stone-work of the window-frame and shot with care until his magazine was empty. Behind him a man, simply grazed on the elbow, was wildly sobbing like a girl. "Damn it, shut up," said Morton, without turning his head. Before him was a vista of a garden, fields, clumps of trees, woods, populated at the time with little fleeting figures.

He grew furious. "Why didn't he send me orders?" he cried aloud. The emphasis on the word "he" was impressive. A mile back on the road a galloper of the Hussars lay dead beside his dead horse.

The man who had been grazed on the elbow still set up his bleat. Morton's fury veered to this soldier. "Can't you shut up? Can't you shut up? Can't you shut up? Fight! That's the thing to do. Fight!"

A bullet struck Morton, and he fell upon the man who had been shot in the throat. There was a sickening moment. Then the sergeant rolled off to a position upon the blood floor. He turned himself with a last effort until he could look at the wounded who were able to look at him.

"Kim up, the Kickers," he said thickly. His arms weakened and he dropped on his face.

After an interval a young subaltern of the enemy's infantry, followed by his eager men, burst into this reeking interior. But just over the threshold he halted before the scene of blood and death. He turned with a shrug to his sergeant. "God, I should have estimated them at least one hundred strong."

WYOMING VALLEY TALES

I.—THE SURRENDER OF FORTY FORT.

Immediately after the battle of 3rd July, my mother said, "We had best take the children and go into the Fort."

But my father replied, "I will not go. I will not leave my property. All that I have in the world is here, and if the savages destroy it they may as well destroy me also."

My mother said no other word. Our household was ever given to stern silence, and such was my training that it did not occur to me to reflect that if my father cared for his property it was not my property, and I was entitled to care somewhat for my life.

Colonel Denison was true to the word which he had passed to me at the Fort before the battle. He sent a messenger to my father, and this messenger stood in the middle of our living-room and spake with a clear, indifferent voice. "Colonel Denison bids me come here and say that John Bennet is a wicked man, and the blood of his own children will be upon his head." As usual, my father said nothing. After the messenger had gone, he remained silent for hours in his chair by the fire, and this stillness was so impressive to his family that even my mother walked on tip-toe as she went about her work. After this long time my father said, "Mary!"

Mother halted and looked at him. Father spoke slowly, and as if every word was wrested from him with violent pangs. "Mary, you take the girls and go to the Fort. I and Solomon and Andrew will go over the mountain to Stroudsberg."

Immediately my mother called us all to set about packing such things as could be taken to the Fort. And by nightfall we had seen them within its pallisade, and my father, myself, and my little brother Andrew, who was only eleven years old, were off over the hills on a long march to the Delaware settlements. Father and I had our rifles, but we seldom dared to fire them, because of the roving bands of Indians. We lived as well as we could on blackberries and raspberries. For the most part, poor little Andrew rode first on the back of my father and then on my back. He was a good little man, and only cried when he would wake in the dead of night very cold and very hungry. Then my father would wrap him in an old grey coat that was so famous in the Wyoming country that there was not even an Indian who did not know of it. But this act he did without any direct display of tenderness, for the fear, I suppose, that he would weaken little Andrew's growing manhood. Now, in these days of safety, and even luxury, I often marvel at the iron spirit of the people of my young days. My father, without his coat and no doubt very cold, would then sometimes begin to pray to his God in the wilderness, but in low voice, because of the Indians. It was July, but even July nights are cold in the pine mountains, breathing a chill which goes straight to the bones.

But it is not my intention to give in this section the ordinary adventures of the masculine part of my family. As a matter of fact, my mother and the girls were undergoing in Forty Fort trials which made as nothing the happenings on our journey, which ended in safety.

My mother and her small flock were no sooner established in the crude quarters within the pallisade than negotiations were opened between Colonel Denison and Colonel Zebulon Butler on the American side, and "Indian Butler" on the British side, for the capitulation of the Fort with such arms and military stores as it contained, the lives of the settlers to be strictly preserved. But "Indian Butler" did not seem to feel free to promise safety for the lives of the Continental Butler and the pathetic little fragment of the regular troops. These men always fought so well against the Indians that whenever the Indians could get them at their mercy there was small chances of anything but a massacre. So every regular left before the surrender; and I fancy that Colonel Zebulon Butler considered himself a much-abused man, for if we had left ourselves entirely under his direction there is no doubt but what we could have saved the valley. He had taken us out on 3rd July because our militia officers had almost threatened him. In the end he had said, "Very well, I can go as far as any of you." I was always on Butler's side of the argument, but owing to the singular arrangement of circumstances, my opinion at the age of sixteen counted upon neither the one side nor the other.

The Fort was left in charge of Colonel Denison. He had stipulated before the surrender that no Indians should be allowed to enter the stockade and molest these poor families of women whose fathers and brothers were either dead or fled over the mountains, unless their physical debility had been such that they were able neither to get killed in the battle nor to take the long trail to the Delaware. Of course, this excepts those men who were with Washington.

For several days the Indians, obedient to the British officers, kept out of the Fort, but soon they began to enter in small bands and went sniffing and poking in every corner to find plunder. Our people had hidden everything as well as they were able, and for a period little was stolen. My mother told me that the first thing of importance to go was Colonel Denison's hunting shirt, made of "fine forty" linen. It had a double cape, and was fringed about the cape and about the wristbands. Colonel Denison at the time was in my mother's cabin. An Indian entered, and, rolling a thieving eye about the place, sighted first of all the remarkable shirt which Colonel Denison was wearing. He seized the shirt and began to tug, while the Colonel backed away, tugging and protesting at the same time. The women folk saw at once that the Colonel would be tomahawked if he did not give up his shirt, and they begged him to do it. He finally elected not to be tomahawked, and came out of his shirt. While my mother unbuttoned the wristbands, the Colonel cleverly dropped into the lap of a certain Polly Thornton a large packet of Continental bills, and his money was thus saved for the settlers.

Colonel Denison had several stormy interviews with "Indian Butler," and the British commander finally ended in frankly declaring that he could do nothing with the Indians at all. They were beyond control, and the defenceless people in the Fort would have to take the consequence. I do not mean that Colonel Denison was trying to recover his shirt; I mean that he was objecting to a situation which was now almost unendurable. I wish to record also that the Colonel lost a large beaver hat. In both cases he willed to be tomahawked and killed rather than suffer the indignity, but mother prevailed over him. I must confess to this discreet age that my mother engaged in fisticuffs with a squaw. This squaw came into the cabin, and, without preliminary discussion, attempted to drag from my mother the petticoat she was wearing. My mother forgot the fine advice she had given to Colonel Denison. She proceeded to beat the squaw out of the cabin, and although the squaw appealed to some warriors who were standing without the warriors only laughed, and my mother kept her petticoat.

The Indians took the feather beds of the people, and, ripping them open, flung the feathers broadcast. Then they stuffed these sacks full of plunder, and flung them across the backs of such of the settlers' horses as they had been able to find. In the old days my mother had had a side saddle, of which she was very proud when she rode to meeting on it. She had also a brilliant scarlet cloak, which every lady had in those days, and which I can remember as one of the admirations of my childhood. One day my mother had the satisfaction of seeing a squaw ride off from the Fort with this prize saddle reversed on a small nag, and with the proud squaw thus mounted wearing the scarlet cloak, also reversed. My sister Martha told me afterwards that they laughed, even in their misfortunes. A little later they had the satisfaction of seeing the smoke from our house and barn arising over the tops of the trees.

When the Indians first began their pillaging, an old Mr. Sutton, who occupied a cabin near my mother's cabin, anticipated them by donning all his best clothes. He had had a theory that the Americans would be free to retain the clothes that they wore. And his best happened to be a suit of Quaker grey, from beaver to boots, in which he had been married. Not long afterwards my mother and my sisters saw passing the door an Indian arrayed in Quaker grey, from beaver to boots. The only odd thing which impressed them was that the Indian had appended to the dress a long string of Yankee scalps. Sutton was a good Quaker, and if he had been wearing the suit there would have been no string of scalps.

They were, in fact, badgered, insulted, robbed by the Indians so openly that the British officers would not come into the Fort at all. They stayed in their camp, affecting to be ignorant of what was happening. It was about all they could do. The Indians had only one idea of war, and it was impossible to reason with them when they were flushed with victory and stolen rum.

The hand of fate fell heavily upon one rogue whose ambition it was to drink everything that the Fort contained. One day he inadvertently came upon a bottle of spirits of camphor, and in a few hours he was dead.

But it was known that General Washington contemplated sending a strong expedition into the valley, to clear it of the invaders and thrash them. Soon there were no enemies in the country save small roving parties of Indians, who prevented work in the fields and burned whatever cabins that earlier torches had missed.

The first large party to come into the valley was composed mainly of Captain Spaulding's company of regulars, and at its head rode Colonel Zebulon Butler. My father, myself, and little Andrew returned with this party to set to work immediately to build out of nothing a prosperity similar to that which had vanished in the smoke.

II.—"OL' BENNET" AND THE INDIANS.

My father was so well known of the Indians that, as I was saying, his old grey coat was a sign through the northern country. I know of no reason for this save that he was honest and obstreperously minded his own affairs, and could fling a tomahawk better than the best Indian. I will not declare upon how hard it is for a man to be honest and to mind his own affairs, but I fully know that it is hard to throw a tomahawk as my father threw it, straighter than a bullet from a duelling pistol. He had always dealt fairly with the Indians, and I cannot tell why they paled him so bitterly, unless it was that when an Indian went foolishly drunk my father would deplore it with his foot, if it so happened that the drunkenness was done in our cabin. It is true to say that when the war came, a singular large number of kicked Indians journeyed from the Canadas to re-visit with torch and knife the scenes of the kicking.

If people had thoroughly known my father he would have had no enemies. He was the best of men. He had a code of behaviour for himself, and for the whole world as well. If people wished his good opinion they only had to do exactly as he did, and to have his views. I remember that once my sister Martha made me a waistcoat of rabbits' skins, and generally it was considered a great ornament. But one day my father espied me in it, and commanded me to remove it for ever. Its appearance was indecent, he said, and such a garment tainted the soul of him who wore it. In the ensuing fortnight a poor pedlar arrived from the Delaware, who had suffered great misfortunes in the snows. My father fed him and warmed him, and when he gratefully departed, gave him the rabbits' skin waistcoat, and the poor man went off clothed indecently in a garment that would taint his soul. Afterwards, in a daring mood, I asked my father why he had so cursed this pedlar, and he recommended that I should study my Bible more closely, and there read that my own devious ways should be mended before I sought to judge the enlightened acts of my elders. He set me to ploughing the upper twelve acres, and I was hardly allowed to loose my grip of the plough handles until every furrow was drawn.

The Indians called my father "Ol' Bennet," and he was known broadcast as a man whose doom was sealed when the redskins caught him. As I have said, the feeling is inexplicable to me. But Indians who had been ill-used and maltreated by downright ruffians, against whom revenge could with a kind of propriety be directed—many of these Indians avowedly gave up a genuine wrong in order to direct a fuller attention to the getting of my father's scalp. This most unfair disposition of the Indians was a great, deep anxiety to all of us up to the time when General Sullivan and his avenging army marched through the valley and swept our tormentors afar.

And yet great calamities could happen in our valley even after the coming and passing of General Sullivan. We were partly mistaken in our gladness. The British force of Loyalists and Indians met Sullivan in one battle, and finding themselves over-matched and beaten, they scattered in all directions. The Loyalists, for the most part, went home, but the Indians cleverly broke up into small bands, and General Sullivan's army had no sooner marched beyond the Wyoming Valley than some of these small bands were back into the valley plundering outlying cabins and shooting people from the thickets and woods that bordered the fields.

General Sullivan had left a garrison at Wilkesbarre, and at this time we lived in its strong shadow. It was too formidable for the Indians to attack, and it could protect all who valued protection enough to remain under its wings, but it could do little against the flying small bands. My father chafed in the shelter of the garrison. His best lands lay beyond Forty Fort, and he wanted to be at his ploughing. He made several brief references to his ploughing that led us to believe that his ploughing was the fundamental principle of life. None of us saw any means of contending him. My sister Martha began to weep, but it no more mattered than if she had began to laugh. My mother said nothing. Aye, my wonderful mother said nothing. My father said he would go plough some of the land above Forty Fort. Immediately this was with us some sort of a law. It was like a rain, or a wind, or a drought.

He went, of course. My young brother Andrew went with him, and he took the new span of oxen and a horse. They began to plough a meadow which lay in a bend of the river above Forty Fort. Andrew rode the horse hitched ahead of the oxen. At a certain thicket the horse shied so that little Andrew was almost thrown down. My father seemed to have begun a period of apprehension at this time, but it was of no service. Four Indians suddenly appeared out of the thicket. Swiftly, and in silence, they pounced with tomahawk, rifle, and knife upon my father and my brother, and in a moment they were captives of the redskins—that fate whose very phrasing was a thrill to the heart of every colonist. It spelled death, or that horrible simple absence, vacancy, mystery, which is harder than death.

As for us, he had told my mother that if he and Andrew were not returned at sundown she might construe a calamity. So at sundown we gave the news to the Fort, and directly we heard the alarm gun booming out across the dusk like a salute to the death of my father, a solemn, final declaration. At the sound of this gun my sisters all began newly to weep. It simply defined our misfortune. In the morning a party was sent out, which came upon the deserted plough, the oxen calmly munching, and the horse still excited and affrighted. The soldiers found the trail of four Indians. They followed the trail some distance over the mountains, but the redskins with their captives had a long start, and pursuit was but useless. The result of this expedition was that we knew at least that father and Andrew had not been massacred immediately. But in those days this was a most meagre consolation. It was better to wish them well dead.

My father and Andrew were hurried over the hills at a terrible pace by the four Indians. Andrew told me afterwards that he could think sometimes that he was dreaming of being carried off by goblins. The redskins said no word, and their mocassined feet made no sound. They were like evil spirits. But it was as he caught glimpses of father's pale face, every wrinkle in it deepened and hardened, that Andrew saw everything in its light. And Andrew was but thirteen years old. It is a tender age at which to be burned at the stake.

In time the party came upon two more Indians, who had as a prisoner a man named Lebbeus Hammond. He had left Wilkesbarre in search of a strayed horse. He was riding the animal back to the Fort when the Indians caught him. He and my father knew each other well, and their greeting was like them.

"What! Hammond! You here?"

"Yes, I'm here."

As the march was resumed, the principal Indian bestrode Hammond's horse, but the horse was very high-nerved and scared, and the bridle was only a temporary one made from hickory withes. There was no saddle. And so finally the principal Indian came off with a crash, alighting with exceeding severity upon his head. When he got upon his feet he was in such a rage that the three captives thought to see him dash his tomahawk into the skull of the trembling horse, and, indeed, his arm was raised for the blow, but suddenly he thought better of it. He had been touched by a real point of Indian inspiration. The party was passing a swamp at the time, so he mired the horse almost up to its eyes, and left it to the long death.

I had said that my father was well known of the Indians, and yet I have to announce that none of his six captors knew him. To them he was a complete stranger, for upon camping the first night they left my father unbound. If they had had any idea that he was "Ol' Bennet" they would never have left him unbound. He suggested to Hammond that they try to escape that night, but Hammond seemed not to care to try it yet.

In time they met a party of over forty Indians, commanded by a Loyalist. In that band there were many who knew my father. They cried out with rejoicing when they perceived him. "Ha!" they shouted, "Ol' Bennet!" They danced about him, making gestures expressive of the torture. Later in the day my father accidentally pulled a button from his coat, and an Indian took it from him.

My father asked to be allowed to have it again, for he was a very careful man, and in those days all good husbands were trained to bring home the loose buttons. The Indians laughed, and explained that a man who was to die at Wyallusing—one day's march—need not be particular about a button.

The three prisoners were now sent off in care of seven Indians, while the Loyalist took the remainder of his men down the valley to further harass the settlers. The seven Indians were now very careful of my father, allowing him scarce a wink. Their tomahawks came up at the slightest sign. At the camp that night they bade the prisoners lie down, and then placed poles across them. An Indian lay upon either end of these poles. My father managed, however, to let Hammond know that he was determined to make an attempt to escape. There was only one night between him and the stake, and he was resolved to make what use he could of it. Hammond seems to have been dubious from the start, but the men of that time were not daunted by broad risks. In his opinion the rising would be a failure, but this did not prevent him from agreeing to rise with his friend. My brother Andrew was not considered at all. No one asked him if he wanted to rise against the Indians. He was only a boy, and supposed to obey his elders. So, as none asked his views, he kept them to himself; but I wager you he listened, all ears, to the furtive consultations, consultations which were mere casual phrases at times, and at other times swift, brief sentences shot out in a whisper.

The band of seven Indians relaxed in vigilance as they approached their own country, and on the last night from Wyallusing the Indian part of the camp seemed much inclined to take deep slumber after the long and rapid journey. The prisoners were held to the ground by poles as on the previous night, and then the Indians pulled their blankets over their heads and passed into heavy sleep. One old warrior sat by the fire as guard, but he seems to have been a singularly inefficient man, for he was continuously drowsing, and if the captives could have got rid of the poles across their chests and legs they would have made their flight sooner.

The camp was on a mountain side amid a forest of lofty pines. The night was very cold, and the blasts of wind swept down upon the crackling, resinous fire. A few stars peeped through the feathery pine branches. Deep in some gulch could be heard the roar of a mountain stream. At one o'clock in the morning three of the Indians arose, and, releasing the prisoners, commanded them to mend the fire. The prisoners brought dead pine branches; the ancient warrior on watch sleepily picked away with his knife at the deer's head which he had roasted; the other Indians retired again to their blankets, perhaps each depending upon the other for the exercise of precautions. It was a tremendously slack business; the Indians were feeling security because they knew that the prisoners were too wise to try to run away.

The warrior on watch mumbled placidly to himself as he picked at the deer's head. Then he drowsed again, just the short nap of a man who had been up too long. My father stepped quickly to a spear, and backed away from the Indian; then he drove it straight through his chest. The Indian raised himself spasmodically, and then collapsed into that camp fire which the captives had made burn so brilliantly, and as he fell he screamed. Instantly his blanket, his hair, he himself began to burn, and over him was my father tugging frantically to get the spear out again.

My father did not recover the spear. It had so gone through the old warrior that it could not readily be withdrawn, and my father left it.

The scream of the watchman instantly aroused the other warriors, who, as they scrambled in their blankets, found over them a terrible white-lipped creature with an axe—an axe, the most appallingly brutal of weapons. Hammond buried his weapon in the head of the leader of the Indians even as the man gave out his first great cry. The second blow missed an agile warrior's head, but caught him in the nape of the neck, and he swung, to bury his face in the red-hot ashes at the edge of the fire.

Meanwhile my brother Andrew had been gallantly snapping empty guns. In fact he snapped three empty guns at the Indians, who were in the purest panic. He did not snap the fourth gun, but took it by the barrel, and, seeing a warrior rush past him, he cracked his skull with the clubbed weapon. He told me, however, that his snapping of the empty guns was very effective, because it made the Indians jump and dodge.

Well, this slaughter continued in the red glare of the fire on the lonely mountain side until two shrieking creatures ran off through the trees, but even then my father hurled a tomahawk with all his strength. It struck one of the fleeing Indians on the shoulder. His blanket dropped from him, and he ran on practically naked.

The three whites looked at each other, breathing deeply. Their work was plain to them in the five dead and dying Indians underfoot. They hastily gathered weapons and mocassins, and in six minutes from the time when my father had hurled the spear through the Indian sentinel they had started to make their way back to the settlements, leaving the camp fire to burn out its short career alone amid the dead.

III.—THE BATTLE OF FORTY FORT.

The Congress, sitting at Philadelphia, had voted our Wyoming country two companies of infantry for its protection against the Indians, with the single provision that we raise the men and arm them ourselves. This was not too brave a gift, but no one could blame the poor Congress, and indeed one could wonder that they found occasion to think of us at all, since at the time every gentleman of them had his coat-tails gathered high in his hands in readiness for flight to Baltimore. But our two companies of foot were no sooner drilled, equipped, and in readiness to defend the colony when they were ordered off down to the Jerseys to join General Washington. So it can be seen what service Congress did us in the way of protection. Thus the Wyoming Valley, sixty miles deep in the wilderness, held its log-houses full of little besides mothers, maids, and children. To the clamour against this situation the badgered Congress could only reply by the issue of another generous order, directing that one full company of foot be raised in the town of Westmoreland for the defence of said town, and that the said company find their own arms, ammunition, and blankets. Even people with our sense of humour could not laugh at this joke.

When the first two companies were forming, I had thought to join one, but my father forbade me, saying that I was too young, although I was full sixteen, tall, and very strong. So it turned out that I was not off fighting with Washington's army when Butler with his rangers and Indians raided Wyoming. Perhaps I was in the better place to do my duty, if I could.

When wandering Indians visited the settlements, their drunkenness and insolence were extreme, but the few white men remained calm, and often enough pretended oblivion to insults which, because of their wives and families, they dared not attempt to avenge. In my own family, my father's imperturbability was scarce superior to my mother's coolness, and such was our faith in them that we twelve children also seemed to be fearless. Neighbour after neighbour came to my father in despair of the defenceless condition of the valley, declaring that they were about to leave everything and flee over the mountains to Stroudsberg. My father always wished them God-speed and said no more. If they urged him to fly also, he usually walked away from them.

Finally there came a time when all the Indians vanished. We rather would have had them tipsy and impudent in the settlements; we knew what their disappearance portended. It was the serious sign. Too soon the news came that "Indian Butler" was on his way.

The valley was vastly excited. People with their smaller possessions flocked into the block-houses, and militia officers rode everywhere to rally every man. A small force of Continentals—regulars of the line—had joined our people, and the little army was now under the command of a Continental officer, Major Zebulon Butler.

I had thought that with all this hubbub of an impending life and death struggle in the valley that my father would allow the work of our farm to slacken. But in this I was notably mistaken. The milking and the feeding and the work in the fields went on as if there never had been an Indian south of the Canadas. My mother and my sisters continued to cook, to wash, to churn, to spin, to dye, to mend, to make soap, to make maple sugar. Just before the break of each day, my younger brother Andrew and myself tumbled out for some eighteen hours' work, and woe to us if we departed the length of a dog's tail from the laws which our father had laid down. It was a life with which I was familiar, but it did seem to me that with the Indians almost upon us he might have allowed me, at least, to go to the Fort and see our men drilling.

But one morning we aroused as usual at his call at the foot of the ladder, and, dressing more quickly than Andrew, I climbed down from the loft to find my father seated by a blazing fire reading by its light in his Bible.

"Son," said he.

"Yes, father?"

"Go and fight."

Without a word more I made hasty preparation. It was the first time in my life that I had a feeling that my father would change his mind. So strong was this fear that I did not even risk a good-bye to my mother and sisters. At the end of the clearing I looked back. The door of the house was open, and in the blazing light of the fire I saw my father seated as I had left him.

At Forty Fort I found between three and four hundred under arms, while the stockade itself was crowded with old men, and women and children. Many of my acquaintances welcomed me; indeed, I seemed to know everybody save a number of the Continental officers. Colonel Zebulon Butler was in chief command, while directly under him was Colonel Denison, a man of the valley, and much respected. Colonel Denison asked news of my father, whose temper he well knew. He said to me—"If God spares Nathan Denison I shall tell that obstinate old fool my true opinion of him. He will get himself and all his family butchered and scalped."

I joined Captain Bidlack's company for the reason that a number of my friends were in it. Every morning we were paraded and drilled in the open ground before the Fort, and I learned to present arms and to keep my heels together, although to this day I have never been able to see any point to these accomplishments, and there was very little of the presenting of arms or of the keeping together of heels in the battle which followed these drills. I may say truly that I would now be much more grateful to Captain Bidlack if he had taught us to run like a wild horse.

There was considerable friction between the officers of our militia and the Continental officers. I believe the Continental officers had stated themselves as being in favour of a cautious policy, whereas the men of the valley were almost unanimous in their desire to meet "Indian Butler" more than half way. They knew the country, they said, and they knew the Indians, and they deduced that the proper plan was to march forth and attack the British force near the head of the valley. Some of the more hot-headed ones rather openly taunted the Continentals, but these veterans of Washington's army remained silent and composed amid more or less wildness of talk. My own concealed opinions were that, although our people were brave and determined, they had much better allow the Continental officers to manage the valley's affairs.

At the end of June, we heard the news that Colonel John Butler, with some four hundred British and Colonial troops, which he called the Rangers, and with about five hundred Indians, had entered the valley at its head and taken Fort Wintermoot after an opposition of a perfunctory character. I could present arms very well, but I do not think that I could yet keep my heels together. But "Indian Butler" was marching upon us, and even Captain Bidlack refrained from being annoyed at my refractory heels.

The officers held councils of war, but in truth both fort and camp rang with a discussion in which everybody joined with great vigour and endurance. I may except the Continental officers, who told us what they thought we should do, and then, declaring that there was no more to be said, remained in a silence which I thought was rather grim. The result was that on the 3rd of July our force of about 300 men marched away, amid the roll of drums and the proud career of flags, to meet "Indian Butler" and his two kinds of savages. There yet remains with me a vivid recollection of a close row of faces above the stockade of Forty Fort which viewed our departure with that profound anxiety which only an imminent danger of murder and scalping can produce. I myself was never particularly afraid of the Indians, for to my mind the great and almost the only military virtue of the Indians was that they were silent men in the woods. If they were met squarely on terms approaching equality, they could always be whipped. But it was another matter to a fort filled with women and children and cripples, to whom the coming of the Indians spelled pillage, arson, and massacre. The British sent against us in those days some curious upholders of the honour of the King, and although Indian Butler, who usually led them, afterwards contended that everything was performed with decency and care for the rules, we always found that such of our dead whose bodies we recovered invariably lacked hair on the tops of their heads, and if worse wasn't done to them we wouldn't even use the word mutilate.

Colonel Zebulon Butler rode along the column when we halted once for water. I looked at him eagerly, hoping to read in his face some sign of his opinions. But on the soldierly mask I could read nothing, although I am certain now that he felt that the fools among us were going to get us well beaten. But there was no vacillation in the direction of our march. We went straight until we could hear through the woods the infrequent shots of our leading party at retreating Indian scouts.

Our Colonel Butler then sent forward four of his best officers, who reconnoitered the ground in the enemy's front like so many engineers marking the place for a bastion. Then each of the six companies were told their place in the line. We of Captain Bidlack's company were on the extreme right. Then we formed in line and marched into battle, with me burning with the high resolve to kill Indian Butler and bear his sword into Forty Fort, while at the same time I was much shaken that one of Indian Butler's Indians might interfere with the noble plan. We moved stealthily among the pine trees, and I could not forbear looking constantly to right and left to make certain that everybody was of the same mind about this advance. With our Captain Bidlack was Captain Durkee of the regulars. He was also a valley man, and it seemed that every time I looked behind me I met the calm eye of this officer, and I came to refrain from looking behind me.

Still, I was very anxious to shoot Indians, and if I had doubted my ability in this direction I would have done myself a great injustice, for I could drive a nail to the head with a rifle ball at respectable range. I contend that I was not at all afraid of the enemy, but I much feared that certain of my comrades would change their minds about the expediency of battle on the 3rd July, 1778.

But our company was as steady and straight as a fence. I do not know who first saw dodging figures in the shadows of the trees in our front. The first fire we received, however, was from our flank, where some hidden Indians were yelling and firing, firing and yelling. We did not mind the war-whoops. We had heard too many drunken Indians in the settlements before the war. They wounded the lieutenant of the company next to ours, and a moment later they killed Captain Durkee. But we were steadily advancing and firing regular volleys into the shifting frieze of figures before us. The Indians gave their cries as if the imps of Hades had given tongue to their emotions. They fell back before us so rapidly and so cleverly that one had to watch his chance as the Indians sped from tree to tree. I had a sudden burst of rapture that they were beaten, and this was accentuated when I stepped over the body of an Indian whose forehead had a hole in it as squarely in the middle as if the location had been previously surveyed. In short, we were doing extremely well.

Soon we began to see the slower figures of white men through the trees, and it is only honest to say that they were easier to shoot. I myself caught sight of a fine officer in a uniform that seemed of green and buff. His sword-belt was fastened by a great shining brass plate, and, no longer feeling the elegancies of marksmanship, I fired at the brass plate. Such was the conformation of the ground between us that he disappeared as if he had sunk in the sea. We, all of us, were loading behind the trees and then charging ahead with fullest confidence.

But suddenly from our own left came wild cries from our men, while at the same time the yells of Indians redoubled in that direction. Our rush checked itself instinctively. The cries rolled toward us. Once I heard a word that sounded like "Quarte." Then, to be truthful, our line wavered. I heard Captain Bidlack give an angry and despairing shout, and I think he was killed before he finished it.

In a word, our left wing had gone to pieces. It was in complete rout. I know not the truth of the matter; but it seems that Colonel Denison had given an order which was misinterpreted for the order to retreat. At any rate, there can be no doubt of how fast the left wing ran away.

We ran away too. The company on our immediate left was the company of regulars, and I remember some red-faced and powder-stained men bellowing at me contemptuously. That company stayed, and, for the most part, died. I don't know what they mustered when we left the Fort, but from the battle eleven worn and ragged men emerged. In my running was wisdom. The country was suddenly full of fleet Indians, upon us with the tomahawk. Behind me as I ran I could hear the screams of men cleaved to the earth. I think the first things that most of us discarded were our rifles. Afterward, upon serious reflection, I could not recall where I gave my rifle to the grass.

I ran for the river. I saw some of our own men running ahead of me and I envied them. My point of contact with the river was the top of a high bank. But I did not hesitate to leap for the water with all my ounces of muscle. I struck out strongly for the other shore. I expected to be shot in the water. Up stream, and down stream, I could hear the crack of rifles, but none of the enemy seemed to be paying direct heed to me. I swam so well that I was soon able to put my feet on the slippery round stones and wade. When I reached a certain sandy beach, I lay down and puffed and blew my exhaustion. I watched the scene on the river. Indians appeared in groups on the opposite bank, firing at various heads of my comrades, who, like me, had chosen the Susquehanna as their refuge. I saw more than one hand fling up and the head turn sideways and sink.

I set out for home. I set out for home in that perfect spirit of dependence which I had always felt toward my father and my mother. When I arrived I found nobody in the living room but my father seated in his great chair and reading his Bible, even as I had left him.

The whole shame of the business came upon me suddenly. "Father," I choked out, "we have been beaten."

"Aye," said he, "I expected it."

LONDON IMPRESSIONS.

CHAPTER I.

London at first consisted of a porter with the most charming manners in the world, and a cabman with a supreme intelligence, both observing my profound ignorance without contempt or humour of any kind observable in their manners. It was in a great resounding vault of a place where there were many people who had come home, and I was displeased because they knew the detail of the business, whereas I was confronting the inscrutable. This made them appear very stony-hearted to the sufferings of one of whose existence, to be sure, they were entirely unaware, and I remember taking great pleasure in disliking them heartily for it. I was in an agony of mind over my baggage, or my luggage, or my—perhaps it is well to shy around this terrible international question; but I remember that when I was a lad I was told that there was a whole nation that said luggage instead of baggage, and my boyish mind was filled at the time with incredulity and scorn. In the present case it was a thing that I understood to involve the most hideous confessions of imbecility on my part, because I had evidently to go out to some obscure point and espy it and claim it, and take trouble for it; and I would rather have had my pockets filled with bread and cheese, and had no baggage at all.

Mind you, this was not at all a homage that I was paying to London. I was paying homage to a new game. A man properly lazy does not like new experiences until they become old ones. Moreover, I have been taught that a man, any man, who has a thousand times more points of information on a certain thing than I have will bully me because of it, and pour his advantages upon my bowed head until I am drenched with his superiority. It was in my education to concede some licence of the kind in this case, but the holy father of a porter and the saintly cabman occupied the middle distance imperturbably, and did not come down from their hills to clout me with knowledge. From this fact I experienced a criminal elation. I lost view of the idea that if I had been brow-beaten by porters and cabmen from one end of the United States to the other end I should warmly like it, because in numbers they are superior to me, and collectively they can have a great deal of fun out of a matter that would merely afford me the glee of the latent butcher.

This London, composed of a porter and a cabman, stood to me subtly as a benefactor. I had scanned the drama, and found that I did not believe that the mood of the men emanated unduly from the feature that there was probably more shillings to the square inch of me than there were shillings to the square inch of them. Nor yet was it any manner of palpable warm-heartedness or other natural virtue. But it was a perfect artificial virtue; it was drill, plain, simple drill. And now was I glad of their drilling, and vividly approved of it, because I saw that it was good for me. Whether it was good or bad for the porter and the cabman I could not know; but that point, mark you, came within the pale, of my respectable rumination.

I am sure that it would have been more correct for me to have alighted upon St. Paul's and described no emotion until I was overcome by the Thames Embankment and the Houses of Parliament. But as a matter of fact I did not see them for some days, and at this time they did not concern me at all. I was born in London at a railroad station, and my new vision encompassed a porter and a cabman. They deeply absorbed me in new phenomena, and I did not then care to see the Thames Embankment nor the Houses of Parliament. I considered the porter and the cabman to be more important.

CHAPTER II.

The cab finally rolled out of the gas-lit vault into a vast expanse of gloom. This changed to the shadowy lines of a street that was like a passage in a monstrous cave. The lamps winking here and there resembled the little gleams at the caps of the miners. They were not very competent illuminations at best, merely being little pale flares of gas that at their most heroic periods could only display one fact concerning this tunnel—the fact of general direction. But at any rate I should have liked to have observed the dejection of a search-light if it had been called upon to attempt to bore through this atmosphere. In it each man sat in his own little cylinder of vision, so to speak.

It was not so small as a sentry-box nor so large as a circus tent, but the walls were opaque, and what was passing beyond the dimensions of his cylinder no man knew.

It was evident that the paving was very greasy, but all the cabs that passed through my cylinder were going at a round trot, while the wheels, shod in rubber, whirred merely like bicycles. The hoofs of the animals themselves did not make that wild clatter which I knew so well. New York, in fact, roars always like ten thousand devils. We have ingenuous and simple ways of making a din in New York that cause the stranger to conclude that each citizen is obliged by statute to provide himself with a pair of cymbals and a drum. If anything by chance can be turned into a noise it is promptly turned. We are engaged in the development of a human creature with very large, sturdy, and doubly-fortified ears.

It was not too late at night, but this London moved with the decorum and caution of an undertaker. There was a silence, and yet there was no silence. There was a low drone, perhaps a humming contributed inevitably by closely-gathered thousands, and yet on second thoughts it was to me silence. I had perched my ears for the note of London, the sound made simply by the existence of five million people in one place. I had imagined something deep, vastly deep, a bass from a mythical organ, but found, as far as I was concerned, only a silence.

New York in numbers is a mighty city, and all day and all night it cries its loud, fierce, aspiring cry, a noise of men beating upon barrels, a noise of men beating upon tin, a terrific racket that assails the abject skies. No one of us seemed to question this row as a certain consequence of three or four million people living together and scuffling for coin, with more agility, perhaps, but otherwise in the usual way. However, after this easy silence of London, which in numbers is a mightier city, I began to feel that there was a seduction in this idea of necessity. Our noise in New York was not a consequence of our rapidity at all. It was a consequence of our bad pavements.

Any brigade of artillery in Europe that would love to assemble its batteries, and then go on a gallop over the land, thundering and thundering, would give up the idea of thunder at once if it could hear Tim Mulligan drive a beer waggon along one of the side streets of cobbled New York.

CHAPTER III.

Finally, a great thing came to pass. The cab horse, proceeding at a sharp trot, found himself suddenly at the top of an incline, where through the rain the pavement shone like an expanse of ice. It looked to me as if there was going to be a tumble. In an accident of such a kind a hansom becomes really a cannon in which a man finds that he has paid shillings for the privilege of serving as a projectile. I was making a rapid calculation of the arc that I would describe in my flight, when the horse met his crisis with a masterly device that I could not have imagined. He tranquilly braced his four feet like a bundle of stakes, and then, with a gentle gaiety of demeanour, he slid swiftly and gracefully to the bottom of the hill as if he had been a toboggan. When the incline ended he caught his gait again with great dexterity, and went pattering off through another tunnel.

I at once looked upon myself as being singularly blessed by this sight. This horse had evidently originated this system of skating as a diversion, or, more probably, as a precaution against the slippery pavement; and he was, of course, the inventor and sole proprietor—two terms that are not always in conjunction. It surely was not to be supposed that there could be two skaters like him in the world. He deserved to be known and publicly praised for this accomplishment. It was worthy of many records and exhibitions. But when the cab arrived at a place where some dipping streets met, and the flaming front of a music-hall temporarily widened my cylinder, behold there were many cabs, and as the moment of necessity came the horses were all skaters. They were gliding in all directions. It might have been a rink. A great omnibus was hailed by a hand under an umbrella on the side walk, and the dignified horses bidden to halt from their trot did not waste time in wild and unseemly spasms. They, too, braced their legs and slid gravely to the end of their momentum.

It was not the feat, but it was the word which had at this time the power to conjure memories of skating parties on moonlit lakes, with laughter ringing over the ice, and a great red bonfire on the shore among the hemlocks.

CHAPTER IV.

A terrible thing in nature is the fall of a horse in his harness. It is a tragedy. Despite their skill in skating there was that about the pavement on the rainy evening which filled me with expectations of horses going headlong. Finally it happened just in front. There was a shout and a tangle in the darkness, and presently a prostrate cab horse came within my cylinder. The accident having been a complete success and altogether concluded, a voice from the side walk said, "Look out, now! Be more careful, can't you?"

I remember a constituent of a Congressman at Washington who had tried in vain to bore this Congressman with a wild project of some kind. The Congressman eluded him with skill, and his rage and despair ultimately culminated in the supreme grievance that he could not even get near enough to the Congressman to tell him to go to Hades.

This cabman should have felt the same desire to strangle this man who spoke from the side walk. He was plainly impotent; he was deprived of the power of looking out. There was nothing now for which to look out. The man on the side walk had dragged a corpse from a pond and said to it, "Be more careful, can't you, or you'll drown?" My cabman pulled up and addressed a few words of reproach to the other. Three or four figures loomed into my cylinder, and as they appeared spoke to the author or the victim of the calamity in varied terms of displeasure. Each of these reproaches was couched in terms that defined the situation as impending. No blind man could have conceived that the precipitate phrase of the incident was absolutely closed. "Look out now, cawnt you?" And there was nothing in his mind which approached these sentiments near enough to tell them to go to Hades.

However, it needed only an ear to know presently that these expressions were formulæ. It was merely the obligatory dance which the Indians had to perform before they went to war. These men had come to help, but as a regular and traditional preliminary they had first to display to this cabman their idea of his ignominy.

The different thing in the affair was the silence of the victim. He retorted never a word. This, too, to me seemed to be an obedience to a recognised form. He was the visible criminal, if there was a criminal, and there was born of it a privilege for them.

They unfastened the proper straps and hauled back the cab. They fetched a mat from some obscure place of succour, and pushed it carefully under the prostrate thing. From this panting, quivering mass they suddenly and emphatically reconstructed a horse. As each man turned to go his way he delivered some superior caution to the cabman while the latter buckled his harness.

CHAPTER V.

There was to be noticed in this band of rescuers a young man in evening clothes and top-hat. Now, in America a young man in evening clothes and a top-hat may be a terrible object. He is not likely to do violence, but he is likely to do impassivity and indifference to the point where they become worse than violence. There are certain of the more idle phases of civilisation to which America has not yet awakened—and it is a matter of no moment if she remains unaware. This matter of hats is one of them. I recall a legend recited to me by an esteemed friend, ex-Sheriff of Tin Can, Nevada. Jim Cortright, one of the best gun-fighters in town, went on a journey to Chicago, and while there he procured a top-hat. He was quite sure how Tin Can would accept this innovation, but he relied on the celerity with which he could get a six-shooter in action. One Sunday Jim examined his guns with his usual care, placed the top-hat on the back of his head, and sauntered coolly out into the streets of Tin Can.

Now, while Jim was in Chicago some progressive citizen had decided that Tin Can needed a bowling alley. The carpenters went to work the next morning, and an order for the balls and pins was telegraphed to Denver. In three days the whole population was concentrated at the new alley betting their outfits and their lives.

It has since been accounted very unfortunate that Jim Cortright had not learned of bowling alleys at his mother's knee nor even later in the mines. This portion of his mind was singularly belated. He might have been an Apache for all he knew of bowling alleys.

In his careless stroll through the town, his hands not far from his belt and his eyes going sideways in order to see who would shoot first at the hat, he came upon this long, low shanty where Tin Can was betting itself hoarse over a game between a team from the ranks of Excelsior Hose Company No. 1 and a team composed from the habitues of the "Red Light" saloon.

Jim, in blank ignorance of bowling phenomena, wandered casually through a little door into what must always be termed the wrong end of a bowling alley. Of course, he saw that the supreme moment had come. They were not only shooting at the hat and at him, but the low-down cusses were using the most extraordinary and hellish ammunition. Still, perfectly undaunted, however, Jim retorted with his two Colts, and killed three of the best bowlers in Tin Can.

The ex-Sheriff vouched for this story. He himself had gone headlong through the door at the firing of the first shot with that simple courtesy which leads Western men to donate the fighters plenty of room. He said that afterwards the hat was the cause of a number of other fights, and that finally a delegation of prominent citizens were obliged to wait upon Cortright and ask him if he wouldn't take that thing away somewhere and bury it. Jim pointed out to them that it was his hat, and that he would regard it as a cowardly concession if he submitted to their dictation in the matter of his headgear. He added that he purposed to continue to wear his top-hat on every occasion when he happened to feel that the wearing of a top-hat was a joy and a solace to him.

The delegation sadly retired, and announced to the town that Jim Cortright had openly defied them, and had declared his purpose of forcing his top-hat on the pained attention of Tin Can whenever he chose. Jim Cortright's plug hat became a phrase with considerable meaning to it.

However, the whole affair ended in a great passionate outburst of popular revolution. Spike Foster was a friend of Cortright, and one day, when the latter was indisposed, Spike came to him and borrowed the hat. He had been drinking heavily at the "Red Light," and was in a supremely reckless mood. With the terrible gear hanging jauntily over his eye and his two guns drawn, he walked straight out into the middle of the square in front of the Palace Hotel, and drew the attention of all Tin Can by a blood-curdling imitation of the yowl of a mountain lion.

This was when the long-suffering populace arose as one man. The top-hat had been flaunted once too often. When Spike Foster's friends came to carry him away they found nearly a hundred and fifty men shooting busily at a mark—and the mark was the hat.

My informant told me that he believed he owed his popularity in Tin Can, and subsequently his election to the distinguished office of Sheriff, to the active and prominent part he had taken in the proceedings.

The enmity to the top-hat expressed by the convincing anecdote exists in the American West at present, I think, in the perfection of its strength; but disapproval is not now displayed by volleys from the citizens, save in the most aggravating cases. It is at present usually a matter of mere jibe and general contempt. The East, however, despite a great deal of kicking and gouging, is having the top-hat stuffed slowly and carefully down its throat, and there now exist many young men who consider that they could not successfully conduct their lives without this furniture.

To speak generally, I should say that the headgear then supplies them with a kind of ferocity of indifference. There is fire, sword, and pestilence in the way they heed only themselves. Philosophy should always know that indifference is a militant thing. It batters down the walls of cities, and murders the women and children amid flames and the purloining of altar vessels. When it goes away it leaves smoking ruins, where lie citizens bayoneted through the throat. It is not a children's pastime like mere highway robbery.

Consequently in America we may be much afraid of these young men. We dive down valleys so that we may not kow-tow. It is a fearsome thing.

Taught thus a deep fear of the top-hat in its effect upon youth, I was not prepared for the move of this particular young man when the cab-horse fell. In fact, I grovelled in my corner that I might not see the cruel stateliness of his passing. But in the meantime he had crossed the street, and contributed the strength of his back and some advice, as well as the formal address, to the cabman on the importance of looking out immediately.

I felt that I was making a notable collection. I had a new kind of porter, a cylinder of vision, horses that could skate, and now I added a young man in a top-hat who would tacitly admit that the beings around him were alive. He was not walking a churchyard filled with inferior headstones. He was walking the world, where there were people, many people.

But later I took him out of the collection. I thought he had rebelled against the manner of a class, but I soon discovered that the top-hat was not the property of a class. It was the property of rogues, clerks, theatrical agents, damned seducers, poor men, nobles, and others. In fact, it was the universal rigging. It was the only hat; all other forms might as well be named ham, or chops, or oysters. I retracted my admiration of the young man because he may have been merely a rogue.

CHAPTER VI.

There was a window whereat an enterprising man by dodging two placards and a calendar was entitled to view a young woman. She was dejectedly writing in a large book. She was ultimately induced to open the window a trifle. "What nyme, please?" she said wearily. I was surprised to hear this language from her. I had expected to be addressed on a submarine topic. I have seen shell fishes sadly writing in large books at the bottom of a gloomy aquarium who could not ask me what was my "nyme."

At the end of the hall there was a grim portal marked "Lift." I pressed an electric button and heard an answering tinkle in the heavens. There was an upholstered settle near at hand, and I discovered the reason. A deer-stalking peace drooped upon everything, and in it a man could invoke the passing of a lazy pageant of twenty years of his life.

The dignity of a coffin being lowered into a grave surrounded the ultimate appearance of the lift. The expert we in America call the elevator-boy stepped from the car, took three paces forward, faced to attention, and saluted. This elevator-boy could not have been less than sixty years of age; a great white beard streamed towards his belt. I saw that the lift had been longer on its voyage than I had suspected.

Later in our upward progress a natural event would have been an establishment of social relations. Two enemies imprisoned together during the still hours of a balloon journey would, I believe, suffer a mental amalgamation. The overhang of a common fate, a great principal fact, can make an equality and a truce between any pair. Yet, when I disembarked, a final survey of the grey beard made me recall that I had failed even to ask the boy whether he had not taken probably three trips on this lift.

My windows overlooked simply a great sea of night, in which were swimming little gas fishes.

CHAPTER VII.

I have of late been led to wistfully reflect that many of the illustrators are very clever. In an impatience, which was denoted by a certain economy of apparel, I went to a window to look upon day-lit London. There were the 'buses parading the streets with the miens of elephants. There were the police looking precisely as I had been informed by the prints. There were the sandwich-men. There was almost everything.

But the artists had not told me the sound of London. Now, in New York the artists are able to pourtray sound, because in New York a dray is not a dray at all; it is a great potent noise hauled by two or more horses. When a magazine containing an illustration of a New York street is sent to me, I always know it beforehand. I can hear it coming through the mails. As I have said previously, this which I must call sound of London was to me only a silence.

Later, in front of the hotel a cabman that I hailed said to me—"Are you gowing far, sir? I've got a byby here, and want to giv'er a bit of a blough." This impressed me as being probably a quotation from an early Egyptian poet, but I learned soon enough that the word "byby" was the name of some kind or condition of horse. The cabman's next remark was addressed to a boy who took a perilous dive between the byby's nose and a cab in front. "That's roight. Put your head in there and get it jammed—a whackin good place for it, I should think." Although the tone was low and circumspect, I have never heard a better off-handed declamation. Every word was cut clear of disreputable alliances with its neighbours. The whole thing was as clean as a row of pewter mugs. The influence of indignation upon the voice caused me to reflect that we might devise a mechanical means of inflaming some in that constellation of mummers which is the heritage of the Anglo-Saxon race.

Then I saw the drilling of vehicles by two policemen. There were four torrents converging at a point, and when four torrents converge at one point engineering experts buy tickets for another place.

But here, again, it was drill, plain, simple drill. I must not falter in saying that I think the management of the traffic—as the phrase goes—to be distinctly illuminating and wonderful. The police were not ruffled and exasperated. They were as peaceful as two cows in a pasture.

I remember once remarking that mankind, with all its boasted modern progress, had not yet been able to invent a turnstile that will commute in fractions. I have now learned that 756 rights-of-way cannot operate simultaneously at one point. Right-of-way, like fighting women, requires space. Even two rights-of-way can make a scene which is only suited to the tastes of an ancient public.

This truth was very evidently recognised. There was only one right-of-way at a time. The police did not look behind them to see if their orders were to be obeyed; they knew they were to be obeyed. These four torrents were drilling like four battalions. The two blue-cloth men manœuvred them in solemn, abiding peace, the silence of London.

I thought at first that it was the intellect of the individual, but I looked at one constable closely and his face was as afire with intelligence as a flannel pin-cushion. It was not the police, and it was not the crowd. It was the police and the crowd. Again, it was drill.

CHAPTER VIII.

I have never been in the habit of reading signs. I don't like to read signs. I have never met a man that liked to read signs. I once invented a creature who could play the piano with a hammer, and I mentioned him to a professor in Harvard University whose peculiarity was Sanscrit. He had the same interest in my invention that I have in a certain kind of mustard. And yet this mustard has become a part of me. Or, I have become a part of this mustard. Further, I know more of an ink, a brand of hams, a kind of cigarette, and a novelist than any man living. I went by train to see a friend in the country, and after passing through a patent mucilage, some more hams, a South African Investment Company, a Parisian millinery firm, and a comic journal, I alighted at a new and original kind of corset. On my return journey the road almost continuously ran through soap.

I have accumulated superior information concerning these things, because I am at their mercy. If I want to know where I am I must find the definitive sign. This accounts for my glib use of the word mucilage, as well as the titles of other staples.

I suppose even the Briton in mixing his life must sometimes consult the labels on 'buses and streets and stations, even as the chemist consults the labels on his bottles and boxes. A brave man would possibly affirm that this was suggested by the existence of the labels.

The reason that I did not learn more about hams and mucilage in New York seems to me to be partly due to the fact that the British advertiser is allowed to exercise an unbridled strategy in his attack with his new corset or whatever upon the defensive public. He knows that the vulnerable point is the informatory sign which the citizen must, of course, use for his guidance, and then, with horse, foot, guns, corsets, hams, mucilage, investment companies, and all, he hurls himself at the point.

Meanwhile I have discovered a way to make the Sanscrit scholar heed my creature who plays the piano with a hammer.

NEW YORK SKETCHES

STORIES TOLD BY AN ARTIST IN NEW YORK

A Tale about How "Great Grief" got His Holiday Dinner.

Wrinkles had been peering into the little dry-goods box that acted as a cupboard.

"There are only two eggs and a half of a loaf of bread left," he announced brutally.

"Heavens!" said Warwickson, from where he lay smoking on the bed. He spoke in his usual dismal voice. By it he had earned his popular name of Great Grief.

Wrinkles was a thrifty soul. A sight of an almost bare cupboard maddened him. Even when he was not hungry, the ghosts of his careful ancestors caused him to rebel against it. He sat down with a virtuous air. "Well, what are we going to do?" he demanded of the others. It is good to be the thrifty man in a crowd of unsuccessful artists, for then you can keep the others from starving peacefully. "What are we going to do?"

"Oh, shut up, Wrinkles," said Grief from the bed. "You make me think."

Little Pennoyer, with head bended afar down, had been busily scratching away at a pen and ink drawing. He looked up from his board to utter his plaintive optimism.

"The Monthly Amazement may pay me to-morrow. They ought to. I've waited over three months now. I'm going down there to-morrow, and perhaps I'll get it."

His friends listened to him tolerantly, but at last Wrinkles could not omit a scornful giggle. He was such an old man, almost twenty-eight, and he had seen so many little boys be brave. "Oh, no doubt, Penny, old man." Over on the bed Grief croaked deep down in his throat. Nothing was said for a long time thereafter.

The crash of the New York streets came faintly. Occasionally one could hear the tramp of feet in the intricate corridors of this begrimed building that squatted, slumbering and aged, between two exalted commercial structures that would have had to bend afar down to perceive it. The light snow beat pattering into the window corners, and made vague and grey the vista of chimneys and roofs. Often the wind scurried swiftly and raised a long cry.

Great Grief leaned upon his elbow. "See to the fire, will you, Wrinkles?"

Wrinkles pulled the coal-box out from under the bed and threw open the stove door preparatory to shovelling some fuel. A red glare plunged in the first faint shadow of dusk. Little Pennoyer threw down his pen and tossed his drawing over on the wonderful heap of stuff that hid the table. "It's too dark to work." He lit his pipe and walked about, stretching his shoulders like a man whose labour was valuable.

When dusk came it saddened these youths. The solemnity of darkness always caused them to ponder. "Light the gas, Wrinkles," said Grief.

The flood of orange light showed clearly the dull walls lined with scratches, the tousled bed in one corner, the mass of boxes and trunks in another, the little fierce stove, and the wonderful table. Moreover, there were some wine-coloured draperies flung in some places, and on a shelf, high up, there was a plaster cast dark with dust in the creases. A long stove-pipe wandered off in the wrong direction, and then twined impulsively toward a hole in the wall. There were some extensive cobwebs on the ceilings.

"Well, let's eat," said Grief.

Later, there came a sad knock at the door. Wrinkles, arranging a tin pail on the stove, little Pennoyer busy at slicing the bread, and Great Grief affixing the rubber tube to the gas stove, yelled: "Come in!"

The door opened and Corinson entered dejectedly. His overcoat was very new. Wrinkles flashed an envious glance at it, but almost immediately he cried: "Hello, Corrie, old boy!"

Corinson sat down and felt around among the pipes until he found a good one. Great Grief had fixed the coffee to boil on the gas stove, but he had to watch it closely, for the rubber tube was short, and a chair was balanced on a trunk, and then the gas stove was balanced on the chair. Coffee making was a feat.

"Well," said Grief, with his back turned, "how goes it, Corrie? How's Art, hey?" He fastened a terrible emphasis upon the word.

"Crayon portraits," said Corinson.

"What?" They turned towards him with one movement, as if from a lever connection. Little Pennoyer dropped his knife.

"Crayon portraits," repeated Corinson. He smoked away in profound cynicism. "Fifteen dollars a week or more this time of year, you know." He smiled at them like a man of courage.

Little Pennoyer picked up his knife again. "Well, I'll be blowed," said Wrinkles. Feeling it incumbent upon him to think, he dropped into a chair and began to play serenades on his guitar and watch to see when the water for the eggs would boil. It was a habitual pose.

Great Grief, however, seemed to observe something bitter in the affair. "When did you discover that you couldn't draw?" he said stiffly.

"I haven't discovered it yet," replied Corinson, with a serene air. "I merely discovered that I would rather eat."

"Oh!" said Grief.

"Hand me the eggs, Grief," said Wrinkles. "The water's boiling."

Little Pennoyer burst into the conversation. "We'd ask you to dinner, Corrie, but there's only three of us and there's two eggs. I dropped a piece of bread on the floor, too. I'd shy one."

"That's all right, Penny," said the other; "don't trouble yourself. You artists should never be hospitable. I'm going anyway. I've got to make a call. Well, good night, boys. I've got to make a call. Drop in and see me."

When the door closed upon him, Grief said: "The coffee's done; I hate that fellow. That overcoat cost thirty dollars, if it cost a red. His egotism is so tranquil. It isn't like yours, Wrinkles. He—"

The door opened again and Corinson thrust in his head. "Say, you fellows, you know it's Thanksgiving to-morrow?"

"Well, what of it?" demanded Grief.

Little Pennoyer said: "Yes, I know it is, Corrie, I thought of it this morning."

"Well, come out and have a table d'hote with me to-morrow night. I'll blow you off in good style."

While Wrinkles played an exuberant air on his guitar, little Pennoyer did part of a ballet. They cried ecstatically: "Will we? Well, I guess yes?"

When they were alone again, Grief said: "I'm not going, anyhow. I hate that fellow."

"Oh, fiddle," said Wrinkles. "You're an infernal crank. And besides, where's your dinner coming from to-morrow night if you don't go? Tell me that."

Little Pennoyer said: "Yes, that's so, Grief. Where's your dinner coming from if you don't go?"

Grief said: "Well, I hate him, anyhow."

* * * * * * *

As to Payment of the Rent.

Little Pennoyer's four dollars could not last for ever. When he received it he and Wrinkles and Great Grief went to a table d'hote. Afterwards little Pennoyer discovered that only two dollars and a half remained. A small magazine away down town had accepted one out of the six drawings that he had taken them, and later had given him four dollars for it. Penny was so disheartened when he saw that his money was not going to last for ever, that even with two dollars and a half in his pockets, he felt much worse than when he was penniless, for at that time he anticipated twenty-four. Wrinkles lectured upon "Finance."

Great Grief said nothing, for it was established that when he received six dollar cheques from comic weeklies he dreamed of renting studios at seventy-five dollars per month, and was likely to go out and buy five dollars' worth of second-hand curtains and plaster casts.

When he had money Penny always hated the cluttered den in the old building. He desired to go out and breathe boastfully like a man. But he obeyed Wrinkles, the elder and the wise, and if you had visited that room about ten o'clock of a morning or about seven of an evening you would have thought that rye bread, frankfurters, and potato salad from Second Avenue were the only foods in the world.

Purple Sanderson lived there too, but then he really ate. He had learned parts of the gasfitter's trade before he came to be such a great artist, and when his opinions disagreed with that of every art manager in New York, he went to see a plumber, a friend of his, for whose opinion he had a great respect. In consequence, he frequented a very great restaurant on Twenty-third Street, and sometimes on Saturday nights he openly scorned his companions.

Purple was a good fellow, Grief said, but one of his singularly bad traits was that he always remembered everything. One night, not long after little Pennoyer's great discovery, Purple came in, and as he was neatly hanging up his coat, said: "Well, the rent will be due in four days."

"Will it?" demanded Penny, astounded. Penny was always astounded when the rent came due. It seemed to him the most extraordinary occurrence.

"Certainly it will," said Purple, with the irritated air of a superior financial man.

"My soul!" said Wrinkles.

Great Grief lay on the bed smoking a pipe and waiting for fame. "Oh, go home, Purple. You resent something. It wasn't me, it was the calendar."

"Try and be serious a moment, Grief."

"You're a fool, Purple."

Penny spoke from where he was at work. "Well, if those Amazement Magazine people pay me when they said they would I'll have money then."

"So you will, dear," said Grief, satirically. "You'll have money to burn. Did the Amazement people ever pay you when they said they would? You're wonderfully important all of a sudden, it seems to me. You talk like an artist."

Wrinkles, too, smiled at little Pennoyer. "The Established Magazine people wanted Penny to hire models and make a try for them too. It will only cost him a big blue chip. By the time he has invested all the money he hasn't got and the rent is two weeks' overdue, he will be able to tell the landlord to wait seven months until the Monday morning after the publication. Go ahead, Penny."

It was the habit to make game of little Pennoyer. He was always having gorgeous opportunities, with no opportunity to take advantage of his opportunities.

Penny smiled at them, his tiny, tiny smile of courage.

"You're a confident little cuss," observed Grief, irrelevantly.

"Well, the world has no objection to your being confident also, Grief," said Purple.

"Hasn't it?" said Grief. "Well, I want to know."

Wrinkles could not be light-spirited long. He was obliged to despair when occasion offered. At last he sank down in a chair and seized his guitar.

"Well, what's to be done?" he said. He began to play mournfully.

"Throw Purple out," mumbled Grief from the bed.

"Are you fairly certain that you will have money then, Penny?" asked

Purple.

Little Pennoyer looked apprehensive. "Well, I don't know," he said.

And then began that memorable discussion, great in four minds. The tobacco was of the "Long John" brand. It smelled like burning mummies.

A Dinner on Sunday Evening.

Once Purple Sanderson went to his home in St. Lawrence county to enjoy some country air, and, incidentally, to explain his life failure to his people. Previously, Great Grief had given him odds that he would return sooner than he had planned, and everybody said that Grief had a good bet. It is not a glorious pastime, this explaining of life failures.

Later, Great Grief and Wrinkles went to Haverstraw to visit Grief's cousin and sketch. Little Pennoyer was disheartened, for it is bad to be imprisoned in brick and dust and cobbles when your ear can hear in the distance the harmony of the summer sunlight upon leaf and blade of green. Besides, he did not hear Wrinkles and Grief discoursing and quarrelling in the den, and Purple coming in at six o'clock with contempt.

On Friday afternoon he discovered that he only had fifty cents to last until Saturday morning, when he was to get his cheque from the Gamin. He was an artful little man by this time, however, and it is as true as the sky that when he walked toward the Gamin office on Saturday he had twenty cents remaining.

The cashier nodded his regrets, "Very sorry, Mr.—er—Pennoyer, but our pay-day, you know, is on Monday. Come around any time after ten."

"Oh, it don't matter," said Penny. As he walked along on his return he reflected deeply how he could invest his twenty cents in food to last until Monday morning any time after ten. He bought two coffee cakes in a third avenue bakery. They were very beautiful. Each had a hole in the centre, and a handsome scallop all around the edges.

Penny took great care of those cakes. At odd times he would rise from his work and go to see that no escape had been made. On Sunday he got up at noon and compressed breakfast and noon into one meal. Afterwards he had almost three-quarters of a cake still left to him. He congratulated himself that with strategy he could make it endure until Monday morning any time after ten.

At three in the afternoon there came a faint-hearted knock. "Come in," said Penny. The door opened and old Tim Connegan, who was trying to be a model, looked in apprehensively. "I beg pardon, sir," he said at once.

"Come in, Tim, you old thief," said Penny. Tim entered slowly and bashfully. "Sit down," said Penny. Tim sat down and began to rub his knees, for rheumatism had a mighty hold upon him.

Penny lit his pipe and crossed his legs. "Well, how goes it?"

Tim moved his square jaw upward and flashed Penny a little glance.

"Bad?" said Penny.

The old man raised his hand impressively. "I've been to every studio in the hull city, and I never see such absences in my life. What with the seashore and the mountains, and this and that resort, I think all the models will be starved by fall. I found one man in up on Fifty-seventh Street. He ses to me: 'Come around Tuesday—I may want yez and I may not.' That was last week. You know, I live down on the Bowery, Mr. Pennoyer, and when I got up there on Tuesday, he ses: 'Confound you, are you here again?' ses he. I went and sat down in the park, for I was too tired for the walk back. And there you are, Mr. Pennoyer. What with trampin' around to look for men that are thousand miles away, I'm near dead."

"It's hard," said Penny.

"It is, sir. I hope they'll come back soon. The summer is the death of us all, sir; it is. Sure, I never know where my next meal is coming until I get it. That's true."

"Had anything to-day?"

"Yes, sir, a little."

"How much?"

"Well, sir, a lady gave me a cup of coffee this morning. It was good, too, I'm telling you."

Penny went to his cupboard. When he returned, he said: "Here's some cake."

Tim thrust forward his hands, palms erect. "Oh, now, Mr. Pennoyer, I couldn't. You—"

"Go ahead. What's the odds?"

"Oh, now."

"Go ahead, you old bat."

Penny smoked.

When Tim was going out, he turned to grow eloquent again. "Well, I can't tell you how much I'm obliged to you, Mr. Pennoyer. You—"

"Don't mention it, old man."

Penny smoked.

THE SILVER PAGEANT.

"It's rotten," said Grief.

"Oh, it's fair, old man. Still, I would not call it a great contribution to American art," said Wrinkles.

"You've got a good thing, Gaunt, if you go at it right," said little Pennoyer.

These were all volunteer orations. The boys had come in one by one and spoken their opinions. Gaunt listened to them no more than if they had been so many match-peddlers. He never heard anything close at hand, and he never saw anything excepting that which transpired across a mystic wide sea. The shadow of his thoughts was in his eyes, a little grey mist, and, when what you said to him had passed out of your mind, he asked: "Wha—a—at?" It was understood that Gaunt was very good to tolerate the presence of the universe, which was noisy and interested in itself. All the younger men, moved by an instinct of faith, declared that he would one day be a great artist if he would only move faster than a pyramid. In the meantime he did not hear their voices. Occasionally when he saw a man take vivid pleasure in life, he faintly evinced an admiration. It seemed to strike him as a feat. As for him, he was watching that silver pageant across a sea.

When he came from Paris to New York somebody told him that he must make his living. He went to see some book publishers, and talked to them in his manner—as if he had just been stunned. At last one of them gave him drawings to do, and it did not surprise him. It was merely as if rain had come down.

Great Grief went to see him in his studio, and returned to the den to say: "Gaunt is working in his sleep. Somebody ought to set fire to him."

It was then that the others went over and smoked, and gave their opinions of a drawing. Wrinkles said: "Are you really looking at it, Gaunt? I don't think you've seen it yet, Gaunt?"

"What?"

"Why don't you look at it?"

When Wrinkles departed, the model, who was resting at that time, followed him into the hall and waved his arms in rage. "That feller's crazy. Yeh ought t' see—" and he recited lists of all the wrongs that can come to models.

It was a superstitious little band over in the den. They talked often of Gaunt. "He's got pictures in his eyes," said Wrinkles. They had expected genius to blindly stumble at the perface and ceremonies of the world, and each new flounder by Gaunt made a stir in the den. It awed them, and they waited.

At last one morning Gaunt burst into the room. They were all as dead men.

"I'm going to paint a picture." The mist in his eyes was pierced by a Coverian gleam. His gestures were wild and extravagant. Grief stretched out smoking on the bed, Wrinkles and little Pennoyer working at their drawing-boards tilted against the table—were suddenly frozen. If bronze statues had come and danced heavily before them, they could not have been thrilled further.

Gaunt tried to tell them of something, but it became knotted in his throat, and then suddenly he dashed out again.

Later they went earnestly over to Gaunt's studio. Perhaps he would tell them of what he saw across the sea.

He lay dead upon the floor. There was a little grey mist before his eyes.

When they finally arrived home that night they took a long time to undress for bed, and then came the moment when they waited for some one to put out the gas. Grief said at last, with the air of a man whose brain is desperately driven: "I wonder—I—what do you suppose he was going to paint?"

Wrinkles reached and turned out the gas, and from the sudden profound darkness, he said: "There is a mistake. He couldn't have had pictures in his eyes."

A STREET SCENE IN NEW YORK.

The man and the boy conversed in Italian, mumbling the soft syllables and making little, quick egotistical gestures. Suddenly the man glared and wavered on his limbs for a moment as if some blinding light had flashed before his vision; then he swayed like a drunken man and fell. The boy grasped his arm convulsively, and made an attempt to support his companion so that the body slid to the side-walk with an easy motion like a corpse sinking into the sea. The boy screamed.

Instantly people from all directions turned their gaze upon that figure prone upon the side-walk. In a moment there was a dodging, peering, pushing crowd about the man. A volley of questions, replies, speculations flew to and fro among all the bobbing heads.

"What's th' matter? what's th' matter?"

"Oh, a jag, I guess!"

"Aw, he's got a fit!"

"What's th' matter? what's th' matter?"

Two streams of people coming from different directions met at this point to form a great crowd. Others came from across the street.

Down under their feet, almost lost under this mass of people, lay a man, hidden in the shadows caused by their forms, which, in fact, barely allowed a particle of light to pass between them. Those in the foremost rank bended down eagerly, anxious to see everything. Others behind them crowded savagely like starving men fighting for bread. Always, the question could be heard flying in the air. "What's th' matter." Some, near to the body, and perhaps feeling the danger of being forced over upon it, twisted their heads and protested violently to those unheeding ones who were scuffling in the rear: "Say, quit yer shovin', can't yeh? What do yeh want, anyhow? Quit!"

Somebody back in the throng suddenly said: "Say, young feller, cheese that pushin'! I ain't no peach!"

Another voice said: "Well, dat's all right—"

The boy who had been with the Italian was standing helplessly, a frightened look in his eyes, and holding the man's hand. Sometimes he looked about him dumbly, with indefinite hope, as if he expected sudden assistance to come from the clouds. The men about him frequently jostled him until he was obliged to put his hand upon the breast of the body to maintain his balance. Those nearest the man upon the sidewalk at first saw his body go through a singular contortion. It was as if an invisible hand had reached up from the earth and had seized him by the hair. He seemed dragged slowly, pitilessly backward, while his body stiffened convulsively, his hands clenched, and his arms swung rigidly upward. Through his pallid, half-closed lids one could see the steel-coloured, assassin-like gleam of his eye, that shone with a mystic light as a corpse might glare at those live ones who seemed about to trample it under foot. As for the men near, they hung back, appearing as if they expected it might spring erect and grab them. Their eyes, however, were held in a spell of fascination. They scarce seemed to breathe. They were contemplating a depth into which a human being had sunk, and the marvel of this mystery of life or death held them chained. Occasionally from the rear a man came thrusting his way impetuously, satisfied that there was a horror to be seen, and apparently insane to get a view of it. More self-contained men swore at these persons when they tread upon their toes.

The street cars jingled past this scene in endless parade. Occasionally, down where the elevated road crossed the street, one could hear sometimes a thunder, suddenly begun and suddenly ended. Over the heads of the crowd hung an immovable canvas sign: "Regular Dinner twenty cents."

The body on the pave seemed like a bit of debris sunk in this human ocean.

But after the first spasm of curiosity had passed away, there were those in the crowd who began to bethink themselves of some way to help. A voice called out: "Rub his wrists." The boy and a man on the other side of the body began to rub the wrists and slap the palms of the man. A tall German suddenly appeared, and resolutely began to push the crowd back. "Get back there—get back," he repeated continually while he pushed at them. He seemed to have authority; the crowd obeyed him. He and another man knelt down by the man in the darkness and loosened his shirt at the throat. Once they struck a match and held it close to the man's face. This livid visage suddenly appearing under their feet in the light of the match's yellow glare, made the crowd shudder. Half articulate exclamations could be heard. There were men who nearly created a riot in the madness of their desire to see the thing.

Meanwhile others had been questioning the boy. "What's his name? Where does he live?"

Then a policeman appeared. The first part of this little drama had gone on without his assistance, but now he came, striding swiftly, his helmet towering over the crowd and shading that impenetrable police face. He charged the crowd as if he were a squadron of Irish Lancers. The people fairly withered before this onslaught. Occasionally he shouted: "Come, make way there. Come, now!" He was evidently a man whose life was half-pestered out of him by people who were sufficiently unreasonable and stupid as to insist on walking in the streets. He felt the rage toward them that a placid cow feels toward the flies that hover in clouds and disturb its repose. When he arrived at the centre of the crowd he first said, threateningly: "What's th' matter here?" And then when he saw that human bit of wreckage at the bottom of the sea of men, he said to it: "Come, git up out that! Git out a here!"

Whereupon hands were raised in the crowd and a volley of decorated information was blazed at the officer.

"Ah, he's got a fit, can't yeh see?"

"He's got a fit!"

"What th'ell yeh doin'? Leave 'im be!"

The policeman menaced with a glance the crowd from whose safe precincts the defiant voices had emerged.

A doctor had come. He and the policeman bended down at the man's side. Occasionally the officer reared up to create room. The crowd fell away before his admonitions, his threats, his sarcastic questions, and before the sweep of those two huge buckskin gloves.

At last the peering ones saw the man on the side-walk begin to breathe heavily, strainedly, as if he had just come to the surface from some deep water. He uttered a low cry in his foreign way. It was like a baby's squeal or the side wail of a little storm-tossed kitten. As this cry went forth to all those eager ears the jostling, crowding recommenced again furiously, until the doctor was obliged to yell warningly a dozen times. The policeman had gone to send the ambulance call.

Then a man struck another match, and in its meagre light the doctor felt the skull of the prostrate man carefully to discover if any wound had been caused by his fall to the stone side-walk. The crowd pressed and crushed again. It was as if they fully expected to see blood by the light of the match, and the desire made them appear almost insane. The policeman returned and fought with them. The doctor looked up occasionally to scold and demand room.

At last, out of the faint haze of light far up the street, there came the sound of a gong beating rapidly. A monstrous truck loaded to the sky with barrels scurried to one side with marvellous agility. And then the black waggon, with its gleam of gold lettering and bright brass gong, clattered into view, the horse galloping. A young man, as imperturbable almost as if he were at a picnic, sat upon the rear seat. When they picked up the limp body, from which came little moans and howls, the crowd almost turned into a mob. When the ambulance started on its banging and clanging return, they stood and gazed until it was quite out of sight. Some resumed their way with an air of relief. Others still continued to stare after the vanished ambulance and its burden as if they had been cheated, as if the curtain had been rung down on a tragedy that was but half completed; and this impenetrable blanket intervening between a sufferer and their curiosity seemed to make them feel an injustice.

MINETTA LANE, NEW YORK.

Its Worst Days have Now Passed Away.

But its Inhabitants Still Include Many whose Deeds are Evil.

The Celebrated Resort of Mammy Ross.

Minetta Lane is a small and becobbled valley between hills and dingy brick. At night the street lamps, burning dimly, cause the shadows to be important, and in the gloom one sees groups of quietly conversant negroes, with occasionally the gleam of a passing growler. Everything is vaguely outlined and of uncertain identity, unless, indeed, it be the flashing buttons and shield of the policeman on his coast. The Sixth Avenue horse-cars jingle past one end of the lane, and a block eastward the little thoroughfare ends in the darkness of M'Dougall Street.

One wonders how such an insignificant alley could get such an assuredly large reputation, but, as a matter of fact, Minetta Lane and Minetta Street, which leads from it southward to Bleecker Street, were, until a few years ago, two of the most enthusiastically murderous thoroughfares in New York. Bleecker Street, M'Dougall Street, and nearly all the streets thereabouts were most unmistakably bad; the other streets went away and hid. To gain a reputation in Minetta Lane in those days a man was obliged to commit a number of furious crimes, and no celebrity was more important than the man who had a good honest killing to his credit. The inhabitants, for the most part, were negroes, and they represented the very worst element of their race. The razor habit clung to them with the tenacity of an epidemic, and every night the uneven cobbles felt blood. Minetta Lane was not a public thoroughfare at this period. It was a street set apart, a refuge for criminals. Thieves came here preferably with their gains, and almost any day peculiar sentences passed among the inhabitants. "Big Jim turned a thousand last night." "No-Toe's made another haul." And the worshipful citizens would make haste to be present at the consequent revel.

As has been said, Minetta Lane was then no thoroughfare. A peaceable citizen chose to make a circuit rather than venture through this place, that swarmed with the most dangerous people in the city. Indeed, the thieves of the district used to say: "Once get in the lane and you're all right." Even a policeman in chase of a criminal would probably shy away instead of pursuing him into the lane. The odds were too great against a lone officer.

Sailors, and any men who might appear to have money about them, were welcomed with all proper ceremony at the terrible dens of the lane. At departure they were fortunate if they still retained their teeth. It was the custom to leave very little else to them. There was every facility for the capture of coin, from trap-doors to plain ordinary knock-out drops.

And yet Minetta Lane is built on the grave of Minetta Brook, where, in olden times, lovers walked under the willows on the bank, and Minetta Lane, in later times, was the home of many of the best families of the town.

A negro named Bloodthirsty was perhaps the most luminous figure of Minetta Lane's aggregation of desperadoes. Bloodthirsty supposedly is alive now, but he has vanished from the lane. The police want him for murder. Bloodthirsty is a large negro, and very hideous. He has a rolling eye that shows white at the wrong time, and his neck, under the jaw, is dreadfully scarred and pitted.

Bloodthirsty was particularly eloquent when drunk, and in the wildness of a spree he would rave so graphically about gore that even the habitated wool of old timers would stand straight.

Bloodthirsty meant most of it, too. That is why his orations were impressive. His remarks were usually followed by the wide, lightning sweep of his razor. None cared to exchange epithets with Bloodthirsty. A man in a boiler iron suit would walk down to City Hall and look at the clock before he would ask the time of day from the single-minded and ingenuous Bloodthirsty.

After Bloodthirsty, in combative importance, came No-Toe Charley. Singularly enough, Charley was called No-Toe Charley because he did not have a toe on his feet. Charley was a small negro, and his manner of amusement befitting a smaller man. Charley was more wise, more sly, more round-about than the other man. The path of his crimes was like a corkscrew in architecture, and his method led him to make many tunnels. With all his cleverness, however, No-Toe was finally induced to pay a visit to the gentlemen in the grim, grey building up the river—Sing Sing.

Black-Cat was another famous bandit who made the land his home. Black-Cat is dead. Jube Tyler has been sent to prison, and after mentioning the recent disappearance of Old Man Spriggs it may be said that the lane is now destitute of the men who once crowned it with a glory of crime. It is hardly essential to mention Guinea Johnson.

Guinea is not a great figure. Guinea is just an ordinary little crook. Sometimes Guinea pays a visit to his friends, the other little crooks who make homes in the lane, but he himself does not live there, and with him out of it there is now no one whose industry's unlawfulness has yet earned him the dignity of a nickname. Indeed, it is difficult to find people now who remember the old gorgeous days, although it is but two years since the lane shone with sin like a new head-light. But after a search the reporter found three.

Mammy Ross is one of the last relics of the days of slaughter still living there. Her weird history also reaches back to the blossoming of the first members of the Whyo gang in the Old Sixth Ward, and her mind is stored with bloody memories. She at one time kept a sailors' boarding-house near the Tombs prison, and the accounts of all the festive crimes of that neighbourhood in ancient years roll easily from her tongue. They killed a sailor man every day, and pedestrians went about the streets wearing stoves for fear of the handy knives. At the present day the route to Mammy's home is up a flight of grimy stairs that are pasted on the outside of an old and tottering frame house. Then there is a hall blacker than a wolf's throat, and this hall leads to a little kitchen where Mammy usually sits groaning by the fire. She is, of course, very old, and she is also very fat. She seems always to be in great pain. She says she is suffering from "de very las' dregs of de yaller fever."

During the first part of a reporter's recent visit, old Mammy seemed most dolefully oppressed by her various diseases. Her great body shook and her teeth clicked spasmodically during her long and painful respirations. From time to time she reached her trembling hand and drew a shawl closer about her shoulders. She presented as true a picture of a person undergoing steady, unchangeable, chronic pain as a patent medicine firm could wish to discover for miraculous purposes. She breathed like a fish thrown out on the bank, and her old head continually quivered in the nervous tremors of the extremely aged and debilitated person. Meanwhile her daughter hung over the stove and placidly cooked sausages.

Appeals were made to the old woman's memory. Various personages who had been sublime figures of crime in the long-gone days were mentioned to her, and presently her eyes began to brighten. Her head no longer quivered. She seemed to lose for a period her sense of pain in the gentle excitement caused by the invocation of the spirits of her memory.

It appears that she had had a historic quarrel with Apple Mag. She first recited the prowess of Apple Mag; how this emphatic lady used to argue with paving stones, carving knives, and bricks. Then she told of the quarrel; what Mag said; what she said. It seems that they cited each other as spectacles of sin and corruption in more fully explanatory terms than are commonly known to be possible. But it was one of Mammy's most gorgeous recollections, and, as she told it, a smile widened over her face.

Finally she explained her celebrated retort to one of the most illustrious thugs that had blessed the city in bygone days. "Ah says to 'im, ah says: 'You—you'll die in yer boots like Gallopin' Thompson—dat's what you'll do. You des min' dat', honey. Ah got o'ny one chile, an' he ain't nuthin' but er cripple; but le'me tel' you, man, dat boy'll live t' pick de feathers f'm de goose dat'll eat de grass dat grows over your grave, man.' Dat's what I tol' 'm. But—law sake—how I know dat in less'n three day, dat man be lying in de gutter wif a knife stickin' out'n his back. Lawd, no, I sholy never s'pected noting like dat."

These reminiscences, at once maimed and reconstructed, have been treasured by old Mammy as carefully, as tenderly, as if they were the various little tokens of an early love. She applies the same black-handed sentiment to them, and, as she sits groaning by the fire, it is plainly to be seen that there is only one food for her ancient brain, and that is the recollection of the beautiful fights and murders of the past.

On the other side of the lane, but near Mammy's house, Pop Babcock keeps a restaurant. Pop says it is a restaurant, and so it must be one; but you could pass there ninety times each day and never know you were passing a restaurant. There is one obscure little window in the basement, and if you went close and peered in you might, after a time, be able to make out a small, dusty sign, lying amid jars on a dusty shelf. This sign reads: "Oysters in every style." If you are of a gambling turn of mind, you will probably stand out in the street and bet yourself black in the face that there isn't an oyster within a hundred yards. But Pop Babcock made that sign, and Pop Babcock could not tell an untruth. Pop is a model of all the virtues which an inventive fate has made for us. He says so.

As far as goes the management of Pop's restaurant, it differs from Sherry's. In the first place, the door is always kept locked. The wardmen of the Fifteenth precinct have a way of prowling through the restaurant almost every night, and Pop keeps the door locked in order to keep out the objectionable people that cause the wardmen's visits. He says so. The cooking stove is located in the main room of the restaurant, and it is placed in such a strategic manner that it occupies about all the space that is not already occupied by a table, a bench, and two chairs. The table will, on a pinch, furnish room for the plates of two people if they are willing to crowd. Pop says he is the best cook in the world.

When questioned concerning the present condition of the lane, Pop said: "Quiet! Quiet! Lo'd save us, maybe it ain't. Quiet! Quiet!" His emphasis was arranged crescendo, until the last word was really a vocal explosion. "Why, dish er' lane ain't nohow like what it uster be—no, indeed it ain't. No, sir. 'Deed it ain't. Why, I kin remember when dey was a-cuttin' an' a-slashin' long yere all night. 'Deed dey wos. My-my, dem times was different. Dat der Kent, he kep' de place at Green Gate cou't down yer ol' Mammy's—an' he was a hard baby—'deed he was—an' ol' Black-Cat an' ol' Bloodthirsty, dey was a-comin' round yere a-cuttin', an' a-slashin', an' a-cuttin', an' a-slashin'. Didn't dar' say boo to a goose in dose days, dat you didn't, less'n you lookin' fer a scrap. No, sir." Then he gave information concerning his own prowess at that time. Pop is about as tall as a picket of an undersized fence. "But dey didn't have nothin' ter say ter me. No, sir, 'deed dey didn't. I would lay down fer none of 'em. No, sir. Dey knew my gait, 'deed dey did. Man, man, many's de time I buck up agin 'em."

At this time Pop had three customers in his place, one asleep on the bench, one asleep on two chairs, and one asleep on the floor behind the stove.

But there is one who lends dignity of the real bevel-edged type to Minetta Lane, and that man is Hank Anderson. Hank, of course, does not live in the lane, but the shadows of his social perfections fall upon it as refreshingly as a morning dew.

Hank gave a dance twice in each week at a hall hard by in M'Dougall Street, and the dusky aristocracy of the neighbourhood know their guiding beacon. Moreover, Hank holds an annual ball in Forty-fourth Street. Also, he gives a picnic each year to the Montezuma Club, when he again appears as a guiding beacon. This picnic is usually held on a barge, and the excursion is a very joyous one. Some years ago it required the entire reserve squad of an up-town police precinct to properly control the enthusiasm of the gay picnickers, but that was an exceptional exuberance, and no measure of Hank's ability for management.

He is really a great manager. He was Boss Tweed's body-servant in the days when Tweed was a political prince, and any one who saw Bill Tweed through a spy-glass learned the science of leading, pulling, driving, and hauling men in a way to keep the men ignorant of it. Hank imbibed from this fount of knowledge, and he applied his information in Thompson Street. Thompson Street salaamed. Presently he bore a proud title: "The Mayor of Thompson Street." Dignities from the principal political organisations of the city adorned his brow, and he speedily became illustrious.

Hank knew the lane well in its direful days. As for the inhabitants, he kept clear of them, and yet in touch with them, according to a method that he might have learned in the Sixth ward. The Sixth ward was a good place in which to learn that trick. Anderson can tell many strange tales and good of the lane, and he tells them in the graphic way of his class. "Why, they could steal your shirt without moving a wrinkle on it."

The killing of Joe Carey was the last murder that happened in the Minettas. Carey had what might be called a mixed-ale difference with a man named Kenny. They went out to the middle of Minetta Street to affably fight it out and determine the justice of the question.

In the scrimmage Kenny drew a knife, thrust quickly, and Carey fell. Kenny had not gone a hundred feet before he ran into the arms of a policeman.

There is probably no street in New York where the police keep closer watch than they do in Minetta Lane. There was a time when the inhabitants had a profound and reasonable contempt for the public guardians, but they have it no longer apparently. Any citizen can walk through there at any time in perfect safety, unless, perhaps, he should happen to get too frivolous. To be strictly accurate, the change began under the reign of police Captain Chapman. Under Captain Groo, a commander of the Fifteenth precinct, the lane donned a complete new garb. Its denizens brag now of its peace, precisely as they once bragged of its war. It is no more a bloody lane. The song of the razor is seldom heard. There are still toughs and semi-toughs galore in it, but they can't get a chance with the copper looking the other way. Groo got the poor lane by the throat. If a man should insist upon becoming a victim of the badger game, he could probably succeed, upon search in Minetta Lane, as indeed, he could on any of the great avenues, but then Minetta Lane is not supposed to be a pearly street of Paradise.

In the meantime the Italians have begun to dispute the possession of the lane with the negroes. Green Gate Court is filled with them now, and a row of houses near the M'Dougall Street corner is occupied entirely by Italian families. None of them seem to be over fond of the old Mulberry Bend fashion of life, and there are no cutting affrays among them worth mentioning. It is the original negro element that makes the trouble when there is trouble.

But they are happy in this condition are these people. The most extraordinary quality of the negro is his enormous capacity for happiness under most adverse circumstances. Minetta Lane is a place of poverty and sin, but these influences cannot destroy the broad smile of the negro—a vain and simple child, but happy. They all smile here, the most evil as well as the poorest. Knowing the negro, one always expects laughter from him, be he ever so poor, but it was a new experience to see a broad grin on the face of the devil. Even old Pop Babcock had a laugh as fine and mellow as would be the sound of falling glass, broken saints from high windows, in the silence of some great cathedral's hollow.

THE ROOF GARDENS AND GARDENERS OF NEW YORK.

A Phase of New York Life as Seen by a Close Observer.

When the hot weather comes the roof gardens burst into full bloom, and if an inhabitant of Chicago should take flight on his wings over this city, he would observe six or eight flashing spots in the darkness, spots as radiant as crowns. These are the roof gardens, and if a giant had flung a handful of monstrous golden coins upon the sombre-shadowed city he could not have benefited the metropolis more, although he would not have given the same opportunity to various commercial aspirants to charge a price and a half for everything. There are two classes of men—reporters and central office detectives—who do not mind these prices because they are very prodigal of their money.

Now is the time of the girl with the copper voice, the Irishman with circular whiskers, and the minstrel who had a reputation in 1833. To the street the noise of the band comes down on the wind in fitful gusts, and at the brilliantly illuminated rail there is suggestion of many straw hats.

One of the main features of the roof garden is the waiter, who stands directly in front of you whenever anything interesting transpires on the stage. This waiter is three hundred feet high and seventy-two feet wide. His finger can block your view of the golden-haired soubrette, and when he waves his arm the stage disappears as if by a miracle. What particularly fascinates you is his lack of self-appreciation. He doesn't know that his length over all is three hundred feet, and that his beam is seventy-two feet. He only knows that while the golden-haired soubrette is singing her first verse he is depositing beer on the table before some thirsty New Yorkers. He only knows that during the third verse the thirsty New Yorkers object to the roof-garden prices. He does not know that behind him are some fifty citizens who ordinarily would not give three whoops to see the golden-haired soubrette, but who, under these particular circumstances, are kept from swift assassination by sheer force of the human will. He gives an impressive exhibition of a man who is regardless of consequences, oblivious to everything save his task, which is to provide beer. Some day there may be a wholesale massacre of roof-garden waiters, but they will die with astonished faces and with questions on their lips. Skulls so steadfastly opaque defy axes, or any of the other methods which the populace occasionally use to cure colossal stupidity.

Between numbers on an ordinary roof-garden programme, the orchestra sometimes plays what the more enlightened and wary citizens of the town call a "beer overture." But, for reasons which no civil service commission could give, the waiter does not choose this time to serve the thirsty. No; he waits until the golden-haired soubrette appears, he waits until the haggard audience has goaded itself into some interest in the proceedings. Then he gets under way. Then he comes forth and blots out the stage. In case of war, all roof-garden waiters should be recruited in a special regiment and sent out in advance of everything. There is a peculiar quality of bullet-proofness about them which would turn a projectile pale.

If you have strategy enough in your soul you may gain furtive glimpses of the stage, despite the efforts of the waiters, and then, with something to engage the attention when the attention grows weary of the mystic wind, the flashing yellow lights, the music, and the undertone of the far street's roar, you should be happy.

Far up into the night there is a wildness, a temper to the air which suggests tossing tree boughs and the swift rustle of grass. The New Yorker, whose business will not allow him to go out to nature, perhaps, appreciates these little opportunities to go up to nature, although doubtless he thinks he goes to see the show.

One season two new roof gardens have opened. The one at the top of Grand Central Palace is large enough for a regimental drill room. The band is imprisoned still higher in a turreted affair, and a person who prefers gentle and unobtrusive amusement can gain deep pleasure and satisfaction from watching the leader of this band gesticulating upon the heavens. His figure is silhouetted beautifully against the sky, and every gesture in which he wrings noise from his band is interestingly accentuated.

The other new roof garden was Oscar Hammerstein's Olympia, which blazes on Broadway.

Oscar originally made a great reputation for getting out injunctions. All court judges in New York worked overtime when Oscar was in this business. He enjoined everybody in sight. He had a special machine made—"Drop a nickel in the judge and get an injunction." Then he sent a man to Washington for twenty-two thousand dollars' worth of nickels. In Harlem, where he then lived, it rained orders of the court every day at twelve o'clock. The street-cleaning commission was obliged to enlist a special force to deal with Oscar's injunctions. Citizens meeting on the street never said: "Good morning, how do you feel to-day?" They always said: "Good morning, have you been enjoined yet to-day?" When a man perhaps wished to enter a little game of draw, the universal form was changed when he sent a note to his wife: "Dear Louise, I have received an order of the court restraining me from coming home to dinner to-night. Yours, George."

But Oscar changed. He smashed his machine, girded himself, and resolved to provide the public with amusement. And now we see this great mind applying itself to a roof garden with the same unflagging industry and boundless energy which had previously expressed itself in injunctions. The Olympia, his new roof garden, is a feat. It has an exuberance which reminds one of the Union Depot train-shed of some western city. The steel arches of the roof make a wide and splendid sweep, and over in the corner there are real swans swimming in real water. The whole structure glares like a conflagration with the countless electric lights. Oscar has caused the execution of decorative paintings upon the walls. If he had caused the execution of the decorative painters he would have done better; but a man who has devoted the greater part of his life to the propagation of injunctions is not supposed to understand that wall decoration which appears to have been done with a nozzle is worse than none. But if carpers say that Oscar failed in his landscapes, none can say that he failed in his measurements of the popular mind. The people come in swarms to the Olympia. Two elevators are busy at conveying them to where the cool and steady night-wind insults the straw hat; and the scene here during the popular part of the evening is perhaps more gaudy and dazzling than any other in New York.

The bicycle has attained an economic position of vast importance. The roof garden ought to attain such a position, and it doubtless will soon—as we give it the opportunity it desires.

The Arab or the Moor probably invented the roof garden in some long-gone centuries, and they are at this day inveterate roof gardeners. The American, surprisingly belated—for him, has but recently seized upon the idea, and its development here has been only partial. The possibilities of the roof garden are still unknown.

Here is a vast city in which thousands of people in summer half stifle, cry out continually for air, fresher air. Just above their heads is what might be called a county of unoccupied land. It is not ridiculously small when compared with the area of New York county itself. But it is as lonely as a desert, this region of roofs. It is as untrodden as the corners of Arizona. Unless a man be a roof gardener, he knows practically nothing of this land.

Down in the slums necessity forces a solution of problems. It drives the people to the roofs. An evening upon a tenement roof with the great golden march of the stars across the sky, and Johnnie gone for a pail of beer, is not so bad if you have never seen the mountains nor heard, to your heart, the slow, sad song of the pines.

IN THE BROADWAY CARS.

Panorama of a Day from the Down-town Rush of the Morning to the Uninterrupted Whirr of the Cable at Night—The Man, and the Woman, and the Conductor.

The cable cars come down Broadway as the waters come down at Lodore. Years ago Father Knickerbocker had convulsions when it was proposed to lay impious rails on his sacred thoroughfare. At the present day the cars, by force of column and numbers, almost dominate the great street, and the eye of even an old New Yorker is held by these long yellow monsters which prowl intently up and down, up and down, in a mystic search.

In the grey of the morning they come out of the up-town, bearing janitors, porters, all that class which carries the keys to set alive the great down-town. Later, they shower clerks. Later still, they shower more clerks. And the thermometer which is attached to a conductor's temper is steadily rising, rising, and the blissful time arrives when everybody hangs to a strap and stands on his neighbour's toes. Ten o'clock comes, and the Broadway cars, as well as elevated cars, horse cars, and ferryboats innumerable, heave sighs of relief. They have filled lower New York with a vast army of men who will chase to and fro and amuse themselves until almost nightfall.

The cable car's pulse drops to normal. But the conductor's pulse begins now to beat in split seconds. He has come to the crisis in his day's agony. He is now to be overwhelmed with feminine shoppers. They all are going to give him two-dollar bills to change. They all are going to threaten to report him. He passes his hand across his brow and curses his beard from black to grey and from grey to black.

Men and women have different ways of hailing a car. A man—if he is not an old choleric gentleman, who owns not this road but some other road—throws up a timid finger, and appears to believe that the King of Abyssinia is careering past on his war-chariot, and only his opinion of other people's Americanism keeps him from deep salaams. The gripman usually jerks his thumb over his shoulder and indicates the next car, which is three miles away. Then the man catches the last platform, goes into the car, climbs upon some one's toes, opens his morning paper, and is happy.

When a woman hails a car there is no question of its being the King of Abyssinia's war-chariot. She has bought the car for three dollars and ninety-eight cents. The conductor owes his position to her, and the gripman's mother does her laundry. No captain in the Royal Horse Artillery ever stops his battery from going through a stone house in a way to equal her manner of bringing that car back on its haunches. Then she walks leisurely forward, and after scanning the step to see if there is any mud upon it, and opening her pocket-book to make sure of a two-dollar bill, she says: "Do you give transfers down Twenty-eighth Street?"

Some time the conductor breaks the bell strap when he pulls it under these conditions. Then, as the car goes on, he goes and bullies some person who had nothing to do with the affair.

The car sweeps on its diagonal path through the Tenderloin with its hotels, its theatres, its flower shops, its 10,000,000 actors who played with Booth and Barret. It passes Madison Square and enters the gorge made by the towering walls of great shops. It sweeps around the double curve at Union Square and Fourteenth Street, and a life insurance agent falls in a fit as the car dashes over the crossing, narrowly missing three old ladies, two old gentlemen, a newly-married couple, a sandwich man, a newsboy, and a dog. At Grace Church the conductor has an altercation with a brave and reckless passenger who beards him in his own car, and at Canal Street he takes dire vengeance by tumbling a drunken man on to the pavement. Meanwhile, the gripman has become involved with countless truck drivers, and inch by inch, foot by foot, he fights his way to City Hall Park. On past the Post Office the car goes, with the gripman getting advice, admonition, personal comment, an invitation to fight from the drivers, until Battery Park appears at the foot of the slope, and as the car goes sedately around the curve the burnished shield of the bay shines through the trees.

It is a great ride, full of exciting actions. Those inexperienced persons who have been merely chased by Indians know little of the dramatic quality which life may hold for them. These jungle of men and vehicles, these cañons of streets, these lofty mountains of iron and cut stone—a ride through them affords plenty of excitement. And no lone panther's howl is more serious in intention than the howl of the truck driver when the cable car bumps one of his rear wheels.

Owing to a strange humour of the gods that make our comfort, sailor hats with wide brims come into vogue whenever we are all engaged in hanging to cable-car straps. There is only one more serious combination known to science, but a trial of it is at this day impossible. If a troupe of Elizabethan courtiers in large ruffs should board a cable car, the complication would be a very awesome one, and the profanity would be in old English, but very inspiring. However, the combination of wide-brimmed hats and crowded cable cars is tremendous in its power to cause misery to the patient New York public.

Suppose you are in a cable car, clutching for life and family a creaking strap from overhead. At your shoulder is a little dude in a very wide-brimmed straw hat with a red band. If you were in your senses you would recognise this flaming band as an omen of blood. But you are not in your senses; you are in a Broadway cable car. You are not supposed to have any senses. From the forward end you hear the gripman uttering shrill whoops and running over citizens. Suddenly the car comes to a curve. Making a swift running start, it turns three hand-springs, throws a cart wheel for luck, bounds into the air, hurls six passengers over the nearest building, and comes down a-straddle of the track. That is the way in which we turn curves in New York.

Meanwhile, during the car's gamboling, the corrugated rim of the dude's hat has swept naturally across your neck, and has left nothing for your head to do but to quit your shoulders. As the car roars your head falls into the waiting arms of the proper authorities. The dude is dead; everything is dead. The interior of the car resembles the scene of the battle of Wounded Knee, but this gives you small satisfaction.

There was once a person possessing a fund of uncanny humour who greatly desired to import from past ages a corps of knights in full armour. He then purposed to pack the warriors into a cable car and send them around a curve. He thought that he could gain much pleasure by standing near and listening to the wild clash of steel upon steel—the tumult of mailed heads striking together, the bitter grind of armoured legs bending the wrong way. He thought that this would teach them that war is grim.

Towards evening, when the tides of travel set northward, it is curious to see how the gripman and conductor reverse their tempers. Their dispositions flop over like patent signals. During the down-trip they had in mind always the advantages of being at Battery Park. A perpetual picture of the blessings of Battery Park was before them, and every delay made them fume—made this picture all the more alluring. Now the delights of up-town appear to them. They have reversed the signs on the cars; they have reversed their aspirations. Battery Park has been gained and forgotten. There is a new goal. Here is a perpetual illustration which the philosophers of New York may use.

In the Tenderloin, the place of theatres, and of the restaurant where gayer New York does her dining, the cable cars in the evening carry a stratum of society which looks like a new one, but it is of the familiar strata in other clothes. It is just as good as a new stratum, however, for in evening dress the average man feels that he has gone up three pegs in the social scale, and there is considerable evening dress about a Broadway car in the evening. A car with its electric lamp resembles a brilliantly-lighted salon, and the atmosphere grows just a trifle strained. People sit more rigidly, and glance sidewise, perhaps, as if each was positive of possessing social value, but was doubtful of all others. The conductor says: "Ah, gwan. Git off th' earth." But this is to a man at Canal Street. That shows his versatility. He stands on the platform and beams in a modest and polite manner into the car. He notes a lifted finger and grabs swiftly for the bell strap. He reaches down to help a woman aboard. Perhaps his demeanour is a reflection of the manner of the people in the car. No one is in a mad New York hurry; no one is fretting and muttering; no one is perched upon his neighbour's toes. Moreover, the Tenderloin is a glory at night. Broadway of late years has fallen heir to countless signs illuminated with red, blue, green, and gold electric lamps, and the people certainly fly to these as the moths go to a candle. And perhaps the gods have allowed this opportunity to observe and study the best-dressed crowds in the world to operate upon the conductor until his mood is to treat us with care and mildness.

Late at night, after the diners and theatre-goers have been lost in Harlem, various inebriate persons may perchance emerge from the darker regions of Sixth Avenue and swing their arms solemnly at the gripman. If the Broadway cars run for the next 7000 years this will be the only time when one New Yorker will address another in public without an excuse sent direct from heaven. In these cars late at night it is not impossible that some fearless drunkard will attempt to inaugurate a general conversation. He is quite willing to devote his ability to the affair. He tells of the fun he thinks he has had; describes his feelings; recounts stories of his dim past. None reply, although all listen with every ear. The rake probably ends by borrowing a match, lighting a cigar, and entering into a wrangle with the conductor with an abandon, a ferocity, and a courage that do not come to us when we are sober.

In the meantime the figures on the street grow fewer and fewer. Strolling policemen test the locks of the great dark-fronted stores. Nighthawk cabs whirl by the cars on their mysterious errands. Finally the cars themselves depart in the way of the citizen, and for the few hours before dawn a new sound comes into the still thoroughfare—the cable whirring in its channel underground.

THE ASSASSIN IN MODERN BATTLES.

The Torpedo Boat Destroyers that "Perform in the Darkness. An Act which Is more Peculiarly Murderous than most Things in War."

In the past century the gallant aristocracy of London liked to travel down the south bank of the Thames to Greenwich Hospital, where venerable pensioners of the crown were ready to hire telescopes at a penny each, and with these telescopes the lords and ladies were able to view at a better advantage the dried and enchained corpses of pirates hanging from the gibbets on the Isle of Dogs. In those times the dismal marsh was inhabited solely by the clanking figures whose feet moved in the wind like rather poorly-constructed weather cocks.

But even the Isle of Dogs could not escape the appetite of an expanding London. Thousands of souls now live on it, and it has changed its character from that of a place of execution, with mist, wet with fever, coiling forever from the mire and wandering among the black gibbets, to that of an ordinary, squalid, nauseating slum of London, whose streets bear a faint resemblance to that part of Avenue A which lies directly above Sixtieth Street in New York.

Down near the water front one finds a long brick building, three-storeyed and signless, which shuts off all view of the river. The windows, as well as the bricks, are very dirty, and you see no sign of life, unless some smudged workman dodges in through a little door. The place might be a factory for the making of lamps or stair rods, or any ordinary commercial thing. As a matter of fact, the building fronts the shipyard of Yarrow, the builder of torpedo boats, the maker of knives for the nations, the man who provides everybody with a certain kind of efficient weapon. One then remembers that if Russia fights England, Yarrow meets Yarrow; if Germany fights France, Yarrow meets Yarrow; if Chili fights Argentina, Yarrow meets Yarrow.

Besides the above-mentioned countries Yarrow has built torpedo boats for Italy, Austria, Holland, Japan, China, Ecuador, Brazil, Costa Rica, and Spain. There is a keeper of a great shop in London who is known as the

Universal Provider. If a general conflagration of war should break out in the world, Yarrow would be known as one of the Universal Warriors, for it would practically be a battle between Yarrow, Armstrong, Krupp, and a few other firms. This is what makes interesting the dinginess of the cantonment on the Isle of Dogs.

The great Yarrow forte is to build speedy steamers of a tonnage of not more than 240 tons. This practically includes only yachts, launches, tugs, torpedo boat destroyers, torpedo boats, and of late shallow-draught gunboats for service on the Nile, Congo, and Niger. Some of the gunboats that shelled the dervishes from the banks of the Nile below Khartoum were built by Yarrow. Yarrow is always in action somewhere. Even if the firm's boats do not appear in every coming sea combat, the ideas of the firm will, for many nations, notably France and Germany, have bought specimens of the best models of Yarrow construction in order to reduplicate and reduplicate them in their own yards.

When the great fever to possess torpedo boats came upon the Powers of Europe, England was at first left far in the rear. Either Germany or France to-day has in her fleet more torpedo boats than has England. The British tar is a hard man to oust out of a habit. He had a habit of thinking that his battleships and cruisers were the final thing in naval construction. He scoffed at the advent of the torpedo boat. He did not scoff intelligently but because, mainly, he hated to be forced to change his ways.

You will usually find an Englishman balking and kicking at innovation up to the last moment. It takes him some years to get an idea into his head, and when finally it is inserted, he not only respects it, he reveres it. The Londoners have a fire brigade which would interest the ghost of a Babylonian, as an example of how much the method of extinguishing fires could degenerate in two thousand years, and in 1897, when a terrible fire devastated a part of the city, some voices were raised challenging the efficiency of the fire brigade. But that part of the London County Council which corresponds to fire commissioners in United States laid their hands upon their hearts and solemnly assured the public that they had investigated the matter, and had found the London fire brigade to be as good as any in the world. There were some isolated cases of dissent, but the great English public as a whole placidly accepted these assurances concerning the activity of the honoured corps.

For a long time England blundered in the same way over the matter of torpedo boats. They were authoritatively informed that there was nothing in all the talk about torpedo boats. Then came a great popular uproar, in which people tumbled over each other to get to the doors of the Admiralty and howl about torpedo boats. It was an awakening as unreasonable as had been the previous indifference and contempt. Then England began to build. She has never overtaken France or Germany in the number of torpedo boats, but she now heads the world with her collection of that marvel of marine architecture—the torpedo boat destroyer. She has about sixty-five of these vessels now in commission, and has about as many more in course of building.

People ordinarily have a false idea of the appearance of a destroyer. The common type is longer than an ordinary gunboat—a long, low, graceful thing, flying through the water at fabulous speed, with a great curve of water some yards back of the bow, and smoke flying horizontally from the three or four stacks.

Bushing this way and that way, circling, dodging, turning, they are like demons.

The best kind of modern destroyer has a length of 220 feet, with a beam of 26½ feet. The horse-power is about 6500, driving the boat at a speed of thirty-one knots or more. The engines are triple-expansion, with water tube boilers. They carry from 70 to 100 tons of coal, and at a speed of eight or nine knots can keep the sea for a week; so they are independent of coaling in a voyage of between 1300 and 1500 miles. They carry a crew of three or four officers, and about forty men.

They are armed usually with one twelve-pounder gun, and from three to five six-pounder guns, besides their equipment of torpedoes. Their hulls and top hamper are painted olive, buff, or preferably slate, in order to make them hard to find with the eye at sea.

Their principal functions, theoretically, are to discover and kill the enemy's torpedo boats, guard and scout for the main squadron, and perform messenger service. However, they are also torpedo boats of a most formidable kind, and in action will be found carrying out the torpedo boat idea in an expanded form. Four destroyers of this type building at the Yarrow yards were for Japan (1898).

The modern European ideal of a torpedo boat is a craft 152 feet long, with a beam of 15¼ feet. When the boat is fully loaded a speed of 24 knots is derived from her 2000 horse-power engines. The destroyers are twin screw, whereas the torpedo boats are commonly propelled by a single screw. The speed of twenty knots is for a run of three hours. These boats are not designed to keep at sea for any great length of time, and cannot raid toward a distant coast without the constant attendance of a cruiser to keep them in coal and provisions. Primarily they are for defence. Even with destroyers, England, in lately reinforcing her foreign stations, has seen fit to send cruisers in order to provide help for them in stormy weather.

Some years ago it was thought the proper thing to equip torpedo craft with rudders, which would enable them to turn in their own length when running at full speed. Yarrow found this to result in too much broken steering gear, and the firm's boats now have smaller rudders, which enable them to turn in a larger circle.

At one time a torpedo boat steaming at her best gait always carried a great bone in her teeth. During manœuvres the watch on the deck of a battleship often discovered the approach of the little enemy by the great white wave which the boat rolled at her bows during her headlong rush. This was mainly because the old-fashioned boats carried two torpedo tubes set in the bows, and the bows were consequently bluff.

The modern boat carries the great part of her armament amidships and astern on swivels, and her bow is like a dagger. With no more bow-waves, and with these phantom colours of buff, olive, bottle-green, or slate, the principal foe to a safe attack at night is bad firing in the stoke-room, which might cause flames to leap out of the stacks.

A captain of an English battleship recently remarked: "See those five destroyers lying there? Well, if they should attack me I would sink four of them, but the fifth one would sink me."

This was repeated to Yarrow's manager, who said: "He wouldn't sink four of them if the attack were at night and the boats were shrewdly and courageously handled." Anyhow, the captain's remark goes to show the wholesome respect which the great battleship has for these little fliers.

The Yarrow people say there is no sense in a torpedo flotilla attack on anything save vessels. A modern fortification is never built near enough to the water for a torpedo explosion to injure it, and, although some old stone flush-with-the-water castle might be badly crumpled, it would harm nobody in particular, even if the assault were wholly successful.

Of course, if a torpedo boat could get a chance at piers and dock gates they would make a disturbance, but the chance is extremely remote if the defenders have ordinary vigilance and some rapid fire guns. In harbour defence the searchlight would naturally play a most important part, whereas at sea experts are beginning to doubt its use as an auxiliary to the rapid fire guns against torpedo boats. About half the time it does little more than betray the position of the ship. On the other hand, a port cannot conceal its position anyhow, and searchlights would be invaluable for sweeping the narrow channels.

There could be only one direction from which the assault could come, and all the odds would be in favour of the guns on shore. A torpedo boat commander knows this perfectly. What he wants is a ship off at sea with a nervous crew staring into the encircling darkness from any point in which the terror might be coming.

Hi, then, for a grand, bold, silent rush and the assassin-like stab.

In stormy weather life on board a torpedo boat is not amusing. They tumble about like bucking bronchos, especially if they are going at anything like speed. Everything is battened down as if it were soldered, and the watch below feel that they are living in a football, which is being kicked every way at once.

And finally, while Yarrow and other great builders can make torpedo craft which are wonders of speed and manœuvring power, they cannot make that high spirit of daring and hardihood which is essential to a success.

That must exist in the mind of some young lieutenant who, knowing well that if he is detected, a shot or so from a rapid fire gun will cripple him if it does not sink him absolutely, nevertheless goes creeping off to sea to find a huge antagonist and perform stealthily in the darkness an act which is more peculiarly murderous than most things in war.

If a torpedo boat is caught within range in daylight, the fighting is all over before it begins. Any common little gunboat can dispose of it in a moment if the gunnery is not too Chinese.

IRISH NOTES

I.—AN OLD MAN GOES WOOING.

The melancholy fisherman made his way through a street that was mainly as dark as a tunnel. Sometimes an open door threw a rectangle of light upon the pavement, and within the cottages were scenes of working women and men, who comfortably smoked and talked. From them came the sounds of laughter and the babble of children. Each time the old man passed through one of the radiant zones the light etched his face in profile with touches flaming and sombre until there was a resemblance to a stern and mournful Dante portrait.

Once a whistling lad came through the darkness. He peered intently for purposes of recognition. "Good avenin', Mickey," he cried cheerfully. The old man responded with a groan, which intimated that the lamentable reckless optimism of the youth had forced from him an expression of an emotion that he had been enduring in saintly patience and silence. He continued his pilgrimage toward the kitchen of the village inn.

The kitchen is a great and worthy place. The long range with its lurid heat continually emits the fragrance of broiling fish, roasting mutton, joints, and fowl. The high black ceiling is ornamented with hams and flitches of bacon. There is a long, dark bench against one wall, and it is fronted by a dark table, handy for glasses of stout. On an old mahogany dresser rows of plates face the distant range, and reflect the red shine of the peat. Smoke which has in it the odour of an American forest fire eddies through the air. The great stones of the floor are scarred by the black mud from the inn yard. And here the gossip of a country-side goes on amid the sizzle of broiling fish and the loud protesting splutter of joints taken from the oven.

When the old man reached the door of this paradise, he stopped for a moment with his finger on the latch. He sighed deeply; evidently he was undergoing some lachrymose reflection. For somewhere overhead in the inn he could hear the wild clamour of dining pig-buyers, men who were come for the pig fair to be held on the morrow. Evidently in the little parlour of the inn these men were dining amid an uproar of shouted jests and laughter. The revelry sounded like the fighting of two mobs amid a rain of missiles and crash of shop windows. The old man raised his hand as if, unseen there in the darkness, he was going to solemnly damn the dinner of the pig-buyers.

Within the kitchen Nora, tall, strong, intrepid, approached the fiery stove in the manner of a boxer. Her left arm was held high to guard her face, which was already crimson from the blaze. With a flourish of her apron she achieved a great brown humming joint from the oven, and, emerging a glowing and triumphant figure from the steam and smoke and rapid play of heat, she slid the pan upon the table, even as she saw the old man standing within the room and lugubriously cleaning the mud from his boots. "Tis you, Mickey?" she said.

He made no reply until he had found his way to the long bench. "It is," he said then. It was clear that in the girl's opinion he had gained some kind of strategic advantage. The sanctity of her kitchen was successfully violated, but the old man betrayed no elation. Lifting one knee and placing it over the other, he grunted in the blissful weariness of a venerable labourer returned to his own fireside. He coughed dismally. "Ah, 'tis no good a man gits from fishin' these days. I moind the toimes whin they would be hoppin' up clear o' the wather, there was that little room fur thim. I would be likin' a bottle o' stout."

"Niver fear you, Mickey," answered the girl. Swinging here and there in the glare of the fire, Nora, with her towering figure and bare brawny arms, was like a feminine blacksmith at a forge. The old man, pallid, emaciated, watched her from the shadows at the other side of the room. The lines from the sides of his nose to the corners of his mouth sank low to an expression of despair deeper than any moans. He should have been painted upon the door of a tomb with wringing willows arched above him and men in grey robes slowly booming the drums of death. Finally he spoke. "I would be likin' a bottle o' stout, Nora, me girrl," he said.

"Niver fear you, Mickey," again she replied with cheerful obstinacy. She was admiring her famous roast, which now sat in its platter on the rack over the range. There was a lull in her tumultuous duties. The old man coughed and moved his foot with a scraping sound on the stones. The noise of dining pig-buyers, now heard through doors and winding corridors of the inn, was a roll of far-away storm.

A woman in a dark dress entered the kitchen and keenly examined the roast and Nora's other feats. "Mickey here would be wantin' a bottle o' stout," said the girl to her mistress. The woman turned towards the spectral figure in the gloom, and regarded it quietly with a clear eye. "Have yez the money, Mickey?" repeated the woman of the house.

Profoundly embittered, he replied in short terms, "I have."

"There now," cried Nora, in astonishment and admiration. Poising a large iron spoon, she was motionless, staring with open mouth at the old man. He searched his pockets slowly during a complete silence in the kitchen. He brought forth two coppers and laid them sadly, reproachfully, and yet defiantly on the table.

"There now," cried Nora, stupefied.

They brought him a bottle of the black brew, and Nora poured it out for him with her own red hand, which looked to be as broad as his chest. A collar of brown foam curled at the top of the glass. With measured moments the old man filled a short pipe. There came a sudden howl from another part of the inn. One of the pig-buyers was at the head of the stairs bawling for the mistress. The two women hurriedly freighted themselves with the roast and the vegetables, and sprang with them to placate the pig-buyers. Alone, the old man studied the gleam of the fire on the floor. It faded and brightened in the way of lightning at the horizon's edge.

When Nora returned, the strapping grenadier of a girl was blushing and giggling. The pig-buyers had been humorous. "I moind the toime—" began the man sorrowfully. "I moind the toime whin yea was a wee bit of a girrl,

Nora, an' wouldn't be havin' words wid min loike thim buyers."

"I moind the toime whin yea could attind to your own affairs, ye ould skileton," said the girl promptly. He made a gesture, which may have expressed his stirring grief at the levity of the new generation, and then lapsed into another stillness.

The girl, a giantess, carrying, lifting, pushing, an incarnation of dauntless labour, changing the look of the whole kitchen with a moment's manipulation of her great arms, did not heed the old man for a long time. When she finally glanced toward him, she saw that he was sunk forward with his grey face on his arms. A growl of heavy breathing ascended. He was asleep.

She marched to him and put both hands to his collar. Despite his feeble and dreamy protestations, she dragged him out from behind the table and across the floor. She opened the door and thrust him into the night.

II.—BALLYDEHOB.

The illimitable inventive incapacity of the excursion companies has made many circular paths throughout Ireland, and on these well-pounded roads the guardians of the touring public may be seen drilling the little travellers in squads. To rise in rebellion, to face the superior clerk in his bureau, to endure his smile of pity and derision, and finally to wring freedom from him, is as difficult in some parts of Ireland as it is in all parts of Switzerland. To see the tourists chained in gangs and taken to see the Lakes of Killarney is a sad spectacle, because these people believe that they are learning Ireland, even as men believe that they are studying America when they contemplate the Niagara Falls.

But afterwards, if one escapes, one can go forth, unguided, untaught and alone, and look at Ireland. The joys of the pig-market, the delirium of a little tap-room filled with brogue, the fierce excitement of viewing the Royal Irish Constabulary fishing for trout, the whole quaint and primitive machinery of the peasant life—its melancholy, its sunshine, its humour—all this is then the property of the man who breaks like a Texan steer out of the pens and corrals of the tourist agencies. For what syndicate of maiden ladies—it is these who masquerade as tourist agencies—what syndicate of maiden ladies knows of the existence, for instance, of Ballydehob?

One has a sense of disclosure at writing the name of Ballydehob. It was really a valuable secret. There is in Ballydehob not one thing that is commonly pointed out to the stranger as a thing worthy of a half-tone reproduction in a book. There is no cascade, no peak, no lake, no guide with a fund of useless information, no gamins practised in the seduction of tourists. It is not an exhibit, an entry for a prize, like a heap of melons or cow. It is simply an Irish village wherein live some three hundred Irish and four constables.

If one or two prayer-towers spindled above Ballydehob it would be a perfect Turkish village. The red tiles and red bricks of England do not appear at all. The houses are low, with soiled white walls. The doors open abruptly upon dark old rooms. Here and there in the street is some crude cobbling done with round stones taken from the bed of a brook. At times there is a great deal of mud. Chickens depredate warily about the doorsteps, and intent pigs emerge for plunder from the alleys. It is unavoidable to admit that many people would consider Ballydehob quite too grimy.

Nobody lives here that has money. The average English tradesman with his back-breaking respect for this class, his reflex contempt for that class, his reverence for the tin gods, could here be a commercial lord and bully the people in one or two ways, until they were thrown back upon the defence which is always near them, the ability to cut his skin into strips with a wit that would be a foreign tongue to him. For amid his wrongs and his rights and his failures—his colossal failures—the Irishman retains this delicate blade for his enemies, for his friends, for himself, the ancestral dagger of fast sharp speaking from fast sharp seeing—an inheritance which could move the world. And the Royal Irish Constabulary fished for trout in the adjacent streams.

Mrs. Kearney keeps the hotel. In Ireland male innkeepers die young. Apparently they succumb to conviviality when it is presented to them in the guise of a business duty. Naturally honest, temperate men, their consciences are lulled to false security by this idea of hard drinking being necessary to the successful keeping of a public-house. It is very terrible.

But they invariably leave behind them capable widows, women who do not recognise conviviality as a business obligation. And so all through Ireland one finds these brisk widows keeping hotels with a precision that is almost military.

In Kearney's there is always a wonderful collection of old women, bent figures shrouded in shawls who reach up scrawny fingers to take their little purchases from Mary Agnes, who presides sometimes at the bar, but more often at the shop that fronts it in the same room. In the gloom of a late afternoon these old women are as mystic as the swinging, chanting witches on a dark stage when the thunder-drum rolls and the lightning flashes by schedule. When a grey rain sweeps through the narrow street of Ballydehob, and makes heavy shadows in Kearney's tap-room, these old creatures, with their high mournful voices, and the mystery of their shawls, their moans and aged mutterings when they are obliged to take a step, raise the dead superstitions from the bottom of a man's mind.

"My boy," remarked my London friend cheerfully, "these might have furnished sons to be Aldermen or Congressmen in the great city of New York."

"Aldermen or Congressmen of the great city of New York always take care of their mothers," I answered meekly.

On a barrel, over in a corner, sat a yellow-bearded Irish farmer in tattered clothes who wished to exchange views on the Armenian massacres. He had much information and a number of theories in regard to them. He also advanced the opinion that the chief political aim of Russia at present is in the direction of China, and that it behoved other Powers to keep an eye on her. He thought the revolutionists in Cuba would never accept autonomy at the hands of Spain. His pipe glowed comfortably from his corner; waving the tuppenny glass of stout in the air, he discoursed on the business of the remote ends of the earth with the glibness of a fourth secretary of Legation. Here was a little farmer, digging betimes in a forlorn patch of wet ground, a man to whom a sudden two shillings would appear as a miracle, a ragged, unkempt peasant, whose mind roamed the world like the soul of a lost diplomat. This unschooled man believed that the earth was a sphere inhabited by men that are alike in the essentials, different in the manners, the little manners, which are accounted of such great importance by the emaciated. He was to a degree capable of knowing that he lived on a sphere and not on the apex of a triangle.

And yet, when the talk had turned another corner, he confidently assured the assembled company that a hair from a horse's tail when thrown in a brook would turn shortly to an eel.

III.—THE ROYAL IRISH CONSTABULARY.

The newspapers called it a Veritable Arsenal. There was a description of how the sergeant of Constabulary had bent an ear to receive whispered information of the concealed arms, and had then marched his men swiftly and by night to surround a certain house. The search elicited a double-barrelled breech-loading shot-gun, some empty shells, powder, shot, and a loading machine. The point of it was that some of the Irish papers called it a Veritable Arsenal, and appeared to congratulate the Government upon having strangled another unhappy rebellion in its nest. They floundered and misnamed and mis-reasoned, and made a spectacle of the great modern craft of journalism, until the affair of this poor poacher was too absurd to be pitiable, and Englishmen over their coffee next morning must have almost believed that the prompt action of the Constabulary had quelled a rising. Thus it is that the Irish fight the Irish.

One cannot look Ireland straight in the face without seeing a great many constables. The country is dotted with little garrisons. It must have been said a thousand times that there is an absolute military occupation. The fact is too plain.

The constable himself becomes a figure interesting in its isolation. He has in most cases a social position which is somewhat analogous to that of a Turk in Thessaly. But then, in the same way, the Turk has the Turkish army. He can have battalions as companions and make the acquaintance of brigades. The constable has the Constabulary, it is true; but to be cooped with three or four others in a small white-washed iron-bound house on some bleak country side is not an exact parallel to the Thessalian situation. It looks to be a life that is infinitely lonely, ascetic, and barren. Two keepers of a lighthouse at a bitter end of land in a remote sea will, if they are properly let alone, make a murder in time. Five constables imprisoned 'mid a folk that will not turn a face toward them, five constables planted in a populated silence, may develop an acute and vivid economy, dwell in scowling dislike. A religious asylum in a snow-buried mountain pass will breed conspiring monks. A separated people will beget an egotism that is almost titanic. A world floating distinctly in space will call itself the only world. The progression is perfect.

But the constables take the second degree. They are next to the lighthouse keepers. The national custom of meeting stranger and friend alike on the road with a cheery greeting like "God save you" is too kindly and human a habit not to be missed. But all through the South of Ireland one sees the peasant turn his eyes pretentiously to the side of the road at the passing of the constable. It seemed to be generally understood that to note the presence of a constable was to make a conventional error. None looked, nodded, or gave sign. There was a line drawn so sternly that it reared like a fence. Of course, any police force in any part of the world can gather at its heels a riff-raff of people, fawning always on a hand licensed to strike that would be larger than the army of the Potomac, but of these one ordinarily sees little. The mass of the Irish strictly obey the stern tenet. One hears often of the ostracism or other punishment that befell some girl who was caught flirting with a constable.

Naturally the constable retreats to his pride. He is commonly a soldierly-looking chap, straight, lean, long-strided, well set-up. His little saucer of a forage cap sits obediently on his ear, as it does for the British soldier. He swings a little cane. He takes his medicine with a calm and hard face, and evidently stares full into every eye. But it is singular to find in the situation of the Royal Irish Constabulary the quality of pathos.

It is not known if these places in the South of Ireland are called disturbed districts. Over them hangs the peace of Surrey, but the word disturbance has an elastic arrangement by which it can be made to cover anything. All of the villages visited garrisoned from four to ten men. They lived comfortably in their white houses, strolled in pairs over the country roads, picked blackberries, and fished for trout. If at some time there came a crisis, one man was more than enough to surround it. The remaining nine add dignity to the scene. The crisis chiefly consisted of occasional drunken men who were unable to understand the local geography on Saturday nights.

The note continually struck was that each group of constables lived on a little social island, and there was no boat to take them off. There has been no such marooning since the days of the pirates. The sequestration must be complete when a man with a dinky little cap on his ear is not allowed to talk to the girls.

But they fish for trout. Isaac Walton is the father of the Royal Irish Constabulary. They could be seen on any fine day whipping the streams from source to mouth. There was one venerable sergeant who made a rod less than a yard long. With a line of about the same length attached to this rod, he hunted the gorse-hung banks of the little streams in the hills. An eight-inch ribbon of water lined with masses of heather and gorse will be accounted contemptible by a fisherman with an ordinary rod. But it was the pleasure of the sergeant to lay on his stomach at the side of such a stream and carefully, inch by inch, scout his hook through the pools. He probably caught more trout than any three men in county Cork. He fished more than any twelve men in the county Cork. Some people had never seen him in any other posture but that of crowding forward on his stomach to peer into a pool. They did not believe the rumour that he sometimes stood or walked like a human.

IV.—A FISHING VILLAGE.

The brook curved down over the rocks, innocent and white, until it faced a little strand of smooth gravel and flat stones. It turned then to the left, and thereafter its guilty current was tinged with the pink of diluted blood. Boulders standing neck-deep in the water were rimmed with red; they wore bloody collars whose tops marked the supreme instant of some tragic movement of the stream. In the pale green shallows of the bay's edge, the outward flow from the criminal little brook was as eloquently marked as if a long crimson carpet had been laid upon the waters. The scene of the carnage was the strand of smooth gravel and flat stones, and the fruit of the carnage was cleaned mackerel.

Far to the south, where the slate of the sea and the grey of the sky wove together, could be seen Fastnet Rock, a mere button on the moving, shimmering cloth, while a liner, no larger than a needle, spun a thread of smoke aslant. The gulls swept screaming along the dull line of the other shore of roaring Water Bay, and near the mouth of the brook circled among the fishing boats that lay at anchor, their brown, leathery sails idle and straight. The wheeling, shrieking tumultuous birds stared with their hideous unblinking eyes at the Capers—men from Cape Clear—who prowled to and fro on the decks amid shouts and the creak of the tackle. Shoreward, a little shrivelled man, overcome by a profound melancholy, fished hopelessly from the end of the pier. Back of him, on a hillside, sat a white village, nestled among more trees than is common in this part of Southern Ireland.

A dinghy sculled by a youth in a blue jersey wobbled rapidly past the pier-head and stopped at the foot of the moss-green, dank, stone steps, where the waves were making slow but regular leaps to mount higher, and then falling back gurgling, choking, and waving the long, dark seaweeds. The melancholy fisherman walked over to the top of the steps. The young man was fastening the painter of his boat in an iron ring. In the dinghy were three round baskets heaped high with mackerel. They glittered like masses of new silver coin at times, and then other lights of faint carmine and peacock blue would chase across the sides of the fish in a radiance that was finer than silver.

The melancholy fisherman looked at this wealth. He shook his head mournfully. "Ah, now, Denny. This would not be a very good kill."

The young man snorted indignantly at his fellow-townsman. "This will be th' bist kill th' year, Mickey. Go along now."

The melancholy old man became immersed in deeper gloom. "Shure I have been in th' way of seein' miny a grand day whin th' fish was runnin' sthrong in these wathers, but there will be no more big kills here. No more. No more." At the last his voice was only a dismal croak.

"Come along outa that now, Mickey," cried the youth impatiently. "Come away wid you."

"All gone now. A-ll go-o-ne now!" The old man wagged his grey head, and, standing over the baskets of fishes, groaned as Mordecai groaned for his people.

"'Tis you would be cryin' out, Mickey, whativer," said the youth with scorn. He was giving his basket into the hands of five incompetent but jovial little boys to carry to a waiting donkey cart.

"An' why should I not?" said the old man sternly. "Me—in want—"

As the youth swung his boat swiftly out toward an anchored smack, he made answer in a softer tone. "Shure, if yez got for th' askin', 'tis you, Mickey, that would niver be in want." The melancholy old man returned to his line. And the only moral in this incident is that the young man is the type that America procures from Ireland, and the old man is one of the home types, bent, pallid, hungry, disheartened, with a vision that magnifies with a microscope glance any fly-wing of misfortune, and heroically and conscientiously invents disasters for the future. Usually the thing that remains to one of this type is a sympathy as quick and acute for others as is his pity for himself.

The donkey with his cart-load of gleaming fish, and escorted by the whooping and laughing boys, galloped along the quay and up a street of the village until he was turned off at the gravelly strand, at the point where the colour of the brook was changing. Here twenty people of both sexes and all ages were preparing the fish for market. The mackerel, beautiful as fire-etched salvers, first were passed to a long table, around which worked as many women as could have elbow room. Each one could clean a fish with two motions of the knife. Then the washers, men who stood over the troughs filled with running water from the brook, soused the fish until the outlet became a sinister element that in an instant changed the brook from a happy thing of gorse and heather of the hills to an evil stream, sullen and reddened. After being washed, the fish were carried to a group of girls with knives, who made the cuts that enabled each fish to flatten out in the manner known of the breakfast table. And after the girls came the men and boys, who rubbed each fish thoroughly with great handfuls of coarse salt, which was whiter than snow, and shone in the daylight from a multitude of gleaming points, diamond-like. Last came the packers, drilled in the art of getting neither too few nor too many mackerel into a barrel, sprinkling constantly prodigal layers of brilliant salt. There were many intermediate corps of boys and girls carrying fish from point to point, and sometimes building them in stacks convenient to the hands of the more important labourers.

A vast tree hung its branches over the place. The leaves made a shadow that was religious in its effect, as if the spot was a chapel consecrated to labour. There was a hush upon the devotees. The women at the large table worked intently, steadfastly, with bowed heads. Their old petticoats were tucked high, showing the coarse brogans which they wore—and the visible ankles were proportioned to the brogans as the diameter of a straw is to that of a half-crown. The national red under-petticoat was a fundamental part of the scene.

Just over the wall, in the sloping street, could be seen the bejerseyed Capers, brawny, and with shocks of yellow beard. They paced slowly to and fro amid the geese and children. They, too, spoke little, even to each other; they smoked short pipes in saturnine dignity and silence. It was the fish. They who go with nets upon the reeling sea grow still with the mystery and solemnity of the trade. It was Brittany; the first respectable catch of the year had changed this garrulous Irish hamlet into a hamlet of Brittany.

The Capers were waiting for high tide. It had seemed for a long time that, for the south of Ireland, the mackerel had fled in company with potato; but here, at any rate, was a temporary success, and the occasion was momentous. A strolling Caper took his pipe and pointed with the stem out upon the bay. There was little wind, but an ambitious skipper had raised his anchor, and the craft, her strained brown sails idly swinging, was drifting away on the first oily turn of the tide.

On the top of the pier the figure of the melancholy old man was portrayed upon the polished water. He was still dangling his line hopelessly. He gazed down into the misty water. Once he stirred and murmured: "Bad luck to thim." Otherwise he seemed to remain motionless for hours. One by one the fishing-boats floated away. The brook changed its colour, and in the dusk showed a tumble of pearly white among the rocks.

A cold night wind, sweeping transversely across the pier, awakened perhaps the rheumatism in the old man's bones. He arose and, mumbling and grumbling, began to wind his line. The waves were lashing the stones. He moved off towards the intense darkness of the village streets.

SULLIVAN COUNTY SKETCHES

FOUR MEN IN A CAVE.

Likewise Four Queens, and a Sullivan County Hermit.

The moon rested for a moment on the top of a tall pine on a hill.

The little man was standing in front of the campfire making orations to his companions.

"We can tell a great tale when we get back to the city if we investigate this thing," said he, in conclusion.

They were won.

The little man was determined to explore a cave, because its black mouth had gaped at him. The four men took lighted pine-knot and clambered over boulders down a hill. In a thicket on the mountainside lay a little tilted hole. At its side they halted.

"Well?" said the little man.

They fought for last place and the little man was overwhelmed. He tried to struggle from under by crying that if the fat, pudgy man came after, he would be corked. But he finally administered a cursing over his shoulder and crawled into the hole. His companions gingerly followed.

A passage, the floor of damp clay and pebbles, the walls slimy, green-mossed, and dripping, sloped downward. In the cave atmosphere the torches became studies in red blaze and black smoke.

"Ho!" cried the little man, stifled and bedraggled, "let's go back." His companions were not brave. They were last. The next one to the little man pushed him on, so the little man said sulphurous words and cautiously continued his crawl.

Things that hung seemed to be on the wet, uneven ceiling, ready to drop upon the men's bare necks. Under their hands the clammy floor seemed alive and writhing. When the little man endeavoured to stand erect the ceiling forced him down. Knobs and points came out and punched him. His clothes were wet and mud-covered, and his eyes, nearly blinded by smoke, tried to pierce the darkness always before his torch.

"Oh, I say, you fellows, let's go back," cried he. At that moment he caught the gleam of trembling light in the blurred shadows before him.

"Ho!" he said, "here's another way out."

The passage turned abruptly. The little man put one hand around the corner, but it touched nothing. He investigated and discovered that the little corridor took a sudden dip down a hill. At the bottom shone a yellow light.

The little man wriggled painfully about, and descended feet in advance. The others followed his plan. All picked their way with anxious care. The traitorous rocks rolled from beneath the little man's feet and roared thunderously below him. Lesser stone, loosened by the men above him, hit him on the back. He gained seemingly firm foothold, and, turning half-way about, swore redly at his companions for dolts and careless fools. The pudgy man sat, puffing and perspiring, high in the rear of the procession. The fumes and smoke from four pine-knots were in his blood. Cinders and sparks lay thick in his eyes and hair. The pause of the little man angered him.

"Go on, you fool," he shouted. "Poor, painted man, you are afraid."

"Ho!" said the little man. "Come down here and go on yourself, imbecile!"

The pudgy man vibrated with passion. He leaned downward. "Idiot—!"

He was interrupted by one of his feet which flew out and crashed into the man in front of and below. It is not well to quarrel upon a slippery incline, when the unknown is below. The fat man, having lost the support of one pillar-like foot, lurched forward. His body smote the next man, who hurtled into the next man. Then they all fell upon the cursing little man.

They slid in a body down over the slippery, slimy floor of the passage. The stone avenue must have wibble-wobbled with the rush of this ball of tangled men and strangled cries. The torches went out with the combined assault upon the little man. The adventurers whirled to the unknown in darkness. The little man felt that he was pitching to death, but even in his convolutions he bit and scratched at his companions, for he was satisfied that it was their fault. The swirling mass went some twenty feet, and lit upon a level, dry place in a strong, yellow light of candles. It dissolved and became eyes.

The four men lay in a heap upon the floor of a grey chamber. A small fire smouldered in the corner, the smoke disappearing in a crack. In another corner was a bed of faded hemlock boughs and two blankets. Cooking utensils and clothes lay about, with boxes and a barrel.

Of these things the four men took small cognisance. The pudgy man did not curse the little man, nor did the little swear, in the abstract. Eight widened eyes were fixed upon the centre of the room of rocks.

A great, grey stone, cut squarely, like an altar, sat in the middle of the floor. Over it burned three candles, in swaying tin cups hung from the ceiling. Before it, with what seemed to be a small volume clasped in his yellow fingers, stood a man. He was an infinitely sallow person in the brown-checked shirt of the ploughs and cows. The rest of his apparel was boots. A long grey beard dangled from his chin. He fixed glinting, fiery eyes upon the heap of men, and remained motionless. Fascinated, their tongues cleaving, their blood cold, they arose to their feet. The gleaming glance of the recluse swept slowly over the group until it found the face of the little man. There it stayed and burned.

The little man shrivelled and crumpled as the dried leaf under the glass.

Finally, the recluse slowly, deeply spoke. It was a true voice from a cave, cold, solemn, and damp.

"It's your ante," he said.

"What?" said the little man.

The hermit tilted his beard and laughed a laugh that was either the chatter of a banshee in a storm or the rattle of pebbles in a tin box. His visitors' flesh seemed ready to drop from their bones.

They huddled together and cast fearful eyes over their shoulders. They whispered.

"A vampire!" said one.

"A ghoul!" said another.

"A Druid before the sacrifice," murmured another.

"The shade of an Aztec witch doctor," said the little man.

As they looked, the inscrutable face underwent a change. It became a livid background for his eyes, which blazed at the little man like impassioned carbuncles. His voice arose to a howl of ferocity. "It's your ante!" With a panther-like motion he drew a long, thin knife and advanced, stooping. Two cadaverous hounds came from nowhere, and, scowling and growling, made desperate feints at the little man's legs. His quaking companions pushed him forward.

Tremblingly he put his hand to his pocket.

"How much?" he said, with a shivering look at the knife that glittered.

The carbuncles faded.

"Three dollars," said the hermit, in sepulchral tones which rang against the walls and among the passages, awakening long-dead spirits with voices. The shaking little man took a roll of bills from a pocket and placed "three ones" upon the altar-like stone. The recluse looked at the little volume with reverence in his eyes. It was a pack of playing cards.

Under the three swinging candles, upon the altar-like stone, the grey beard and the agonised little man played at poker. The three other men crouched in a corner, and stared with eyes that gleamed with terror. Before them sat the cadaverous hounds licking their red lips. The candles burned low, and began to flicker. The fire in the corner expired.

Finally, the game came to a point where the little man laid down his hand and quavered: "I can't call you this time, sir. I'm dead broke."

"What?" shrieked the recluse. "Not call me! Villain! Dastard! Cur! I have four queens, miscreant." His voice grew so mighty that it could not fit his throat. He choked, wrestling with his lungs for a moment. Then the power of his body was concentrated in a word: "Go!"

He pointed a quivering, yellow finger at a wide crack in the rock. The little man threw himself at it with a howl. His erstwhile frozen companions felt their blood throb again. With great bounds they plunged after the little man. A minute of scrambling, falling, and pushing brought them to open air. They climbed the distance to their camp in furious springs.

The sky in the east was a lurid yellow. In the west the footprints of departing night lay on the pine trees. In front of their replenished camp fire sat John Willerkins, the guide.

"Hello!" he shouted at their approach. "Be you fellers ready to go deer huntin'?"

Without replying, they stopped and debated among themselves in whispers.

Finally, the pudgy man came forward.

"John," he inquired, "do you know anything peculiar about this cave below here?"

"Yes," said Willerkins at once; "Tom Gardner."

"What?" said the pudgy man.

"Tom Gardner."

"How's that?"

"Well, you see," said Willerkins slowly, as he took dignified pulls at his pipe, "Tom Gardner was once a fambly man, who lived in these here parts on a nice leetle farm. He uster go away to the city orften, and one time he got a-gamblin' in one of them there dens. He wentter the dickens right quick then. At last he kum home one time and tol' his folks he had up and sold the farm and all he had in the worl'. His leetle wife she died then. Tom he went crazy, and soon after—"

The narrative was interrupted by the little man, who became possessed of devils.

"I wouldn't give a cuss if he had left me 'nough money to get home on the doggoned, grey-haired red pirate," he shrilled, in a seething sentence. The pudgy man gazed at the little man calmly and sneeringly.

"Oh, well," he said, "we can tell a great tale when we get back to the city after having investigated this thing."

"Go to the devil," replied the little man.

THE MESMERIC MOUNTAIN.

A Tale of Sullivan County.

On the brow of a pine-plumed hillock there sat a little man with his back against a tree. A venerable pipe hung from his mouth, and smoke-wreaths curled slowly skyward. He was muttering to himself with his eyes fixed on an irregular black opening in the green wall of forest at the foot of the hill. Two vague waggon ruts led into the shadows. The little man took his pipe in his hands and addressed the listening pines.

"I wonder what the devil it leads to," said he.

A grey, fat rabbit came lazily from a thicket and sat in the opening. Softly stroking his stomach with his paw, he looked at the little man in a thoughtful manner. The little man threw a stone, and the rabbit blinked and ran through an opening. Green, shadowy portals seemed to close behind him.

The little man started. "He's gone down that roadway," he said, with ecstatic mystery to the pines. He sat a long time and contemplated the door to the forest. Finally, he arose, and awakening his limbs, started away. But he stopped and looked back.

"I can't imagine what it leads to," muttered he. He trudged over the brown mats of pine needles, to where, in a fringe of laurel, a tent was pitched, and merry flames caroused about some logs. A pudgy man was fuming over a collection of tin dishes. He came forward and waved a plate furiously in the little man's face.

"I've washed the dishes for three days. What do you think I am—"

He ended a red oration with a roar: "Damned if I do it any more."

The little man gazed dim-eyed away. "I've been wonderin' what it leads to."

"What?"

"That road out yonder. I've been wonderin' what it leads to. Maybe, some discovery or something," said the little man.

The pudgy man laughed. "You're an idiot. It leads to ol' Jim Boyd's over on the Lumberland Pike."

"Ho!" said the little man, "I don't believe that."

The pudgy man swore. "Fool, what does it lead to, then?"

"I don't know just what, but I'm sure it leads to something great or something. It looks like it."

While the pudgy man was cursing, two more men came from obscurity with fish dangling from birch twigs. The pudgy man made an obviously herculean struggle and a meal was prepared. As he was drinking his cup of coffee, he suddenly spilled it and swore. The little man was wandering off.

"He's gone to look at that hole," cried the pudgy man.

The little man went to the edge of the pine-plumed hillock, and, sitting down, began to make smoke and regard the door to the forest. There was stillness for an hour. Compact clouds hung unstirred in the sky. The pines stood motionless, and pondering.

Suddenly the little man slapped his knee and bit his tongue. He stood up and determinedly filled his pipe, rolling his eye over the bowl to the doorway. Keeping his eyes fixed he slid dangerously to the foot of the hillock and walked down the waggon ruts. A moment later he passed from the noise of the sunshine to the gloom of the woods.

The green portals closed, shutting out live things. The little man trudged on alone.

Tall tangled grass grew in the roadway, and the trees bended obstructing branches. The little man followed on over pine-clothed ridges and down through water-soaked swales. His shoes were cut by rocks of the mountains, and he sank ankle-deep in mud and moss of swamps. A curve just ahead lured him miles.

Finally, as he wended the side of a ridge, the road disappeared from beneath his feet. He battled with hordes of ignorant bushes on his way to knolls and solitary trees which invited him. Once he came to a tall, bearded pine. He climbed it, and perceived in the distance a peak. He uttered an ejaculation and fell out.

He scrambled to his feet, and said: "That's Jones's Mountain, I guess. It's about six miles from our camp as the crow flies."

He changed his course away from the mountain, and attacked the bushes again. He climbed over great logs, golden-brown in decay, and was opposed by thickets of dark-green laurel. A brook slid through the ooze of a swamp; cedars and hemlocks hung their sprays to the edges of pools.

The little man began to stagger in his walk. After a time he stopped and mopped his brow.

"My legs are about to shrivel up and drop off," he said.... "Still if I keep on in this direction, I am safe to strike the Lumberland Pike before sundown."

He dived at a clump of tag-alders, and emerging, confronted Jones's Mountain.

The wanderer sat down in a clear place and fixed his eyes on the summit. His mouth opened widely, and his body swayed at times. The little man and the peak stared in silence.

A lazy lake lay asleep near the foot of the mountain. In its bed of water-grass some frogs leered at the sky and crooned. The sun sank in red silence, and the shadows of the pines grew formidable. The expectant hush of evening, as if some thing were going to sing a hymn, fell upon the peak and the little man.

A leaping pickerel off on the water created a silver circle that was lost in black shadows. The little man shook himself and started to his feet, crying: "For the love of Mike, there's eyes in this mountain! I feel 'em! Eyes!"

He fell on his face.

When he looked again, he immediately sprang erect and ran.

"It's comin'!"

The mountain was approaching.

The little man scurried, sobbing through the thick growth. He felt his brain turning to water. He vanquished brambles with mighty bounds.

But after a time he came again to the foot of the mountain.

"God!" he howled, "it's been follerin' me." He grovelled.

Casting his eyes upward made circles swirl in his blood.

"I'm shackled I guess," he moaned. As he felt the heel of the mountain about crush his head, he sprang again to his feet. He grasped a handful of small stones and hurled them.

"Damn you," he shrieked loudly. The pebbles rang against the face of the mountain.

The little man then made an attack. He climbed with hands and feet wildly. Brambles forced him back and stones slid from beneath his feet. The peak swayed and tottered, and was ever about to smite with a granite arm. The summit was a blaze of red wrath.

But the little man at last reached the top. Immediately he swaggered with valour to the edge of the cliff. His hands were scornfully in his pockets.

He gazed at the western horizon, edged sharply against a yellow sky. “Ho!” he said. “There’s Boyd’s house and the Lumberland Pike.”

The mountain under his feet was motionless.

MISCELLANEOUS

THE SQUIRE'S MADNESS.

Linton was in his study remote from the interference of domestic sounds. He was writing verses. He was not a poet in the strict sense of the word, because he had eight hundred a year and a manor-house in Sussex. But he was devoted, at any rate, and no happiness was for him equal to the happiness of an imprisonment in this lonely study. His place had been a semi-fortified house in the good days when every gentleman was either abroad with a bared sword hunting his neighbours or behind oak-and-iron doors and three-feet walls while his neighbours hunted him. But in the life of Linton it may be said that the only part of the house which remained true to the idea of fortification was the study, which was free only to Linton's wife and certain terriers. The necessary appearance from time to time of a servant always grated upon Linton as much as if from time to time somebody had in the most well-bred way flung a brick through the little panes of his window.

This window looked forth upon a wide valley of hop-fields and sheep-pastures, dipping and rising this way and that way, but always a valley until it reached a high far away ridge upon which stood the upright figure of a windmill, usually making rapid gestures as if it were an excited sentry warning the old grey house of coming danger. A little to the right, on a knoll, red chimneys and parts of red-tiled roofs appeared among trees, and the venerable square tower of the village church rose above them.

For ten years Linton had left vacant Oldrestham Hall, and when at last it became known that he and his wife were to return from an incomprehensible wandering, the village, which for four centuries had turned a feudal eye toward the Hall, was wrung with a prospect of change, a proper change. The great family pew in Oldrestham church would be occupied each Sunday morning by a fat, happy-faced, utterly squire-looking man, who would be dutifully at his post when the parish was stirred by a subscription list. Then, for the first time in many years, the hunters would ride in the early morning merrily out through the park, and there would be also shooting parties, and in the summer groups of charming ladies would be seen walking the terrace, laughing on the lawns and in the rose gardens. The village expected to have the perfectly legal and fascinating privilege of discussing the performances of its own gentry.

The first intimation of calamity was in the news that Linton had rented all the shooting. This prepared the people for the blow, and it fell when they sighted the master of Oldrestham Hall. The older villagers remembered then that there had been nothing in the youthful Linton to promise a fat, happy-faced, dignified, hunting, shooting over-lord, but still they could not but resent the appearance of the new squire. There was no conceivable reason for his looking like a gaunt ascetic, who would surprise nobody if he borrowed a sixpence from the first yokel he met in the lanes.

Linton was in truth three inches more than six feet in height, but he had bowed himself to five feet eleven inches. His hair shocked out in front like hay, and under it were two spectacled eyes which never seemed to regard anything with particular attention. His face was pale and full of hollows, and the mouth apparently had no expression save a chronic pout of the under-lip. His hands were large and raw boned but uncannily white. His whole bent body was thin as that of a man from a long sick-bed, and all was finished by two feet which for size could not be matched in the county.

He was very awkward, but apparently it was not so much a physical characteristic as it was a mental inability to consider where he was going or what he was doing. For instance, when passing through a gate it was not uncommon for him to knock his side viciously against one of the posts. This was because he dreamed almost always, and if there had been forty gates in a row he would not then have noted them more than he did the one. As far as the villagers and farmers were concerned he never came out of this manner save in wide-apart cases, when he had forced upon him either some great exhibition of stupidity or some faint indication of double-dealing, and then this smouldering man flared out encrimsoning his immediate surrounding with a brief fire of ancestral anger. But the lapse back to indifference was more surprising. It was far quicker than the flare in the beginning. His feeling was suddenly ashes at the moment when one was certain it would lick the sky.

Some of the villagers asserted that he was mad. They argued it long in the manner of their kind, repeating, repeating, and repeating, and when an opinion confusingly rational appeared they merely shook their heads in pig-like obstinacy. Anyhow, it was historically clear that no such squire had before been in the line of Lintons of Oldrestham Hall, and the present incumbent was a shock.

The servants at the Hall—notably those who lived in the country-side—came in for a lot of questioning, and none were found too backward in explaining many things which they themselves did not understand. The household was most irregular. They all confessed that it was really so uncustomary that they did not know but what they would have to give notice. The master was probably the most extraordinary man in the whole world. The butler said that Linton would drink beer with his meals day in and day out like any carrier resting at a pot-house. It didn't matter even if the meal were dinner. Then suddenly he would change his tastes to the most valuable wines, and in ten days would make the wine-cellar look as if it had been wrecked at sea. What was to be done with a gentleman of that kind? The butler said for his part he wanted a master with habits, and he protested that Linton did not have a habit to his name, at least, none that could properly be called a habit.

Barring the cook, the entire establishment agreed categorically with the butler. The cook didn't agree because she was a very good cook indeed, which she thought entitled her to be extremely aloof from the other servants' hall opinions.

As for the squire's lady, they described her as being not much different from the master. At least she gave support to his most unusual manner of life, and evidently believed that whatever he chose to do was quite correct.

Linton had written—

"The garlands of her hair are snakes,

Black and bitter are her hating eyes,

A cry the windy death-hall makes,

O, love, deliver us.

The flung cup rolls to her sandal's tip,

His arm—"

Whereupon his thought fumed over the next two lines, coursing like greyhounds, after a fugitive vision of a writhening lover with the foam of poison on his lips dying at the feet of the woman. Linton arose, lit a cigarette, placed it on the window ledge, took another cigarette, looked blindly for the matches, thrust a spiral of paper into the flame of the log fire, lit the second cigarette, placed it toppling on a book and began a search among his pipes for one that would draw well. He gazed at his pictures, at the books on the shelves, out at the green spread of country-side, all without taking mental note. At the window ledge he came upon the first cigarette, and in a matter of fact way he returned it to his lips, having forgotten that he had forgotten it.

There was a sound of steps on the stone floor of the quaint little passage that led down to his study, and turning from the window he saw that his wife had entered the room and was looking at him strangely.

"Jack," she said in a low voice, "what is the matter?"

His eyes were burning out from under his shock of hair with a fierceness that belied his feeling of simple surprise. "Nothing is the matter," he answered. "Why do you ask?"

She seemed immensely concerned, but she was visibly endeavouring to hide her concern as well as to abate it.

"I—I thought you acted queerly."

He answered: "Why no. I'm not acting queerly. On the contrary," he added smiling, "I'm in one of my most rational moods."

Her look of alarm did not subside. She continued to regard him with the same stare. She was silent for a time and did not move. His own thoughts had quite returned to a contemplation of a poisoned lover, and he did not note the manner of his wife. Suddenly she came to him, and laying a hand on his arm said, "Jack, you are ill?"

"Why no, dear," he said with a first impatience, "I'm not ill at all. I never felt better in my life." And his mind beleaguered by this pointless talk strove to break through to its old contemplation of the poisoned lover. "Hear what I have written." Then he read—

"The garlands of her hair are snakes,

Black and bitter are her hating eyes,

A cry the windy death-hall makes,

O, love, deliver us.

The flung cup rolls to her sandal's tip,

His arm—"

Linton said: "I can't seem to get the lines to describe the man who is dying of the poison on the floor before her. Really I'm having a time with it. What a bore. Sometimes I can write like mad and other times I don't seem to have an intelligent idea in my head."

He felt his wife's hand tighten on his arm and he looked into her face. It was so alight with horror that it brought him sharply out of his dreams. "Jack," she repeated tremulously, "you are ill."

He opened his eyes in wonder. "Ill! ill? No; not in the least!"

"Yes, you are ill. I can see it in your eyes. You—act so strangely."

"Act strangely? Why, my dear, what have I done? I feel quite well. Indeed, I was never more fit in my life."

As he spoke he threw himself into a large wing chair and looked up at his wife, who stood gazing at him from the other side of the black oak table upon which Linton wrote his verses.

"Jack, dear," she almost whispered, "I have noticed it for days," and she leaned across the table to look more intently into his face. "Yes, your eyes grow more fixed every day—you—you—your head, does it ache, dear?"

Linton arose from his chair and came around the big table toward his wife. As he approached her, an expression akin to terror crossed her face and she drew back as in fear, holding out both hands to ward him off.

He had been smiling in the manner of a man reassuring a frightened child, but at her shrinking from his outstretched hand he stopped in amazement. "Why, Grace, what is it? tell me."

She was glaring at him, her eyes wide with misery. Linton moved his left hand across his face, unconsciously trying to brush from it that which alarmed her.

"Oh, Jack, you must see some one; I am wretched about you. You are ill!"

"Why, my dear wife," he said, "I am quite, quite well; I am anxious to finish these verses but words won't come somehow, the man dying—"

"Yes, that is it, you cannot remember, you see that you cannot remember. You must see a doctor. We will go up to town at once," she answered quickly.

"'Tis true," he thought, "that my memory is not as good as it used to be. I cannot remember dates, and words won't fit in somehow. Perhaps I don't take enough exercise, dear; is that what worries you?" he asked.

"Yes, yes, dear, you do not go out enough," said his wife. "You cling to this room as the ivy clings to the walls—but we must go to London, you must see some one; promise me that you will go, that you will go immediately."

Again Linton saw his wife look at him as one looks at a creature of pity. The faint lines from her nose to the corners of her mouth deepened as if she were in physical pain; her eyes, open to their fullest extent, had in them the expression of a mother watching her dying babe. What was this strange wall that had suddenly raised itself between them? Was he ill? No; he never was in better health in his life. He found himself vainly searching for aches in his bones. Again he brushed away this thing which seemed to be upon his face. There must be something on my face, he thought, else why does she look at me with such hopeless despair in her eyes; these kindly eyes that had hitherto been so responsive to each glance of his own. Why did she think that he was ill? She who knew well his every mood. Was he mad? Did this thing of the poisoned cup that rolled to her sandal's tip—and her eyes, her hating eyes, mean that his—no, it could not be. He fumbled among the papers on the table for a cigarette. He could not find one. He walked to the huge fireplace and peered near-sightedly at the ashes on the hearth.

"What, what do you want, Jack? Be careful! The fire!" cried his wife.

"Why, I want a cigarette," he said.

She started, as if he had spoken roughly to her. "I will get you some, wait, sit quietly, I will bring you some," she replied as she hastened through the small passage-way up the stone steps that led from his study.

Linton stood with his back still bent, in the posture of a man picking something from the ground. He did not turn from the fireplace until the echo of his wife's foot-fall on the stone floors had died away. Then he straightened himself and said, "Well, I'm damned!" And Linton was not a man who swore.

* * * * * * *

A month later the Squire and his wife were on their way to London to consult the great brain specialist, Doctor Redmond. Linton now believed that "something" was wrong with him. His wife's anxiety, which she could no longer conceal, forced him to this conclusion; "something" was wrong. Until these few last weeks Linton's wife had managed her household with the care and wisdom of a Chatelaine of mediæval times. Each day was planned for certain duties in house or village. She had theories as to the management and education of the village children, and this work occupied much of her time. She was the antithesis of her husband. He, a weaver of dream-stories, she of that type of woman who has ideas of the emancipation of women and who believe the problem could be solved by training the minds of the next generation of mothers. Linton was not interested in these questions, but he would smile indulgently at his wife as she talked of the equality of mind of the sexes and the public part in the world's history which would be played by the women of the future.

There was no talk of this kind now. The household management fell into the hands of servants. Night and day his wife watched Linton. He would awaken in the night to find her face close to his own, her eyes burning with feverish anxiety.

"What is it, Grace?" he would cry, "have I said anything? What is the reason you watch me in this fashion, dear?"

And she would sob, "Jack, you are ill, dear, you are ill; we must go to town, we must, indeed."

Then he would soothe her with fond words and promise that he would go to London.

This present journey was the outcome of those weeks of watching and fear in Linton's wife's mind.

* * * * * * *

Linton's wife was trembling violently as he helped her down from the cab in front of Doctor Redmond's door. They had made an appointment, so that they were sure of little delay before the portentous interview.

A small page in blue livery opened the door and ushered them into a waiting-room. Mrs. Linton dropped heavily into a chair, looking with a frightened air from side to side and biting her under lip nervously. She was moaning half under her breath, "Oh, Jack, you are ill, you are ill."

A short stout man with clean-shaven face and scanty black hair entered the room. His nose was huge and misshapen and his mouth was a straight firm line. Overhanging black brows tried in vain to shadow the piercing dark eyes, that darted questioning looks at every one, seeming to search for hidden thoughts as a flash-light from the conning tower of a ship searches for the enemy in time of war.

He advanced toward Mrs. Linton with outstretched hand. "Mrs. Linton?" he said. "Ah!"

She almost jumped from her chair as he came near her, crying, "Oh, doctor, my husband is ill, very ill, very ill!"

Again Doctor Redmond with his eyes fixed upon her face ejaculated, "Ah!" Turning to Linton he said, "Please wait here, Squire; I will first talk to your wife. Will you step into my study, madam?" he said to Mrs. Linton, bowing courteously.

Linton's wife ran into the room which the doctor pointed toward as his study.

Linton waited. He moved softly about the room looking at the photographs of Greek ruins which adorned the walls. He stopped finally before a large picture of the Gate of Hadrian. He travelled once more into his dream country. His fancy painted in the figures of men and women who had passed through that gate. He had forgotten his fear of the blotting out of his mind that could conjure these glowing colours. He had forgotten himself.

From this dream he was recalled to the present by a hand being placed gently upon his arm. He half turned and saw the doctor regarding him with sympathetic eyes.

"Come, my dear sir, come into my study," said the doctor. "I have asked your wife to await us here." Linton then turned fully toward the centre of the room and found that his wife was seated quietly by a table. Doctor Redmond bowed low to Mrs. Linton as he passed her, and Linton waved his hand, smiled, and said, "Only a moment, dear." She did not reply. The door closed behind them.

"Be seated, my dear sir," said the doctor, drawing forward a chair, "be seated. I want to say something to you, but you must drink this first." He handed Linton a small glass of brandy.

Linton sat down, took the glass mechanically, and gulped the brandy in one great swallow. The doctor stood by the mantel and said slowly, "I rejoice to say to you, sir, that I have never met a man more sound mentally than yourself"—

Linton half started from his chair.

"Stop!" said the doctor, "I have not yet finished—but it is my painful duty to tell you the truth—It is your WIFE WHO IS MAD! MAD AS A HATTER!"

A DESERTION.

The yellow gas-light that came with an effect of difficulty through the dust-stained windows on either side of the door, gave strange hues to the faces and forms of the three women who stood gabbling in the hall-way of the tenement. They made rapid gestures, and in the background their enormous shadows mingled in terrific conflict.

"Aye, she ain't so good as he thinks she is, I'll bet. He can watch over 'er an' take care of 'er all he pleases, but when she wants t' fool 'im, she'll fool 'im. An' how does he know she ain't foolin' 'im now?"

"Oh, he thinks he's keepin' 'er from goin' t' th' bad, he does. Oh, yes. He ses she's too purty t' let run round alone. Too purty! Huh! My Sadie—"

"Well, he keeps a clost watch on 'er, you bet. O'ny las' week, she met my boy Tim on th' stairs, an' Tim hadn't said two words to 'er b'fore th' ol' man begin to holler. 'Dorter, dorter, come here, come here!'"

At this moment a young girl entered from the street, and it was evident from the injured expression suddenly assumed by the three gossipers that she had been the object of their discussion. She passed them with a slight nod, and they swung about into a row to stare after her.

On her way up the long flights the girl unfastened her veil. One could then clearly see the beauty of her eyes, but there was in them a certain furtiveness that came near to marring the effects. It was a peculiar fixture of gaze, brought from the street, as of one who there saw a succession of passing dangers with menaces aligned at every corner.

On the top floor, she pushed open a door and then paused on the threshold, confronting an interior that appeared black and flat like a curtain. Perhaps some girlish idea of hobgoblins assailed her then, for she called in a little breathless voice, "Daddie!"

There was no reply. The fire in the cooking-stove in the room crackled at spasmodic intervals. One lid was misplaced, and the girl could now see that this fact created a little flushed crescent upon the ceiling. Also, a series of tiny windows in the stove caused patches of red upon the floor. Otherwise, the room was heavily draped with shadows.

The girl called again, "Daddie!"

Yet there was no reply.

"Oh, Daddie!"

Presently she laughed as one familiar with the humours of an old man. "Oh, I guess yer cussin' mad about yer supper, dad," she said, and she almost entered the room, but suddenly faltered, overcome by a feminine instinct to fly from this black interior, peopled with imagined dangers.

Again she called, "Daddie!" Her voice had an accent of appeal. It was as if she knew she was foolish but yet felt obliged to insist upon being reassured. "Oh, daddie!"

Of a sudden a cry of relief, a feminine announcement that the stars still hung, burst from her. For, according to some mystic process, the smouldering coals of the fire went aflame with sudden, fierce brilliance, splashing parts of the walls, the floor, the crude furniture, with a hue of blood-red. And in the light of this dramatic outburst of light, the girl saw her father seated at a table with his back turned toward her.

She entered the room, then, with an aggrieved air, her logic evidently concluding that somebody was to blame for her nervous fright. "Oh, yer on'y sulkin' 'bout yer supper. I thought mebbe ye'd gone somewheres."

Her father made no reply. She went over to a shelf in the corner, and, taking a little lamp, she lit it and put it where it would give her light as she took off her hat and jacket in front of the tiny mirror. Presently, she began to bustle among the cooking utensils that were crowded into the sink, and as she worked she rattled talk at her father, apparently disdaining his mood.

"I'd 'a come home earlier t'night, dad, o'ny that fly foreman, he kep' me in th' shop 'til half-past six. What a fool. He came t' me, yeh know, an' he ses, 'Nell, I wanta give yeh some brotherly advice.' Oh, I know him an' his brotherly advice. 'I wanta give yeh some brotherly advice. Yer too purty, Nell,' he ses, 't' be workin' in this shop an' paradin' through the streets alone, without somebody t' give yeh good brotherly advice, an' I wanta warn yeh, Nell. I'm a bad man, but I ain't as bad as some, an' I wanta warn yeh.' 'Oh, g'long 'bout yer business,' I ses. I know 'im. He's like all of 'em, o'ny he's a little slyer. I know 'im. 'You g'long 'bout yer business,' I ses. Well, he ses after a while that he guessed some evenin' he'd come up an' see me. 'Oh, yeh will,' I ses, 'yeh will? Well, you jest let my ol' man ketch yeh comin' foolin' 'round our place. Yeh'll wish yeh went t' some other girl t' give brotherly advice.' 'What th' 'ell do I care fer yer father?' he ses. 'What's he t' me?' 'If he throws yeh down stairs, yeh'll care for 'im,' I ses. 'Well,' he ses, 'I'll come when 'e ain't in, b' Gawd, I'll come when 'e ain't in.' 'Oh, he's allus in when it means takin' care 'a me,' I ses. 'Don't yeh fergit it either. When it comes t' takin' care 'a his dorter, he's right on deck every single possible time.'"

After a time, she turned and addressed cheery words to the old man. "Hurry up th' fire, daddie! We'll have supper pretty soon."

But still her father was silent, and his form in its sullen posture was motionless.

At this, the girl seemed to see the need of the inauguration of a feminine war against a man out of temper. She approached him breathing soft, coaxing syllables.

"Daddie! Oh, Daddie! O—o—oh, Daddie!"

It was apparent from a subtle quality of valour in her tones that this manner of onslaught upon his moods had usually been successful, but to-night it had no quick effect. The words, coming from her lips, were like the refrain of an old ballad, but the man remained stolid.

"Daddie! My Daddie! Oh, Daddie are yeh mad at me, really—truly mad at me!"

She touched him lightly upon the arm. Should he have turned then he would have seen the fresh, laughing face, with dew-sparkling eyes, close to his own.

"Oh, Daddie! My Daddie! Pretty Daddie!"

She stole her arm about his neck, and then slowly bended her face toward his. It was the action of a queen who knows that she reigns notwithstanding irritations, trials, tempests.

But suddenly, from this position, she leaped backward with the mad energy of a frightened colt. Her face was in this instant turned to a grey, featureless thing of horror. A yell, wild and hoarse as a brute-cry, burst from her. "Daddie!" She flung herself to a place near the door, where she remained, crouching, her eyes staring at the motionless figure, spattered by the quivering flashes from the fire. Her arms extended, and her frantic fingers at once besought and repelled. There was in them an expression of eagerness to caress and an expression of the most intense loathing. And the girl's hair that had been a splendour, was in these moments changed to a disordered mass that hung and swayed in witchlike fashion.

Again, a terrible cry burst from her. It was more than the shriek of agony—it was directed, personal, addressed to him in the chair, the first word of a tragic conversation with the dead.

It seemed that when she had put her arm about its neck, she had jostled the corpse in such a way, that now she and it were face to face. The attitude expressed an intention of arising from the table. The eyes, fixed upon hers, were filled with an unspeakable hatred.

* * * * * * *

The cries of the girl aroused thunders in the tenement. There was a loud slamming of doors, and presently there was a roar of feet upon the boards of the stairway. Voices rang out sharply.

"What is it?"

"What's th' matter?"

"He's killin' her!"

"Slug 'im with anythin' yeh kin lay hold of, Jack."

But over all this came the shrill shrewish tones of a woman. "Ah, th' damned ol' fool, he's drivin' 'er inteh th' street—that's what he's doin.' He's drivin' 'er inteh th' street."

HOW THE DONKEY LIFTED THE HILLS.

Many people suppose that the donkey is lazy. This is a great mistake. It is his pride.

Years ago, there was nobody quite so fine as the donkey. He was a great swell in those times. No one could express an opinion of anything without the donkey showing where he was in it. No one could mention the name of an important personage without the donkey declaring how well he knew him.

The donkey was, above all things, a proud and aristocratic beast.

One day a party of animals were discussing one thing and another, until finally the conversation drifted around to mythology.

"I have always admired that giant, Atlas," observed the ox in the course of the conversation. "It was amazing how he could carry things."

"Oh, yes, Atlas," said the donkey, "I knew him very well. I once met a man and we got talking of Atlas. I expressed my admiration for the giant and my desire to meet him some day, if possible. Whereupon the man said there was nothing quite so easy. He was sure that his dear friend, Atlas, would be happy to meet so charming a donkey. Was I at leisure next Monday? Well, then, could I dine with him upon that date? So, you see, it was all arranged. I found Atlas to be a very pleasant fellow."

"It has always been a wonder to me how he could have carried the earth on his back," said the horse.

"Oh, my dear sir, nothing is more simple," cried the donkey. "One has only to make up one's mind to it, and then—do it. That is all. I am quite sure that if I wished I could carry a range of mountains upon my back."

All the others said, "Oh, my!"

"Yes, I could," asserted the donkey, stoutly. "It is merely a question of making up one's mind. I will bet."

"I will wager also," said the horse. "I will wager my ears that you can't carry a range of mountains upon your back."

"Done," cried the donkey.

Forthwith the party of animals set out for the mountains. Suddenly, however, the donkey paused and said, "Oh, but look here. Who will place this range of mountains upon my back? Surely I can not be expected to do the loading also."

Here was a great question. The party consulted. At length the ox said, "We will have to ask some men to shovel the mountain upon the donkey's back."

Most of the others clapped their hoofs or their paws and cried, "Ah, that is the thing."

The horse, however, shook his head doubtfully. "I don't know about these men. They are very sly. They will introduce some deviltry into the affair."

"Why, how silly," said the donkey. "Apparently you do not understand men. They are the most gentle, guileless creatures."

"Well," retorted the horse, "I will doubtless be able to escape since I am not to be encumbered with any mountains. Proceed."

The donkey smiled in derision at these observations by the horse.

Presently they came upon some men who were labouring away like mad, digging ditches, felling trees, gathering fruits, carrying water, building huts.

"Look at these men, would you," said the horse. "Can you trust them after this exhibition of their depravity? See how each one selfishly—"

The donkey interrupted with a loud laugh.

"What nonsense!"

And then he cried out to the men, "Ho, my friends, will you please come and shovel a range of mountains upon my back?"

"What?"

"Will you please come and shovel a range of mountains upon my back?"

The men were silent for a time. Then they went apart and debated. They gesticulated a great deal.

Some apparently said one thing and some another. At last they paused and one of their number came forward.

"Why do you wish a range of mountains shovelled upon your back?"

"It is a wager," cried the donkey.

The men consulted again. And as the discussion became older, their heads went closer and closer together, until they merely whispered, and did not gesticulate at all. Ultimately they cried, "Yes, certainly we will shovel a range of mountains upon your back for you."

"Ah, thanks," said the donkey.

"Here is surely some deviltry," said the horse behind his hoof to the ox.

The entire party proceeded then to the mountains. The donkey drew a long breath and braced his legs.

"Are you ready?" asked the men.

"All ready," cried the donkey.

The men began to shovel.

The dirt and stones flew over the donkey's back in showers. It was not long before his legs were hidden. Presently only his neck and head remained in view. Then at last this wise donkey vanished. There had been made no great effect upon the range of mountains. They still towered toward the sky.

The watching crowd saw a heap of dirt and stones make a little movement and then was heard a muffled cry. "Enough! Enough! It was not two ranges of mountains! It is not fair! It is not fair!"

But the men only laughed as they shovelled on.

"Enough! Enough! Oh, woe is me—thirty snow-capped peaks upon my little back. Ah, these false, false men! Oh, virtuous, wise, and holy men, desist."

The men again laughed. They were as busy as fiends with their shovels.

"Ah, brutal, cowardly, accursed men; ah, good, gentle, and holy men, please remove some of those damnable peaks. I will adore your beautiful shovels forever. I will be slave to the beckoning of your little fingers. I will no longer be my own donkey—I will be your donkey."

The men burst into a triumphant shout and ceased shovelling.

"Swear it, mountain-carrier."

"I swear! I swear! I swear!"

The other animals scampered away then, for these men in their plots and plans were very terrible. "Poor old foolish fellow," cried the horse; "he may keep his ears. He will need them to hear and count the blows that are now to fall upon him."

The men unearthed the donkey. They beat him with their shovels. "Ho, come on, slave." Encrusted with earth, yellow-eyed from fright, the donkey limped toward his prison. His ears hung down like leaves of the plantain during the great rain.

So, now, when you see a donkey with a church, a palace, and three villages upon his back, and he goes with infinite slowness, moving but one leg at a time, do not think him lazy. It is his pride.

A MAN BY THE NAME OF MUD.

Deep in a leather chair, the Kid sat looking out at where the rain slanted before the dull brown houses and hammered swiftly upon an occasional lonely cab. The happy crackle from the great and glittering fireplace behind him had evidently no meaning of content for him. He appeared morose and unapproachable, and when a man appears morose and unapproachable it is a fine chance for his intimate friends. Three or four of them discovered his mood, and so hastened to be obnoxious.

"What's wrong, Kid? Lost your thirst?"

"He can never be happy again. He has lost his thirst."

"That's right, Kid. When you quarrel with a man who can whip you, resort to sarcastic reflection and distance."

They cackled away persistently, but the Kid was mute and continued to stare gloomily at the street.

Once a man who had been writing letters looked up and said, "I saw your friend at the Comique the other night." He waited a moment and then added, "In back."

The Kid wheeled about in his chair at this information, and all the others saw then that it was important. One man said with deep intelligence, "Ho, ho, a woman, hey? A woman's come between the two Kids. A woman. Great, eh?" The Kid launched a glare of scorn across the room, and then turned again to a contemplation of the rain. His friends continued to do all in their power to worry him, but they fell ultimately before his impregnable silence.

As it happened, he had not been brooding upon his friend's mysterious absence at all. He had been concerned with himself. Once in a while he seemed to perceive certain futilities and lapsed them immediately into a state of voiceless dejection. These moods were not frequent.

An unexplained thing in his mind, however, was greatly enlightened by the words of the gossip. He turned then from his harrowing scrutiny of the amount of pleasure he achieved from living, and settled into a comfortable reflection upon the state of his comrade, the other Kid.

Perhaps it could be indicated in this fashion: "Went to Comique, I suppose. Saw girl. Secondary part, probably. Thought her rather natural. Went to Comique again. Went again. One time happened to meet omnipotent and good-natured friend. Broached subject to him with great caution. Friend said—'Why, certainly, my boy, come round to-night, and I'll take you in back. Remember, it's against all rules, but I think that in your case, etc.' Kid went. Chorus girls winked same old wink. 'Here's another dude on the prowl.' Kid aware of this, swearing under his breath and looking very stiff. Meets girl. Knew beforehand that the footlights might have sold him, but finds her very charming. Does not say single thing to her which she naturally expected to hear. Makes no reference to her beauty nor her voice—if she has any. Perhaps takes it for granted that she knows. Girl don't exactly love this attitude, but then feels admiration, because after all she can't tell whether he thinks her nice or whether he don't. New scheme this. Worked by occasional guys in Rome and Egypt, but still, new scheme. Kid goes away. Girl thinks. Later, nails omnipotent and good-natured friend. 'Who was that you brought back?' 'Oh, him? Why, he—' Describes the Kid's wealth, feats, and virtues—virtues of disposition. Girl propounds clever question—'Why did he wish to meet me?' Omnipotent person says, 'Damned if I know.'"

Later, Kid asks girl to supper. Not wildly anxious, but very evident that he asks her because he likes her. Girl accepts; goes to supper. Kid very good comrade and kind. Girl begins to think that here at last is a man who understands her. Details ambitions—long, wonderful ambitions. Explains her points of superiority over the other girls of stage. Says their lives disgust her. She wants to work and study and make something of herself. Kid smokes vast number of cigarettes. Displays and feels deep sympathy. Recalls, but faintly, that he has heard it on previous occasions. They have an awfully good time. Part at last in front of apartment house. "Good-night, old chap." "Good-night." Squeeze hands hard. Kid has no information at all about kissing her good-night, but don't even try. Noble youth. Wise youth. Kid goes home and smokes. Feels strong desire to kill people who say intolerable things of the girl in rows. "Narrow, mean, stupid, ignorant, damnable people." Contemplates the broad, fine liberality of his experienced mind.

Kid and girl become very chumy. Kid like a brother. Listens to her troubles. Takes her out to supper regularly and regularly. Chorus girls now tacitly recognise him as the main guy. Sometimes, may be, girl's mother sick. Can't go to supper. Kid always very noble. Understands perfectly the probabilities of there being others. Lays for 'em, but makes no discoveries.

Begins to wonder whether he is a winner or whether she is a girl of marvellous cleverness. Can't tell. Maintains himself with dignity, however. Only occasionally inveighs against the men who prey upon the girls of the stage. Still noble.

Time goes on. Kid grows less noble. Perhaps decides not to be noble at all, or as little as he can. Still inveighs against the men who prey upon the girls of the stage. Thinks the girl stunning. Wants to be dead sure there are no others. Once suspects it, and immediately makes the colossal mistake of his life. Takes the girl to task. Girl won't stand it for a minute. Harangues him. Kid surrenders and pleads with her—pleads with her. Kid's name is mud.

A POKER GAME.

Usually a poker game is a picture of peace. There is no drama so low-voiced and serene and monotonous. If an amateur loser does not softly curse, there is no orchestral support. Here is one of the most exciting and absorbing occupations known to intelligent American manhood; here a year's reflection is compressed into a moment of thought; here the nerves may stand on end and scream to themselves, but a tranquillity as from heaven is only interrupted by the click of chips. The higher the stakes the more quiet the scene; this is a law that applies everywhere save on the stage.

And yet sometimes in a poker game things happen. Everybody remembers the celebrated corner on bay rum that was triumphantly consummated by Robert F. Cinch, of Chicago, assisted by the United States Courts and whatever other federal power he needed. Robert F. Cinch enjoyed his victory four months. Then he died, and young Bobbie Cinch came to New York in order to more clearly demonstrate that there was a good deal of fun in twenty-two million dollars.

Old Henry Spuytendyvil owns all the real estate in New York save that previously appropriated by the hospitals and Central Park. He had been a friend of Bob's father. When Bob appeared in New York, Spuytendyvil entertained him correctly. It came to pass that they just naturally played poker.

One night they were having a small game in an up-town hotel. There were five of them, including two lawyers and a politician. The stakes depended on the ability of the individual fortune.

Bobbie Cinch had won rather heavily. He was as generous as sunshine, and when luck chases a generous man it chases him hard, even though he cannot bet with all the skill of his opponents.

Old Spuytendyvil had lost a considerable amount. One of the lawyers from time to time smiled quietly, because he knew Spuytendyvil well, and he knew that anything with the name of loss attached to it sliced the old man's heart into sections.

At midnight Archie Bracketts, the actor, came into the room. "How you holding 'em, Bob?" said he.

"Pretty well," said Bob.

"Having any luck, Mr. Spuytendyvil?"

"Blooming bad," grunted the old man.

Bracketts laughed and put his foot on the round of Spuytendyvil's chair. "There," said he, "I'll queer your luck for you." Spuytendyvil sat at the end of the table. "Bobbie," said the actor, presently, as young Cinch won another pot, "I guess I better knock your luck." So he took his foot from the old man's chair and placed it on Bob's chair. The lad grinned good-naturedly and said he didn't care.

Bracketts was in a position to scan both of the hands. It was Bob's ante, and old Spuytendyvil threw in a red chip. Everybody passed out up to Bobbie. He filled in the pot and drew a card.

Spuytendyvil drew a card. Bracketts, looking over his shoulder, saw him holding the ten, nine, eight, and seven of diamonds. Theatrically speaking, straight flushes are as frequent as berries on a juniper tree, but as a matter of truth the reason that straight flushes are so admired is because they are not as common as berries on a juniper tree. Bracketts stared; drew a cigar slowly from his pocket, and placing it between his teeth forgot its existence.

Bobbie was the only other stayer. Bracketts flashed an eye for the lad's hand and saw the nine, eight, six, and five of hearts. Now, there are but six hundred and forty-five emotions possible to the human mind, and Bracketts immediately had them all. Under the impression that he had finished his cigar, he took it from his mouth and tossed it toward the grate without turning his eyes to follow its flight.

There happened to be a complete silence around the green-clothed table. Spuytendyvil was studying his hand with a kind of contemptuous smile, but in his eyes there perhaps was to be seen a cold, stern light expressing something sinister and relentless.

Young Bob sat as he had sat. As the pause grew longer, he looked up once inquiringly at Spuytendyvil.

The old man reached for a white chip. "Well, mine are worth about that much," said he, tossing it into the pot. Thereupon he leaned back comfortably in his chair and renewed his stare at the five straight diamond. Young Bob extended his hand leisurely toward his stack. It occurred to Bracketts that he was smoking, but he found no cigar in his mouth.

The lad fingered his chips and looked pensively at his hand. The silence of those moments oppressed Bracketts like the smoke from a conflagration.

Bobbie Cinch continued for some moments to coolly observe his cards. At last he breathed a little sigh and said, "Well, Mr. Spuytendyvil, I can't play a sure thing against you." He threw in a white chip. "I'll just call you. I've got a straight flush." He faced down his cards.

Old Spuytendyvil's fear, horror, and rage could only be equalled in volume to a small explosion of gasolene. He dashed his cards upon the table. "There!" he shouted, glaring frightfully at Bobbie. "I've got a straight flush, too! And mine is Jack high!"

Bobbie was at first paralysed with amazement, but in a moment he recovered, and apparently observing something amusing in the situation he grinned.

Archie Bracketts, having burst his bond of silence, yelled for joy and relief. He smote Bobbie on the shoulder. "Bob, my boy," he cried exuberantly, "you're no gambler, but you're a mighty good fellow, and if you hadn't been you would be losing a good many dollars this minute."

Old Spuytendyvil glowered at Bracketts. "Stop making such an infernal din, will you, Archie," he said morosely. His throat seemed filled with pounded glass. "Pass the whisky."

THE SNAKE.

Where the path wended across the ridge, the bushes of huckle-berry and sweet fern swarmed at it in two curling waves until it was a mere winding line traced through a tangle. There was no interference by clouds, and as the rays of the sun fell full upon the ridge, they called into voice innumerable insects which chanted the heat of the summer day in steady, throbbing, unending chorus.

A man and a dog came from the laurel thickets of the valley where the white brook brawled with the rocks. They followed the deep line of the path across the ridge. The dog—a large lemon and white setter—walked, tranquilly meditative, at his master's heels.

Suddenly from some unknown and yet near place in advance there came a dry, shrill whistling rattle that smote motion instantly from the limbs of the man and the dog. Like the fingers of a sudden death, this sound seemed to touch the man at the nape of the neck, at the top of the spine, and change him, as swift as thought, to a statue of listening horror, surprise, rage. The dog, too—the same icy hand was laid upon him, and he stood crouched and quivering, his jaw dropping, the froth of terror upon his lips, the light of hatred in his eyes.

Slowly the man moved his hands toward the bushes, but his glance did not turn from the place made sinister by the warning rattle. His fingers, unguided, sought for a stick of weight and strength. Presently they closed about one that seemed adequate, and holding this weapon poised before him, the man moved slowly forward, glaring. The dog with his nervous nostrils fairly fluttering moved warily, one foot at a time, after his master.

But when the man came upon the snake, his body underwent a shock as if from a revelation, as if after all he had been ambushed. With a blanched face, he sprang forward, and his breath came in strained gasps, his chest heaving as if he were in the performance of an extraordinary muscular trial. His arm with the stick made a spasmodic, defensive gesture.

The snake had apparently been crossing the path in some mystic travel when to his sense there came the knowledge of the coming of his foes. The dull vibration perhaps informed him, and he flung his body to face the danger. He had no knowledge of paths; he had no wit to tell him to slink noiselessly into the bushes. He knew that his implacable enemies were approaching; no doubt they were seeking him, hunting him. And so he cried his cry, an incredibly swift jangle of tiny bells, as burdened with pathos as the hammering upon quaint cymbals by the Chinese at war—for, indeed, it was usually his death-music.

"Beware! Beware! Beware!"

The man and the snake confronted each other. In the man's eyes were hatred and fear. In the snake's eyes were hatred and fear. These enemies manœuvred, each preparing to kill. It was to be a battle without mercy. Neither knew of mercy for such a situation. In the man was all the wild strength of the terror of his ancestors, of his race, of his kind. A deadly repulsion had been handed from man to man through long dim centuries. This was another detail of a war that had begun evidently when first there were men and snakes. Individuals who do not participate in this strife incur the investigations of scientists. Once there was a man and a snake who were friends, and at the end, the man lay dead with the marks of the snake's caress just over his East Indian heart. In the formation of devices, hideous and horrible, Nature reached her supreme point in the making of the snake, so that priests who really paint hell well fill it with snakes instead of fire. These curving forms, these scintillant colourings create at once, upon sight, more relentless animosities than do shake barbaric tribes. To be born a snake is to be thrust into a place a-swarm with formidable foes. To gain an appreciation of it, view hell as pictured by priests who are really skilful.

As for this snake in the pathway, there was a double curve some inches back of its head, which, merely by the potency of its lines, made the man feel with tenfold eloquence the touch of the death-fingers at the nape of his neck. The reptile's head was waving slowly from side to side and its hot eyes flashed like little murder-lights. Always in the air was the dry, shrill whistling of the rattles.

"Beware! Beware! Beware!"

The man made a preliminary feint with his stick. Instantly the snake's heavy head and neck were bended back on the double curve and instantly the snake's body shot forward in a low, straight, hard spring. The man jumped with a convulsive chatter and swung his stick. The blind, sweeping blow fell upon the snake's head and hurled him so that steel-coloured plates were for a moment uppermost. But he rallied swiftly, agilely, and again the head and neck bended back to the double curve, and the steaming, wide-open mouth made its desperate effort to reach its enemy. This attack, it could be seen, was despairing, but it was nevertheless impetuous, gallant, ferocious, of the same quality as the charge of the lone chief when the walls of white faces close upon him in the mountains. The stick swung unerringly again, and the snake, mutilated, torn, whirled himself into the last coil.

And now the man went sheer raving mad from the emotions of his forefathers and from his own. He came to close quarters. He gripped the stick with his two hands and made it speed like a flail. The snake, tumbling in the anguish of final despair, fought, bit, flung itself upon this stick which was taking his life.

At the end, the man clutched his stick and stood watching in silence. The dog came slowly and with infinite caution stretched his nose forward, sniffing. The hair upon his neck and back moved and ruffled as if a sharp wind was blowing. The last muscular quivers of the snake were causing the rattles to still sound their treble cry, the shrill, ringing war chant and hymn of the grave of the thing that faces foes at once countless, implacable, and superior.

"Well, Rover," said the man, turning to the dog with a grin of victory, "we'll carry Mr. Snake home to show the girls."

His hands still trembled from the strain of the encounter, but he pried with his stick under the body of the snake and hoisted the limp thing upon it. He resumed his march along the path, and the dog walked, tranquilly meditative, at his master's heels.

A SELF-MADE MAN.

An Example of Success that Any One can Follow.

Tom had a hole in his shoe. It was very round and very uncomfortable, particularly when he went on wet pavements. Rainy days made him feel that he was walking on frozen dollars, although he had only to think for a moment to discover he was not.

He used up almost two packs of playing cards by means of putting four cards at a time inside his shoe as a sort of temporary sole, which usually lasted about half a day. Once he put in four aces for luck. He went down town that morning and got refused work. He thought it wasn't a very extraordinary performance for a young man of ability, and he was not sorry that night to find his packs were entirely out of aces.

One day Tom was strolling down Broadway. He was in pursuit of work, although his pace was slow. He had found that he must take the matter coolly. So he puffed tenderly at a cigarette and walked as if he owned stock. He imitated success so successfully, that if it wasn't for the constant reminder (king, queen, deuce, and tray) in his shoe, he would have gone into a store and bought something.

He had borrowed five cents that morning off his landlady, for his mouth craved tobacco. Although he owed her much for board, she had unlimited confidence in him, because his stock of self-assurance was very large indeed. And as it increased in a proper ratio with the amount of his bills, his relations with her seemed on a firm basis. So he strolled along and smoked with his confidence in fortune in nowise impaired by his financial condition.

Of a sudden he perceived on old man seated upon a railing and smoking a clay pipe.

He stopped to look, because he wasn't in a hurry, and because it was an unusual thing on Broadway to see old men seated upon railings and smoking clay pipes.

And to his surprise the old man regarded him very intently in return. He stared, with a wistful expression, into Tom's face, and he clasped his hands in trembling excitement.

Tom was filled with astonishment at the old man's strange demeanour. He stood puffing at his cigarette, and tried to understand matters. Failing, he threw his cigarette away, took a fresh one from his pocket, and approached the old man.

"Got a match?" he inquired, pleasantly.

The old man, much agitated, nearly fell from the railing as he leaned dangerously forward.

"Sonny, can you read?" he demanded in a quavering voice.

"Certainly, I can," said Tom, encouragingly. He waived the affair of the match.

The old man fumbled in his pocket. "You look honest, sonny. I've been looking for an honest feller fur a'most a week. I've set on this railing fur six days," he cried, plaintively.

He drew forth a letter and handed it to Tom. "Read it fur me, sonny, read it," he said, coaxingly.

Tom took the letter and leaned back against the railings. As he opened it and prepared to read, the old man wriggled like a child at a forbidden feast.

Thundering trucks made frequent interruptions, and seven men in a hurry jogged Tom's elbow, but he succeeded in reading what follows:—

Office of Ketchum R. Jones, Attorney-at-Law,

Tin Can, Nevada, May 19, 18—.

Rufus Wilkins, Esq.

Dear Sir,—I have as yet received no acknowledgment of the draft from the sale of the north section lots, which I forwarded to you on 25th June. I would request an immediate reply concerning it.

Since my last I have sold the three corner lots at five thousand each. The city grew so rapidly in that direction that they were surrounded by brick stores almost before you would know it. I have also sold for four thousand dollars the ten acres of out-laying sage bush, which you once foolishly tried to give away. Mr. Simpson, of Boston, bought the tract. He is very shrewd, no doubt, but he hasn't been in the west long. Still, I think if he holds it for about a thousand years, he may come out all right.

I worked him with the projected-horse-car-line gag.

Inform me of the address of your New York attorneys, and I will send on the papers. Pray do not neglect to write me concerning the draft sent on 25th June.

In conclusion, I might say that if you have any eastern friends who are after good western investments inform them of the glorious future of Tin Can. We now have three railroads, a bank, an electric light plant, a projected horse-car line, and an art society. Also, a saw manufactory, a patent car-wheel mill, and a Methodist Church. Tin Can is marching forward to take her proud stand as the metropolis of the west. The rose-hued future holds no glories to which Tin Can does not—

Tom stopped abruptly. "I guess the important part of the letter came first," he said.

"Yes," cried the old man, "I've heard enough. It is just as I thought. George has robbed his dad."

The old man's frail body quivered with grief. Two tears trickled slowly down the furrows of his face.

"Come, come, now," said Tom, patting him tenderly on the back. "Brace up, old feller. What you want to do is to get a lawyer and go put the screws on George."

"Is it really?" asked the old man, eagerly.

"Certainly, it is," said Tom.

"All right," cried the old man, with enthusiasm. "Tell me where to get one." He slid down from the railing and prepared to start off.

Tom reflected. "Well," he said, finally, "I might do for one myself."

"What," shouted the old man in a voice of admiration, "are you a lawyer as well as a reader?"

"Well," said Tom again, "I might appear to advantage as one. All you need is a big front," he added, slowly. He was a profane young man.

The old man seized him by the arm. "Come on, then," he cried, "and we'll go put the screws on George."

Tom permitted himself to be dragged by the weak arms of his companion around a corner and along a side street. As they proceeded, he was internally bracing himself for a struggle, and putting large bales of self-assurance around where they would be likely to obstruct the advance of discovery and defeat.

By the time they reached a brown-stone house, hidden away in a street of shops and warehouses, his mental balance was so admirable that he seemed to be in possession of enough information and brains to ruin half of the city, and he was no more concerned about the king, queen, deuce, and tray than if they had been discards that didn't fit his draw. He infused so much confidence and courage into his companion, that the old man went along the street, breathing war, like a decrepit hound on the scent of new blood.

He ambled up the steps of the brown-stone house as if he were charging earthworks. He unlocked the door and they passed along a dark hallway. In a rear room they found a man seated at table engaged with a very late breakfast. He had a diamond in his shirt front and a bit of egg on his cuff.

"George," said the old man in a fierce voice that came from his aged throat with a sound like the crackle of burning twigs, "here's my lawyer, Mr. er—ah—Smith, and we want to know what you did with the draft that was sent on 25th June."

The old man delivered the words as if each one was a musket shot.

George's coffee spilled softly upon the tablecover, and his fingers worked convulsively upon a slice of bread. He turned a white, astonished face toward the old man and the intrepid Thomas.

The latter, straight and tall, with a highly legal air, stood at the old man's side. His glowing eyes were fixed upon the face of the man at the table. They seemed like two little detective cameras taking pictures of the other man's thoughts.

"Father, what d—do you mean," faltered George, totally unable to withstand the two cameras and the highly legal air.

"What do I mean?" said the old man with a feeble roar as from an ancient lion. "I mean that draft—that's what I mean. Give it up or we'll—we'll"—he paused to gain courage by a glance at the formidable figure at his side—"we'll put the screws on you."

"Well, I was—I was only borrowin' it for 'bout a month," said George.

"Ah," said Tom.

George started, glared at Tom, and then began to shiver like an animal with a broken back. There were a few moments of silence. The old man was fumbling about in his mind for more imprecations. George was wilting and turning limp before the glittering orbs of the valiant attorney. The latter, content with the exalted advantage he had gained by the use of the expression "Ah," spoke no more, but continued to stare.

"Well," said George, finally, in a weak voice, "I s'pose I can give you a cheque for it, 'though I was only borrowin' it for 'bout a month. I don't think you have treated me fairly, father, with your lawyers and your threats, and all that. But I'll give you the cheque."

The old man turned to his attorney. "Well?" he asked.

Tom looked at the son and held an impressive debate with himself. "I think we may accept the cheque," he said coldly after a time.

George arose and tottered across the room. He drew a cheque that made the attorney's heart come privately into his mouth. As he and his client passed triumphantly out, he turned a last highly legal glare upon George that reduced that individual to a mere paste.

On the side-walk the old man went into a spasm of delight and called his attorney all the admiring and endearing names there were to be had.

"Lord, how you settled him," he cried ecstatically.

They walked slowly back toward Broadway. "The scoundrel," murmured the old man. "I'll never see 'im again. I'll desert 'im. I'll find a nice quiet boarding-place and—"

"That's all right," said Tom. "I know one. I'll take you right up," which he did.

He came near being happy ever after. The old man lived at advanced rates in the front room at Tom's boarding-house. And the latter basked in the proprietress' smiles, which had a commercial value, and were a great improvement on many we see.

The old man, with his quantities of sage bush, thought Thomas owned all the virtues mentioned in high-class literature, and his opinion, too, was of commercial value. Also, he knew a man who knew another man who received an impetus which made him engage Thomas on terms that were highly satisfactory. Then it was that the latter learned he had not succeeded sooner because he did not know a man who knew another man.

So it came to pass that Tom grew to be Thomas G. Somebody. He achieved that position in life from which he could hold out for good wines when he went to poor restaurants. His name became entangled with the name of Wilkins in the ownership of vast and valuable tracts of sage bush in Tin Can, Nevada.

At the present day he is so great that he lunches frugally at high prices. His fame has spread through the land as a man who carved his way to fortune with no help but his undaunted pluck, his tireless energy, and his sterling integrity.

Newspapers apply to him now, and he writes long signed articles to struggling young men, in which he gives the best possible advice as to how to become wealthy. In these articles, he, in a burst of glorification, cites the king, queen, deuce, and tray, the four aces, and all that. He alludes tenderly to the nickel he borrowed and spent for cigarettes as the foundation of his fortune.

"To succeed in life," he writes, "the youth of America have only to see an old man seated upon a railing and smoking a clay pipe. Then go up and ask him for a match."

A TALE OF MERE CHANCE.

Being an Account of the Pursuit of the Tiles, the Statement of the Clock, and the Grip of a Coat of Orange Spots, together with some Criticism of a Detective said to be Carved from an Old Table-leg.

Yes, my friend, I killed the man, but I would not have been detected in it were it not for some very extraordinary circumstances. I had long considered this deed, but I am a delicate and sensitive person, you understand, and I hesitated over it as the diver hesitates on the brink of a dark and icy mountain pool. A thought of the shock of the contact holds one back.

As I was passing his house one morning, I said to myself, "Well, at any rate, if she loves him, it will not be for long." And after that decision I was not myself, but a sort of a machine.

I rang the bell and the servants admitted me to the drawing-room. I waited there while the old tall clock placidly ticked its speech of time. The rigid and austere chairs remained in possession of their singular imperturbability, although, of course, they were aware of my purpose, but the little white tiles of the floor whispered one to another and looked at me. Presently he entered the room, and I, drawing my revolver, shot him. He screamed—you know that scream—mostly amazement—and as he fell forward his blood was upon the little white tiles. They huddled and covered their eyes from this rain. It seemed to me that the old clock stopped ticking as a man may gasp in the middle of a sentence, and a chair threw itself in my way as I sprang toward the door.

A moment later, I was walking down the street, tranquil, you understand,

and I said to myself, "It is done. Long years from this day I will say to her that it was I who killed him. After time has eaten the conscience of the thing, she will admire my courage."

I was elated that the affair had gone off so smoothly, and I felt like returning home and taking a long, full sleep, like a tired working man. When people passed me, I contemplated their stupidity with a sense of satisfaction.

But those accursed little white tiles.

I heard a shrill crying and chattering behind me, and, looking back, I saw them, blood-stained and impassioned, raising their little hands and screaming "Murder! It was he!" I have said that they had little hands. I am not sure of it, but they had some means of indicating me as unerringly as pointing fingers. As for their movement, they swept along as easily as dry, light leaves are carried by the wind. Always they were shrilly piping their song of my guilt.

My friend, may it never be your fortune to be pursued by a crowd of little blood-stained tiles. I used a thousand means to be free from the clash-clash of these tiny feet. I ran through the world at my best speed, but it was no better than that of an ox, while they, my pursuers, were always fresh, eager, relentless.

I am an ingenious person, and I used every trick that a desperate, fertile man can invent. Hundreds of times I had almost evaded them when some smouldering, neglected spark would blaze up and discover me.

I felt that the eye of conviction would have no terrors for me, but the eyes of suspicion which I saw in city after city, on road after road, drove me to the verge of going forward and saying, "Yes, I have murdered."

People would see the following, clamorous troops of blood-stained tiles, and give me piercing glances, so that these swords played continually at my heart. But we are a decorous race, thank God. It is very vulgar to apprehend murderers on the public streets. We have learned correct manners from the English. Besides, who can be sure of the meaning of clamouring tiles? It might be merely a trick in politics.

Detectives? What are detectives? Oh, yes, I have read of them and their deeds, when I come to think of it. The prehistoric races must have been remarkable. I have never been able to understand how the detective navigated in stone boats. Still, specimens of their pottery excavated in Taumalipas show a remarkable knowledge of mechanics. I remember the little hydraulic—what's that? Well, what you say may be true, my friend, but I think you dream.

The little stained tiles. My friend, I stopped in an inn at the ends of the earth, and in the morning they were there flying like little birds and pecking at my window.

I should have escaped. Heavens, I should have escaped. What was more simple? I murdered and then walked into the world, which is wide and intricate.

Do you know that my own clock assisted in the hunting of me? They asked what time I left my home that morning, and it replied at once, "Half-after eight." The watch of a man I had chanced to pass near the house of the crime told the people "Seven minutes after nine." And, of course, the tall, old clock in the drawing-room went about day after day repeating, "Eighteen minutes after nine."

Do you say that the man who caught me was very clever? My friend, I have lived long, and he was the most incredible blockhead of my experience. An enslaved, dust-eating Mexican vaquero wouldn't hitch his pony to such a man. Do you think he deserves credit for my capture? If he had been as pervading as the atmosphere, he would never have caught me. If he was a detective, as you say, I could carve a better one from an old table-leg. But the tiles. That is another matter. At night I think they flew in long high flock, like pigeons. In the day, little mad things, they murmured on my trail like frothy-mouthed weasels.

I see that you note these great, round, vividly orange spots on my coat. Of course, even if the detective were really carved from an old table-leg, he could hardly fail to apprehend a man thus badged. As sores come upon one in the plague so came these spots upon my coat. When I discovered them, I made effort to free myself of this coat. I tore, tugged, wrenched at it, but around my shoulders it was like a grip of a dead man's arms. Do you know that I have plunged into a thousand lakes? I have smeared this coat with a thousand paints. But day and night the spots burn like lights. I might walk from this jail to-day if I could rid myself of this coat, but it clings—clings—clings.

At any rate, the person you call a detective was not so clever to discover a man in a coat of spotted orange, followed by shrieking, blood-stained tiles. Yes, that noise from the corridor is most peculiar. But they are always there, muttering and watching, clashing and jostling. It sounds as if the dishes of Hades were being washed. Yet I have become used to it. Once, indeed, in the night, I cried out to them, "In God's name, go away, little blood-stained tiles." But they doggedly answered, "It is the law."

AT CLANCY'S WAKE.

SCENE—*Room in the house of the lamented Clancy. The curtains are pulled down. A perfume of old roses and whisky hangs in the air. A weeping woman in black it seated at a table in the centre. A group of wide-eyed children are sobbing in a corner. Down the side of the room is a row of mourning friends of the family. Through an open door can be seen, half hidden in shadows, the silver and black of a coffin.*

Widow—Oh, wirra, wirra, wirra!

Children—B-b boo-hoo-hoo!

Friends (conversing in low tones)—Yis, Moike Clancy was a foine mahn, sure! None betther! No, I don't t'ink so. Did he? Sure, all th' elictions! He was th' bist in the warrud! He licked 'im widin an inch of his loife, aisy, an' th' other wan a big, shtrappin' buck of a mahn, an' him jes' free of th' pneumonia! Yis, he did! They carried th' warrud by six hunder! Yis, he was a foine mahn. None betther. Gawd sav' 'im!

(*Enter* Mr. Slick, *of the "Daily Blanket," shown in by a maid-servant, whose hair has become disarranged through much tear-shedding. He is attired in a suit of grey check, and wears a red rose in his buttonhole.*)

Mr. Slick—Good afternoon, Mrs. Clancy. This is a sad misfortune for you, isn't it?

Widow—Oh, indade, indade, young mahn, me poor heart is bruk.

Mr. Slick—Very sad, Mrs. Clancy. A great misfortune, I'm sure. Now, Mrs. Clancy, I've called to—

Widow—Little did I t'ink, young mahn, win they brought poor Moike in that it was th' lasht!

Mr. Slick (with conviction)—True! True! Very true, indeed. It was a great grief to you, Mrs. Clancy. I've called this morning, Mrs. Clancy, to see if I could get from you a short obituary notice for the Blanket if you could—

Widow—An' his hid was done up in a rag, an' he was cursin' frightful. A damned Oytalian lit fall th' hod as Moike was walkin' pasht as dacint as you plaze. Win they carried 'im in, him all bloody, an' ravin' tur'ble 'bout Oytalians, me heart was near bruk, but I niver tawt—I niver tawt—I—I niver—(Breaks forth into a long, forlorn cry. The children join in, and the chorus echoes wailfully through the rooms.)

Mr. Slick (as the yell, in a measure, ceases)—Yes, indeed, a sad, sad affair. A terrible misfortune. Now, Mrs. Clancy—

Widow (turning suddenly)—Mary Ann. Where's thot lazy divil of a Mary Ann? (As the servant appears.) Mary Ann, bring th' bottle! Give th' gintlemin a dhrink!... Here's to Hiven savin' yez, young mahn. (Drinks.)

Mr. Slick (drinks)—A noble whisky, Mrs. Clancy. Many thanks. Now, Mrs. Clancy—

Widow—Take anodder wan! Take anodder wan! (Fills his glass.)

Mr. Slick (impatiently)—Yes, certainly, Mrs. Clancy, certainly. (He drinks.) Now, could you tell me, Mrs. Clancy, where your late husband was—

Widow—Who—Moike? Oh, young mahn, yez can just say thot he was the foinest mahn livin' an' breathin', an' niver a wan in th' warrud was betther. Oh, but he had th' tindther heart for 'is fambly, he did. Don't I remimber win he clipped little Patsey wid th' bottle, an' didn't he buy th' big rockin'-horse th' minit he got sober? Sure he did. Pass th' bottle, Mary Ann! (Pours a beer-glass about half-full for her guest.)

Mr. Slick (taking a seat)—True, Mr. Clancy was a fine man, Mrs. Clancy—a very fine man. Now, I—

Widow (plaintively)—An' don't yez loike th' rum? Dhrink th' rum, mahn! It was me own Moike's fav'rite bran'. Well I remimber win he fotched it home, an' half th' demijohn gone a'ready, an' him a-cursin' up th' stairs as dhrunk as Gawd plazed. It was a—Dhrink th' rum, young mahn, dhrink th' rum! If he cud see yez now, Moike Clancy wud git up from 'is—

Mr. Slick (desperately)—Very well, very well, Mrs. Clancy. Here's your good health. Now, can you tell me, Mrs. Clancy, when was Mr. Clancy born?

Widow—Win was he borrun. Sure, divil a bit do I care win he was borrun. He was th' good mahn to me an' his childher; an' Gawd knows I don't care win he was borrun. Mary Ann, pass th' bottle! Wud yez kape th' gintlemin starvin' for a dhrink here in Moike Clancy's own house? Gawd save yez.

(*When the bottle appears she pours a huge quantity out for her guest.*)

Mr. Slick—Well, then, Mrs. Clancy, where was he born?

Widow (staring)—In Oirland, mahn, in Oirland! Where did yez t'ink? (Then, in sudden, wheedling tones.) An' ain't yez goin' to dhrink th' rum? Are yez goin' to shirk th' good whisky what was th' pride of Moike's life, an' him gettin' full on it an' breakin' th' furnitir t'ree nights a week hard-runnin'? Shame an yez, an' Gawd save yer soul. Dhrink it oop now, there's a dear, dhrink it oop now, an' say: "Moike Clancy, be all th' powers in th' shky, Hiven sind yez rist!"

Mr. Slick—(to himself)—Holy smoke! (He drinks, then regards the glass for a long time.) ... Well, now, Mrs. Clancy, give me your attention for a moment, please. When did—

Widow—An' oh, but he was a power in th' warrud! Divil a mahn cud vote right widout Moike Clancy at 'is elbow. An' in th' calkus, sure didn't Mulrooney git th' nominashun jes' by raison of Moike's atthackin' th' opposashun wid th' shtove-poker. Mulrooney got it as aisy as dhirt, wid Moike rowlin' under th' tayble wid th' other candeedate. He was a good sit'zen, was Moike—divil a wan betther.

Mr. Slick *spends some minutes in collecting his faculties.*

Mr. Slick (after he decides that he has them collected)—Yes, yes, Mrs. Clancy, your husband's h-highly successful pol-pol-political career was w-well known to the public; but what I want to know is—what I want to know—(Pauses to consider.)

Widow (finally)—Pass th' glasses, Mary Ann, yez lazy divil; give th' gintlemin a dhrink! Here (tendering him a glass), take anodder wan to Moike Clancy, an' Gawd save yez for yer koindness to a poor widee woman!

Mr. Slick (after solemnly regarding the glass)—Certainly, I—I'll take a drink. Certainly, M—Mish Clanshy. Yes, certainly, Mish Clanshy. Now, Mish Clanshy, w-w-wash was Mr. Clanshy's n-name before he married you, Mish Clanshy?

Widow (astonished)—Why, divil a bit else but Clancy.

Mr. Slick (after reflection)—Well, but I mean—I mean, Mish Clanshy, I mean—what was date of birth? Did marry you 'fore then, or d-did marry you when 'e was born in N' York, Mish Clanshy?

Widow—Phwat th' divil—

Mr. Slick (with dignity)—Ansher my queshuns, pleash, Mish Clanshy. Did 'e bring chil'en withum f'm Irelan', or was you, after married in N' York, mother those chil'en 'e brought f'm Irelan'?

Widow—Be th' powers above, I—

Mr. Slick (with gentle patience)—I don't shink y' unnerstan' m' queshuns, Mish Clanshy. What I wanna fin' out is, what was 'e born in N' York for when he, before zat, came f'm Irelan'? Dash what puzzels me. I-I'm completely puzzled. An' alsho, I wanna fin' out—I wanna fin' out, if poshble—zat is, if it's poshble shing, I wanna fin' out—I wanna fin' out—if poshble—I wanna-shay, who the blazesh is dead here, anyhow?

AN EPISODE OF WAR.

The lieutenant's rubber blanket lay on the ground, and upon it he had poured the company's supply of coffee. Corporals and other representatives of the grimy and hot-throated men who lined the breastwork had come for each squad's portion.

The lieutenant was frowning and serious at this task of division. His lips pursed as he drew with his sword various crevices in the heap until brown squares of coffee, astoundingly equal in size, appeared on the blanket. He was on the verge of a great triumph in mathematics, and the corporals were thronging forward, each to reap a little square, when suddenly the lieutenant cried out and looked quickly at a man near him as if he suspected it was a case of personal assault. The others cried out also when they saw blood upon the lieutenant's sleeve.

He has winced like a man stung, swayed dangerously, and then straightened. The sound of his hoarse breathing was plainly audible. He looked sadly, mystically, over the breastwork at the green face of a wood, where now were many little puffs of white smoke. During this moment the men about him gazed statue-like and silent, astonished and awed by this catastrophe which happened when catastrophes were not expected—when they had leisure to observe it.

As the lieutenant stared at the wood, they too swung their heads, so that for another instant all hands, still silent, contemplated the distant forest as if their minds were fixed upon the mystery of a bullet's journey.

The officer had, of course, been compelled to take his sword into his left hand. He did not hold it by the hilt. He gripped it at the middle of the blade, awkwardly. Turning his eyes from the hostile wood, he looked at the sword as he held it there, and seemed puzzled as to what to do with it, where to put it. In short, this weapon had of a sudden become a strange thing to him. He looked at it in a kind of stupefaction, as if he had been endowed with a trident, a sceptre, or a spade.

Finally he tried to sheath it. To sheath a sword held by the left hand, at the middle of the blade, in a scabbard hung at the left hip, is a feat worthy of a sawdust ring. This wounded officer engaged in a desperate struggle with the sword and the wobbling scabbard, and during the time of it he breathed like a wrestler.

But at this instant the men, the spectators, awoke from their stone-like poses and crowded forward sympathetically. The orderly-sergeant took the sword and tenderly placed it in the scabbard. At the time, he leaned nervously backward, and did not allow even his finger to brush the body of the lieutenant. A wound gives strange dignity to him who bears it. Well men shy from this new and terrible majesty. It is as if the wounded man's hand is upon the curtain which hangs before the revelations of all existence—the meaning of ants, potentates, wars, cities, sunshine, snow, a feather dropped from a bird's wing; and the power of it sheds radiance upon a bloody form, and makes the other men understand sometimes that they are little. His comrades look at him with large eyes thoughtfully. Moreover, they fear vaguely that the weight of a finger upon him might send him headlong, precipitate the tragedy, hurl him at once into the dim, grey unknown. And so the orderly-sergeant, while sheathing the sword, leaned nervously backward.

There were others who proffered assistance. One timidly presented his shoulder and asked the lieutenant if he cared to lean upon it, but the latter waved him away mournfully. He wore the look of one who knows he is the victim of a terrible disease and understands his helplessness. He again stared over the breastwork at the forest, and then turning went slowly rearward. He held his right wrist tenderly in his left hand as if the wounded arm was made of very brittle glass.

And the men in silence stared at the wood, then at the departing lieutenant—then at the wood, then at the lieutenant.

As the wounded officer passed from the line of battle, he was enabled to see many things which as a participant in the fight were unknown to him. He saw a general on a black horse gazing over the lines of blue infantry at the green woods which veiled his problems. An aide galloped furiously, dragged his horse suddenly to a halt, saluted, and presented a paper. It was, for a wonder, precisely like an historical painting.

To the rear of the general and his staff a group, composed of a bugler, two or three orderlies, and the bearer of the corps standard, all upon maniacal horses, were working like slaves to hold their ground, preserve their respectful interval, while the shells boomed in the air about them, and caused their chargers to make furious quivering leaps.

A battery, a tumultuous and shining mass, was swirling toward the right. The wild thud of hoofs, the cries of the riders shouting blame and praise, menace and encouragement, and, last, the roar of the wheels, the slant of the glistening guns, brought the lieutenant to an intent pause. The battery swept in curves that stirred the heart; it made halts as dramatic as the crash of a wave on the rocks, and when it fled onward, this aggregation of wheels, levers, motors, had a beautiful unity, as if it were a missile. The sound of it was a war-chorus that reached into the depths of man's emotion.

The lieutenant, still holding his arm as if it were of glass, stood watching this battery until all detail of it was lost, save the figures of the riders, which rose and fell and waved lashes over the black mass.

Later, he turned his eyes toward the battle where the shooting sometimes crackled like bush-fires, sometimes sputtered with exasperating irregularity, and sometimes reverberated like the thunder. He saw the smoke rolling upward and saw crowds of men who ran and cheered, or stood and blazed away at the inscrutable distance.

He came upon some stragglers, and they told him how to find the field hospital. They described its exact location. In fact, these men, no longer having part in the battle, knew more of it than others. They told the performance of every corps, every division, the opinion of every general. The lieutenant, carrying his wounded arm rearward, looked upon them with wonder.

At the roadside a brigade was making coffee and buzzing with talk like a girls' boarding-school. Several officers came out to him and inquired concerning things of which he knew nothing. One, seeing his arm, began to scold. "Why, man, that's no way to do. You want to fix that thing." He appropriated the lieutenant and the lieutenant's wound. He cut the sleeve and laid bare the arm, every nerve of which softly fluttered under his touch. He bound his handkerchief over the wound, scolding away in the meantime. His tone allowed one to think that he was in the habit of being wounded every day. The lieutenant hung his head, feeling, in this presence, that he did not know how to be correctly wounded.

The low white tents of the hospital were grouped around an old school-house. There was here a singular commotion. In the foreground two ambulances interlocked wheels in the deep mud. The drivers were tossing the blame of it back and forth, gesticulating and berating, while from the ambulances, both crammed with wounded, there came an occasional groan. An interminable crowd of bandaged men were coming and going. Great numbers sat under the trees nursing heads or arms or legs. There was a dispute of some kind raging on the steps of the school-house. Sitting with his back against a tree a man with a face as grey as a new army blanket was serenely smoking a corn-cob pipe. The lieutenant wished to rush forward and inform him that he was dying.

A busy surgeon was passing near the lieutenant. "Good-morning," he said, with a friendly smile. Then he caught sight of the lieutenant's arm and his face at once changed. "Well, let's have a look at it." He seemed possessed suddenly of a great contempt for the lieutenant. This wound evidently placed the latter on a very low social plane. The doctor cried out impatiently, "What mutton-head had tied it up that way anyhow?" The lieutenant answered, "Oh, a man."

When the wound was disclosed the doctor fingered it disdainfully. "Humph," he said. "You come along with me and I'll 'tend to you." His voice contained the same scorn as if he were saying, "You will have to go to jail."

The lieutenant had been very meek, but now his face flushed, and he looked into the doctor's eyes. "I guess I won't have it amputated," he said.

"Nonsense, man! Nonsense! Nonsense!" cried the doctor. "Come along, now. I won't amputate it. Come along. Don't be a baby."

"Let go of me," said the lieutenant, holding back wrathfully, his glance fixed upon the door of the old school-house, as sinister to him as the portals of death.

And this is the story of how the lieutenant lost his arm. When he reached home, his sisters, his mother, his wife, sobbed for a long time at the sight of the flat sleeve. "Oh, well," he said, standing shamefaced amid these tears, "I don't suppose it matters so much as all that."

THE VOICE OF THE MOUNTAIN.

The old man Popocatepetl was seated on a high rock with his white mantle about his shoulders. He looked at the sky, he looked at the sea, he looked at the land—nowhere could he see any food. And he was very hungry, too.

Who can understand the agony of a creature whose stomach is as large as a thousand churches, when this same stomach is as empty as a broken water jar?

He looked longingly at some island in the sea. "Ah, those flat cakes! If I had them." He stared at storm-clouds in the sky. "Ah, what a drink is there." But the King of Everything, you know, had forbidden the old man Popocatepetl to move at all, because he feared that every footprint would make a great hole in the land. So the old fellow was obliged to sit still and wait for his food to come within reach. Any one who has tried this plan knows what intervals lie between meals.

Once his friend, the little eagle, flew near, and Popocatepetl called to him. "Ho, tiny bird, come and consider with me as to how I shall be fed."

The little eagle came and spread his legs apart and considered manfully, but he could do nothing with the situation. "You see," he said, "this is no ordinary hunger which one goat will suffice—"

Popocatepetl groaned an assent.

"—but it is an enormous affair," continued the little eagle, "which requires something like a dozen stars. I don't see what can be done unless we get that little creature of the earth—that little animal with two arms, two legs, one head, and a very brave air, to invent something. He is said to be very wise."

"Who claims it for him?" asked Popocatepetl.

"He claims it for himself," responded the eagle.

"Well, summon him. Let us see. He is doubtless a kind little animal, and when he sees my distress he will invent something."

"Good!" The eagle flew until he discovered one of these small creatures. "Oh, tiny animal, the great chief Popocatepetl summons you!"

"Does he, indeed!"

"Popocatepetl, the great chief," said the eagle again, thinking that the little animal had not heard rightly.

"Well, and why does he summon me?"

"Because he is in distress, and he needs your assistance."

The little animal reflected for a time, and then said, "I will go."

When Popocatepetl perceived the little animal and the eagle he stretched forth his great, solemn arms. "Oh, blessed little animal with two arms, two legs, a head, and a very brave air, help me in my agony. Behold I, Popocatepetl, who saw the King of Everything fashioning the stars, I, who knew the sun in his childhood, I, Popocatepetl, appeal to you, little animal. I am hungry."

After a while the little animal asked: "How much will you pay?"

"Pay?" said Popocatepetl.

"Pay?" said the eagle.

"Assuredly," quoth the little animal, "pay!"

"But," demanded Popocatepetl, "were you never hungry? I tell you I am hungry, and is your first word then 'pay'?"

The little animal turned coldly away. "Oh, Popocatepetl, how much wisdom has flown past you since you saw the King of Everything fashioning the stars and since you knew the sun in his childhood? I said pay, and, moreover, your distress measures my price. It is our law. Yet it is true that we did not see the King of Everything fashioning the stars. Nor did we know the sun in his childhood."

Then did Popocatepetl roar and shake in his rage. "Oh, louse—louse—louse! Let us bargain then! How much for your blood?" Over the little animal hung death.

But he instantly bowed himself and prayed: "Popocatepetl, the great, you who saw the King of Everything fashioning the stars, and who knew the sun in his childhood, forgive this poor little animal. Your sacred hunger shall be my care. I am your servant."

"It is well," said Popocatepetl at once, for his spirit was ever kindly. "And now, what will you do?"

The little animal put his hand upon his chin and reflected. "Well, it seems you are hungry, and the King of Everything has forbidden you to go for food in fear that your monstrous feet will riddle the earth with holes. What you need is a pair of wings."

"A pair of wings!" cried Popocatepetl delightedly.

"A pair of wings!" screamed the eagle in joy.

"How very simple, after all."

"And yet how wise!"

"But," said Popocatepetl, after the first outburst, "who can make me these wings?"

The little animal replied: "I and my kind are great, because at times we can make one mind control a hundred thousand bodies. This is the secret of our performance. It will be nothing for us to make wings for even you, great Popocatepetl. I and my kind will come"—continued the crafty, little animal—"we will come and dwell on this beautiful plain that stretches from the sea to the sea, and we will make wings for you."

Popocatepetl wished to embrace the little animal. "Oh, glorious! Oh, best of little brutes! Run! run! run! Summon your kind, dwell in the plain and make me wings. Ah, when once Popocatepetl can soar on his wings from star to star, then, indeed—"

* * * * * * *

Poor old stupid Popocatepetl! The little animal summoned his kind, they dwelt on the plains, they made this and they made that, but they made no wings for Popocatepetl.

And sometimes when the thunderous voice of the old peak rolls and rolls, if you know that tongue, you can hear him say: "Oh, traitor! Traitor! Traitor! Where are my wings? My wings, traitor! I am hungry! Where are my wings?"

But the little animal merely places his finger beside his nose and winks.

"Your wings, indeed, fool! Sit still and howl for them! Old idiot!"

WHY DID THE YOUNG CLERK SWEAR? OR, THE UNSATISFACTORY FRENCH.

All was silent in the little gent's furnishing store. A lonely clerk with a blonde moustache and a red necktie raised a languid hand to his brow and brushed back a dangling lock. He yawned and gazed gloomily at the blurred panes of the windows.

Without, the wind and rain came swirling round the brick buildings and went sweeping over the streets. A horse-car rumbled stolidly by. In the mud on the pavements, a few pedestrians struggled with excited umbrellas.

"The deuce!" remarked the clerk. "I'd give ten dollars if somebody would come in and buy something, if 'twere only cotton socks."

He waited amid the shadows of the grey afternoon. No customers came. He heaved a long sigh and sat down on a high stool. From beneath a stack of unlaundried shirts he drew a French novel with a picture on the cover.

He yawned again, glanced lazily toward the street, and settled himself as comfortable as the gods would let him upon the high stool.

He opened the book and began to read. Soon it could have been noticed that his blonde moustache took on a curl of enthusiasm, and the refractory locks on his brow showed symptoms of soft agitation.

"Silvere did not see the young girl for some days," read the clerk. "He was miserable. He seemed always to inhale that subtle perfume from her hair. At night he saw her eyes in the stars.

"His dreams were troubled. He watched the house. Heloise did not appear. One day he met Vibert. Vibert wore a black frock-coat. There were wine-stains on the right breast. His collar was soiled. He had not shaved.

"Silvere burst into tears. 'I love her! I love her! I shall die!' Vibert laughed scornfully. His necktie was second-hand. Idiotic, this boy in love. Fool! Simpleton! But at last he pitied him. She goes to the music-teacher's every morning. Silly Silvere embraced him.

"The next day Silvere waited at the street corner. A vendor was selling chestnuts. Two gamins were fighting in an alley. A woman was scrubbing some steps. This great Paris throbbed with life.

"Heloise came. She did not perceive Silvere. She passed with a happy smile on her face. She looked fresh, fair, innocent. Silvere felt himself swooning. 'Ah, my God!'

"She crossed the street. The young man received a shock that sent the warm blood to his brain. It had been raining. There was mud. With one slender hand Heloise lifted her skirts. Silvere leaning forward, saw her—"

A young man in a wet mackintosh came into the little gent's furnishing store.

"Ah, beg pardon," said he to the clerk, "but do you have an agency for a steam laundry here? I have been patronising a Chinaman down th' avenue for some time, but he—what? No? You have none here? Well, why don't you start one, anyhow? It'd be a good thing in this neighbourhood. I live just round the corner, and it'd be a great thing for me. I know lots of people who would—what? Oh, you don't? Oh!"

As the young man in the wet mackintosh retreated, the clerk with a blonde moustache made a hungry grab at the novel. He continued to read: "Handkerchief fall in a puddle. Silvere sprang forward. He picked up the handkerchief. Their eyes met. As he returned the handkerchief, their hands touched. The young girl smiled. Silvere was in ecstacies. 'Ah, my God!'

"A baker opposite was quarrelling over two sous with an old woman.

"A grey-haired veteran with a medal upon his breast and a butcher's boy were watching a dog-fight. The smell of dead animals came from adjacent slaughter-houses. The letters on the sign over the tinsmith's shop on the corner shone redly like great clots of blood. It was hell on roller skates."

Here the clerk skipped some seventeen chapters descriptive of a number of intricate money transactions, the moles on the neck of a Parisian dressmaker, the process of making brandy, the milk-leg of Silvere's aunt, life in the coal-pits, and scenes in the Chamber of Deputies. In these chapters the reputation of the architect of Charlemagne's palace was vindicated, and it was explained why Heloise's grandmother didn't keep her stockings pulled up.

Then he proceeded: "Heloise went to the country. The next day Silvere followed. They met in the fields. The young girl had donned the garb of the peasants. She blushed. She looked fresh, fair, innocent. Silvere felt faint with rapture. 'Ah, my God!'

"She had been running. Out of breath, she sank down in the hay. She held out her hand. 'I am so glad to see you.' Silvere was enchanted at this vision. He bended toward her. Suddenly he burst into tears. 'I love you! I love you! I love you!' he stammered.

"A row of red and white shirts hung on a line some distance away. The third shirt from the left had a button off the neck. A cat on the rear steps of a cottage near the shirt was drinking milk from a platter. The north-east portion of the platter had a crack in it.

"'Heloise!' Silvere was murmuring hoarsely. He leaned toward her until his warm breath moved the curls on her neck. 'Heloise!' murmured Jean."

"Young man," said an elderly gentleman with a dripping umbrella to the clerk with a blonde moustache, "have you any night-shirts open front and back? Eh? Night-shirts open front and back, I said. D'you hear, eh? Night-shirts open front and back. Well, then, why didn't you say so? It would pay you to be a trifle more polite, young man. When you get as old as I am, you will find out that it pays to—what? I didn't see you adding any column of figures. In that case I am sorry. You have no night-shirts open front and back, eh? Well, good-day."

As the elderly gentleman vanished, the clerk with a blonde moustache grasped the novel like some famished animal. He read on: "A peasant stood before the two children. He wrung his hands. 'Have you seen a stray cow?' 'No,' cried the children in the same breath. The peasant wept. He wrung his hands. It was a supreme moment.

"'She loves me!' cried Silvere to himself, as he changed his clothes for dinner.

"It was evening. The children sat by the fire-place. Heloise wore a gown of clinging white. She looked fresh, fair, innocent. Silvere was in raptures. 'Ah, my God!'

"Old Jean, the peasant, saw nothing. He was mending harness. The fire crackled in the fire-place. The children loved each other. Through the open door to the kitchen came the sound of old Marie shrilly cursing the geese who wished to enter. In front of the window two pigs were quarrelling over a vegetable. Cattle were lowing in a distant field. A hay-waggon creaked slowly past. Thirty-two chickens were asleep in the branches of a tree. This subtle atmosphere had a mighty effect upon Heloise. It was beating down her self-control. She felt herself going. She was choking.

"The young girl made an effort. She stood up. 'Good-night, I must go.' Silvere took her hand. 'Heloise,' he murmured. Outside the two pigs were fighting.

"A warm blush overspread the young girl's face. She turned wet eyes toward her lover. She looked fresh, fair, innocent. Silvere was maddened. 'Ah, my God!'

"Suddenly the young girl began to tremble. She tried vainly to withdraw her hand. But her knee—"

"I wish to get my husband some shirts," said a shopping-woman with six bundles. The clerk with a blonde moustache made a private gesture of despair, and rapidly spread a score of different-patterned shirts upon the counter. "He's very particular about his shirts," said the shopping-woman. "Oh, I don't think any of these will do. Don't you keep the Invincible brand? He only wears that kind. He says they fit him better. And he's very particular about his shirts. What? You don't keep them? No? Well, how much do you think they would come at?" "Haven't the slightest idea." "Well, I suppose I must go somewhere else, then. Um, good-day."

The clerk with the blonde moustache was about to make further private gestures of despair, when the shopping-woman with six bundles turned and went out. His fingers instantly closed nervously over the book. He drew it from its hiding-place, and opened it at the place where he had ceased. His hungry eyes seemed to eat the words upon the page. He continued: "—struck cruelly against a chair. It seemed to awaken her. She started. She burst from the young man's arms. Outside the two pigs were grunting amiably.

"Silvere took his candle. He went toward his room. He was in despair. 'Ah, my God!'

"He met the young girl on the stairs. He took her hand. Tears were raining down his face. 'Heloise!' he murmured.

"The young girl shivered. As Silvere put his arms about her, she faintly resisted. This embrace seemed to sap her life. She wished to die. Her thoughts flew back to the old well and the broken hayrakes at Plassans.

"The young girl looked fresh, fair, innocent 'Heloise!' murmured Silvere. The children exchanged a long, clinging kiss. It seemed to unite their souls.

"The young girl was swooning. Her head sank on the young man's shoulder. There was nothing in space except these warm kisses on her neck. Silvere enfolded her. 'Ah, my God!'"

"Say, young fellow," said a youth with a tilted cigar to the clerk with a blonde moustache, "where th'll is Billie Carcart's joint round here? Know?"

"Next corner," said the clerk fiercely.

"Oh, th'll," said the youth, "yehs needn't git gay. See! When a feller asts a civil question yehs needn't git gay. See! Th'll!"

The youth stood and looked aggressive for a moment. Then he went away.

The clerk seemed almost to leap upon the book. His feverish fingers twirled the pages. When he found his place he glued his eyes to it. He read:

"Then a great flash of lightning illumined the hall-way. It threw livid hues over a row of flowerpots in the window-seat. Thunder shook the house to its foundation. From the kitchen arose the voice of old Marie in prayer.

"Heloise screamed. She wrenched herself from the young man's arms. She sprang inside her room. She locked the door. She flung herself face downward on the bed. She burst into tears. She looked fresh, fair, innocent.

"The rain pattering upon the thatched roof sounded in the stillness like the footsteps of spirits. In the sky toward Paris there shone a crimson light.

"The chickens had all fallen from the tree. They stood, sadly, in a puddle. The two pigs were asleep under the porch.

"Upstairs, in the hall-way, Silvers was furious."

The clerk with a blonde moustache gave here a wild scream of disappointment. He madly hurled the novel with the picture on the cover from him. He stood up and said: "Damn!"

THE VICTORY OF THE MOON.

The Strong Man of the Hills lost his wife. Immediately he went abroad, calling aloud. The people all crouched afar in the dark of their huts, and cried to him when he was yet a long distance away: "No, no, great chief, we have not even seen the imprint of your wife's sandal in the sand. If we had seen it, you would have found us bowed down in worship before the marks of her ten glorious brown toes, for we are but poor devils of Indians, and the grandeur of the sun rays on her hair would have turned our eyes to dust."

"Her toes are not brown. They are pink," said the Strong Man from the Hills. "Therefore do I believe that you speak the truth when you say you have not seen her, good little men of the valley. In this matter of her great loveliness, however, you speak a little too strongly. As she is no longer among my possessions, I have no mind to hear her praised. Whereabouts is the best man of you?"

None of them had stomach for this honour at the time. They surmised that the Strong Man of the Hills had some plan for combat, and they knew that the best of them would have in this encounter only the strength of the meat in the grip of the fire. "Great King," they said, in one voice, "there is no best man here."

"How is this?" roared the Strong Man. "There must be one who excels. It is a law. Let him step forward then."

But they solemnly shook their heads. "There is no best man here."

The Strong Man turned upon them so furiously that many fell to the ground. "There must be one. Let him step forward." Shivering, they huddled together and tried, in their fear, to thrust each other toward the Strong Man.

At this time a young philosopher approached the throng slowly. The philosophers of that age were all young men in the full heat of life. The old greybeards were, for the most part, very stupid, and were so accounted.

"Strong Man from the Hills," said the young philosopher, "go to yonder brook and bathe. Then come and eat of this fruit. Then gaze for a time at the blue sky and the green earth. Afterward I have something to say to you."

"You are not so wise that I am obliged to bathe before listening to you?" demanded the Strong Man, insolently.

"No," said the young philosopher. All the people thought this reply very strange.

"Why, then, must I bathe and eat of fruit and gaze at the earth and the sky?"

"Because they are pleasant things to do."

"Have I, do you think, any thirst at this time for pleasant things?"

"Bathe, eat, gaze," said the young philosopher with a gesture.

The Strong Man did, indeed, whirl his bronzed and terrible limbs in the silver water. Then he lay in the shadow of a tree and ate the cool fruit and gazed at the sky and the earth. "This is a fine comfort," he said. After a time he suddenly struck his forehead with his finger. "By the way, did I tell you that my wife had fled from me?"

"I know it," said the young philosopher.

Later the Strong Man slept peacefully. The young philosopher smiled.

But in the night the little men of the valley came clamouring: "Oh, Strong Man of the Hills, the moon derides you!"

The philosopher went to them in the darkness. "Be still, little people. It is nothing. The derision of the moon is nothing."

But the little men of the valley would not cease their uproar. "Oh, Strong Man! Strong Man, awake! Awake! The moon derides you!"

Then the Strong Man aroused and shook his locks away from his eyes. "What is it, good little men of the valley?"

"Oh, Strong Man, the moon derides you! Oh, Strong Man!"

The Strong Man looked, and there, indeed, was the moon laughing down at him. He sprang to his feet and roared. "Ah, old, fat, lump of moon, you laugh! Have you seen my wife?"

The moon said no word, but merely smiled in a way that was like a flash of silver bars.

"Well, then, moon, take this home to her," thundered the Strong Man, and he hurled his spear.

The moon clapped both hands to its eye, and cried: "Oh! Oh!"

The little people of the valley cried: "Oh, this is terrible, Strong Man! He has smitten our sacred moon in the eye!"

The young philosopher cried nothing at all.

The Strong Man threw his coat of crimson feathers upon the ground. He took his knife and felt its edge. "Look you, philosopher," he said. "I have lost my wife, and the bath, the meal of fruit in the shade, the sight of sky and earth are still good to me, but when this false moon derides me, there must be a killing."

"I understand you," said the young philosopher.

The Strong Man ran off into the night. The little men of the valley clapped their hands in ecstacy and terror. "Ah! ah! what a battle will there be!"

The Strong Man went into his own hills and gathered there many great rocks and trunks of trees. It was strange to see him erect upon a peak of the mountains and hurling these things at the moon. He kept the air full of them.

"Fat moon, come closer," he shouted. "Come closer, and let it be my knife against your knife. Oh, to think that we are obliged to tolerate such an old, fat, stupid, lazy, good-for-nothing moon. You are ugly as death, while I—Oh, moon, you stole my beloved, and it was nothing, but when you stole my beloved and laughed at me, it became another matter. And yet you are so ugly, so fat, so stupid, so lazy, so good-for-nothing. Ah, I shall go mad! Come closer, moon, and let me examine your round, grey skull with this club."

And he always kept the air full of great missiles.

The moon merely laughed, and said: "Why should I come closer?"

Wildly did the Strong Man pile rock upon rock. He builded him a tower that was the father of all towers. It made the mountains to appear to be babes. Upon the summit of it he swung his great club and flourished his knife.

The little men in the valley far below beheld a great storm, and at the end of it they said: "Look, the moon is dead." The cry went to and fro on the earth: "The moon is dead!"

The Strong Man went to the home of the moon. She, the sought one, lay upon a cloud, and her little foot dangled over the side of it. The Strong Man took this little foot in his two hands and kissed it. "Ah, beloved!" he moaned, "I would rather this little foot was upon my dead neck than that moon should ever have the privilege of seeing it."

She leaned over the edge of the cloud and gazed at him. "How dusty you are. Why do you puff so? Veritably, you are an ordinary person. Why did I ever find you interesting?"

The Strong Man flung his knife into the air and turned back toward the earth. "If the young philosopher had been at my elbow," he reflected, bitterly, "I would doubtless have gone at the matter in another way. What does my strength avail me in this contest?"

The battered moon, limping homeward, replied to the Strong Man from the Hills: "Aye, surely. My weakness is in this thing as strong as your strength. I am victor with ugliness, my age, my stoutness, my laziness, my good-for-nothingness. Woman is woman. Men are equal in everything save good fortune. I envy you not."

THE END.

About Author

In 1896, Crane endured a highly publicized scandal after appearing as a witness in the trial of a suspected prostitute, an acquaintance named Dora Clark. Late that year he accepted an offer to travel to Cuba as a war correspondent. As he waited in Jacksonville, Florida for passage, he met Cora Taylor, with whom he began a lasting relationship. En route to Cuba, Crane's vessel the SS Commodore sank off the coast of Florida, leaving him and others adrift for 30 hours in a dinghy. Crane described the ordeal in "The Open Boat". During the final years of his life, he covered conflicts in Greece (accompanied by Cora, recognized as the first woman war correspondent) and later lived in England with her. He was befriended by writers such as Joseph Conrad and H. G. Wells. Plagued by financial difficulties and ill health, Crane died of tuberculosis in a Black Forest sanatorium in Germany at the age of 28.

At the time of his death, Crane was considered an important figure in American literature. After he was nearly forgotten for two decades, critics revived interest in his life and work. Crane's writing is characterized by vivid intensity, distinctive dialects, and irony. Common themes involve fear, spiritual crises and social isolation. Although recognized primarily for The Red Badge of Courage, which has become an American classic, Crane is also known for his poetry, journalism, and short stories such as "The Open Boat", "The Blue Hotel", "The Bride Comes to Yellow Sky", and The Monster. His writing made a deep impression on 20th-century writers, most prominent among them Ernest Hemingway, and is thought to have inspired the Modernists and the Imagists.

Early years

Stephen Crane was born on November 1, 1871, in Newark, New Jersey, to Jonathan Townley Crane, a minister in the Methodist Episcopal church, and Mary Helen Peck Crane, daughter of a clergyman, George Peck. He was the fourteenth and last child born to the couple. At 45, Helen Crane had suffered the early deaths of her previous four children, each of whom died within one year of birth. Nicknamed "Stevie" by the family, he joined eight surviving brothers and sisters—Mary Helen, George Peck, Jonathan Townley, William Howe, Agnes Elizabeth, Edmund Byran, Wilbur Fiske, and Luther.

The Cranes were descended from Jaspar Crane, a founder of New Haven Colony, who had migrated there from England in 1639. Stephen was named for a putative founder of Elizabethtown, New Jersey, who had, according to family tradition, come from England or Wales in 1665, as well as his great-great-grandfather Stephen Crane (1709–1780), a Revolutionary War patriot who served as New Jersey delegate to the First Continental Congress in Philadelphia. Crane later wrote that his father, Dr. Crane, "was a great, fine, simple mind," who had written numerous tracts on theology. Although his mother was a popular spokeswoman for the Woman's Christian Temperance Union and a highly religious woman, Crane wrote that he did not believe "she was as narrow as most of her friends or family." The young Stephen was raised primarily by his sister Agnes, who was 15 years his senior. The family moved to Port Jervis, New York, in 1876, where Dr. Crane became the pastor of Drew Methodist Church, a position that he retained until his death.

As a child, Stephen was often sickly and afflicted by constant colds. When the boy was almost two, his father wrote in his diary that his youngest son became "so sick that we are anxious about him." Despite his fragile nature, Crane was an intelligent child who taught himself to read before the age of four. His first known inquiry, recorded by his father, dealt with writing; at the age of three, while imitating his brother Townley's writing, he asked his mother, "how do you spell O?" In December 1879, Crane wrote a poem about wanting a dog for Christmas. Entitled "I'd Rather Have –", it is his first surviving poem. Stephen was not regularly enrolled in school until January 1880, but he had no difficulty in completing two grades in six weeks. Recalling this feat, he wrote that it "sounds like the lie of a fond mother at a teaparty, but I do remember that I got ahead very fast and that father was very pleased with me."

Dr. Crane died on February 16, 1880, at the age of 60; Stephen was eight years old. Some 1,400 people mourned Dr. Crane at his funeral, more than double the size of his congregation. After her husband's death, Mrs. Crane moved to Roseville, near Newark, leaving Stephen in the care of his older brother Edmund, with whom the young boy lived with cousins in Sussex County. He next lived with his brother William, a lawyer, in Port Jervis for several years.

His older sister Helen took him to Asbury Park to be with their brother Townley and his wife, Fannie. Townley was a professional journalist; he headed the Long Branch department of both the New-York Tribune and the Associated Press, and also served as editor of the Asbury Park Shore Press. Agnes, another Crane sister, joined the siblings in New Jersey. She took a position at Asbury Park's intermediate school and moved in with Helen to care for the young Stephen.

Within a couple of years, the Crane family suffered more losses. First, Townley and his wife lost their two young children. His wife Fannie died of Bright's disease in November 1883. Agnes Crane became ill and died on June 10, 1884, of meningitis at the age of 28.

Schooling

Crane wrote his first known story, "Uncle Jake and the Bell Handle", when he was 14. In late 1885, he enrolled at Pennington Seminary, a ministry-focused coeducational boarding school 7 miles (11 km) north of Trenton. His father had been principal there from 1849 to 1858. Soon after her youngest son left for school, Mrs. Crane began suffering what the Asbury Park Shore Press reported as "a temporary aberration of the mind." She had apparently recovered by early 1886, but later that year, her son, 23-year-old Luther Crane, died after falling in front of an oncoming train while working as a flagman for the Erie Railroad. It was the fourth death in six years among Stephen's immediate family.

After two years, Crane left Pennington for Claverack College, a quasi-military school. He later looked back on his time at Claverack as "the happiest period of my life although I was not aware of it." A classmate remembered him as a highly literate but erratic student, lucky to pass examinations in math and science, and yet "far in advance of his fellow students in his knowledge of History and Literature", his favorite subjects. While he held an impressive record on the drill field and baseball diamond, Crane generally did not excel in the classroom. Not having a middle name, as was customary among other students, he took to signing his name "Stephen T. Crane" in order "to win recognition as a regular fellow". Crane was seen as friendly, but also moody and rebellious. He sometimes skipped class in order to play baseball, a game in which he starred as catcher. He was also greatly interested in the school's military training program. He rose rapidly in the ranks of the student battalion. One classmate described him as "indeed physically attractive without being handsome", but he was aloof, reserved and not generally popular at Claverack. Although academically weak, Crane gained experience at Claverack that provided background (and likely some anecdotes from the Civil War veterans on the staff) that proved useful when he came to write The Red Badge of Courage.

In mid-1888, Crane became his brother Townley's assistant at a New Jersey shore news bureau, working there every summer until 1892. Crane's first publication under his byline was an article on the explorer Henry M. Stanley's famous quest to find the Scottish missionary David Livingstone in Africa. It appeared in the February 1890 Claverack College Vidette. Within a few months, Crane was persuaded by his family to forgo a military career and transfer to Lafayette College in Easton, Pennsylvania, in order to pursue a mining engineering degree. He registered at Lafayette on September 12, and promptly became involved in extracurricular activities; he took up baseball again and joined the largest fraternity, Delta Upsilon. He also joined both rival literary societies, named for (George) Washington and (Benjamin) Franklin. Crane infrequently attended classes and ended the semester with grades for four of the seven courses he had taken.

After one semester, Crane transferred to Syracuse University, where he enrolled as a non-degree candidate in the College of Liberal Arts. He roomed in the Delta Upsilon fraternity house and joined the baseball team. Attending just one class (English Literature) during the middle trimester, he remained in residence while taking no courses in the third semester.

Concentrating on his writing, Crane began to experiment with tone and style while trying out different subjects. He published his fictional story, "Great Bugs of Onondaga," simultaneously in the Syracuse Daily Standard and the New York Tribune. Declaring college "a waste of time", Crane decided to become a full-time writer and reporter. He attended a Delta Upsilon chapter meeting on June 12, 1891, but shortly afterward left college for good.

Full-time writer

In the summer of 1891, Crane often camped with friends in the nearby area of Sullivan County, New York, where his brother Edmund occupied a house obtained as part of their brother William's Hartwood Club (Association) land dealings. He used this area as the geographic setting for several short stories, which were posthumously published in a collection under the title Stephen Crane: Sullivan County Tales and Sketches. Crane showed two of these works to Tribune editor Willis Fletcher Johnson, a friend of the family, who accepted them for the publication. "Hunting Wild Dogs" and "The Last of the Mohicans" were the first of fourteen unsigned Sullivan County sketches and tales that were published in the Tribune between February and July 1892. Crane also showed Johnson an early draft of his first novel, Maggie: A Girl of the Streets.

Later that summer, Crane met and befriended author Hamlin Garland, who had been lecturing locally on American literature and the expressive arts; on August 17 he gave a talk on novelist William Dean Howells, which Crane wrote up for the Tribune. Garland became a mentor for and champion of the young writer, whose intellectual honesty impressed him. Their relationship suffered in later years, however, because Garland disapproved of Crane's alleged immorality, related to his living with a woman married to another man.

Stephen moved into his brother Edmund's house in Lakeview, a suburb of Paterson, New Jersey, in the fall of 1891. From here he made frequent trips into New York City, writing and reporting particularly on its impoverished tenement districts. Crane focused particularly on The Bowery, a small and once prosperous neighborhood in the southern part of Manhattan. After the Civil War, Bowery shops and mansions had given way to saloons, dance halls, brothels and flophouses, all of which Crane frequented. He later said he did so for research. He was attracted to the human nature found in the slums, considering it "open and plain, with nothing hidden". Believing nothing honest and unsentimental had been written about the Bowery, Crane became determined to do so himself; this was the setting of his first novel. On December 7, 1891, Crane's mother died at the age of 64, and the 20-year-old appointed Edmund as his guardian.

Despite being frail, undernourished and suffering from a hacking cough, which did not prevent him from smoking cigarettes, in the spring of 1892 Crane began a romance with Lily Brandon Munroe, a married woman who was estranged from her husband. Although Munroe later said Crane "was not a handsome man", she admired his "remarkable almond-shaped gray eyes." He begged her to elope with him, but her family opposed the match because Crane lacked money and prospects, and she declined. Their last meeting likely occurred in April 1898, when he again asked her to run away with him and she again refused.

Such an assemblage of the spraddle-legged men of the middle class, whose hands were bent and shoulders stooped from delving and constructing, had never appeared to an Asbury Park summer crowd, and the latter was vaguely amused.

— Stephen Crane, account of the JOUAM parade as it appeared in the Tribune

Between July 2 and September 11, 1892, Crane published at least ten news reports on Asbury Park affairs. Although a Tribune colleague stated that Crane "was not highly distinguished above any other boy of twenty who had gained a reputation for saying and writing bright things," that summer his reporting took on a more skeptical, hypocrisy-deflating tone. A storm of controversy erupted over a report he wrote on the Junior Order of United American Mechanics' American Day Parade, entitled "Parades and Entertainments". Published on August 21, the report juxtaposes the "bronzed, slope-shouldered, uncouth" marching men "begrimed with dust" and the spectators dressed in "summer gowns, lace parasols, tennis trousers, straw hats and indifferent smiles". Believing they were being ridiculed, some JOUAM marchers were outraged and wrote to the editor. The owner of the Tribune, Whitelaw Reid, was that year's Republican vice-presidential candidate, and this likely increased the sensitivity of the paper's management to the issue. Although Townley wrote a piece for the Asbury Park Daily Press in his brother's defense, the Tribune quickly apologized to its readers, calling Stephen Crane's piece "a bit of random correspondence, passed inadvertently by the copy editor". Hamlin Garland and biographer John Barry attested that Crane told them he had been dismissed by the Tribune, although Willis Fletcher Johnson later denied this. The paper did not publish any of Crane's work after 1892.

Life in New York

Crane struggled to make a living as a free-lance writer, contributing sketches and feature articles to various New York newspapers. In October 1892, he moved into a rooming house in Manhattan whose boarders were a group of medical students. During this time, he expanded or entirely reworked Maggie: A Girl of the Streets, which is about a girl who "blossoms in a mud-puddle" and becomes a pitiful victim of circumstance. In the winter of 1893, Crane took the manuscript of Maggie to Richard Watson Gilder, who rejected it for publication in The Century Magazine.

Crane decided to publish it privately, with money he had inherited from his mother. The novel was published in late February or early March 1893 by a small printing shop that usually printed medical books and religious tracts. The typewritten title page for the Library of Congress copyright application read simply: "A Girl of the Streets, / A Story of New York. / —By—/Stephen Crane." The name "Maggie" was added to the title later. Crane used the pseudonym "Johnston Smith" for the novel's initial publication, later telling friend and artist Corwin Knapp Linson that the nom de plume was the "commonest name I could think of. I had an editor friend named Johnson, and put in the "t", and no one could find me in the mob of Smiths." Hamlin Garland reviewed the work in the June 1893 issue of The Arena, calling it "the most truthful and unhackneyed study of the slums I have yet read, fragment though it is." Despite this early praise, Crane became depressed and destitute from having spent $869 for 1,100 copies of a novel that did not sell; he ended up giving a hundred copies away. He would later remember "how I looked forward to publication and pictured the sensation I thought it would make. It fell flat. Nobody seemed to notice it or care for it... Poor Maggie! She was one of my first loves."

In March 1893, Crane spent hours lounging in Linson's studio while having his portrait painted. He became fascinated with issues of the Century that were largely devoted to famous battles and military leaders from the Civil War. Frustrated with the dryly written stories, Crane stated, "I wonder that some of those fellows don't tell how they felt in those scraps. They spout enough of what they did, but they're as emotionless as rocks." Crane returned to these magazines during subsequent visits to Linson's studio, and eventually the idea of writing a war novel overtook him. He would later state that he "had been unconsciously working the detail of the story out through most of his boyhood" and had imagined "war stories ever since he was out of knickerbockers." This novel would ultimately become The Red Badge of Courage.

A river, amber-tinted in the shadow of its banks, purled at the army's feet; and at night, when the stream had become of a sorrowful blackness, one could see across it the red, eyelike gleam of hostile camp-fires set in the low brows of distant hills.

— Stephen Crane, The Red Badge of Courage

From the beginning, Crane wished to show how it felt to be in a war by writing "a psychological portrayal of fear." Conceiving his story from the point of view of a young private who is at first filled with boyish dreams of the glory of war and then quickly becomes disillusioned by war's reality, Crane borrowed the private's surname, "Fleming", from his sister-in-law's maiden name. He later said that the first paragraphs came to him with "every word in place, every comma, every period fixed." Working mostly nights, he wrote from around midnight until four or five in the morning. Because he could not afford a typewriter, he wrote carefully in ink on legal-sized paper, seldom crossing through or interlining a word. If he did change something, he would rewrite the whole page.

While working on his second novel, Crane remained prolific, concentrating on publishing stories to stave off poverty; "An Experiment in Misery", based on Crane's experiences in the Bowery, was printed by the New York Press. He also wrote five or six poems a day. In early 1894, he showed some of his poems or "lines" as he called them, to Hamlin Garland, who said he read "some thirty in all" with "growing wonder." Although Garland and William Dean Howells encouraged him to submit his poetry for publication, Crane's free verse was too unconventional for most. After brief wrangling between poet and publisher, Copeland & Day accepted Crane's first book of poems, The Black Riders and Other Lines, although it would not be published until after The Red Badge of Courage. He received a 10 percent royalty and the publisher assured him that the book would be in a form "more severely classic than any book ever yet issued in America."

In the spring of 1894, Crane offered the finished manuscript of The Red Badge of Courage to McClure's Magazine, which had become the foremost magazine for Civil War literature. While McClure's delayed giving him an answer on his novel, they offered him an assignment writing about the Pennsylvania coal mines. "In the Depths of a Coal Mine", a story with pictures by Linson, was syndicated by McClure's in a number of newspapers, heavily edited. Crane was reportedly disgusted by the cuts, asking Linson: "Why the hell did they send me up there then? Do they want the public to think the coal mines gilded ball-rooms with the miners eating ice-cream in boiled shirt-fronts?"

Sources report that following an encounter with a male prostitute that spring, Crane began a novel on the subject entitled Flowers of Asphalt, which he later abandoned. The manuscript has never been recovered.

After discovering that McClure's could not afford to pay him, Crane took his war novel to Irving Bacheller of the Bacheller-Johnson Newspaper Syndicate, which agreed to publish The Red Badge of Courage in serial form. Between the third and the ninth of December 1894, The Red Badge of Courage was published in some half-dozen newspapers in the United States.

Although it was greatly cut for syndication, Bacheller attested to its causing a stir, saying "its quality [was] immediately felt and recognized." The lead editorial in the Philadelphia Press of December 7 said that Crane "is a new name now and unknown, but everybody will be talking about him if he goes on as he has begun".

Travels and fame

At the end of January 1895, Crane left on what he called "a very long and circuitous newspaper trip" to the west. While writing feature articles for the Bacheller syndicate, he traveled to Saint Louis, Missouri, Nebraska, New Orleans, Galveston, Texas and then Mexico City. Irving Bacheller would later state that he "sent Crane to Mexico for new color", which the author found in the form of Mexican slum life. Whereas he found the lower class in New York pitiful, he was impressed by the "superiority" of the Mexican peasants' contentment and "even refuse[d] to pity them."

Returning to New York five months later, Crane joined the Lantern (alternately spelled "Lanthom" or "Lanthorne") Club organized by a group of young writers and journalists. The Club, located on the roof of an old house on William Street near the Brooklyn Bridge, served as a drinking establishment of sorts and was decorated to look like a ship's cabin. There Crane ate one good meal a day, although friends were troubled by his "constant smoking, too much coffee, lack of food and poor teeth", as Nelson Greene put it. Living in near-poverty and greatly anticipating the publication of his books, Crane began work on two more novels: The Third Violet and George's Mother.

The Black Riders was published by Copeland & Day shortly before his return to New York in May, but it received mostly criticism, if not abuse, for the poems' unconventional style and use of free verse. A piece in the Bookman called Crane "the Aubrey Beardsley of poetry," and a commentator from the Chicago Daily Inter-Ocean stated that "there is not a line of poetry from the opening to the closing page. Whitman's Leaves of Grass were luminous in comparison. Poetic lunacy would be a better name for the book." In June, the New York Tribune dismissed the book as "so much trash." Crane was pleased that the book was "making some stir".

In contrast to the reception for Crane's poetry, The Red Badge of Courage was welcomed with acclaim after its publication by Appleton in September 1895. For the next four months, the book was in the top six on various bestseller lists around the country. It arrived on the literary scene "like a flash of lightning out of a clear winter sky", according to H. L. Mencken, who was about 15 at the time. The novel also became popular in Britain; Joseph Conrad, a future friend of Crane, wrote that the novel "detonated... with the impact and force of a twelve-inch shell charged with a very high explosive." Appleton published two, possibly three, printings in 1895 and as many as eleven more in 1896. Although some critics considered the work overly graphic and profane, it was widely heralded for its realistic portrayal of war and unique writing style. The Detroit Free Press declared that The Red Badge would give readers "so vivid a picture of the emotions and the horrors of the battlefield that you will pray your eyes may never look upon the reality."

Wanting to capitalize on the success of The Red Badge, McClure Syndicate offered Crane a contract to write a series on Civil War battlefields. Because it was a wish of his to "visit the battlefield—which I was to describe—at the time of year when it was fought", Crane agreed to take the assignment. Visiting battlefields in Northern Virginia, including Fredericksburg, he would later produce five more Civil War tales: "Three Miraculous Soldiers", "The Veteran", "An Indiana Campaign", "An Episode of War" and The Little Regiment.

Scandal

At the age of 24, Crane, who was reveling in his success, became involved in a highly publicized case involving a suspected prostitute named Dora Clark. At 2 a.m. on September 16, 1896, he escorted two chorus girls and Clark from New York City's Broadway Garden, a popular "resort" where he had interviewed the women for a series he was writing. As Crane saw one woman safely to a streetcar, a plainclothes policeman named Charles Becker arrested the other two for solicitation; Crane was threatened with arrest when he tried to interfere. One of the women was released after Crane confirmed her erroneous claim that she was his wife, but Clark was charged and taken to the precinct. Against the advice of the arresting sergeant, Crane made a statement confirming Dora Clark's innocence, stating that "I only know that while with me she acted respectably, and that the policeman's charge was false." On the basis of Crane's testimony, Clark was discharged. The media seized upon the story; news spread to Philadelphia, Boston and beyond, with papers focusing on Crane's courage. The Stephen Crane story, as it became known, soon became a source for ridicule; the Chicago Dispatch in particular quipped that "Stephen Crane is respectfully informed that association with women in scarlet is not necessarily a 'Red Badge of Courage' ".

A couple of weeks after her trial, Clark pressed charges of false arrest against the officer who had arrested her. The next day, the officer physically attacked Clark in the presence of witnesses for having brought charges against him. Crane, who initially went briefly to Philadelphia to escape the pressure of publicity, returned to New York to give testimony at Becker's trial despite advice given to him from Theodore Roosevelt, who was Police Commissioner at the time and a new acquaintance of Crane. The defense targeted Crane: police raided his apartment and interviewed people who knew him, trying to find incriminating evidence in order to lessen the effect of his testimony. A vigorous cross-examination took place that sought to portray Crane as a man of dubious morals; while the prosecution proved that he frequented brothels, Crane claimed this was merely for research purposes. After the trial ended on October 16, the arresting officer was exonerated, and Crane's reputation was ruined.

Cora Taylor and the Commodore shipwreck

None of them knew the color of the sky. Their eyes glanced level and were fastened upon the waves that swept toward them. These waves were of the hue of slate, save for the tops, which were of foaming white, and all of the men knew the colors of the sea.

— Stephen Crane, "The Open Boat"

Given $700 in Spanish gold by the Bacheller-Johnson syndicate to work as a war correspondent in Cuba as the Spanish–American War was pending, the 25-year-old Crane left New York on November 27, 1896, on a train bound for Jacksonville, Florida. Upon arrival in Jacksonville, he registered at the St. James Hotel under the alias of Samuel Carleton to maintain anonymity while seeking passage to Cuba. While waiting for a boat, he toured the city and visited the local brothels. Within days he met 31-year-old Cora Taylor, proprietor of the downtown bawdy house Hotel de Dream. Born into a respectable Boston family, Taylor (whose legal name was Cora Ethel Stewart) had already had two brief marriages; her first husband, Vinton Murphy, divorced her on grounds of adultery. In 1889, she had married British Captain Donald William Stewart. She left him in 1892 for another man, but was still legally married. By the time Crane arrived, Taylor had been in Jacksonville for two years. She lived a bohemian lifestyle, owned a hotel of assignation, and was a well-known and respected local figure. The two spent much time together while Crane awaited his departure. He was finally cleared to leave for the Cuban port of Cienfuegos on New Year's Eve aboard the SS Commodore.

The ship sailed from Jacksonville with 27 or 28 men and a cargo of supplies and ammunition for the Cuban rebels. On the St. Johns River and less than 2 miles (3.2 km) from Jacksonville, Commodore struck a sandbar in a dense fog and damaged its hull. Although towed off the sandbar the following day, it was beached again in Mayport and again damaged. A leak began in the boiler room that evening and, as a result of malfunctioning water pumps, the ship came to a standstill about 16 miles (26 km) from Mosquito Inlet. As the ship took on more water, Crane described the engine room as resembling "a scene at this time taken from the middle kitchen of hades." Commodore's lifeboats were lowered in the early hours of the morning on January 2, 1897 and the ship ultimately sank at 7 a.m. Crane was one of the last to leave the ship in a 10-foot (3.0 m) dinghy. In an ordeal that he recounted in the short story "The Open Boat", Crane and three other men (including the ship's Captain) floundered off the coast of Florida for a day and a half before trying to land the dinghy at Daytona Beach. The small boat overturned in the surf, forcing the exhausted men to swim to shore; one of them died. Having lost the gold given to him for his journey, Crane wired Cora Taylor for help. She traveled to Daytona and returned to Jacksonville with Crane the next day, only four days after he had left on the Commodore.

The disaster was reported on the front pages of newspapers across the country. Rumors that the ship had been sabotaged were widely circulated but never substantiated. Portrayed favorably and heroically by the press, Crane emerged from the ordeal with his reputation enhanced, if not restored, after the battering he had received in the Dora Clark affair. Meanwhile, Crane's affair with Taylor blossomed.

Three seasons of archaeological investigation were conducted in 2002-04 to examine and document the exposed remains of a wreck near Ponce Inlet, FL conjectured to be that of the SS Commodore. The collected data, and other accumulated evidence, finally substantiated the identification of the Commodore beyond a reasonable doubt.

Greco-Turkish War

Despite contentment in Jacksonville and the need for rest after his ordeal, Crane became restless. He left Jacksonville on January 11 for New York City, where he applied for a passport to Cuba, Mexico and the West Indies. Spending three weeks in New York, he completed "The Open Boat" and periodically visited Port Jervis to see family. By this time, however, blockades had formed along the Florida coast as tensions rose with Spain, and Crane concluded that he would never be able to travel to Cuba. He sold "The Open Boat" to Scribner's for $300 in early March. Determined to work as a war correspondent, Crane signed on with William Randolph Hearst's New York Journal to cover the impending Greco-Turkish conflict. He brought along Taylor, who had sold the Hotel de Dream in order to follow him.

On March 20, they sailed first to England, where Crane was warmly received. They arrived in Athens in early April; between April 17 (when Turkey declared war on Greece) and April 22, Crane wrote his first published report of the war, "An Impression of the 'Concert' ". When he left for Epirus in the northwest, Taylor remained in Athens, where she became the Greek war's first woman war correspondent. She wrote under the pseudonym "Imogene Carter" for the New York Journal, a job that Crane had secured for her. They wrote frequently, traveling throughout the country separately and together. The first large battle that Crane witnessed was the Turks' assault on General

Constantine Smolenski's Greek forces at Velestino. Crane wrote, "It is a great thing to survey the army of the enemy. Just where and how it takes hold upon the heart is difficult of description." During this battle, Crane encountered "a fat waddling puppy" that he immediately claimed, dubbing it "Velestino, the Journal dog". Greece and Turkey signed an armistice on May 20, ending the 30-day war; Crane and Taylor left Greece for England, taking two Greek brothers as servants and Velestino the dog with them.

Spanish–American War

After staying in Limpsfield, Surrey, for a few days, Crane and Taylor settled in Ravensbrook, a plain brick villa in Oxted. Referring to themselves as Mr. and Mrs. Crane, the couple lived openly in England, but Crane concealed the relationship from his friends and family in the United States. Admired in England, Crane thought himself attacked back home: "There seem so many of them in America who want to kill, bury and forget me purely out of unkindness and envy and—my unworthiness, if you choose", he wrote. Velestino the dog sickened and died soon after their arrival in England, on August 1. Crane, who had a great love for dogs, wrote an emotional letter to a friend an hour after the dog's death, stating that "for eleven days we fought death for him, thinking nothing of anything but his life." The Limpsfield-Oxted area was home to members of the socialist Fabian Society and a magnet for writers such as Edmund Gosse, Ford Madox Ford and Edward Garnett. Crane also met the Polish-born novelist Joseph Conrad in October 1897, with whom he would have what Crane called a "warm and endless friendship".

Although Crane was confident among peers, strong negative reviews of the recently published The Third Violet were causing his literary reputation to dwindle. Reviewers were also highly critical of Crane's war letters, deeming them self-centered. Although The Red Badge of Courage had by this time gone through fourteen printings in the United States and six in England, Crane was running out of money. To survive financially, he worked at a feverish pitch, writing prolifically for both the English and the American markets. He wrote in quick succession stories such as The Monster, "The Bride Comes to Yellow Sky", "Death and the Child" and "The Blue Hotel".

Crane began to attach price tags to his new works of fiction, hoping that "The Bride", for example, would fetch $175.

As 1897 ended, Crane's money crisis worsened. Amy Leslie, a reporter from Chicago and a former lover, sued him for $550. The New York Times reported that Leslie gave him $800 in November 1896 but that he'd repaid only a quarter of the sum. In February he was summoned to answer Leslie's claim. The claim was apparently settled out of court, because no record of adjudication exists. Meanwhile, Crane felt "heavy with troubles" and "chased to the wall" by expenses. He confided to his agent that he was $2,000 in debt but that he would "beat it" with more literary output.

Soon after the USS Maine exploded in Havana Harbor on February 15, 1898, under suspicious circumstances, Crane was offered a £60 advance by Blackwood's Magazine for articles "from the seat of war in the event of a war breaking out" between the United States and Spain. His health was failing, and it is believed that signs of his pulmonary tuberculosis, which he may have contracted in childhood, became apparent. With almost no money coming in from his finished stories, Crane accepted the assignment and left Oxted for New York. Taylor and the rest of the household stayed behind to fend off local creditors. Crane applied for a passport and left New York for Key West two days before Congress declared war. While the war idled, he interviewed people and produced occasional copy.

In early June, he observed the establishment of an American base in Cuba when Marines seized Guantánamo Bay. He went ashore with the Marines, planning "to gather impressions and write them as the spirit moved." Although he wrote honestly about his fear in battle, others observed his calmness and composure. He would later recall "this prolonged tragedy of the night" in the war tale "Marines Signaling Under Fire at Guantanamo". After showing a willingness to serve during fighting at Cuzco, Cuba, by carrying messages to company commanders, Crane was officially cited for his "material aid during the action".

He continued to report upon various battles and the worsening military conditions and praised Theodore Roosevelt's Rough Riders, despite past tensions with the Commissioner. In early July, Crane was sent to the United States for medical treatment for a high fever. He was diagnosed with yellow fever, then malaria. Upon arrival in Old Point Comfort, Virginia, he spent a few weeks resting in a hotel. Although Crane had filed more than twenty dispatches in the three months he had covered the war, the World's business manager believed that the paper had not received its money's worth and fired him. In retaliation, Crane signed with Hearst's New York Journal with the wish to return to Cuba. He traveled first to Puerto Rico and then to Havana. In September, rumors began to spread that Crane, who was working anonymously, had either been killed or disappeared. He sporadically sent out dispatches and stories; he wrote about the mood in Havana, the crowded city sidewalks, and other topics, but he was soon desperate for money again. Taylor, left alone in England, was also penniless. She became frantic with worry over her lover's whereabouts; they were not in direct communication until the end of the year. Crane left Havana and arrived in England on January 11, 1899.

Death

Rent on Ravensbrook had not been paid for a year. Upon returning to England, Crane secured a solicitor to act as guarantor for their debts, after which Crane and Taylor relocated to Brede Place. This manor in Sussex, which dated to the 14th century and had neither electricity nor indoor plumbing, was offered to them by friends at a modest rent. The relocation appeared to give hope to Crane, but his money problems continued. Deciding that he could no longer afford to write for American publications, he concentrated on publishing in English magazines.

Crane pushed himself to write feverishly during the first months at Brede; he told his publisher that he was "doing more work now than I have at any other period in my life". His health worsened, and by late 1899 he was asking friends about health resorts. The Monster and Other Stories was in production and War Is Kind, his second collection of poems, was published in the United States in May. None of his books after The Red Badge of Courage had sold well, and he bought a typewriter to spur output. Active Service, a novella based on Crane's correspondence experience, was published in October. The New York Times reviewer questioned "whether the author of 'Active Service' himself really sees anything remarkable in his newspapery hero."

In December, the couple held an elaborate Christmas party at Brede, attended by Conrad, Henry James, H. G. Wells and other friends; it lasted several days. On December 29 Crane suffered a severe pulmonary hemorrhage. In January 1900 he'd recovered sufficiently to work on a new novel, The O'Ruddy, completing 25 of the 33 chapters. Plans were made for him to travel as a correspondent to Gibraltar to write sketches from Saint Helena, the site of a Boer prison, but at the end of March and in early April he suffered two more hemorrhages. Taylor took over most of Crane's correspondence while he was ill, writing to friends for monetary aid. The couple planned to travel on the continent, but Conrad, upon visiting Crane for the last time, remarked that his friend's "wasted face was enough to tell me that it was the most forlorn of all hopes."

On May 28, the couple arrived at Badenweiler, Germany, a health spa on the edge of the Black Forest. Despite his weakened condition, Crane continued to dictate fragmentary episodes for the completion of The O'Ruddy. He died on June 5, 1900, at the age of 28. In his will he left everything to Taylor, who took his body to New Jersey for burial. Crane was interred in Evergreen Cemetery in what is now Hillside, New Jersey.

Style and technique

Stephen Crane's fiction is typically categorized as representative of Naturalism, American realism, Impressionism or a mixture of the three. Critic Sergio Perosa, for example, wrote in his essay, "Stephen Crane fra naturalismo e impressionismo," that the work presents a "symbiosis" of Naturalistic ideals and Impressionistic methods. When asked whether or not he would write an autobiography in 1896, Crane responded that he "dare not say that I am honest. I merely say that I am as nearly honest as a weak mental machinery will allow." Similarities between the stylistic techniques in Crane's writing and Impressionist painting—including the use of color and chiaroscuro—are often cited to support the theory that Crane was not only an Impressionist but also influenced by the movement. H. G. Wells remarked upon "the great influence of the studio" on Crane's work, quoting a passage from The Red Badge of Courage as an example: "At nightfall the column broke into regimental pieces, and the fragments went into the fields to camp. Tents sprang up like strange plants. Camp fires, like red, peculiar blossoms, dotted the night.... From this little distance the many fires, with the black forms of men passing to and fro before the crimson rays, made weird and satanic effects." Although no direct evidence exists that Crane formulated a precise theory of his craft, he vehemently rejected sentimentality, asserting that "a story should be logical in its action and faithful to character. Truth to life itself was the only test, the greatest artists were the simplest, and simple because they were true."

Poet and biographer John Berryman suggested that there were three basic variations, or "norms", of Crane's narrative style. The first, being "flexible, swift, abrupt and nervous", is best exemplified in The Red Badge of Courage, while the second ("supple majesty") is believed to relate to "The Open Boat", and the third ("much more closed, circumstantial and 'normal' in feeling and syntax") to later works such as The Monster. Crane's work, however, cannot be determined by style solely on chronology. Not only does his fiction not take place in any particular region with similar characters, but it varies from serious in tone to reportorial writing and light fiction. Crane's writing, both fiction and nonfiction, is consistently driven by immediacy and is at once concentrated, vivid and intense. The novels and short stories contain poetic characteristics such as shorthand prose, suggestibility, shifts in perspective and ellipses between and within sentences. Similarly, omission plays a large part in Crane's work; the names of his protagonists are not commonly used and sometimes they are not named at all.

Crane was often criticized by early reviewers for his frequent incorporation of everyday speech into dialogue, mimicking the regional accents of his characters with colloquial stylization. This is apparent in his first novel, in which Crane ignored the romantic, sentimental approach of slum fiction; he instead concentrated on the cruelty and sordid aspects of poverty, expressed by the brashness of the Bowery's crude dialect and profanity, which he used lavishly. The distinct dialect of his Bowery characters is apparent at the beginning of the text; the title character admonishes her brother saying: "Yeh knows it puts mudder out when yes comes home half dead, an' it's like we'll all get a poundin'."

Major themes

Crane's work is often thematically driven by Naturalistic and Realistic concerns, including ideals versus realities, spiritual crises and fear. These themes are particularly evident in Crane's first three novels, Maggie: A Girl of the Streets, The Red Badge of Courage and George's Mother. The three main characters search for a way to make their dreams come true, but ultimately suffer from crises of identity. Crane was fascinated by war and death, as well as fire, disfigurement, fear and courage, all of which inspired him to write many works based on these concepts. In The Red Badge of Courage, the main character both longs for the heroics of battle but ultimately fears it, demonstrating the dichotomy of courage and cowardice. He experiences the threat of death, misery and a loss of self.

Extreme isolation from society and community is also apparent in Crane's work. During the most intense battle scenes in The Red Badge of Courage, for example, the story's focus is mainly "on the inner responses of a self unaware of others". In "The Open Boat", "An Experiment in Misery" and other stories, Crane uses light, motion and color to express degrees of epistemological uncertainty. Similar to other Naturalistic writers, Crane scrutinizes the position of man, who has been isolated not only from society, but also from God and nature. "The Open Boat", for example, distances itself from Romantic optimism and affirmation of man's place in the world by concentrating on the characters' isolation.

While he lived, Stephen Crane was denominated by critical readers a realist, a naturalist, an impressionist, symbolist, Symboliste, expressionist and ironist; his posthumous life was enriched by critics who read him as nihilistic, existentialist, a neo-Romantic, a sentimentalist, protomodernist, pointilliste, visionist, imagist and, by his most recent biographer, a "bleak naturalist." At midcentury he was a "prediscipline of the New Criticism"; by its end he was "a proto-deconstructionist anti-artist hero" who had "leapfrogged modernism, landing on postmodernist ground." Or, as Sergio Perosa wrote in 1964, "The critic wanders in a labyrinth of possibilities, which every new turn taken by Crane's fiction seems to explode or deny."

One undeniable fact about Crane's work, as Anthony Splendora noted in 2015, is that Death haunts it; like a threatening eclipse it overshadows his best efforts, each of which features the signal demise of a main character. Allegorically, "The Blue Hotel," at the pinnacle of the short story form, may even be an autothanatography, the author's intentional exteriorization or objectification, in this case for the purpose of purgation, of his own impending death. Crane's "Swede" in that story can be taken, following current psychoanalytical theory, as a surrogative, sacrificial victim, ritually to be purged.

Transcending this "dark circumstance of composition," Crane had a particular telos and impetus for his creation: beyond the tautologies that all art is alterity and to some formal extent mimesis, Crane sought and obviously found "a form of catharsis" in writing. This view accounts for his uniqueness, especially as operative through his notorious "disgust" with his family's religion, their "vacuous, futile psalm-singing". His favorite book, for example, was Mark Twain's Life on the Mississippi, in which God is mentioned only twice—once as irony and once as "a swindle." Not only did Crane call out God specifically with the lines "Well then I hate thee / righteous image" in "The Black Riders" (1895), but even his most hopeful tropes, such as the "comradeship" of his "Open Boat" survivors, make no mention of deity, specifying only "indifferent nature." His antitheism is most evident in his characterization of the human race as "lice clinging to a space-lost bulb," a climax-nearing speech in "The Blue Hotel," Ch. VI. It is possible that Crane utilized religion's formal psychic space, now suddenly available resulting from the recent "Death of God", as a milieu for his compensative art.

Novels

Beginning with the publication of Maggie: A Girl of the Streets in 1893, Crane was recognized by critics mainly as a novelist. Maggie was initially rejected by numerous publishers because of its atypical and true-to-life depictions of class warfare, which clashed with the sentimental tales of that time. Rather than focusing on the very rich or middle class, the novel's characters are lower-class denizens of New York's Bowery. The main character, Maggie, descends into prostitution after being led astray by her lover. Although the novel's plot is simple, its dramatic mood, quick pace and portrayal of Bowery life have made it memorable. Maggie is not merely an account of slum life, but also represents eternal symbols. In his first draft, Crane did not give his characters proper names. Instead, they were identified by epithets: Maggie, for example, was the girl who "blossomed in a mud-puddle" and Pete, her seducer, was a "knight". The novel is dominated by bitter irony and anger, as well as destructive morality and treacherous sentiment. Critics would later call the novel "the first dark flower of American Naturalism" for its distinctive elements of naturalistic fiction.

Written thirty years after the end of the Civil War and before Crane had any experience of battle, The Red Badge of Courage was innovative stylistically as well as psychologically. Often described as a war novel, it focuses less on battle and more on the main character's psyche and his reactions and responses in war. It is believed that Crane based the fictional battle in the novel on that of Chancellorsville; he may also have interviewed veterans of the 124th New York Volunteer Infantry Regiment, commonly known as the Orange Blossoms, in Port Jervis, New York. Told in a third-person limited point of view, it reflects the private experience of Henry Fleming, a young soldier who flees from combat. The Red Badge of Courage is notable in its vivid descriptions and well-cadenced prose, both of which help create suspense within the story. Similarly, by substituting epithets for characters' names ("the youth", "the tattered soldier"), Crane injects an allegorical quality into his work, making his characters point to a specific characteristic of man. Like Crane's first novel, The Red Badge of Courage has a deeply ironic tone which increases in severity as the novel progresses. The title of the work is ironic; Henry wishes "that he, too, had a wound, a red badge of courage", echoing a wish to have been wounded in battle. The wound he does receive (from the rifle butt of a fleeing Union soldier) is not a badge of courage but a badge of shame.

The novel expresses a strong connection between humankind and nature, a frequent and prominent concern in Crane's fiction and poetry throughout his career. Whereas contemporary writers (Ralph Waldo Emerson, Nathaniel Hawthorne, Henry David Thoreau) focused on a sympathetic bond on the two elements, Crane wrote from the perspective that human consciousness distanced humans from nature. In The Red Badge of Courage, this distance is paired with a great number of references to animals, and men with animalistic characteristics: people "howl", "squawk", "growl", or "snarl".

Since the resurgence of Crane's popularity in the 1920s, The Red Badge of Courage has been deemed a major American text. The novel has been anthologized numerous times, including in the 1942 collection Men at War: The Best War Stories of All Time, edited by Ernest Hemingway. In the introduction, Hemingway wrote that the novel "is one of the finest books of our literature, and I include it entire because it is all as much of a piece as a great poem is."

Crane's later novels have not received as much critical praise. After the success of The Red Badge of Courage, Crane wrote another tale set in the Bowery. George's Mother is less allegorical and more personal than his two previous novels, and it focuses on the conflict between a church-going, temperance-adhering woman (thought to be based on Crane's mother) and her single remaining offspring, who is a naive dreamer. Critical response to the novel was mixed. The Third Violet, a romance that he wrote quickly after publishing The Red Badge of Courage, is typically considered as Crane's attempt to appeal to popular audiences. Crane considered it a "quiet little story." Although it contained autobiographical details, the characters have been deemed inauthentic and stereotypical. Crane's second to last novel, Active Service, revolves around the Greco-Turkish War of 1897, with which the author was familiar. Although noted for its satirical take on the melodramatic and highly passionate works that were popular of the nineteenth century, the novel was not successful. It is generally accepted by critics that Crane's work suffered at this point due to the speed which he wrote in order to meet his high expenses. His last novel, a suspenseful and picaresque work entitled The O'Ruddy, was finished posthumously by Robert Barr and published in 1903.

Short fiction

Crane wrote many different types of fictional pieces while indiscriminately applying to them terms such as "story", "tale" and "sketch". For this reason, critics have found clear-cut classification of Crane's work problematic. While "The Open Boat" and "The Bride Comes to Yellow Sky" are often considered short stories, others are variously identified.

In an 1896 interview with Herbert P. Williams, a reporter for the Boston Herald, Crane said that he did "not find that short stories are utterly different in character from other fiction. It seems to me that short stories are the easiest things we write." During his brief literary career, he wrote more than a hundred short stories and fictional sketches. Crane's early fiction was based in camping expeditions in his teen years; these stories eventually became known as The Sullivan County Tales and Sketches. He considered these "sketches", which are mostly humorous and not of the same caliber of work as his later fiction, to be "articles of many kinds," in that they are part fiction and part journalism.

The subject matter for his stories varied extensively. His early New York City sketches and Bowery tales accurately described the results of industrialization, immigration and the growth of cities and their slums. His collection of six short stories, The Little Regiment, covered familiar ground with the American Civil War, a subject for which he became famous with The Red Badge of Courage. Although similar to Crane's noted novel, The Little Regiment was believed to lack vigor and originality. Realizing the limitations of these tales, Crane wrote: "I have invented the sum of my invention with regard to war and this story keeps me in internal despair."

The Open Boat and Other Tales of Adventure (1898) contains thirteen short stories that deal with three periods in Crane's life: his Asbury Park boyhood, his trip to the West and Mexico in 1895, and his Cuban adventure in 1897. This collection was well received and included several of his most critically successful works. His 1899 collection, The Monster and Other Stories, was similarly well received.

Two posthumously published collections were not as successful. In

August 1900 The Whilomville Stories were published, a collection of thirteen stories that Crane wrote during the last year of his life. The work deals almost exclusively with boyhood, and the stories are drawn from events occurring in Port Jervis, where Crane lived from the age of six to eleven. Focusing on small-town America, the stories tend toward sentimentality, but remain perceptive of the lives of children. Wounds in the Rain, published in September 1900, contains fictional tales based on Crane's reports for the World and the Journal during the Spanish–American War. These stories, which Crane wrote while desperately ill, include "The Price of the Harness" and "The Lone Charge of William B. Perkins" and are dramatic, ironic and sometimes humorous.

Despite Crane's prolific output, only four stories--"The Open Boat", "The Blue Hotel", "The Bride Comes to Yellow Sky", and The Monster—have received extensive attention from scholars. H. G. Wells considered "The Open Boat" to be "beyond all question, the crown of all his work", and it is one of the most frequently discussed of Crane's works.

Poetry

Many red devils ran from my heart

And out upon the page.

They were so tiny

The pen could mash them.

And many struggled in the ink.

It was strange

To write in this red muck

Of things from my heart.

— Stephen Crane

Crane's poems, which he preferred to call "lines", are typically not given as much scholarly attention as his fiction; no anthology contained Crane's verse until 1926. Although it is not certain when Crane began to write poetry seriously, he once said that his overall poetic aim was "to give my ideas of life as a whole, so far as I know it". The poetic style used in both of his books of poetry, The Black Riders and Other Lines and War is Kind, was unconventional for the time in that it was written in free verse without rhyme, meter, or even titles for individual works. They are typically short in length; although several poems, such as "Do not weep, maiden, for war is kind", use stanzas and refrains, most do not. Crane also differed from his peers and poets of later generations in that his work contains allegory, dialectic and narrative situations.

Critic Ruth Miller claimed that Crane wrote "an intellectual poetry rather than a poetry that evokes feeling, a poetry that stimulates the mind rather than arouses the heart". In the most complexly organized poems, the significance of the states of mind or feelings is ambiguous, but Crane's poems tend to affirm certain elemental attitudes, beliefs, opinions and stances toward God, man and the universe. The Black Riders in particular is essentially a dramatic concept and the poems provide continuity within the dramatic structure. There is also a dramatic interplay in which there is frequently a major voice reporting an incident seen ("In the desert / I saw a creature, naked, bestial") or experienced ("A learned man came to me once"). The second voice or additional voices represent a point of view which is revealed to be inferior; when these clash, a dominant attitude emerges.

Legacy

In four years, Crane published five novels, two volumes of poetry, three short story collections, two books of war stories, and numerous works of short fiction and reporting. Today he is mainly remembered for The Red Badge of Courage, which is regarded as an American classic. The novel has been adapted several times for the screen, including John Huston's 1951 version. By the time of his death, Crane had become one of the best known writers of his generation. His eccentric lifestyle, frequent newspaper reporting, association with other famous authors, and expatriate status made him somewhat of an international celebrity. Although most stories about his life tended toward the romantic, rumors about his alleged drug use and alcoholism persisted long after his death.

By the early 1920s, Crane and his work were nearly forgotten. It was not until Thomas Beer published his biography in 1923, which was followed by editor Wilson Follett's The Work of Stephen Crane (1925–1927), that Crane's writing came to the attention of a scholarly audience. Crane's reputation was then enhanced by faithful support from writer friends such as Joseph Conrad, H. G. Wells and Ford Madox Ford, all of whom either published recollections or commented upon their time with Crane. John Berryman's 1950 biography of Crane further established him as an important American author. Since 1951 there has been a steady outpouring of articles, monographs and reprints in Crane scholarship.

Today, Crane is considered one of the most innovative writers of the 1890s. His peers, including Conrad and James, as well as later writers such as Robert Frost, Ezra Pound and Willa Cather, hailed Crane as one of the finest creative spirits of his time. His work was described by Wells as "the first expression of the opening mind of a new period, or, at least, the early emphatic phase of a new initiative." Wells said that "beyond dispute", Crane was "the best writer of our generation, and his untimely death was an irreparable loss to our literature." Conrad wrote that Crane was an "artist" and "a seer with a gift for rendering the significant on the surface of things and with an incomparable insight into primitive emotions". Crane's work has proved inspirational for future writers; not only have scholars drawn similarities between Hemingway's A Farewell to Arms and The Red Badge of Courage, but Crane's fiction is thought to have been an important inspiration for Hemingway and his fellow Modernists. In 1936, Hemingway wrote in The Green Hills of Africa that "The good writers are Henry James, Stephen Crane, and Mark Twain. That's not the order they're good in. There is no order for good writers." Crane's poetry is thought to have been a precursor to the Imagist movement, and his short fiction has also influenced American literature. "The Open Boat", "The Blue Hotel", The Monster and "The Bride Comes to Yellow Sky" are generally considered by critics to be examples of Crane's best work.

Several institutions and places have endeavored to keep Crane's legacy alive. Badenweiler and the house where he died became something of a tourist attraction for its fleeting association with the American author; Alexander Woollcott attested to the fact that, long after Crane's death, tourists would be directed to the room where he died. Columbia University Rare Book and Manuscript Library has a collection of Crane and Taylor's personal correspondence dating from 1895 to 1908. Near his brother Edmund's Sullivan County home in New York, where Crane stayed for a short time, a pond is named after him. The Stephen Crane House in Asbury Park, New Jersey, where the author lived with his siblings for nine years, is operated as a museum dedicated to his life and work. Syracuse University has an annual Stephen Crane Lecture Series which is sponsored by the Dikaia Foundation.

Columbia University purchased much of the Stephen Crane materials held by Cora Crane at her death. The Crane Collection is one of the largest in the nation of his materials. Columbia University had an exhibit: 'The Tall Swift Shadow of a Ship at Night': Stephen and Cora Crane, November 2, 1995 through February 16, 1996, about the lives of the couple, featuring letters and other documents and memorabilia. (Source: Wikipedia)

Lightning Source UK Ltd.
Milton Keynes UK
UKHW012226301119
354485UK00001B/88/P

9 789353 839178